THE ROGUE'S LAST SCANDAL

BOOK THREE, SONS OF THE SPY LORD

ALINA K. FIELD

Dedication

To the savers, the memoirists, the letter-writers, the genealogists, and all the quiet historians who make the past come alive.

Like any good rogue, he was after a lady.

Saving a young heiress from wedding a scoundrel might just ease Charley Everly's boredom with his current assignment. He's been looking for a lady: beautiful, rich, Spanish, and the key to a traitor.

Could Grace Kingsley be the one?

Falling—literally—into the arms of the *ton*'s most outrageous rogue seems a risky path of escape, but Maria Graciela Kingsley y Romero has no other choice. Only the great Earl of Shaldon can help her, and he is not to be found.

So his son will have to do.

CHAPTER ONE

London, 1821

His lady had not made an appearance tonight, not that he'd have any reason to expect her at a Kingsley soirée.

Charles Rupert Armstrong Everly took a long drag upon his cigarillo and surveyed the shadowed tangles of the garden.

Lady Kingsley had failed to place inviting lanterns outside to lure ball-goers into wickedness. And in all the preparations for the Kingsleys' grand party, no servant had been sent to sweep away dead leaves from the previous autumn, or chase away whatever vermin were rustling around in them.

Of course, Lady Kingsley had also discouragingly locked the ballroom's terrace doors.

He and his old school chum, Quentin Penderbrook, had required little more than a minor diversion and their wits to manage the Kingsley servants and the flimsy terrace door lock.

"Kingsley is pockets to let, I hear," Penderbrook said. "Wonder how he financed this grand display?" He took a long drag. "The heiress, I suppose. As my aunt used to say, you need money to draw in the grand mark."

"Your aunt was a font of wisdom."

Penderbrook laughed. "Outspoken, she was, for a clergyman's wife. It's a pity I don't have a title. I wonder if my chance of a position in the Home Office would suffice for the Kingsleys? From what I saw, the girl looks to be a beauty."

Charley tapped off a bit of ash. "She looks to be a handful."

His friend laughed. "You didn't see her up close, as I did, Everly."

That was true enough. They'd been dragged off to this ball by his sister, Lady Perpetua Everly, and had arrived blessedly late. From the crowded distance of the ballroom floor, the heiress's back bore the usual outline of white muslin and piled up hair. "I'm speaking from general principles. Spanish women."

"Ah. Spanish women. Well, you would know."

He would, and he did. He was looking for a Spanish woman, wealthy and beautiful. He had tracked down more than a few in this pre-coronation social whirl.

"She'll be miserable if he throws her to that slimy fish," Penderbrook said.

The door clicked behind them and a lady appeared, the light behind her shadowing her face. Nothing, however—not the furbelows and flounces on her white dress, not the dim light—nothing could hide that figure.

Speech failed him—as it never did. He dropped his tobacco and bowed, his eyes traveling over her, down and up. She was exquisite.

She cast a trembling glance back, and he caught his breath, tasting the fear rolling off her.

A ray of light from the ballroom flashed in her eyes as they widened.

Before he could even stutter, she put a finger to her lips and disappeared down the crumbled stairs to the brush below, as quick and as wispy as a water wraith, albeit a curvy one.

"Well." Penderbrook dropped his own cigarillo and ground it with the heel of his scuffed dancing slipper.

Almost never at a loss for words was his friend Penderbrook. And if he thought to pursue the young lady, he would have to knock Charley out of the way.

The terrace door slammed open and all of his senses went to high alert.

"Come to join us?" Penderbrook's words rolled out smoothly over the roiling tension. "Dreadfully hot in there," he drawled.

"Smoking?"

That voice. Charley would recognize it anywhere, even without the dripping disdain, forged by the self-serving corruption of a smuggler's lordship.

He'd met this particular slimy fish previously in Brussels.

Charley staggered against the crumbling terrace wall, slipped a flask from his pocket and swigged it.

"A flask? At a ball, Everly?" The man moved closer.

"Why, by Jove, it's Gregory Carvelle." Charley wiped his mouth and managed a belch. "Penderbrook, let me introduce you. I have not seen you since Brussels. Lady Devonshire's ball, wasn't it. What *have* you been up to all these many years, old man?"

"You are drunk."

"Drunk?" Penderbrook said. "No one could be drunk on Kingsley's lemonade. Not even Everly here, who we know cannot hold his liquor. I say, Everly, why not let your man here have one of those excellent Spanish cigars? Join us, Carvelle."

"I will not. I am looking for a young lady. Has anyone else come out?"

Charley laughed, and threw back his head, projecting his voice to the garden. "*Ah, April, dressed in all his trim, hath put a spirit of youth in everything.*"

"Shakespeare," Penderbrook explained. "The sonnets."

"Indeed," Charley laughed again. "Is the young lady pretty?"

Penderbrook joined in with the laughter and snatched the flask. "If a girl had come out here, Everly would have pushed me back inside. Now that you have someone else to entertain you, Everly, I shall find some lemonade and doctor it up."

"Don't let my sister catch you at it. She'll roast you for a week."

Penderbrook laughed as if he hadn't a care in the world, as if he wasn't leaving Charley alone with a disreputable thug.

As if there wasn't a beautiful woman hiding in the wild scrub below them.

His friend had made it known he was angling for a spot in the Earl of Shaldon's service, desperately, from what Charley could surmise. If only Pender knew how dreadfully tedious it could be, working for Father. Chasing down a Spanish woman who was the key to a spy had proved to be less than heroic.

Though perhaps, this wouldn't be one of those times.

Charley pulled a case from another pocket his clever tailor had managed to craft for him. "Will you have one of these tiny cigars?"

Carvelle waved him away. "I'm surprised you are here tonight, and not off at Mivart's swinging your way down from the Duquesa's hotel window. But, oh yes—the Duque has arrived in town, hasn't he."

Charley laughed. "Has he? I'm not keeping track, Carvelle, but I see you are."

"I make it my business to keep track of many things. How is your father, the great Lord Shaldon?"

"Father? I imagine you must know."

"He is in Bath."

"Quite. Ill enough to take the waters."

The other man's lips turned up unpleasantly. "Your brother must be counting the hours until his succession."

Heat spiked within him. "Perhaps." He made himself drawl lazily. "Bakeley and I do not speak much." It was not entirely a lie. Since his recent marriage, his elder brother, Viscount Bakeley, was busy with affairs of the heart.

That marriage, however, had restored the relationship between father and son. One thing Charley knew for sure, Bakeley did not wish his father dead.

"And what will become of you, eh, once the great *diplomat,* Lord Shaldon, is not around to pull his strings for you?"

"Have you not heard, Carvelle? I've entered Parliament. A politician never starves."

"A smart politician. Not a drunken gambler who spends his time jumping through the beds of married women. You will need to marry money."

Well, and wasn't that interesting—the man was feeling very confident to speak so bluntly, the ignorant ass. Drunk or sober, another man might have called Carvelle out.

Charley managed a hiccup. "Have you got someone in mind for me?"

Again, that sneer.

He hiccupped again and tapped a finger against his cheek. "I hear Kingsley's ward is very rich."

Carvelle's hand locked around Charley's wrist. "You are not to touch her."

His blood rose as he studied the hand grasping his. He counted to three, silently, forced it down. Made himself laugh.

Duty required him to let it be. This time.

The door rattled and a cloud of emerald silk filled the doorway.

"Gregory." Lady Kingsley advanced on them bringing with her a gagging cloud of lavender. "Sir." She curtsied her deference to the son of a powerful and very rich earl. "Gregory, you've not found her?"

"No."

Her plump little hands clenched as tightly as the bodice displaying her generous wares, as tightly as her scowl. She was a handsome enough woman, even now, if one could stomach a social-climbing harpy.

"This is the want of a rod," she said.

Charley's ears pricked up, aware that the wildlife in the untamed garden had gone silent.

"Which I have not, nor will not spare, nor should you, Gregory, when..."

She must have remembered his aristocratic presence, and with her pause he staggered again, bracing himself on the balustrade.

Her back stiffened. "Perhaps we should check again in the nursery. I will go myself. Carvelle, you are wanted inside by my husband."

Charley let the door shut on them and waited. The night time noises rose again—the clattering of wheels on a nearby street, a watchman's call, a breeze fluttering the new leaves of the untamed foliage.

"I hear there is a packet running daily from Portsmouth to Calais," he said.

The bushes below rustled. He hurried down the terrace stairs.

CHAPTER TWO

The brick against her back was cold, stirring the ache in her wounded heart, soaking the dampness into her soul.

A packet running daily from Portsmouth to Calais. And he'd quoted from the Sonnets. She sighed and rubbed her fists against her cheeks.

She could not leave. She must not cry.

His smell reached her before his footsteps, tobacco and leather, like her papa's, and some subtle masculine scent unique to this man. She inhaled deeply and squeezed her eyes a moment.

Hold the waterworks, my Gracie.

When she looked, he stood more than an arm's length away. The blood danced in her veins and her breath tightened. Tall and broad shouldered, she had seen that his hair was a thick tawny brown, and he was handsome as sin.

Everly, his name was. Son of Lord Shaldon, Carvelle had said. She made herself breathe and waited.

As did he, respectful, watchful. Not, she decided, drunk. That had been a feint, and why?

Because he was smart, because he could recognize evil. Which did not mean he was himself to be trusted.

She curtsied. "Lord Everly."

"I do not wish to disappoint," he said softly, "but I am only a mister. Mr. Charles Everly."

The test had produced humor. Perhaps he *would* help her.

"And I am a simple miss. Miss Maria Graciela Kingsley y Romero." She held out her hand.

"*Señorita.*" He bent over her white glove and kissed it.

Warmth bloomed where his lips touched silk, soaked through the thin covering, rippled up her arm, and, even after he'd released her, caused a shiver to tumble through her.

"You are cold." He started to disrobe.

"No please. You must stay dressed." *We both must.*

Or must they? Would a scandal in the garden with a notorious rogue, with *this* notorious rogue, cause Carvelle to cry off? He had implied that Mr. Everly was having an affair with a Duquesa. He had told Mr. Everly not to touch *her*, Graciela.

She thought of little Reina. And the witch's rod, and she hugged herself tighter.

"*Por favor, señor. Ayudame.*" *Please sir, help me.*

Charley moved closer and took both of her hands. The thin gloves only amplified the chill of her. Fear had made her slip into Spanish.

He was looking for a Spanish woman, wealthy and beautiful. Not this Spanish woman, who he well knew was not really Spanish, but a product of an Englishman and a creole woman of New Spain.

He moved her into a thread of light and examined her again. A great deal of skin showed above her bosom. She didn't look like she'd felt the other lady's rod, not lately anyway.

"I will help you," he said in Spanish. "Will you leave with me? I will take you directly to my brother and his wife." His eldest brother, Bink, was in town. He and his wife Paulette would take in the girl and hold their curiosity until a later time.

She shook her head. "No. I thank you." She had found her English again. "I did not arrive alone and I cannot leave without the others who accompanied me."

That was news, and surprising, to boot. A villain generally dispensed with his victim's allies quickly. "He will sack your servants as soon as you are gone."

Again, that quick head shake. "There is a child. I am her guardian."

A child. Lady Kingsley was going to the nursery. Children were the best of leverages, if one's victim cared about them at all.

A window creaked somewhere above them. "Please," she whispered, "I wish very much to meet your father. Can you kindly arrange it?"

That sent a prickle through him. His father had many friends and many enemies. In truth, his father had never said whether her father, Captain Tristan Kingsley, was either. They'd never talked about the man at all. "You are all politeness," he said, stalling.

Her mouth firmed. "I am not polite, *señor*. I am desperate." She pulled her hands away. "I cannot be seen with you."

"Wait." He touched her bare arm, above the buttoned glove. "He's in Bath. I'll find a way when he returns."

"That will be too late."

"Then *I'll* help you."

She looked up at him. "My father said I could trust your father. I am not so sure about you."

His reputation had preceded him, as it always did. The feckless, whoring, drunken younger son of one of England's greatest. Only occasionally did he regret his ill repute. Only occasionally did it work against him. Like now.

"I will help you, and I will not importune you in any way. You can trust me. Have you a plan?"

She straightened. She hesitated, and then tucked her hand around his arm. "Tonight, I will raise the false flag. I will play the coward and faint. You may catch me if you will." They proceeded up the stairs and at the top she stopped. "Please. No duels. I do not wish any more blood upon my conscience."

"Me? Duel? With whom? Carvelle?"

She nodded.

He released her hand, took a step back, and smiled. "I prefer to deal with villains in a more expedient way."

That did not cheer her as he'd hoped. Instead her mouth firmed more. Before she could speak the door opened and Penderbrook walked out with Charley's sister, Perry.

Charley made the introductions and watched Miss Kingsley attempt polite small talk. She was no better at it than his passionate, opinionated, intelligent sister, who quickly surmised a problem.

"There you are, Grace." Lady Kingsley barreled through the doors. "We have been looking all over for you. Where have you been?"

Perry moved into her path before she could snatch up Miss Kingsley. "She was with me." Perry smiled and pushed up her spectacles.

She used them to ward off all the idiots after her grand dowry, but Charley knew she only fiddled with them like this when she was nervous.

"I am most anxious to visit the Caribbean and Mexico someday. And, oh, my dear Miss Kingsley, I heard the news about your father's ship. I feel certain the report must be mistaken. Why, how many times, Charley, did we receive word that Father was dead? And he wasn't. And our brother's wife, Sirena—her brother was reported dead, and it is a marvel how that turned out. You must not lose hope, Miss Kingsley."

Dear Perry. She was far too *feeling* for the bloodless *ton,* even the members who lurked around the fringes of high society.

Miss Kingsley blinked tears that Charley decided were real.

"You are so very kind." She smiled up at Perry and slid the warm glance to Charley, briefly, briefly before it extinguished.

His nerves tingled. Miss Kingsley might be making her first bows in London, but she'd been out in some kind of society before. At some time in her past, she'd practiced sending gentlemen that sort of look.

And of course, she'd spent considerable time on a privateer's ship.

"We must go in now, Grace," Lady Kingsley said through clenched teeth.

Miss Kingsley stared up at Perry. "I shall never forget your kindness."

"Of course you won't." Perry squeezed both of her hands. "I shall remind you of it at every opportunity, when we shop, or go for ices, or to the theater. I cannot wait to meet your father when he returns, and I know my father will be delighted to meet you when he returns from Bath."

That was laying it on rather thickly. Somehow, his sister had sniffed out Miss Kingsley's dilemma and was coming to her aid. If Perry had been born male, and if she exercised just a bit more daring, she'd be the true successor of Shaldon, the great manipulator.

Perry sent him a smile. "Do you not agree, brother?"

He leveled a gaze at Miss Kingsley. "I most certainly agree. In fact, I shall send Father a message. He might be able to do some good in searching out information on your father."

"You must not let them put these ideas into your head, Grace. Your father is dead. You must not hold onto false hope." Lady Kingsley elbowed Perry aside. "I know you mean well, Lady Perpetua, but it is not kindness to keep our Grace in a state of impossible hope. Now we must go in. The world is waiting."

She led the girl off.

"Nicely done, Perry," he whispered, and shuffled off after the damsel in distress.

Lady Kingsley steered her prisoner so quickly through the crowded dance floor she would have eluded a man with less experience chasing women.

Earlier, he'd noted that this crowd of dandified coats and sprigged up muslins was not the smartest of the *ton*. Country nabobs, rising industrialists, and the sort of nagging noseys who expected a drama—and who were not to be disappointed tonight—populated the room. He saw only a few of Perry's bluestocking friends, and none from the ranks of the foreign diplomatic corps.

She'd nabbed him and Pender just as they'd been heading out for a round of their usual haunts, insisting she wanted to meet the young lady. Perhaps she really was considering escape from the traps of marriage and a voyage to the new world, in which case, their goals might align.

He held that thought for later. The huntress and her prey had reached Lord Kingsley, and next to him, Carvelle stood in disdainful stillness. He couldn't see her face, but Miss Kingsley's back told an eloquent story.

Oh, it was a lovely, creamy, straight back, and one could tell from the mound of hair arranged upon her head that once the pins were removed, an abundance of shiny dark silk would fall at least to her waist.

Carvelle, he decided, would not be allowed to run his fingers through those tresses.

He bowed his way past a clammy matron with a magnificent bosom, moving nearer. Lord Kingsley signaled and the music came to a sudden stop.

"Ladies and gentlemen." The man's booming voice could halt a full stampede. No doubt his would be the loudest in the Lords if he bothered to speak up with an idea of his own.

The crowd hushed and leaned closer. Charley jostled his way even nearer.

Lady Kingsley turned her ward to face the crowd, and he could see a pale cheek, the corner of her full lips drawn down, eyelashes fluttering lower.

Kingsley pushed back his wide shoulders and thrust out his ample belly, hands folded behind his back at parade rest. "I have an important announcement to make. No sense delaying. My ward here, my cousin, the late Captain Kingsley's daughter, and Mr. Gregory Carvelle, are to be married."

Sharp breaths, murmurs and scattered applause broke out. Even this crowd knew it was wrong. Charley pushed his way through them.

Carvelle reached for the lady. She rounded her shoulders squirming away.

A step closer to Charley. Close enough that when she folded, it was he who caught her.

CHAPTER THREE

Graciela pulled her thin dressing gown tighter around her and shivered.

The brush stroking through her hair stopped. "You tremble. It was less chilled in the nursery. Let us go and join Juan and Reina there."

Her maid's rapid Spanish touched her heart as the clipped English of her guardians never could.

"No wonder your papa left this country. There is not enough fuel in all of the universe to take the chill from this place."

And we would not be allowed to burn it even if we could find some. She had thought the absence of coal was because of Lord Kingsley's financial difficulties, but since her father's disappearance several weeks earlier, money had started to flow into this house.

Her money. None of it had been spent to warm her bedchamber. Not even during the passage through the Straits of Magellan had she felt this cold.

"Where is your other guardian?" the servant asked. "Why does he not come to help you?"

She had asked only once about Lord Farnsworth, the other trustee designated by her father. The beatings had started after that.

"I am sorry Papa has put you and Juan through this, Francisca."

The tortoiseshell brush clacked onto the scarred dressing table, the large vase of flowers there jumping and rattling. Wiry arms came around her and tugged her to a thin chest, Francisca's thin bones pressed against her back. "Juan and I made a promise, and we would never leave you or Reina. We will not leave you to the mercy of this lord and his witch of a wife, that *tlahuelpuchi*. She will not gobble Reina for dinner when the moon is full. We will suffer through this together. You must leave their house soon, before she turns her stick on the little one. I know he is not a desirable man, but I have seen many girls survive bad spouses. We will be with you."

"I will not marry him. And if I did, there is no guarantee he would not send you and Reina away."

The older woman tensed. Francisca and her husband Juan had been with her since before she could remember. Uncertain of the *inglés* her mother was marrying, they had come along with the new bride, two proud *meztisos* who would never be servile enough for aristocrats of any country. Papa had always understood them and their loyalty. Papa was one of a kind.

"How will we get away, then, and where will we go?"

A distant murmur in the hallway raised an alarm within her.

Graciela gripped both of the maid's hands. "Did you come down in time to see the man who carried me into the parlor?"

Francisca's eyes narrowed. "Who is this man to you?"

The voices drew closer. Soon the key would click within the lock. "He will help us. Listen. His father is Lord Shaldon. Papa said we could trust him. Lord Shaldon who has a grand house near Berkeley Square. Remember. Say it."

Francisca glanced to the door. "Lord Shaldon. Berkeley Square."

"Papa said he will help us. Papa said go to him if ever I have need."

Francisca's eyes glinted and her mouth set in the fierce line of her *Yaqui* warrior forebears. "Shaldon. Berkley Square."

"Tell the servants here that Lord Kingsley ordered you, Juan, and Reina away, tonight, and then leave with the clothes on your back. Wrap Reina in her shawl so she will be comforted and sleep, and go, before they realize you are escaping."

She saw the maid's hesitation.

"They will throw Reina into the street. You must save her." The key slipped the lock and she rushed on. "Tell Juan he must get her away. The streets are not safe for a child alone. Do whatever it takes to make him go with you."

The door flew open and Lord Kingsley's bulk filled the doorway of her bedchamber.

He had come himself this time. Graciela shot to her feet. "*How dare you.*"

Her voice shook and she hated it. Papa would not be so weak. It was the fault of resorting to womanly devices, fainting when she should fight.

But no, hadn't Papa outrun his enemies when his powder was low and the sickness was high? On several occasions he'd even run up a flag that was not his own.

But he had done it with strength, and a plan, and never with sniveling.

"How dare I?" Kingsley crossed the room in two strides. She saw his lady behind him, still in her green gown. They'd neither of them changed. And the lady held the dreaded cane.

The flesh on Graciela's back rippled. Thin and supple, this cane was not meant to support a woman, but to break a girl. And this time, with Lord Kingsley wielding the switch, it would be no minor swatting.

"Get out," Kingsley shouted at Francisca.

Francisca could take a beating, that Graciela knew. She'd seen the marks from something long, long ago, before Francisca came to serve Mama.

A ship captain's daughter could survive also. Had she not seen a man flogged when Papa'd had no other choice? She'd sneaked up on deck to watch, biting back her own terror, amazed at the rebellious sailor's refusal to scream. Had he screamed, surely the lashes would have been less, would have hurt less—Papa was not like this cousin of his, taking pleasure in giving pain.

She hugged Francisca tightly and set her lips to her ear. "Get Juan. Save the child. Go to the Lord's house right now. I will join you." Neither Kingsley or his lady had any Spanish, yet she whispered.

Francisca had seen the cane, and she balked.

Kingsley pulled back his fist and Graciela dodged in front of the maid. The blow glanced over her jaw, sending her into the dressing table.

Brushes and bottles flew to the floor, lavender scent wafting up in a cloud.

"Not in the face," Lady Kingsley squawked.

"For all that is holy, go before he tries to kill you all," Graciela shouted in rapid Spanish. "You know what to do. I must give them their pound of flesh. Do not turn back. Do not ask the neighbors for help. Do not let yourselves be taken. Save the child."

Francisca's mouth firmed and she nodded.

Her guardian crowded closer, his gaze bouncing from the maid to Graciela, his thick scowl darkening. He probably thought she was cursing him.

Lady Kingsley grabbed her husband's arm and tugged him back, and Francisca was gone.

She fisted her hands and fought for a breath. She must buy the maid time to convince Juan, gather the child, and get away. She must not scream, else Juan would want to barge in.

She rubbed her cheek where the blow had struck. Whether it would bruise, she did not know. She hoped it would, enough so that none of Lady Kingsley's paint would cover it. Then she would not have to go to their stupid parties.

"Shall I remove the dressing gown for my next beating?" she asked.

"You spoiled, spiteful, disrespectful girl. My husband took you in when no one else would."

"Are you not the head of the Kingsley family, Lord Kingsley? My papa told me it is what heads of families are supposed to do. He told me it would be no trouble as he would provide you with money for my care."

"And that is what his lordship is doing. Arranging a good marriage for you."

"My papa promised I would never be forced to marry against my will. And I do not wish to marry that man."

Lord Kingsley snatched the cane from his wife's hand. "You will marry Gregory Carvelle." He slapped the wood against his palm.

She drew in a long breath. "There are men in my country who beat their wives and the children entrusted to their care." And their servants, but she would not mention that. No need to put ideas into their heads, not until Francisca got away.

"This is your country now."

This cold, disdainful place? Never. "But my papa did not respect those men. He sometimes had to beat one of his crew. But beating a woman, he said, is the work of a coward."

His lordship advanced, and she stepped behind a chair.

"I must say this, Lord Kingsley, so we know where we stand. My papa, when he returns—"

"He's dead," Lady Kingsley said. "Captain Llewellyn has made port in Falmouth and will—"

"Shut up, Blanche," Kingsley said.

She caught her breath, hope stirring, as Lady Kingsley spluttered.

"Your father is most assuredly dead," Kingsley said.

She stood taller. "No one has found a body, have they? When my papa returns, when he learns of your beatings, he will not resort to lawsuits or legal proceedings. He will take that cane and use it on you, my lord."

Lord Kingsley's face grew impossibly redder. Perhaps she could coax him into an apoplexy right here in her bedchamber. In all the confusion, she could easily get away.

"I have seen him do such to men who would harm me or my mother. He will not call you out to a duel of honor, for there is no honor in a man who would beat a ward in his care."

The cane swung and she ducked and ran, hopping upon the bed.

"Especially not a ward whose money he was making free use of."

Lady Kingsley had circled the bed. She was trapped.

"You, he will not beat, Lady Kingsley, but you will wish that he had."

Thwack.

She jumped away from the cane.

"I gather that Carvelle's lust is for my money and not my person." She gasped as the cane struck her leg. "Careful. You must not prevent me from walking the aisle of your despicable English church."

She hopped to the footboard and over it. A blow landed on her back.

"Not so hard," her ladyship shouted. A dispute erupted between the two of them, and the next blow was softer.

She had said her piece. She must give them their blood so the others had time to escape. She must hold their attention.

With the next crack, sharp pain laced her skin and she bit back a scream. The next one carved deeper, stung harder. A hand clamped her shoulder and tugged at her robe, ripping the thin silk while she clung to the footboard, like that sailor on Papa's ship, tied to the mast.

Squeezing her eyes and lips shut, she held on, enduring. She must save the people she loved.

CHAPTER FOUR

"Get your gloomy self up from my sofa and share my toast." Penderbrook's voice pierced the fog in Charley's head.

When he opened his eyes, his friend waved to him from the table. The aroma of coffee wafted to him, and he sat up. Penderbrook's small, comfortable drawing room was strewn with papers and books, and carelessly discarded clothing.

Some of the clothing was his. He'd shed his coats, and his shirt bloused over his trousers. "Am I drunk?" he asked.

"Not very. Nor was I. You were no fun last night, Everly. That funk you were in was a bore. I'm sure the lady is out of range of your concern now. Whatever scolding she was to have has already taken place. Come and eat."

Details of the night before came to him. Miss Kingsley had been dead weight in his arms, a very vital, nubile, soul-stirring dead weight. Her guardian's red face and bulging veins had left no doubt of her fate. Yet, he'd gone along with Perry elbowing him aside to offer her own assistance while Penderbrook pulled him away.

And from a distance, Carvelle's glare had followed him. Hostile before, he would now be an avowed enemy.

Damn, damn, damn. As sure as Charley was, at least most of the time, a gentleman, Carvelle was not getting that girl.

He hoisted himself up and took a sip of the coffee set out for him, his fog clearing more.

There was something murky about the whole arrangement of Miss Kingsley's life and impending marriage. His funk after they left the ball had been the result of the great matter of thinking through the facts.

He was a ponderer, not a good trait for a spy— and he had a few scars to prove it—but it would do for a diplomat. Someday, he would sit in a tropical office, an ocean breeze blowing over him from the veranda doors, a domesticated lizard staring down at him from the whitewashed wall, while he sipped a rum-laced beverage and considered some treaty or other.

Perhaps that was what Captain Kingsley was doing now. Miss Kingsley was right—he might be alive. The report of a rich father's demise at sea could be easily arranged. In Kingsley's case another privateer had limped into a port with the news of the Captain's death on his sinking ship. And almost as soon as Lord Kingsley had learned of it, he'd set that great ball and the engagement in motion.

The girl had reason to be angry.

"No need to dress." Penderbrook waved a hand over his own attire, a dark dressing gown.

Penderbrook's all-around manservant—valet, butler, and footman—entered, carrying a covered tray. The scent of meat wafted up and drew his thoughts away from the lady.

"You're a good man, Pender."

"And perhaps I'll need a loan next quarter day." Penderbrook slid a news sheet over to him and pointed to a column of print. "How quickly they get out this drivel."

Charley squinted at the paper. It was a scandal sheet, and the breathless text told the story of an unnamed and reluctant heiress fainting dead away at her own betrothal ball. The paper noted that the handsome young man who had caught the swooner was not her intended, but a notorious man about town with whom she had been seen entering the ballroom from the garden.

He cursed and tossed the paper aside.

A plate of food slid toward him. "Eat. You'll think more clearly."

Charley rose and found his shoes and his coats.

"Off your feed, Everly? This girl has struck a chord within you. Are you perhaps smitten?"

He took a deep breath and finished buttoning his waistcoat. *This is the want of a rod. Which I have not spared.*

He had a very good memory. "They are beating her into this, Pender."

Penderbrook dropped his fork. "Surely not?" His eyes narrowed. "Or..." His mouth firmed. "Whatever you are planning, count me in."

Lloyd, the family's long-time butler, opened the door of the Shaldon townhouse for Charley and wished him a good morning.

He had hoped to slip in unobtrusively, but it was just as well. "I need to send an express to

Lord Shaldon," he said. "I will be but a few minutes."

"Certainly, sir. But perhaps—Lady Perpetua has already sent Lord Shaldon and Lord Bakeley urgent messages earlier this morning."

Squeals, like the shrieks of a cat-fight, raced through the hall. The sound had emanated from one of the chambers at the back of the large Shaldon townhouse. He raised an eyebrow at the butler.

"Lady Perpetua is in the morning room, waiting for you."

With a cat? Before he could ask, the butler disappeared.

Charley strode down the hallway, nodding at bowing footmen and curtseying maids, more servants than were needed to dust, mop, and shine. The hair on his neck prickled.

None of Shaldon House's servants were simple domestics, and a great many more of them than usual were up and about early.

Another loud shriek quickened his pace. He pushed through the door.

Perry, her skirts rucked up, her hair bedraggled, her spectacles missing, sat on the floor. And he sensed another presence in the corner, but before he could look, a bundle of dark hair rushed him and latched onto his leg, bursting with cackling laughter.

It was a child, less than knee-height. It turned up its chin and stared up at him, brown eyes shining. A grin split its face, revealing a scattering of tiny white teeth.

It was a very pretty child. With flowing dark curls and short skirts over miniature black boots, it could be either a female or an unbreeched male.

It hugged his leg tighter and settled a cheek on his calf. With that affectionate gesture and that wicked, winsome grin, this must be a female.

"Charley." Perry pushed to her feet. "Oh, Charley, I'm so glad you're home."

"Cha," the child said. "Cha. Cha. Cha." She unlatched from his leg and reached her arms up.

A thin, foreign-looking woman, the dark wraith from the corner, moved into his vision, beckoning the child. "Reina."

Queen. A prickling within sent blood accelerating and pounding into his ears. His mind raced through the facts, the possibilities and the actions needed. No wonder Perry had called for Father and their brother Bakeley.

Charley scooped up the little one. "You are very noisy."

She chortled, stuffed her fist in her mouth, and began to gnaw.

"I take her, my lord," the thin woman said.

Thin and older. Perhaps fifty. She must be the child's nanny, a native servant brought along. And whose child was this? No one had said.

"I am not a lord," Charley said. "I am a simple mister."

Drool leaked down the chubby wrist and dampened his sleeve. She smiled, tucked her head down on his shoulder, wriggled her bottom, and sighed.

The nanny's frown tightened.

"Is Miss Kingsley all right?" he asked.

The woman bit down on her thin lip, and a tremble went through her.

"She is not," Perry said. "I've sent for Father. And I intend to call on Miss Kingsley as soon as is decent. With Sirena gone, I could ask Paulette to accompany me, but I had rather not involve her just yet."

Their eldest brother Bink's wife, Paulette, was expecting again.

"Will you come along with me?" Perry asked.

"I'm not sure I should allow you into that house."

"Try to stop me, brother."

He glanced down at the little girl. Her eyes had closed. She was fair on to napping. He could hand her off to the anxious nanny, but hanging onto her would cure any reticence toward answering questions. Children were excellent leverage.

"*Señora,*" he began. He spoke to her in the Castilian Spanish he'd learned in his travels, possibly an accent different from her own, but she would surely understand it better than his English. "What is your name?"

The dark eyes lit. "I am Francisca. My husband is Juan. We have served Graciela all of her life."

Miss Kingsley's father had not left her entirely friendless. "And where is your husband?"

"He has gone back. He had to go back. He will linger around the mews to see what he may learn."

"Did Lord Kingsley send you away?"

She shook her head and her eyes shimmered.

In his experience, many women used tears as a tool. These looked authentic.

With a deep frown, she squeezed them back. "*She* did. Graciela did. To save the child. She said we must take Reina and come to your father. She said he will help her." She gritted her teeth, her fingers curling into fists. "The Lord came to beat her himself this time. That man, that big fat devil. When the Captain comes he will kill him. Lord or no, cousin or no, he will kill him, or my Juan will."

Or I will. Blood churning, Charley's hand firmed around the child's bottom, and the little one squirmed. He eased in a breath, softening his hold.

The maid's fierceness collapsed also, and she swayed on her feet. Deep, large eyes were ringed with shadows. She'd likely been up all night and needed some rest. He'd need to convince her the child would be safe in the hands of the Shaldon servants while she slept. But before that, he needed every bit of knowledge she and her husband could provide of the Kingsley home and Graciela's location therein.

"Let us all sit," he said.

The woman reached for the baby, but he freed a hand and held it up.

"Let her be for now. I believe she's asleep." He took a seat. "Perry, send someone to fetch Juan." Perry slipped out the door, and he led the maid to a chair. "Please sit. And tell me everything. Leave nothing out. I must know every aspect of the lady's day and where they will be keeping her."

CHAPTER FIVE

"She's not here." Perry glided into the empty space next to Charley.

He'd been quite alone at the center of this society rout, being avoided by the stuffier sort and the young virgins they guarded. Rakes and rogues—people in his league—hadn't been on the guest list, apparently.

But Perry had received an invitation, and once they'd established that the Kingsleys—who hadn't been at home to Perry that day—would attend, he'd determined to escort her.

Perry greeted a passing dowager, as Penderbrook stepped up to join them.

Charley nodded at the older woman and grinned when she cut him and moved on.

"Yet I saw *him* and his lady," Charley said. The *big fat devil* and his wife had arrived in a new coach. He'd overheard two of the matrons buzzing about the coach's mahogany trim and silk shades.

"Yes. The word is Miss Kingsley was not feeling well enough to attend. And I have not seen Carvelle."

Carvelle was not in attendance, nor Miss Kingsley. The skin on his neck twitched, and he caught Penderbrook's eye.

"Do you suppose…" Perry's voice cracked. She took a deep breath.

She didn't need to express the worry. It electrified the air around them. In fact, alarm bells were now clanging in his head.

"Shall we be off?" Penderbrook asked.

"Excellent idea. Will you escort Perry home?"

Perry's lips firmed, and he sighed.

"Fine. But promise you'll do as I say."

As soon as the elderly maid had tucked her into her bed and clicked the lock on her door, Graciela rose, relit her candle, and dressed herself in her most practical gown. She rummaged in her trunk for the pair of *pantalones* that she had worn under her dresses during parts of her sea voyage, pulled them on, and then fastened her half boots. She found the pouch with her jewelry and coins and her mother's slim volume of sonnets, stowed both deep in a pocket, and tied her hair back with a ribbon.

The lovely large Spanish prayer book her father had given her before his departure lay under her pillow. Her eyes clouded as she unfastened the hasp, remembering the words and instructions he'd bestowed with this gift.

She pressed her fists to her eyes and forced the tears back. There was no time for remembering.

The lovely sheathed dagger slipped easily from its hidden space in the spine. She kissed it and tucked it into the sash at her waist.

Then she pulled on her heaviest pelisse, and sorted through her box of hairpins for her picks.

This lock she had not mastered, simply because of interruptions. It could not be so hard. Juan had explained the mechanics mere days ago, after the first time she'd found the door locked, and he'd provided her with tools that he promised would work. With the Kingsleys gone, she would have plenty of time.

She went to the door, setting her ear against it. Some Kingsley forebear in the distant past— one more like her father, perhaps—had built this house solidly. The thick door was no exception. The house had been quiet for some time, the servants off to their final tasks or to bed. They were not entirely a bad sort, the Kingsley servants. The gray-haired maid helping her tonight was hard of hearing and should have been pensioned off long ago, but she had gasped at Graciela's back, and whispered that Juan had been seen in the mews. If that was so, then he had got Reina and Francisca to safety.

That was something, anyway.

She knelt before the door and began to work. After several minutes, she heard a muffled step. An odor seeped under the door and she sprang to her feet, pocketed her picks, and ran for the darkest corner of the room, by her washstand, grabbing a heavy dark shawl from the bedcoverings as she passed, and shrouding herself.

Heart pounding, she held her breath and rested her hand on the hilt of the dagger. *Dios.* Even the man's cologne smelled of rot.

She might hang. These *ingleses* stole all of a woman's money upon marriage and were not any more sanguine about a woman defending herself than the rankest of *dons,* or pirates for that matter.

The door opened and closed, and he filled the room, tainting it.

Anger sparked through her. She did not care if they hanged her. She would have a trial first. She would stand at the King's bench and tell of his lordship's beatings. And then shame, shame on these cold people so lacking in honor.

A numbness started in her hands, and she squeezed it down, remembering her father's lessons. Stab here, to kill a man, and here to disarm him, and here, so that he will never hurt another woman. For this man, it would be all three.

Had not her mother and Consuela shown her how a woman could do hard things?

Her candle rested on her dressing table near to the door. He held another in his hand and approached the bed. Diabolical he was, the candle showing the craters and planes of his face, his crooked nose. Her own nose rebelled at the smell of him, and she pressed her lips together, holding her breath.

She had not taken the time to arrange the bedding. Ah, but it would have been a short-lived feint anyway.

His lips, those thin twisted things, curled up revealing broken teeth, discolored, even in this light.

Her muscles tensed like the hard blade at her waist. Her vision tunneled, her gaze meeting his. The ugly slash widened.

Under her wrappings, she eased the dagger out.

"Not in your bed, Grace?" He moved closer, his gaze sweeping over her. "And dressed. Hmm."

Get out of my bedchamber. She clamped her lips shut on the words. There was no Lady Kingsley behind him to manage his ire. To pump up his greater strength with anger would not be wise.

This time, she must let her blade speak her anger.

"It is very cold in this room," she said.

The leer widened. "I have come to warm you."

His foul breath swarmed around her and she bumped into the washstand, grabbing the pitcher with her free hand and steadying it.

It was a heavy, well-made, rustic thing, and there was still water within.

"I should prefer some coals in the grate."

He chuckled. "No coals, my dear. Just my blackened, devious heart tonight."

"I think not. You must wait for the wedding night."

"The wedding night. Oh ho. Because why? We both know your innocence is not part of the package."

She froze. *Reina.* He was thinking of Reina. Lord and Lady Kingsley had eyed the child askance, but even after the news arrived about Papa's disappearance they had not dared to contradict what they thought was a fiction, that Reina was the daughter of her mother's dearest friend.

She did not have to feign indignation. "*What?*"

"You have got your bastard safely away, I hear. And here you stand, boots and all under that large covering, planning to go and join her."

"She is not my bastard. And it was Lord Kingsley who sent her and my servants away. I am worried sick about them."

"I think you are lying on all counts. But I don't care that your baggage is gone or where she went. She is well out of my hair."

"Her mother's father is a Spanish *don*. Papa pledged to her—"

"But I shall enjoy testing your assertion of innocence."

A shiver went through her and she tried very hard to hold herself still. She had been in this spot on another occasion, with a man who turned out to be just as fearsome. This time no one would come to her rescue. This time she must save herself.

"And screaming will do you no good. Lord Kingsley has dismissed most of the servants tonight."

She gulped hard over a lump in her throat and her trembling—she could not control it—darkened his smile.

He saw her fear. Oh, that was not good.

Or...was it? She bit down on her lip.

"I should prefer you w-woo me properly."

"Properly? Shall I kiss you?"

Her stomach flipped and bile rose in her throat. She swallowed hard. "Sw-sweet talk," she spluttered. "Flowers. P-poems."

"You have your flowers from me, I see, on your dressing table."

Those flowers had been from him? Her gaze darted to the withering blooms. No wonder they had shriveled so quickly.

Her hand tightened on the dagger's hilt. He still held the candle in one hand. He had arrived stripped down to his open waistcoat and his trousers. Somewhere in this house was a servant holding the rest of his clothing. Perhaps he was just outside, guarding her door. She must be careful and silent.

She saw no weapons on him. He was larger than her—most men were—but in the dark...

He leaned close and that breath...*Dios* that breath...

"And anyway, ladies are wooed. Other women are taken."

Rage roared through her. She snatched the pitcher and swung it, water flying. He grabbed for it just as the candle went out, and he lunged at her, straight into the point of her dagger.

He yelped, and the pitcher clattered. She yanked the knife out and ran.

The door was locked. He slammed her to the hard panel driving the blade into the wood.

She must hold tight to the hilt. She must not lose it to him.

"Help." The door muffled her scream, and he bellowed, "Bitch!"

He clawed at her neck, one-handed. She ducked, freed the dagger, and scuttled out of his reach.

One of his hands clutched his belly, but the light from her dressing table candle showed a dark spot spreading beyond the press of his filthy hand.

Her fingers tightened around the hilt, her heart clattering. A stab to the belly, the cloth pushed in—it might fester and kill him, but not soon enough. A man on his feet always had a chance, Papa said.

She edged toward the other candle. She must put it out. Darkness would help her. In the dark, he wouldn't see her blade coming at him. She must stab him again.

Or...he was weakened. She could club him.

The empty grate with its poker was too far away. Her tortoiseshell brush would not fell a strong man.

The vase with his vile, wilted flowers twinkled in the candle light. The vase was a heavy lead crystal.

He staggered but stayed on his feet, just barely. No true pirate was he. No soldier. No *caballero*. Like her guardian, this man beat only those he thought to be weak.

She would never be weak again.

"Go and lie on my bed," she said in a rush. "When they find you there, it will serve just as well to your purpose of ruining me."

He lunged at her, and hit the wall. The darkness of his belly was spreading, two hand widths now.

She must wear him down. "I will call your man to tend to you. He is waiting outside, no?"

He was panting now, great gasps of air, but under the glaze of what must be pain, his eyes hardened.

Ay Dios, she would have to kill him. She would *have* to.

"Your master is hurt," she shouted. No answer. No shuffling feet or pounding on the door. No one was lingering in the hall.

He would have the door key in a pocket, but she did not want to touch the man or his trousers.

"You think your little prick has hurt me?" he growled.

Do not expect your little prick to hurt me. She clamped her lips tightly over the words. Actions must speak more loudly than words, Papa always said.

"Hand over the dagger." He extended a hand streaked with blood. "I will need it to cut off this shirt."

And I will use it to cut off your hand.

He took a step closer. She backed up to the dressing table knocking over the chair. With her free hand she groped behind her, grabbed the candle and swirled it in front of her like a weapon.

His hot breath assaulted her again, the flame died, and she skittered back, dropping the hot wax.

Fingers curled around the wrist of her knife hand, twisting. His other groped for her neck, finding her shoulder.

His smell, oh, his smell. Choking and holding her breath, she fought for control. Pain laced up her arm as he bent back her wrist, her other hand scrabbling across the dressing table.

Rot. Water. Stems scratching. The vase.

As her fingers grasped the thick, smooth lip he gave up trying to find her neck and applied both hands to her wrist, bending the knife back upon her.

She shrieked and jerked her knee into his trousers, hitting a lump like a rock.

Dios. Violence aroused him. "*Pig.*" She struck him there again harder.

He swore, staggered and some of his force waned. And some of hers. Her grip on the knife loosened. She heard it skitter across the floor.

With another curse, he released her wrist.

"*Vile.*" With both hands she hoisted the vase. "*Pig.*" Leaded crystal slammed into his head.

An *oof* popped from his mouth. He lurched and grabbed the edge of the dressing table.

She coshed him again and watched him fold to the floor. With the vase as a shield, she peered closer. Whether his chest moved, it was too dark to tell, and the stench could be him or the rot of the flowers. For a long moment, she waited for him to stir, trying to think.

The dagger. Where was it? It was a treasured gift from Papa and must go with her. She would need it to face other threats on the London streets. She scrabbled over his dark form, expecting his hand to reach out for her ankle, keeping her own hand poised to cosh him again.

When he still didn't stir, a new wave of terror surged in her.

Get away, Graciela. You must get away. If this man was dead, it would be bad for her, but if he lived, it would likely be worse.

She skirted around the narrow bed and swept open her window curtains, her eyes welcoming the dim bit of light. Somewhere in the fog, there must be a moon tonight.

Edging back again, she honed her vision, searching the dark masses at her feet, the wooden flooring, the carpet, the body.

There. At the corner of the bed lay something. She poked with her toe.

She gathered the blade, wiped it on the bedcover and shed the heavy shawl. The dark wool had cushioned her body from the force of the wooden door and protected her wrist from the full impact of his grip. Now, it would only pull her down. She must be light as a cat tonight.

He stirred and she gulped in air, relieved that he lived, terrified he would try to stop her escape.

Finding the key was out of the question, as was taking the time to pick the lock. She tossed the vase on her coverlet, drove the blade into its sheath, tied her skirts at her waist, and opened the window. The light-filled haze stung her nostrils. A faint dusting of coal, lighter now that the cold English spring had arrived, mixed with the jungle scents of Lord Kingsley's garden and a more familiar scent.

The sea. She was three stories up, but no matter. She had climbed the main mast and walked a yard arm more than once in her days when Papa was not looking, and the next chamber over wasn't so far.

Charley paused at the mews to listen. A dim light seeped through the seams of the ramshackle stables behind the ill-kept garden.

Kingsley House was a very large dwelling situated on a respectable older street settled late in the century before last. There'd once been significant wealth here, but it had been lost by the current baron in bad speculation. That much he'd learned in his investigating that day.

At least one horse rustled and stamped in the small stable. Whatever other cattle Lord Kingsley kept were likely off with the new carriage.

A restless horse could be Lord Kingsley's personal mount. Or...

Rattling stopped his thoughts. Dice, it was. A sound he knew well.

"Two sevens," a man grumbled. "You win, and I'm done."

"Give you a chance to win it back. Your master returns at dawn, and mine is busy inside."

The accent was foreign. The chuckle that followed made Charley's skin crawl.

He moved noiselessly through the darkness, picking his way down the crumbled stones of the path from the stables to the house, stopping at the steps that led up to the ballroom terrace. The windowed doors there might be the easiest access. The locks had been flimsy. The ballroom would be unoccupied.

However, he should at least test the door at the servants' entrance. If they were not all gathered there drinking gin while their master was away, he'd prefer to slip in that way. And tonight, he'd gamble his last penny that they were all away.

He looked up at the house. All was dark, not so unusual with the master and mistress out. Not much light was needed to keep Miss Kingsley locked in her room.

Would there be guards set?

He slipped the latch on the door. Unlocked.

In the service entry, he paused to listen.

A dim light emanated from the larger room within—the servants' hall probably. The scent of oil from a lamp tickled his nose.

No noise touched his ears and yet his skin rippled again. He peered through the doorway. The room was deserted.

At this hour at Shaldon House, there'd be a maid mending, or a cluster of servants chatting over their cups, or a footman at work servicing a pistol or honing a blade.

Carvelle was here, and Kingsley *had* sent his servants away. There was a special place in hell for men like them.

Across the room, a shadow edged along the other doorway. Charley eased back into the gloom, his breathing quickening.

Miss Kingsley poked into the room and swept her gaze around it. He dodged out of sight.

A chuckle bubbled up inside him. She'd been fully dressed, her hair was down, and in her hand metal glinted.

Her scent traveled in with her, a floral on top of other baser elements—woman, fear, and...blood.

"It's Charles Everly," he said into the darkness.

No sound, but he could smell the fear spiking.

"My coach is waiting on the corner," he said. "My sister is waiting there also."

Her clothing rustled as though she had decided she was free to make noise, and she stepped closer.

"Are there guards outside?" she whispered.

"A stable hand and another man. Is Carvelle here?"

"Upstairs."

"Dead?"

"No."

They must hurry then. "Stay close. Keep your blade handy."

He heard a sharp intake of breath.

"And don't use it on me. I'm rescuing you."

"I have rescued myself."

So she had. "Now is not the time to argue."

Graciela took two steps to each irritating one of Mr. Everly's, trying to keep up.

"Ungentlemanly," she muttered.

He shushed her.

A plain, unmarked coach sat at the corner, its lights dimmed.

"Stow the knife," he whispered.

Her hands fumbled the blade back into its sheath, while her feet kept moving. As soon as they neared, the groom holding the horses ran to open the door. Everly waved him off, and without dropping the stairs, all but tossed her into the coach. In seconds, they were away.

She was pulled onto a seat. "Are you all right?"

The strained voice next to her was Lady Perpetua's. As her vision adjusted, she saw the glint of the lady's spectacles.

Her heart quaked and a chill went through her. Another man sat in the seat opposite Lady Perpetua. She could not make him out. She was not out of danger yet.

"Yes," she said tensely, and started to shake.

"Change seats with me, Perry." The commanding voice was Mr. Everly's.

The coach teetered as if her own trembles were rattling it.

"Lean forward." A coat, warm, and fragrant, settled over her, and then an arm wrapped her shoulders tucking her against a strong, broad chest.

Mr. Everly's scent filled her anew. She choked, gulping great mouthfuls of it. Her eyes and nose clouded with moisture.

"Shhh," he breathed into her ear. "I smell blood. Are you injured?"

"It is his."

The hand at her shoulder squeezed. "Good."

She closed her eyes and grasped for control. She was quivering and trembling like Reina after a tantrum, and her eyes were beginning to water, and she must not show weakness here.

"She is terrified," Lady Perpetua said. "Do not fret, Miss Kingsley, we have your ward and your servants. They arrived safely last night. The danger is past."

Reina...she'd forgotten to ask. Her heart filled and she could not speak.

"She is not terrified," Mr. Everly went on. "You are experiencing the aftermath of battle, my love. It is very normal. Fighting for one's life upsets the humors. This will pass."

Yes, and of course she knew that from her papa. "It will pass until they come after me."

"Yes, well, you will not stand alone. We will fight them together. I regret we did not come sooner."

"We thought you would be at the rout," the lady said. "Penderbrook and Charley and I were prepared to whisk you away from there. I am so dreadfully sorry."

So, the other man in the coach was his friend. Tears flowed from her. Try as she might, she could not stop them. For the first time in so long, she felt hope. Juan would die for her, she knew, but he was her servant, a man in her care, a man without power, except for his fist and his blade and his honor.

This man who held her, she felt his power, and it was like a balm spreading over the muscles and raw wounds beginning to ache in her back.

She would allow herself these moments of comfort, and as soon as they arrived at the home of the Everlys, she would gather her servants and Reina and leave. Lady Kingsley said that her father's friend, Captain Llewellyn, was at Falmouth. Wherever that was, she would find her way there, and he would help her go home.

The coach stopped and she sat up stiffly and let the groom hand her down the steps. They were in a neighborhood of quiet, darkened houses. The groom stood by at a respectful distance and Mr. Everly took her arm.

The coach rattled and she wheeled around, watching it turn the corner, leaving her alone with Charles Everly and the groom.

Fear swept through her again. Her breath froze.

"We are going to my brother's house," he said, as nonchalantly as if he were speaking of a social call. He stepped out along the pavement. "Once they learn I have taken in your servants, the first place they will look for you is Shaldon House. They cannot legally touch Reina, but you, I am not so sure about. Lord Kingsley is your guardian. Until my father returns I should like you to disappear into a safe house."

"They will know where your brother lives."

"He never actually had the chance to live in this home. It is his *pied-a-terre* when he and his lady desire a break from the busyness at home. Not many know he has it. And we shall move you when the time is right."

They walked down another street and around the corner to an even quieter street of homes, and then down a dark mews to a back gate. He moved silently as a breeze this man, as did his groom, as if they sneaked about quite regularly.

Perhaps he did. Perhaps rakes went into their mistresses' homes by the back door.

He held her elbow and handed a key to the groom.

The door opened on a dim light. "It's Mr. Charles Everly," the groom announced, as if he was calling out the name of a ball guest.

As they entered, the light brightened. A grey-haired servant in shirtsleeves and trousers lowered a musket.

Graciela's heart pounded and she looked again at the groom, who was carrying himself like the chief of one of Papa's boarding parties.

"Mr. Windle," Mr. Everly said placidly but with much volume, "greetings to you and Mrs. Windle. I hope you're well. It's been an age since I've seen the both of you. My brother gave me a key to use his house at any time. Did he inform you?"

The grizzled man's eyes narrowed. A stout older woman popped from behind him, a pistol in her hand. Her gaze darted from the groom, to Mr. Everly, and then landed on Graciela, in her disheveled state.

The rheumy eyes widened. She set the pistol on the table and curtsied.

"Aye, Master Charley. Of course we know you." She nudged her husband aside and drew closer. "The lady is injured. Come, let me see to you, madam."

"Mrs. Windle, the lady's maid will be along shortly to assist her. If you would be so kind as to show us to a bedchamber?"

He meant to accompany her to the bedchamber? But the maid coming must surely be Francisca. Perhaps Lady Perpetua was on her way to Shaldon House to fetch her.

Distrust mixed with relief. She did not think he would attempt to molest her, not in her present condition, and not with these elderly, familiar servants who showed no fear of him nearby, not with Francisca, and surely Juan also, on the way.

But...a kiss...perhaps she would not mind that so much.

Dios, she must not think like that.

As they moved through the kitchen, he gave orders for water to be heated and coal to be brought to her chamber.

His brother kept coal in the house in the spring? Perhaps Shaldon did also, and Reina, wherever they were keeping her, would finally not shiver every night in her sleep.

At the bottom of the servants' staircase, he swept her into his arms.

Pain seared her back and she gasped. He set her back on her feet quickly and glared at her.

"He *did* hurt you."

She shook her head. The housekeeper stood above them, holding a lamp, stiff as Lot's wife, her gaze directed at the landing above them. "It was Kingsley."

"Lady Kingsley?"

She shook her head again. Green muck from the Kingsley garden clung to the sides of his pretty patent shoes. He had large feet. He was all around as large a man as Papa, and right now, as with Papa when he was angry, impressive waves of rage swirled in the air around him, reminding her she was naught but a troublesome girl, a magnet for shame, and weak to boot.

She blinked hard and lifted her chin. "Reina and Francisca and Juan are safe. And I will be fine very soon."

"You will be fine, and you will also be safe," he said through locked jaws. He lifted her by her arms and threw her over his shoulder like a haversack.

"*What—*"

"Shhh. Hold tight."

She clutched at his waist. Blood pounded in her ears, tears filled the back of her nose, and her hair brushed the steps below them. He carried her like a prize, one strong hand bracing her hip, the other wrapped at the back of her knees, and both sending unholy tingles through her.

Dios, this would not do. Her head swam with the pulsing sensations. She must not let him think he could seduce her. She must not.

Across Town....

Carvelle heard the pounding of a great gun, every reverberation crashing through his head. He cursed the powder, cursed the man who had sold it, the mate who had tested it, the sailor who...

He lifted his head and the room teetered as in a bad squall. He swore and...he smelled a rot like channel dredge, only it was mixed with a floral perfume and...

He raised his shoulders and felt a sharp pain in his middens.

A long stream of oaths poured out of him and did not ease the pain. She'd had a blade. Was the bitch still here?

Damp fog prickled his nose. He rolled, wrenched himself to his knees, and squinted into the gloom. The window was wide open. Rattling wheels, the clomping of hooves, grew louder, nearer. It might be the Kingsleys returning home.

He searched his pocket. The key still rested there. Three stories up, would Kingsley's whore have exited out of the window, or was she cowering under the bed?

When she was his, the windows would be barred. When she was his, he'd tie her down and she would take it. When she was his, once he had her money, her father's compliance, and the matters with Lord Kingsley settled, he would dump her and make a proper marriage. A titled lord's daughter, the younger the better. Someone with proper bloodlines for his children.

Until then, the Kingsley chit would do as well as any hole to quench his wick, and one who paid him instead of sucking off his coins.

He slid the blade from his boot and rose. She'd surprised him though. He'd had a whore in Lisbon once who'd tried to rob him, as this one was trying to slip away with the money that should be his. This one would know his wrath also. In the morn, they'd wed, he'd haul her off to Kent and fix her. Her face need not be pretty for their brief marriage, as no man would be looking at her again.

He groaned. "Come help me to my feet, Miss Kingsley. You fight quite well, and I need your help."

Nothing.

He heard a muffled entrance below stairs. Crawling to the bed, he hauled himself up, cursing, and then felt his way around the room until he found a branch of candles and a tinder box on the mantel. Once lit, they showed the room in all its disarray. Unmade bed, a broken pitcher, a downed vase, the flowers scattered all about, and the dark spot upon his belly where new blood oozed and pain pricked him with every breath.

He staggered about, checking every hidey-hole. She was gone.

A red haze cast itself upon his vision. No man or woman got the better of Gregory Carvelle. No stupid, headstrong, spoiled chit of a whore stabbed him and ran away. She would not be allowed to think she could make a fool of him. She was his, that money was his, and she would be knowing it as soon as he'd recovered her.

Carvelle met Kingsley and his lady on the stairs. Lord Kingsley's eyes widened and the woman gasped and clutched the handrail. The single aging servant guiding them almost dropped his candle. All but deaf, he was, Kingsley had promised, as was his wife.

"Get my man from the stables," Carvelle shouted. "And here." He thrust the branch of candles at Kingsley. "We'll go below. You," he said to his pinched-up cow of a cousin, Blanche, her with her scheming, "Get linens and hot water."

Her mouth puckered. "Is Grace—"

"*Now*," he bellowed.

Kingsley pulled a candle from the branch and handed the rest to his wife.

"But the servants are not—"

"Go," her husband said.

"If you've killed her..." She spluttered and threw up her hands, taking her rage with her. Blanche was afraid for her reputation among the other useless nobles.

Afraid was what she should be, questioning him about the chit she couldn't manage.

Kingsley's hand shook while he lit the lamp in his study, throwing glances back at Carvelle.

Carvelle lifted the shirt and gritted his teeth at the pain. He didn't know the hour, but the blood'd had time to congeal.

His man, Kees, appeared.

"Cut this shirt off," Carvelle said. "You'll need to fish out the fibers. Where is that woman with the water?"

"That woman is my wife," Kingsley said. "And what have you done to Miss Kingsley?"

"Bugger your wife, and bugger that whore."

Even in the dim light he could see Kingsley's face flush a dark shade of red. "Made a deal with the devil, haven't you, Kingsley, and you'll just have to walk with it. I'll need a fresh shirt."

Kingsley's mouth firmed, but he left the room.

Kees finished ripping the shirt and stowed his knife.

"And you." He turned on the man. "I can smell the gin on you. You let her walk right past, didn't you?"

Kees frowned. "I did as you told. I tended to the horses. I ignored any noises from in the house."

"You sat in the stables and drank."

The man lifted his shoulder. "No one passed by. Coming or going. It was quiet as death outside." He poked at the skin around the wound. "It is not so bad. I have had worse. I will need a...a something to pull on the thread. Wait here."

As he left, Kingsley returned bearing a stack of white flannels. "The water is boiling. A servant will bring a shirt. Where is she?"

"You tell me. Where would she go?"

"Did you take her first?" Kingsley's mouth twisted.

"We will say that I did. And you might search your garden. She may be splattered below. She went out the window."

Kingsley's eyes widened. "Three stories up?"

"Consider that she was probably allowed to run wild on her father's ships."

"I would have put bars on the windows had I thought of it."

"You didn't need bars until you let her child escape. Find the child, and you'll find the mother."

Kingsley swiped a hand over his face, went to a sideboard and poured two glasses.

"Here." He handed Carvelle a snifter and took a healthy swallow from his own glass.

"Enjoying my brandy, Kingsley? If you want to keep yourself in brandy and your wife in frills, you had best bring that girl to the altar. It will be worse than a debtor's cell for you, Kingsley. The new king may allow one more drawing and quartering."

"You shall be right at my side on the gallows."

Carvelle stood and threw the glass against the empty fireplace. "You dare to threaten me? You forget I have ships and men who serve me. I can be far away from English justice. Perhaps I'll find a true Spanish aristocrat to wed, not your cast-off pirate spawn. Find her."

Kees entered then, carrying a steaming bucket, the elderly manservant in attendance, and Kingsley stalked out

Removing her chemise was not as painful as it had been earlier in the evening at Kingsley House.

Mrs. Windle, who had made no comment at Graciela's lack of stays, had her stand facing the warm fire and peeled the lightweight cotton over her shoulders and down her back. Graciela grasped the cloth in front and covered her breasts. Behind her, gruff, mumbling, half-swallowed oaths poured from the older maidservant.

A soft warmth settled over Graciela, a velvet wrap so plush she rubbed her cheek against it. It smelled of a light lilac perfume. She let the chemise fall to the floor and stepped out of it.

"I should beat the man who did this to you myself if he was here," the servant said. "Has Mr. Everly seen this? No. Of course he hasn't." She clucked her tongue. "Best he not, or he will go a murderin'. Wait here. I have a salve to help the broken places heal and 'twill keep the cloth from sticking. Drink up your tea, my lady."

Graciela smiled. "I am but a miss, Mrs. Windle. Miss Kingsley."

"Aye then, Miss Kingsley. We'll get you fixed up fast."

She went to the door and whispered to the man outside. It was a far longer chat than needed to conduct her business.

Mrs. Windle returned clutching a silver handled hair brush. "There now. Master Charley will get the salve, and I will brush your hair. Please to be seated on this ottoman."

Bemused, Graciela clutched the wrapper closed and settled onto the backless cushion. The little housekeeper had just sent an earl's son on an errand. It was expedient, and he had not balked. Such would never occur at Kingsley House. She did not know what to make of it.

Mrs. Windle's fingers were as gentle as ever Francisca's would be untangling her unruly hair.

This feminine chamber must belong to the lady of the house. The four-poster was not overly large, but would easily accommodate two. The wing chairs and table by the fire would make for a comfortable *tête-à-tête* or dining. She wondered about the couple who used this home but didn't live here, and especially the lady, whose room and hair brush she was usurping.

"Have you served the family a long time?" Graciela asked.

"Aye. Decades."

"Will her ladyship be angry that I am here using her things?"

The hand paused. "Lady Sirena? No. She was in much the same circumstance as you. Lord Bakeley rescued her from a ruckus on the docks and brought her here. They were married the next day."

Awareness raced through her in a jumble of nerves. She could not be carried off into marriage, not by anyone. She would never marry.

Yet...Mr. Everly's gentle touch. His scent. His warmth. And he was handsomer than sin, with his light brown hair and merry eyes. He sent her nerves spinning.

Because he was a rake and a rogue of course, a man who would always have many women falling at his feet. And he would always pick them up in the moment. Each of them. All of them.

She must remember that.

"She had not suffered as you have, though. 'Twas her men who had been beaten, not her. Lord Bakeley and his brother rescued them all."

"Mr. Everly?"

"Ah no, there is another brother, Bink Gibson. He is Lord Shaldon's eldest. Born on the wrong side of the bed, he was. I'm not speaking out of turn; it is but a fact, and a fine man, he is."

"The father has acknowledged him?"

"He has."

Then perhaps Lord Shaldon truly was honorable, and she could indeed trust him, as her father had said.

She thought about the other rescued lady. She would like to hear that story, to help gauge her own danger.

Or perhaps she should just cut to the heart of it. "You've known Mr. Everly for some time?"

"I was a nursery maid when he was young."

"I see." She tried to frame her next question, and was not sure what she wanted to ask.

"He will act a gentleman with you, miss, or I'll have a piece of his hide, I will."

Graciela exhaled. The maid knew of Mr. Everly's reputation and did not approve.

Strong fingers worked her scalp, easing her humors down to her toes. "He has not hurt me." *Yet.* "And I do not wish at all to marry him tomorrow. I am not English. I will return to my own country and the scandal will not matter there, so far away."

"You're not English? I couldn't tell it from your speech, miss. Where is home, if I may be so bold."

"The new country of Mexico. My father was an Englishman who immigrated to New Spain. He is participating in the War of Independence there."

"I have heard summat of it. Lady Sirena was not English either."

"No?"

"She's Irish. The Everly men seem to like... Well, you have naught to fear from our Master Charley." A tap at the door stayed her hand. "And here is our salve."

After a moment the door closed firmly.

Mrs. Windle pushed Graciela's hair away, lowered the top of the robe, and muttered quietly.

Camphor stung her nose, but it was cut with something sweeter. "The smell is quite strong," Graciela said.

"Aye. And it'll sting your flesh for a moment. That'll pass and you'll feel relief."

At the first touch, tears sprang to her eyes. But the sting, as Mrs. Windle had said, soon turned to seeping warmth.

"There now," the older lady said. "I have a fresh new chemise for you here if you'll take off the robe and stand."

Graciela clutched the robe to her chest and glanced over her shoulder. "I thank you. It is our custom to be modest. If you will kindly leave it, I will dress myself."

When the servant had left she quickly donned the clean chemise, wrapped herself in the velvet robe, and went to check the latch on the window.

Perspiration beaded Charley's forehead as he sat in a matching wing chair opposite Miss Kingsley in front of the ebbing fire.

Thank the gods, she'd finally warmed and asked for no more coal. Mrs. Windle had returned the coat he'd wrapped around the young lady, but he'd thrown it over a chair and let the servant glare her disapproval of his shirtsleeves from her perch in the corner of the room.

"Have another sip of the brandy," he said. "It will strengthen the blood."

She looked at him from under her lashes and swirled the liquid in her glass.

"I'm not trying to muddle you. And I *have* sent for Francisca."

Her hand shook when she lifted the glass and he beat down another wave of anger. Besides the bruise beginning to mottle her jawline, her wrist bore a band of bright pink that would bloom to purple, courtesy of her battle with Carvelle. And she sat as erect as the Virgin in a medieval Spanish painting he had seen somewhere.

He'd waited like a schoolboy out in the corridor, while Mrs. Windle had helped Miss Kingsley into some of his sister-in-law's things. The housekeeper had said very little more than muttered oaths as she'd passed him the bloodied flannels and the pink-tinged water, grim-faced and frowning, and sent him on errands as if he were a footman.

He had no idea what Miss Kingsley wore under the velvet dressing gown. He tossed back his drink. Nor could he think about that now.

The girl was clearly hurting.

"We didn't tell your people of our plot to rescue you at the party tonight. They were both collapsing from their worry, and we made them take beds in the nursery. Perry likely had to wake them and give them time to dress. We are a stretch away from Shaldon House, and they would need to travel through the late-night traffic. They'll have to change to a different carriage and take a roundabout way, in case Carvelle's injuries have been discovered and watchers set."

She blew into her glass, studying the rippling liquid, making him smile. She would, perhaps, never fit in here with the Almack's crowd. He counted that a good thing.

"And Reina?"

He heard the worry in her voice. "And that is likely the other holdup. Perry is persuading them that Reina will be safe with her."

Her gaze shot to him.

"She will be. I promise. What do you know about my father, Miss Kingsley?"

She pursed her lips. "He is a powerful lord. And my father apparently trusts him."

"He was a diplomat during the wars. Did you hear much about the wars?" At the flash in her eyes he added, "You would have been but a child then."

"The French killed their king and queen. Then Napoleon took over. He invaded all his neighbors. Lord Wellington went to Spain and defeated him, and they locked him up on an island. Then he escaped, and Wellington fought him at Waterloo. I hope Napoleon dies soon so he will cause no more trouble."

"Your wish may come true soon." Napoleon was gravely ill, had perhaps even died already, or so everyone hoped. "However, we must be sure of it. There was a rumor of Napoleon's death some years ago that caused no end of trouble. Even in death the man is a nuisance. Father has probably sent a man to St. Helena."

"I see." She raised an eyebrow, making him smile.

"My father was more than a diplomat. He directed the services of men and women seeking information on our enemy's activities."

Her eyes widened. *Good.* He had distracted her from her black thoughts.

"Spies?" She laughed ruefully. "How nicely you put it."

She glanced at the fire and then back at him, eyes narrowed.

Time to gabble before she launched questions about his line of employment. "The servants of Shaldon House are carefully screened—for their loyalty first of all, and their discretion, and their skills." The bad apples that had slipped through the net and threatened Bakeley's wife were disposed of. There was no need to share those details and add to Miss Kingsley's worries. "You will see. Perry will keep Reina safe. Perry is quite adept."

"As are you. You are also a spy?"

He took a sip and grinned. "I'm the troublesome younger son. Am I not, Mrs. Windle?"

A loud huff sounded from the corner, a reminder to Miss Kingsley if she needed one.

She set her glass upon the side table. "I note that you did not answer my question."

He should issue a denial, but he did not want to lie unless he must. He lifted his glass and drained the last few drops.

"I take that as a yes. What are you planning to do with me, Mr. Everly?"

"I would like to visit your solicitor." This particular solicitor would likely be known to Bakeley, but Bakeley was in the country. Penderbrook could accompany Charley. He would ask his brother Bink to guard the lady in his absence.

"I will go with you."

"It's the first place they'll expect you to go."

She looked away, thinking.

"Can they snatch me up, do you think? Would they do so?" She stared into the embers and nodded. "Carvelle would. He will marry me, ensure possession of my money, and arrange for me to die painfully."

"He will not marry you. And he will not hurt you. Nor will Lord Kingsley, nor his wife. I will not allow it."

Her mouth firmed. "I want to go home."

"To Kingsley House?"

He knew what she'd meant but he couldn't resist the prod.

She sighed. "To Alta California. I have family there. Cousins."

"Are you not bound for Spain and Reina's family? It's what your maid told me."

She grimaced. Frowned. Firmed her lips. "Papa wrote to them. I do not know if there has been an answer back." Her gaze lifted with a look that reminded him of the little girl back at Shaldon House. "Will you take me to a ship?

Lady Kingsley said that Captain Llewellyn has arrived in Falmouth. You can turn me over to his care. He is my father's friend and—"

"Miss Kingsley—"

"Carvelle has visited my bedchamber, and I am sitting in a house with a notorious rogue with only the servants as chaperones. I am ruined, most thoroughly, according to your stupid English standards. No respectable man will marry me, not even for my money, if Lord Kingsley has not spent it all. I will take what is left and go home, and buy some land and perhaps, someday, find a strong man who I can respect."

"Miss Kingsley—"

"In my country, a woman does not lose all her property to a husband." She flung out a hand. "Girls are sold into marriage, of course, by uncaring fathers to rich old men. It is the way of things. But a woman alone with some wealth may choose." She jumped to her feet and began to pace.

He gave up and lolled back to watch her.

"I will say I am a widow." She paused and braced her hands on the mantel, staring into the hearth. "I shall say Reina is mine. It is what everyone believes anyway."

Guilt niggled him. He had wondered it himself.

She turned, reading his thoughts.

He groped for the right words. "She is the child of your heart."

"Yes." That had pleased her, and tears sprang to her eyes. Her hands twisted at her waist. "Her mother was our dearest friend, recently widowed, who almost died giving birth on our way overland to Veracruz. We fed Reina with the milk of a nanny goat we tethered behind our cart." The hands came apart and formed into white-knuckled fists. "The Kingsleys had naught but contempt for the child. Francisca and Juan did their best to keep her quiet and keep her safe, but her presence was a constant taunt to the Kingsleys' vile tempers. I knew their servants would not stop mine from sneaking away with her. And I knew I could not—could never—marry that odious man who smells like death. I made a sacred promise to protect her."

"Carvelle would not have let you keep her."

But I would. And where had that thought come from?

She pounded the mantel. "I should have killed him."

"You are sure you did not?" He had debated sending an anonymous message to Kingsley at the rout to return home immediately.

"He...he ran into my dagger. Here." She pointed to a spot at her waist. "He did bleed much. He had removed his coats before coming to...to attack me. If they clean the wound well, he should survive." She bit her lip. "I do not think the vase did more than knock him out."

Charley shot from his chair and took her hands. They were cold again, and in the candlelight, her wide eyes gleamed with unshed tears. Her beauty almost undid him.

Almost. He'd had many dealings with this sort of beguilement, enough to know to be wary.

Tears streaked her cheeks, and he pulled her to him. He reached for her back, remembered her injuries, and rested his hands on her shoulders, his fingers tangling in thick locks of hair there, his chin resting on the top of her head. She trembled under his touch, but there was no wailing. Perhaps a girl who'd spent as much time as she had on a ship full of men had learned to throw tantrums quietly. A rush of desire swept through him.

Mrs. Windle cleared her throat loudly.

The reminder helped him recover his breath. "You're very brave, Miss Kingsley. We'll not pretend we don't have obstacles ahead, but you mustn't worry. We'll deal with them and keep Reina safe. If Carvelle comes after you again, I shall kill him myself."

It would, in fact, be his pleasure. He suspected his father would have scores to settle there anyway.

Graciela could not pry her head from the broad chest where it rested, reminded of the solace she'd found there during the journey in the coach. It was as warm and comforting as Papa's embrace, except that the stroking of Mr. Everly's ungloved palms upon her shoulders made her skin ripple.

And didn't frighten her.

Hope bloomed in her. Years ago, when she was no more than a child just starting her courses, a boy they'd met on a stop in one of their journeys had touched her like this. Darkly handsome, he'd stirred feelings in her she'd wanted to explore, until one night after the dancing, Papa had barged into the shed where they were stretched on the hay kissing and pulled him off her.

She closed her eyes and squeezed in the troubling images. How that would have ended, she now knew. No matter how pleasant those feelings stirred by that boy, Papa had been in the right, and she had been in the wrong.

She must be careful. That boy's forthright kisses and fondling hadn't heated her as much as Mr. Everly's simple touches. The wonder of it was, until now, she had barely been able to tolerate a man's hand on her,

Not since Rigo. She dropped her hands and stepped back, letting her gaze fall also. His finger tipped her chin up and she looked into his eyes. They were the same plain brown as her own: thoughtful, hard to read. His hair, many shades lighter than her own, was tousled in the way of the lazy, fashionable men here.

Only, no, that was not the way of Mr. Everly. He was something more than what he seemed. Perhaps trust was possible here.

He smiled at her, and her heart took a great leap in her chest, her breath coming in short gasps. *Perhaps I can feel something with him besides fear.*

She fought to steady her breath. *Dios.* She pushed his hand away. "I want to rest now."

"That is a good idea, miss," the housekeeper said. "Master Charley, you should have a lie-down also."

His serious gaze never left her. "It is an excellent idea."

A river of impossible heat roared through her. She felt herself flush. "Go now."

"I will have your promise first, that you will not go out those windows or otherwise attempt to leave here without me."

"Am I to be your prisoner then?"

"No. Never." He dropped his voice. "Carvelle does not just smell like death. He runs a smuggling ring and some say pirate ships. He is a criminal conspirator of the most dangerous sort. He will want back what he thinks is his."

"I will be no man's property."

"Then let me help you keep your freedom."

Oh. The wind left her anger, and her heart swelled again. At this rate, it would burst. "I could not leave anyway. I have no clothing. Even I would rather not run through the streets of London in a dressing gown."

"We'll find a dress of Lady Sirena's for you and alter it." Mrs. Windle bustled closer. Dark circles smudged her eyes, and in the growing light of dawn, her face looked grayer. "Or, you are closer in figure to Lady Perry. Mayhap your maid will bring something of hers that we can tack up."

"You have not slept either, Mrs. Windle." Graciela looked at Mr. Everly. "Mrs. Windle must rest also. I will not run away, I promise."

Charley paced the corridor of the tidy house waiting for the housekeeper. With another bedchamber on this floor, and probably two more on the next, the tidy little house would be easy enough to protect. It was more than sufficient for a bachelor, but he could see why his sister-in-law, Sirena, had elected to live at Shaldon House. Bakeley's *pied-a-terre* would not be big enough for the family that Perry reported was already on the way.

The door opened and closed with a sharp *snick*.

"You are not going back in there." Mrs. Windle rested her hands on her plump hips. "And you are not going to linger here in this hallway." She wagged a finger. "There is a spark between the two of you."

Not a spark—a conflagration.

"I was waiting for you, Windy." He took her arm. "Come, I'll escort you downstairs. That is where you are headed, is it not? With a visitor here and it almost dawn, you're not off to bed, are you?"

She expelled a long breath and toddled along down the corridor next to him. "I got her settled, though she cannot rest upon that back for a few days. Who would do such a thing?" She shook her head. "Your mother would never have allowed it. She didn't even like me swatting your bottom, Master Charley, and I'm thinking I didn't do enough of it. The stories I hear—"

"Shhh, Windy. You will shame me into taking holy orders."

She frowned up at him.

"I won't dally with her, my word of honor. And Bink will be along shortly, and Perry has sent for Father." He patted her hand. "She's in great danger, but not from me."

She grunted. "I must get the breakfast started. I doubt she'll sleep much and she needs to eat something. Not an ounce of fat on the girl."

Except in all the right places.

CHAPTER EIGHT

Charley found his eldest brother, Bink Gibson, in the kitchen, his large frame folded onto a chair at the servants' table, a steaming cup in front of him. The fragrance of coffee filled the air.

"Coffee for me also, Windle," Charley said.

"What's afoot, Charley?" There was no rancor in the question, and Bink did not get up. All they lacked was a plate of eggs and the morning news sheets.

The back door opened and a dark-eyed, dark-haired man of middle age and some height entered. "All's well on the perimeter." He shook moisture off his hat. "Morning, Charley."

Charley groaned, and relief mixed with...what?

Happy he *should* be that Kincaid, his father's favorite henchman, Bink's uncle by marriage, was along. If there was a villain to be disposed of, Kincaid would step up and oblige. He'd done so for Bink.

But Bink was a veteran of the Peninsula. He'd had nothing to prove.

"And who is watching out for Paulette?" Charley asked.

"As it happens, she's gone down to Sussex for a few days with the Cathmores and Hackwells. Your timing is providential, little brother." He turned and straddled the bench, stretching his long legs. "You've sent for Shaldon, so I take it he's not the villain in this drama."

There was no smile on Bink's lips, but his eyes sparkled. He'd visited this house a few months before, protecting Bakeley's intended from their father.

Kincaid looked from one to the other, his face devoid of expression as usual.

Charley took the cup Windle handed him and tamped down his anger. "There's a lady upstairs whose guardian himself caned her so that she cannot rest on her back. Is that not right, Mrs. Windle?"

"Aye. And I've never seen such on a girl. The man himself should be thrashed."

"All to persuade her to marry the man of his choice."

Kincaid took a deep audible breath, his only reaction. Bink's mouth firmed and he got to his feet. "Let's go to the parlor, and let Mrs. Windle have her kitchen. Kincaid?"

The other man shook his head. "I'll wait here for the others."

"What others?"

"The ones coming from Shaldon House."

Of course. The ones bringing Miss Kingsley's servants.

In the sparsely furnished parlor, Charley lit candles and then paced to the yawning fireplace and back again across the room.

"Who is the prospective groom?" Bink asked.

"Gregory Carvelle."

Bink frowned. "Fill me in."

"A Huguenot smuggler. A weasel in pilgrim's clothing. Some also say he runs an enterprise that extends into the West Indies."

Bink grunted. "Plenty of privateering there also."

With the demise of Spain in the new world, the Caribbean was ripe for exploitation. The newest war against piracy was there.

"And the girl?" Bink asked.

"Graciela Kingsley. The wealthy heir of Captain Kingsley and his Spanish colonial wife. He left for the new world decades ago, took up citizenship and the religion, made a fortune in furs and hides and whatnot." He had found out that much yesterday, though the *whatnot* was still a bit murky.

"The captain who has not returned. I heard he is dead."

Charley walked to the front window and looked out. The fog was lifting, and the day coming might prove to be sunny. Down the street, a boy lingered. He recognized him as one of Bink's grooms, one of his father's former men.

"What's Shaldon got you up to, Charley? All this whoring around is a bit more than your usual. You're walking a fine line with some of these diplomats. Bound to be called out sooner or later, or found with a stiletto in your gut."

There's a Spanish woman, wealthy and beautiful, with the key to a traitor. Newly arrived, exactly when, we don't know. Where, we don't know. Find her.

He tossed back his coffee and set down the cup. Kincaid had started him on this mission and handed it over to Farnsworth a few months ago, before he himself had disappeared on some errand of Father's.

A familiar ache started in the back of his head, flooding him with grim memories, pictures of the rocky shore, of a broken carriage, and the dead...

He took a deep breath. Farnsworth had left, but not before Charley had heard the whispered discussion between him and Shaldon. Whoever this lady was, she might be linked to the traitor who'd sent Lady Shaldon over a cliff edge so many years before.

He'd flirted with ambassadors' wives, paid calls on a visiting merchant's daughter, bedded a lady's maid. He'd thought the Contessa—wealthy, widowed, and well-connected—a likely prospect. Her wealth, however, had proved to be a fiction, and he'd had to duck and weave avoiding the parson's trap.

And the Duquesa de San Sebastiano...between her powerful father and her treacherous husband, she was a walking pot of true danger; beautiful, impenetrable, and well-guarded.

And how she could possibly be the key to a Yorkshire murder years ago, he still couldn't puzzle out.

"Charley? Charles." Bink's voice penetrated his thoughts and he turned. A beam of candlelight set Bink's red hair afire. "Are you planning to wed the girl?"

His chest tightened as if the hand of a genie gripped it and pushed all the hot blood to his head.

Bink grinned.

Damnation. Agents of the Crown did not blush like schoolgirls.

"It's your turn to be matched by our father, you know. You're next."

"No." He shook his head. Father had managed the marriages of Bink and then Bakeley. "I'll not play his marriage game." He had plans. A murder to solve. A world to explore. Wives did not travel well.

Assignments were not to be shared, but of all the people in the world, he felt sure he could trust his brothers, who had both inadvertently found themselves battling villains to protect the ladies they married. The skin on his neck rippled. He swiped a hand over his face. *Damnation.*

"I have a mission. I'm looking for a Spanish woman, wealthy and beautiful. Not *this* Spanish woman, Bink."

"Are you sure? Father set you to this."

He shook his head. "No. It was Kincaid, who handed me off to Farnsworth." Lord Farnsworth was a long associate of Shaldon's. "Who is now off to God-knows-where to check on Napoleon's conspirators. Would that someone could drive a stake through the Corsican's heart and be done with it."

"And yet, I expect Shaldon will know all about this assignment."

"Undoubtedly. But I met Miss Kingsley merely by chance. Perry dragged me off to a ball and the lady asked me for help."

"You let yourself be dragged to a ball?"

"I thought someone I was hoping to meet would be in attendance."

Was that it? He'd had more than one brandy after their dinner that night when Perry had persuaded him to accompany her.

"I see. Her husband had come back to town. So, what's next? You're not going to make this young lady Mrs. Everly. What will you do with her?"

He rubbed his face again. Taking her to Falmouth, turning her over to a sea captain to travel under the protection of only two servants was her wish. It was not something he would do.

"We've sent for Father." Who might or might not be too ill to return immediately. Father was cagey. With Bink, he'd gone so far as to fake his own death. "Until then, I intend to hide her from her guardian. And speak with the solicitor managing her affairs. Lord Kingsley, I believe, is helping himself to her money."

"As he may do."

"For his new town coach?"

Bink's forehead crinkled. "As he may do. Bakeley knows everyone in the City. Every damn solicitor and barrister and banker."

"Perry sent for him also. I know the solicitor's name, though: Watelford."

"Bakeley or Shaldon would know what's what with him."

"Yes. Meanwhile, Penderbrook is investigating him at the club, and is looking into what bank Captain Kingsley might have used. I'll pay a call on the solicitor later."

"I'll go with you."

"I thought to bring Penderbrook."

"I'll go. I'm on a committee looking at some changes in estate law."

Charley laughed. "Of course. I'd forgotten—we're Members of Parliament." It was a useful cover if he would but show up for the tiresome meetings, debates, and votes. "You're brilliant, Bink. It will get us in through the door."

"Yes. And Kincaid and his Scotsmen will keep a sharp eye here. Now, is there a magistrate we can trust?"

"For what?"

"To bring charges against Lord Kingsley. He's the one who beat the girl, isn't he? Or was that Carvelle?"

"It's worse than that. Kingsley left the girl alone in the house and sent the servants away to give Carvelle free access."

Bink cursed and rose and stopped in front of him. A few inches taller, a bit bigger in muscle, his brother, when angered, was a force unto himself.

"He didn't succeed. She says it, and I believe her. She says she stabbed him, and clubbed him, and went out of the window to the next bedchamber." His heart filled. "And to my thinking, any man who would think it mattered is a fool."

"They were forcing the issue, though. True or not, they'll pass the word around to force her to marry him."

"She is not going to marry him."

"Then she won't be marrying any of your blue-bloods, I'm afraid, not with that in the scandal sheets."

It was true, but Graciela had the right of it. If she left England with some of her fortune, she would be a plum pick for some colonial man starved for the company of a pretty woman with some coin in her reticule.

"Yet Carvelle is not one of your nobles, is he?" Bink asked. "Why did they match her with him, I wonder?"

Outside, a bank of fog drifted and light from a street lamp pierced the window. "Bink, I must say it again, you are brilliant." He should have thought of the question himself—would have, had he not been so matrimonially averse, so lacking in sleep, and so determined to find a rich, beautiful *Señorita*.

Lord Kingsley's spending spree hadn't started until after the report of Captain Kingsley's death. The man had the usual broken-down country estate and a house in disrepair. But why was he short on money? He wasn't known at the gambling hells. He hadn't spent on lavish furnishings, a stable, or an errant heir. And if Graciela's guardian needed money, why marry her off and hand her fortune over to a husband?

And why to Carvelle, who was thought to be rich already? Though, in the way of successful criminals everywhere, perhaps that wasn't true at the moment.

Money might be a factor, but his gut told him there was some other urgency driving Lord Kingsley to force Graciela into this particular marriage.

And in that case, there was no sense in waiting for Father.

Charley clapped his brother on the shoulder. "Give me your cup. I'll serve your coffee and we'll get Kincaid to plot with us."

"We're plotting?" The voice was Penderbrook's. "Then I have information you'll want to hear about your solicitor."

Sometime later, across town...

Lord Kingsley scanned the blurry lines of the cheap paper. "Where did you get this?"

"A boy shoved it in the cook's hand and left." Lady Kingsley slammed a fist into her other hand. "I should box her ears for not detaining him, but then we wouldn't be sure what we were eating."

Fingers of pain pulsed in his chest, echoing the aches in his jaw and the tapping behind his eyes. This might well be Carvelle's work. The man had bollocksed up the easy matter of making his bride certain, and now he was trying to extract revenge in the scandal sheets.

"Do not worry, the cook cannot read. She gave this to the housekeeper who can barely read, but who will not talk." She crinkled her brow. "She ran away, did she not, Kingsley? You don't think Carvelle—"

"No." The scandal sheet in front of him said that a wealthy young heiress had disappeared; an heiress whose guardian was beating her, embezzling her funds, and forcing her into a marriage with a man of ill-repute. The implication was foul play. No name that would make the libel actionable had been given, but the *ton* would put their finger on him.

"He wouldn't kill her. He must marry her before she may disappear." And to do that, Carvelle needed her guardian's permission, unless he took her to Scotland. But he, and his principle henchman, had both been in the house the previous night, fuming. He didn't think Carvelle was a good enough actor to fake the anger he'd shown last night. "So only the housekeeper saw this?"

"Yes."

And the housekeeper would now be speculating on why he'd given the entire staff a special outing the night before.

"Shall I send for Carvelle?" Lady Kingsley asked.

The man had a ghastly wound from the chit. He could go to the inn where Carvelle said he was staying. And yet, he was waiting on his own man who was making inquiries in the neighborhood to return.

"No. Have the carriage readied. I shall pay a call on Carvelle, and then meet with Watelford. She'll go to him first." She'd want to check on the fortune the solicitor had under guard. She'd not know that Watelford was his man. There would be no drafts for her to take to McCollum's Bank.

"If she's alive after walking this neighborhood at night," Blanche said.

"She's armed and as ruthless as her father." He should have known. He should have paid closer attention.

"But who is helping her, Kingsley?" A fist came down on the table, plump, but surprisingly powerful. His jaw had encountered it more than once, in one of her tirades. "I searched all her things, read all her papers and books, and found nothing. I was present for all of her callers. She didn't ride with beaus or go shopping with other girls. She had no friends."

"She had the two darkling servants. They planned this. They ran away first, and then her. Find them and we find her."

"They've taken her to some squalid rooms somewhere. She had no money."

He glared at her. "Yes, and she had no weapons either, wife."

She blinked, and quickly recovered her bully stance, always her first approach to a dispute.

She'd been tasked with insuring the obstinate girl's room had no writing paper, no money, no weapons. She'd failed miserably.

Her own day of reckoning would come if they did not find the girl.

"I shall pay calls," she said. "I shall say the chit is still ill." She drew herself higher and balled her fists. "We'll need to put a good face on this. We have done nothing wrong. Once we find the girl, we'll have the wedding here and arrange for a public appearance before Carvelle takes her away." She paused and her plump cheeks, for once, washed pale. "We must make sure her father is truly lost."

He looked down at the scandal sheet. If Tristan Kingsley walked through the door of Kingsley House, he could count out the rest of his life in minutes. He must resolve this. Must resolve his business with Carvelle. Must get the girl married to the man. And then Captain Kingsley—should he miraculously return—could spend his revenge on another man.

"Yes. I've been assured we have nothing to worry about from that quarter."

Charley and his companion sat back in their hackney, trailing at a distance behind the unmarked coach. A boy strode into the street with his broom, halting their progress for the well-dressed pedestrian following him. Charley's driver flung a colorful curse at the street sweeper, and the boy shouted some indecipherable cant in reply.

The heavy black coach stopped in front of a discreetly marked building. *Watelford and Grinley*, the sign would say. He couldn't see it from their station so far down the street, but they had driven by earlier.

A couple exited the vehicle, a handsome strapping gentleman and a lady, Graciela's size, all veiled in black. Juan jumped down from his perch on the coach and came to stand next to them.

The couple looked around, like country folk come to town early for the coronation festivities, making a jaunt to their new solicitor's office, uncertain of their surroundings. The man bent to speak into her ear.

As they approached the door, two men jumped from nowhere and attacked, one large, the other small and swarthy as a Moor, both dressed in wide-legged sailors' slops.

"They're good," Charley said.

"Aye, but we're better," Kincaid muttered from his perch in the driver's box.

Indeed. Before the big man could rip the woman's veils, she'd landed a hard one in his kidneys and Juan was atop him. Other men poured from inside the coach, and the sweeper and his pedestrian joined the fray. In mere moments, they wrestled both men into the carriage. The gentleman and lady retreated down a side street where another coach would be waiting. The sweeper abandoned his broom and shovel, and he and his walker disappeared into the London traffic.

With the street clear, the horse stepped out and Charley leaned back against the squab.

"I see now." Graciela's voice shook. She smoothed an ungloved hand along the rough fabric of her breeches.

The coats she'd acquired from young Roddy stretched tight across her bosom. "Lean back, my dear." He adjusted her hat, and took her hand. She was trembling.

"Will Carvelle and Kingsley be here also?" she asked.

Charley squeezed her hand. "Kingsley is not here now, but our man spotted him returning from some early errand. Carvelle will likely be about though. Ah, there, perhaps."

A coach had stopped around the corner, blocked by a cart that had tangled with another hackney.

His heart raced like a green recruit's. It had been a mad frantic morning, and he hoped this plan would work. He didn't wish to lead either villain to his destination.

"Don't worry," Kincaid said. "We won't be followed."

CHAPTER NINE

Graciela's heart pounded at the sight of the grand house that was Charley's home. Mr. Kincaid stopped the battered carriage in front, and called out a fare to them over his shoulder. No footmen or grooms appeared. She exited the hackney behind Mr. Everly, jumping down without a hand to hold, and took the empty package he handed her, pressing it to her chest as he'd instructed. She handed Kincaid some coins, and followed her master into the grand house.

Inside, a liveried servant reached for the package and quickly averted his eyes.

The hat rose from her head, uncoiling her plaited hair down her back.

Mr. Everly tossed the hat to the servant. "Give Roddy his hat back. Cass, take Miss Kingsley up to the nursery."

Out of thin air, a maid had appeared, as quiet as a ghost. Her heart lifted and she quelled the trembling that threatened. "Yes, please, Cass."

But her feet did not want to work. The grand house was like the palaces of old Spain Papa had seen in his younger days, or like the home of a fairy tale king, and Mr. Everly was the prince who lived here. Marble floors stretched through a high entry hall, and twin stairs led up, cushioned with the Aubusson carpeting so coveted by Lady Kingsley. There was gilding on wood trim, and flocked wallpaper, and delicate footed tables and a vase that was surely Sevres.

His hand touched her waist sending warmth coursing through her. "Go," he commanded. "I must have a word with Perry."

"I have a dress ready for you, miss," the maid said.

"A dress," Charley said, leaning close. "There you go. I won't continue to be tortured by the shapely outlines of your legs."

With Mr. Everly's whisper tickling her ear and fine-tuning her senses, she could make out every finger of his hand through the thin coats.

She lifted her chin and looked over her shoulder. "I may not wish to change. These clothes are so freeing."

No expression touched his face, but his eyes went very dark. And then he grinned. "As you wish. But you smell like horses, hay, and onions."

"Do I?" She sniffed her sleeve and smiled back at him. It was true. And he was kind enough not to mention the musk of the boy whose clothing she wore. "So I do."

His clear gaze sent the air around them humming and heating and she realized she must be blushing. The male servants had slipped away. The maid waited patiently, studying the immaculate floor.

Graciela moved away from his hand which somehow was still connected, as if the heat had branded it in place. "I shall go then to Reina. Please give Lady Perpetua my thanks."

"You may do that yourself in a bit."

His sister would be joining her, but not too soon, she hoped. She needed to spend time with Reina. She needed a private talk with her maid. Juan had agreed to act as a lure today, and he would want to stay for the questioning and take pieces of those men's flesh. She needed him to come to her, as quickly as possible. She needed to make her own plans. "Lead the way, if you please, Cass."

Cool air rushed to where his hand had rested, and she felt suddenly adrift and mentally muddled. She must pull herself together. She must not grow dependent on Charles Everly, especially when he had this effect upon her. Stiffening her spine, she followed the maid.

The large suite of rooms that comprised the nursery was tucked at the back of the house on the uppermost floor below the attic rooms.

"It is a longer walk to this nursery than my voyage to England," Graciela said.

"It's indeed a large house, miss."

"With many windows and doors." Escape would be easy.

The maid stopped at one of those doors, its raised panels darkened by time and regular oiling. "You and the babe, and your people, will be safe here, miss. Mr. Everly will see to it."

The girl's fierce look was belied by a blush. She had a *tendre* for Mr. Everly.

Was he dallying with servants?

"My husband is a footman here. He served Lord Shaldon in the war. You will be safe."

Graciela's heart fluttered. He was not dallying. The servants of Shaldon house were carefully screened, he had said. Loyalty, discretion, skills. This one was of middling height, and—she peered more closely—perhaps not as young as she'd first thought.

"Thank you, then, Cass. It will be good to feel safe for awhile."

She pushed open the door to bright light pouring through the windows. This was a playroom, and had recently been torn asunder, the plunder still scattered about. It was a world away from the grimy, austere attic nursery at Kingsley house. Here there were toys, and games, and paints, and even a pair of hobbyhorses.

She spotted a silent maid on her knees, gathering building bricks. The girl—this one *was* a girl, quite too young for the wars that had ended six years earlier—stood quickly, bobbed, and pointed toward an open doorway.

Graciela hurried through to another room. Her gaze went to the table in the corner. A low affair, it had seating for at least six in child-sized chairs. Francisca huddled there, knees crammed under the table edge, a spoon poised for entry through Reina's rounded lips.

She caught the maid's eye and smiled a greeting. The lines that crinkled the tired corners of Francisca's eyes went deeper.

"*Gracias a Dios*," the maid said.

"Thank God, you are safe also," she answered in Spanish.

"*Y Juan?*"

"He is overjoyed and relieved that he was able to punch someone."

Francisca's frown eased.

"And how is *la Reina*?" Graciela asked.

Reina's faced puffed out like that animal that stored food in its cheek pouches. Gruel ringed her lips.

"Look at you. Will you share with me? I am hungry," she said in English.

Papa had always spoken to her in English, and Mama in Spanish. Reina would learn both English and Spanish as she herself had, except that Juan and Francisca would teach her the Spanish.

The little girl scowled and looked away.

She shooed Francisca and took her seat next to the child. "I think I should like to ride one of the horses out there."

The contents of Reina's mouth oozed down her chin. She jabbed a fist into the air and said "*No.*"

Graciela swallowed a smile. That reply was clear enough in any language. She grabbed the napkin, but the child jerked away, gruel hitting the bib tied at her neck.

Her heart seemed to cave in on itself, like a sinkhole in a desert place. After only two nights apart, Reina felt abandoned.

"I will request you some food." Francisca went to the door, exchanged some words with the maid in the playroom and came back. All the while, Reina's pout didn't lift.

"What in God's name are you wearing?" Francisca asked. "We brought you a dress this morning, and you tried it on, and it fit."

That brought Reina up short and halted the temper that was building.

"The disguise was Mr. Everly's idea, and an excellent one."

"Mr. Everly." The maid clucked and scowled. "It is indecent. What would your father say? *Ay*

Dios. How we have failed you, Juan and I. We promised to look after you. We promised to keep you safe. It is indecent."

Reina's face scrunched, easing Graciela's heart. She smiled at the girl.

"My sweet, I was playing dress-up. We are together now. And I am safe. And you are safe."

Francisca wrung her hands. "Safe. From the lair of one wolf to the lair of another. I do not think...the way he looks at you—"

Throat-clearing, distinct, loud and male, made Francisca's eyes go wide. Reina craned her neck at the sound, her eyes narrowing, then brightening.

"*Cha.*" She shrieked, scooted out of her chair and ran to the doorway where Charley Everly was crouching to receive her.

She is the child of your heart. He understood, because Reina had charmed him too.

Or...he had used his rogue's powers on her.

The girl ran into his open arms and he lifted her up in the air and they both filled this bright room with laughter.

She batted down the spark of jealousy flaring within, balling her fingers to keep from grabbing the child away from him.

"*Aargh,*" he roared.

Reina chortled in reply. She locked her chubby child's arms around his neck and nuzzled there.

Swallowing the lump in her throat made Graciela's eyes start to water. If Charley Everly loved the girl as he seemed to, he would fight to keep her safe and that was really what mattered. Best to be grateful. She forced a smile.

He tucked the little girl closer and looked at Francisca, who glared back. He had heard their conversation. With his hair spiked and waving in complete disarray, he was like a wild lion, or indeed, a tawny-colored wolf.

Yet he did not look as if he were about to devour either of them. His eyes sparkled and reflected back some of the rare golden sunlight. "Juan shall return soon," he said to Francisca in perfect Spanish. "When he returns, you should both rest. It was a very long night. Miss Kingsley will be safe, even from me. And this one..." The corner of one lip twisted up. He laid his palm on the baby's back and Graciela shivered, as if she felt that warm touch herself. "This one has drooled on yet another coat, I fear. We must only protect her from my valet. I shall tell the maids to keep him away from the nursery."

Francisca's lips firmed and she gripped her hands at her waist.

Mr. Everly went to the table and settled his large self into a chair. He looked up at Graciela as if she had protested when in truth she had said nothing. "Don't worry. These chairs survived the worst kind of mischief from Bakeley, Perry and me. They're quite sturdy."

That mischief still glittered in his eyes, and sent her blood dancing through her, sparking hot warmth in her cheeks. His gaze did not leave her face, yet she felt his attention on her in her coats and the tight breeches. Freeing she had said they made her feel. Now she just felt naked.

That warmth turned to anger. It was his attention making her feel that way. It was the way of all men. If she could simply go unnoticed...

"Here you are." Lady Perpetua swept into the room and held Graciela at arms' length. "Oh, you do look very dashing. We shall have to get you back into a dress, else every maid will fall for you as they do for our Roddy." She peered closer. "Graciela—may I call you that? And you must call me Perry. You are quite all right? They are bringing a luncheon up." She smiled. "It will be like old times, Charley, only none of this awful gruel."

"You must dress first," Francisca said, interrupting.

Lady Perry turned kindly eyes on the maid. "Do not worry, Francisca. It is only us. Our brother Mr. Gibson has arrived, and Penderbrook who is a friend. They are both coming up. Mr. Kincaid said he will catch up with us later. I shall stay with Graciela and protect her from the gentlemen."

Graciela marveled—that speech had also been delivered in Spanish and was meant for her understanding as much as Francisca's. Because Charley had not turned away. His gaze still probed her in that intimate way.

"Do you not love wearing pantaloons?" Lady Perry whispered in English. "They are so liberating." She drew a paper from her pocket. It was a news sheet. "Now, you'll sit and I'll show you what we've done, and we'll talk about what we must do next."

CHAPTER TEN

The gentlemen's knees knocked into the table's edge, and Reina insisted on remaining in Mr Everly's lap and helping herself to bits of food from his plate, as she used to do with Graciela's father. No one quite lost their good manners entirely, but it was clear right away, the men were ravenous. All that was needed was to have the room sway to one side and a large splash of seawater arrive through the window, and it would feel much like a meal on her father's ship.

The scandal sheet lay next to her own still almost full plate, and her eyes kept coming back to it.

Shocking Tale of Scandal
Unthought of perhaps in this modern day, Dear Readers, we have just learned of the story of an Heiress confined as it were to a Tower by her Guardian for her unwillingness to be wed to a Man of Ill Repute. We may not mention names here, but we will say that the poor child's only Parent serves the Crown honorably, the Guardian holds one of the

oldest titles of the Realm, and to think of the Duress he has inflicted on the Poor Girl, Duress of such force that one wonders if she may bear the Stripes of it on her Back through the rest of her life. This Writer had prayed that she might find Nine Lives to carry her past the Nine Tails of her Torturer's Wand.

But lo, this Writer has learned that the Unfortunate Girl who did not appear with her Guardians for a recent Society Assembly has DISAPPEARED. One must wonder, after the degree of Displeasure she has inflicted upon her Noble Host, if the last Exercise of Discipline has broken the Delicate Creature entirely. For indeed, it is said that the Noble Lord was waxing so wroth he dismissed all of his retainers the evening the Lovely Creature vanished, and when they returned the next day, her Bedchamber had been the scene of a Violent Struggle and BLOODLETTING, and the Young Lady was GONE and has not since been heard of or SEEN. To the Veracity of these words, I rely on the testimony of an EYEWITNESS.

Her eyes watered reading it. She'd been tossing back and forth between waves of anger and moments of relief at her rescue, and her hand trembled around the fork she was clutching. If Lord Kingsley were here, she would stab him with it.

Put as it was in the news sheet, it was astonishing she'd braved all the peril. Her body had heated and chilled with anger and fear so many times in the last few days she felt like a brittle blade, ready to break.

Mr. Everly's gaze rested upon her, and for that moment, they were the only two people in the room. The concern in his eyes settled over her, as comforting as the strong arm that held Reina in place on his lap.

"Have you had a reply from Lord Shaldon?" Penderbrook asked, bringing her up from her mood.

"Not as yet. That isn't surprising," Lady Perry said.

Mr. Gibson grunted. "Be assured, Shaldon will know exactly what's happening."

Graciela studied the oldest Everly son. He might not carry their name, he might have the exotically fiery hair of the northmen, yet one could not miss his resemblance to the strong-jawed, straight-nosed, firm-lipped siblings. This must be the look of the father. She wondered if there was a portrait of the man somewhere in this great house.

"But Bakeley sent an express," Lady Perry said. "He and Sirena are on their way."

Bakeley was the second son and heir. The Viscount Bakeley whose bed she had napped in early that morning, the rescuer of Lady Sirena.

How wonderful to have brothers and sisters to come to one's aid. She had none of those. She had only her two servants and Reina. She was not part of this house or this great family. When they were finished rescuing her, they would try to begin their own arranging of her life.

She did not belong here. She must not forget that.

Lady Perry reached across Graciela to catch the biscuit sliding from Reina's hand. "You have put her to sleep again, Charley." She laughed.

"I'll take her." Graciela leaned in close. The hand that slid under the child's bottom collided with the solid muscle of Mr. Everly's chest. The other met his wide shoulder. Both collisions induced a riot and leaping of nerves within her. Her cheeks warmed again, but she kept her lashes lowered, her gaze on the sleeping child as she sat back down.

Around her, the others went very still. She blinked hard. *I will not cry.*

"How beautiful she is," Mr. Everly breathed out. When she looked, his gaze was on her, not Reina.

Her heart stuttered and she found herself short of breath.

Yet, she had things she must say. "We have spoken—" She cleared her throat and sipped some more air. "Of the scandal sheet piece and the solicitor's office. What is next in your devious plan for my future?"

Penderbrook chuckled, and Charley made himself grin.

She didn't trust him. Of course she didn't. And he needed her to.

"What do you want to do next, Graciela?" Perry asked.

The lovely lips clamped together, her face crumpling over the child in her lap, like a Madonna thinking ahead to her savior child's fate.

As soon as she'd tamed her emotions, she'd ask for transport to Falmouth. And he wasn't having that.

Charley cleared his throat. "There's the matter of your trust."

Her head shot up.

"The bank," he said. "The bank where the funds are being held. You'll not want to leave all your money here."

With her next breath, her emotions cleared. "Yes."

She *had* been pondering running. It was good she had him to think this through logically.

"Do you know which bank your father was using, Miss Everly?" Bink asked.

"He did tell me. It was a Scottish name." She pursed her lips. "Mack...Mack..." She shook her head. "Mack-something."

"McLintoch," Penderbrook said. "Or, MacIntosh is Bank of Scotland, is he not? Oh, but I believe he's in Edinburgh. As well as...might you be mistaken? Kinnear and Sons—"

"You've done a study of Scottish banks, have you, Pender?" Charley asked.

Pender was looking for a position, any position. And the lady was frowning prodigiously at his friend's doubting.

"I am not mistaken." She waved a hand, juggling the sleeping child. "I will visit them all. McLintock, MacIntosh, Mac—"

"McCollum's," Bink said.

Gracie blinked and nodded. "It might be."

Bink drummed his fingers on the table. "It might well be." Plates and utensils rattled as he lumbered to his feet. "There'll be no need to visit them all. We'll go there first thing tomorrow morning." He excused himself and left.

Charley stood also and signaled to Penderbrook. "I must go change my coat and cravat." He flicked a spot of dried gruel from his shoulder and bowed to Graciela. "Ladies."

Penderbrook hurried out behind him.

"Where are we going?" Penderbrook asked.

"*We* are not going anywhere. *I* am going to change coats, as I said. *You* may proceed to the next bank on your list of prospective employers."

His friend's cheeks reddened, and Charley laughed, slapping him on the shoulder. "I'm roasting you. Of course, you must have a position like a regular gentleman, somewhere in the government. We'll both talk to my father when he returns. Meet me at White's later tonight."

Penderbrook hesitated and nodded. "You're a friend indeed, Everly. I'll keep my ear to the ground. Until later."

Charley hurried to his room, changed, and left the house, before either of the ladies could track him down and demand to come with him.

The approaching hackney squeezed down the mews and stopped at the door where Charley waited. He pulled his cap low and put down the steps, dipping his head like a faithful retainer. Swathed in a gauzy mantilla, the lady stepping down gripped his fingers and tugged him inside the dark stable.

She glanced around the empty stable and pulled his head down and kissed him, a long press of her mobile lips on his, totally without passion on her part, stirring none on his. When she squeezed his arm and stepped away, she glanced over her shoulder at her coach and shut the stable door.

"That was convincing, Duquesa," he said.

The mantilla slipped back to reveal a tiny bonnet perching atop her golden coiffure. Blue eyes dancing, she smiled. "Perhaps someday, Charles Everly, it may be a real kiss."

His thoughts flew to Gracie's petulant mouth, and he reeled them back, forcing a grin. "You must take care. You're playing a dangerous game. And what would your father say if he knew how you were carrying out his mission?"

"He will not care. He knows I will not allow that pig into my bed. As long as I am discreet..." She shrugged.

"Your men are outside?"

"At either end of this street. We may take our time. He will think, when he learns of it, that you have tupped me here. I shall attach a few pieces of straw."

"I fear we don't have that much time. You are blocking the mews at a busy of time of the day."

She slid a hand up his arm and smiled. "It would not take long." With a quick squeeze, her demeanor changed. "But now, we must get to our business." She withdrew a paper from under her redingote.

Charley turned the letter over and studied the plain seal.

"From my father to yours."

"If it came by pouch, The Duque will have read it," he said.

"No. A friend has brought it."

"Is it urgent? Father is in Bath."

She cocked her head and studied him. "You have called him back, no?"

"One of our servants is talking." Bakeley would want to know about that.

A wide smile displayed gleaming white teeth. "It is only a leap of logic from the reports in the scandal sheets." She tapped his arm. "You have dallied with some other young woman. I, perhaps, must have a fit of jealousy."

Voices outside drew their attention, and they waited until they had passed.

"I will save that for our next public meeting. For now, give that letter to him, and for your other request, I've learned that he was held in a farmhouse north of Pamplona, where the exchange was to be. He walked into a trap. The hostage was already dead of a fever. The money went to the French but...he was taken. It was a chance to obtain another ransom. A painting."

His mind flew back to Perry's accusation of theft after their mother's passing.

"What painting?" he asked.

She tapped him again. "You know."

He held her gaze.

Around the same time, Saints Felicity and Perpetua had disappeared from the wall in his mother's bedchamber, replaced by a painting of her three children. Mother never said where the painting had gone.

"That's madness," he said.

"It was Lopez de Arteaga's work, painted in Mexico City and lost with a Spanish ship full of treasure, that is, until your father obtained it."

"A ship belonging to your husband?"

She shrugged again.

"And he has the painting now?"

A knock rattled the door. Charley stepped over to it. A dark-clad man who he recognized as one of the Duquesa's guards whispered that they must leave, that a cart wanted to pass through the mews.

Charley shut the door and turned on her. "Well?"

"No. That is, I do not know where the painting is. But I know that, weeks later, when the painting was delivered, both the messenger and your father ended up in the hands of a French commander, and your father was never released. He escaped."

"You know this how?"

"A peasant boy who worked at the estate."

The door rattled; the Duquesa's guard again. Charley quickly bundled her into the hackney along with her man, closed and locked the mews door, and climbed out through a window. He made his way to the street, whistling and pondering the story the lady had told him.

Later that evening, he caught up with Penderbrook at White's and ordered both of them drinks.

"No family dinner for you tonight?" Penderbrook asked.

"I'll join them in a bit. For now, what have you found?"

"No other McBankers than the one your brother lit upon. Shall I accompany you?"

While the waiter poured their wine, he sat back, thinking. McCollum's was tied in with merchant shipping, that much he'd learned in his afternoon travels. He might as well make quick work of this conversation and go talk to Bink, who he suspected knew something more of this bank than he was mentioning. Perhaps from the Parliamentary work that Charley had been shirking.

"I think not," he said.

A member he didn't know seated himself at the next table, twitching his chair so that one ear was turned their way. Dark hair and a well-tailored dark coat.

He was obviously preparing to eavesdrop.

"I say, Pender," Charley said, too loudly, "will you still insist that Cribb was a better pugilist than Spring?"

The fellow turned full around. "Penderbrook, is it you?" He stood.

A tall athletic body stretched under a lean face with a hawk nose planted between two small dark eyes. A flamboyant gold waistcoat caught the light from the nearest sconce, a contrast to the rest of his darkness.

Penderbrook nodded cordially, his jaw tightening. "Payne-Elsdon," he said.

"Fancy seeing you so soon after that card game at—"

"Yes, yes," Charley interrupted, tossing back some wine and signaling the waiter. "Let's make short work of the introductions and I'll get on to my third drink. I'm Charles Everly."

"Pleased to meet you. I have heard you are blessed with the attentions of a golden-haired angel."

Indeed.

The fellow put his hand on a back of a chair preparing to draw it out and join them.

"This is Major Payne-Elsdon," Penderbrook said. Then he put his attention to gulping the rest of his wine. Though as pale as his face was, it might come back up.

"Major." Charley beamed a smile. "We'd invite you to join us but I'm delving into Penderbrook's expertise for an upcoming wager. Height of secrecy, and all that."

Penderbrook failed to smile. Instead his face paled even more.

Payne-Elsdon's lip curled up. "Maybe you'll have better luck with your boxing bet than cards."

"I say, Payne-Elsdon," Charley said affably, "on active duty, are you?"

He shook his head. "I've sold out my commission."

"Weren't in the Peninsula, were you? Might have run into my brother."

He blinked. "I don't believe I had the pleasure." He flashed a toothy smile. "Though I was there during the war, and more recently."

Charley grinned back while the waiter poured a fresh glass and he mentally connected the dots. He'd heard of a sold-out major, recently returned from some scandal in Spain, a card shark and swordsman who'd maimed a man, all of it hushed up by the victim's family. Pender was swimming in dark waters. "Not likely you'd have met my brother. He was a lowly sergeant then, but Shaldon has lured him into the Everly fold and he's a Member of Parliament now." He raised his glass. "Cheers."

Penderbrook pushed back his chair and stood. His face had recovered some of its color. "I see Gilbert over there and I promised to meet him. Many thanks for the drink, Everly. Do send a note if I'm needed. I am at your service."

The abrupt departure brought a smirk and a raised eyebrow. Charley stood also and leveled a gaze at the man. His appearance at their table tonight—and for that matter at Penderbrook's card table sometime in the recent past—was one more sudden appearance to delve into.

"I suppose I'll have to manage this wager with my own wits," Charley said.

Payne-Elsdon dipped his head, but there was no apology in his expression. "I'd be happy to offer counsel."

He drummed up a grin. "No thanks. I'll ponder out the odds myself."

He waved to Pender as he passed. The bloody fool was playing cards again trying to raise some capital. In spite of his joking, he was too proud to take a loan, preferring to issue vowels to the likes of a shady major, who'd work for the likes of the Duque and who probably marked his cards.

He'd send Pender some work on the morrow, and scrape his own allowance to pay for it.

CHAPTER ELEVEN

Charley tipped back the chair and rested a booted foot on the edge of the library table where one dim candle burned.

The four of them—Bink, Perry, Gracie, and Charley—had dined informally and rather quickly, retiring to the drawing room to plan the trip to the bank.

After, he'd lured Bink to the library to discuss the major. Bink thought he'd heard the name, and promised to make inquiries, without any nosy questions about why Charley wanted to know. Which was much the way Shaldon would have reacted, and wasn't it amazing that the bastard who'd joined the family only two years before should be so much like the father the man had never met. Their brother Bakeley would have spent a full hour trying to winkle out the reason Charley was asking.

He rather liked his new brother.

Bink refilled Charley's brandy glass. "I'm for bed then. Best get some rest yourself. Kingsley and Carvelle will catch up with us soon enough, and even if they don't we'll have Shaldon's tricks to deal with. He'll pop on the scene just as everything is falling apart."

Charley laughed and wished him a good night.

As Bink left, Perry entered.

"She's safely tucked into the blue guest room. Francisca and Juan have the chamber next to her, but they're sleeping in the nursery, I fear."

"Good."

Perry came close and wagged a finger at him, smiling. "Should I lock Graciela's door, Charley?"

No. Never. It's what her captors at Kingsley House had done.

He made himself grin back, as she expected him to.

Perry boosted herself and perched on the edge of the table near where his feet rested. "Look at us. Mother would scold us, wouldn't she?" She tapped the toe of his boot. "Mother would have liked her, I think. Miss Kingsley is a lovely young woman. Quite beautiful. Brave and intelligent. Likes children. And she's wealthy."

His heart had picked up an annoying race along Perry's matrimonial track. He must divert her. "We shall see about her wealth tomorrow."

She sighed. "I do wish I was going along. I'm always left out of the excitement."

"Miss Kingsley will feel better if you are here with the child, marshaling the guards."

He heard the swish of skirts as she swung her legs. "Yes, I suppose. I have bought Juan's goodwill with a pair of the Mantons from Father's cache. Francisca, however, was excoriating him about the danger you pose to her lady." She went very silent for a moment. "But I assured her you will act honorably."

The candle sputtered and outside a distant carriage rattled—one of their neighbors heading out for an evening's amusement. Not Carvelle—his attack would be a silent one.

"Charley?"

He plopped his feet on the floor and stood. "The girl has survived one attempted assault. Do you think *I* would do such a thing to her, Perry?"

Perry dropped down from the table and faced him. "You would not need to. She is half in love with you already. And you are attracted to her, as any man would be. *That* is what Francisca sees."

His hand remembered the tightness of Graciela's back, and the chill of her slender fingers, and the slimness of her waist as he'd lifted her into the coach the night before. His shoulder remembered the touch of her next to him in the narrow hackney. He thought about the fit of the coats over her bosom and the fine turn of her thighs in Roddy's clothing.

He shook his head. "I'm not looking for a wife, Perry." He walked out of the circle of candlelight to the window that looked out over the garden.

"What *do* you intend to do with her?"

What indeed? Miss Kingsley wanted to find Captain Llewellyn, to investigate her father's disappearance, to take the child to her relatives in Spain, to return to Alta California. All of those seemed impulsive, improvident, one might say, impossible.

I will take what is left and go home, and buy some land and perhaps, someday, find a strong man who I can respect.

No, no, that was, in the long term, sensible, and reasonable, and he could not fathom letting her go into another man's arms.

He shook off the unwelcome feeling.

"I intend to take her to the bank tomorrow to find out the state of her accounts. I intend to protect her, her servants, and the child from Carvelle and Kingsley. I intend to make inquiries about her father's supposed disappearance."

"Very well." Perry was finally giving up. "I'm going up."

He heard the click of the door and slid further into the shadows.

Perry was right. Graciela was beautiful. A wealthy, beautiful Spanish woman.

With the key to a spy? No. It couldn't be her. It must certainly be the Duquesa. Farnsworth had set him on this mission, and Farnsworth was Graciela's guardian. If she was a spy, Farnsworth already held the key within his grasp. Besides, she didn't move in the kind of circles where spies hovered. She hadn't been allowed to move freely in any circles at all.

Another noise outside stirred him and he slipped behind the curtain to peer out.

A footman walked by below in the garden, outlined by the dim light of his lantern. Another man walked out, smaller, distinctively limping. It was the head groom.

He released a breath and backed away. And then behind him, he felt a wisp of a draft as if the door had opened.

Shaldon House was not a fortress in any of the normal ways. There were no turrets with gun slits, no moats, no ironwork lacing the window openings, yet Graciela's late-night inspection showed her that the likelihood of Carvelle gaining entrance was small.

As was the likelihood of her, and her servants, and Reina walking out without notice. Alone, she believed it was possible, as it was now possible for her to move freely down the long corridors and flights of carpeted stairs.

And it would have to be a kind of escape. It was clear to her, from Charley and Lady Perry's behavior—she could not walk out of here without a score of armed guards. It was rational, she knew, perhaps even kind, but it still chafed.

They had assigned her a very grand bedchamber, with an anteroom for Francisca and Juan. As she knew they would, her servants had chosen to remain in the nursery, Francisca in a bed near Reina, and Juan upon a pallet on the floor. Conflicted they'd been, though, Francisca convinced that Mr. Everly would try to enter her chamber and ravish her. Her own protestations meant nothing to Francisca. Lady Perry's endorsement had calmed her somewhat, but only Juan's chastisement had silenced her. Mr. Everly was an honorable man, he'd said, and Graciela had proven herself capable of self-defense. And later, after Lady Perry had left, he promised Francisca he would do as Captain Kingsley would to any man who tried to dishonor Graciela.

She was sorry Juan knew about Kingsley's whippings and Carvelle's attack. She would not be able to stop Juan, and the English would hang him. It was another dilemma. She must extract her own revenge, if possible, and get them all away from this place before Juan's life was endangered by his sense of honor.

As she came down the grand stairs, a night porter shot to his feet and she tugged the heavy dressing gown tighter. They had found another set of soft, elegant nightclothes for her. The porter was armed, and though he studied the floor at her slippered feet, he had scanned her too quickly, for weapons, or for nefarious intent.

There'd been nothing improper. This was no privateer's ship.

"All is quiet?" she asked.

"Aye, miss."

Well, then. "I...I am looking for the kitchen."

Without catching her eye, he directed her toward the back of the house. She thanked him and moved on.

The kitchen would be guarded also, perhaps abuzz with guards resting between turns on the watch. That was not for her. She moved along the hall, outside the view of the porter, and began opening doors.

A series of salons, parlors, and eating rooms were quiet, dark. At the back corner of the house, she opened a door and spotted a dim candle. It sputtered in the draft from the door, and her heart skittered with it. The light touched upon rows of books, running off into the dark. The room was otherwise unoccupied. Some foolish soul had left a candle burning among all these valuable tomes.

Fire was a great fear. Smoking below decks had been a punishable offense. The cook fire was always carefully watched.

She slid into the room and closed the door. Perhaps this room had a comfortable chair. Perhaps she could find respite here. In any case, a candle should not be left unguarded in a room like this, in a house like this.

As she neared the taper she saw that it was safely ensconced in a glass bell. She lifted the candle in its holder and looked around.

Volume after volume of rich leather, in all colors, circled the walls, from corner to corner and floor to ceiling—though that last was a guess as she could no way see the height of the shelving around her. She would have to visit this room in the day, to see what books were housed here. Perhaps there would be a volume of Cervantes that she could read to Francisca.

For now, it was the windows she must visit. Tall casement windows, they were. The drop from the first floor would not be much, but perhaps Shaldon had planted some spiky *buganvilla* below.

Although, *buganvilla* might not grow in this cold place, else she would have seen riotous color in someone's garden. There would be some other sort of brambly bush. They would have to wrap Reina in blankets, and still she might cry.

She set the candle down, the light dancing and sparkling on the dark wooden table. Like everything else here, it was meticulously maintained. Except—she peered closer—for a small crescent of dust.

Shivering, she edged toward the window and looked out. The glow there must be the stables.

She slid the window latch and tugged at the window. It moved up without noise, letting in the dank London air.

Behind the house, shrubbery outlined the garden, but this way along the side of the house was clear, and not much of a drop. She rested her forehead on the window sash, letting the cool wood calm her, savoring the scents of new grass and flowers. Lady Perry had said they had roses and lilacs. She would miss those sweet garden smells, once she was free in Captain Llewellyn's ship on the open seas.

Another scent wafted into her awareness and her chest squeezed again, making her heart race.

"You are hiding in the shadows," she whispered. "Are you trying to frighten me?"

Charley Everly moved to her side and rested an elbow on the window ledge.

She looked up at him, and the tightening and racing all but convulsed her. He had shed both his coats. A scruff shadowed his jaw and chin, and his eyes glittered darkly. She heated, and chilled, and heated again.

Dios. She needed to get out of here.

"If you're thinking to jump down there, then yes, I hope I am frightening you."

"Don't be silly. I'm in my nightclothes."

He reached for the plait of hair that dangled over her shoulder and fingered it, his touch racing up the long tail and through her.

She gulped for air. With the talk of her nightclothes, she had given him an indecent opening. He was going to touch more than her hair. Perhaps he would even try to kiss her.

"Your nightclothes. I noticed." The back of his hand brushed her sleeve, sending even more tingles through her. "I imagine the next time you peer out this window, you'll be fully clothed."

Charley watched the movement of her face as she decided how to respond. Miss Kingsley was like most of the other Latin women he had met— fiery, emotional. She lacked the coldness of her father's heritage, the knack for subterfuge. She was aroused, but she didn't want to be, and her feelings were all twisted around how to respond.

He counted the passion as an asset, especially when she was thinking to lie to him.

"I don't like to be caged." The words came on a gaspy, deflating breath.

She had more control than he'd expected.

On the distant street, another carriage rattled the silence.

"Come. Let's move you away from the window."

He took her hand and led her across the room to a set of wing chairs. He remembered her back and seated her on a footstool, taking the chair in front of her.

"In this very room some weeks ago, Sirena was almost killed."

Her head jerked up. The darkness hid her expression, but he knew he'd startled her.

Good. She should be startled.

"Yes. An intruder, a so-called artist who was chalking the ballroom floor, attempted to strangle her. We found that one of our footmen and a groom had been corrupted also. Since then, Bakeley has scrutinized every member of the staff to kingdom come."

Her free hand rubbed at her neck. He pulled it down and held it.

"You are not in a cage, my love. You are protected. They are two completely different things."

A tremble rippled through her and he drew her closer, sliding his hands to her shoulders, as naturally as if she'd been made for him.

She gasped, and he dropped his hands. He'd forgotten her wounds.

Except that, he hadn't touched more than her shoulder. So, she had wounds that were deeper than those on her back.

"Did your brother rescue his lady?" she asked.

"In a manner of speaking. He kept her from hitting that hard ground below when she leaped from the window."

Her low chuckle made him dare to take her hands again.

"And then he carried her off and married her," she said.

"No. They were already married."

She went silent. She was no longer shaking, and her hands had warmed. He slid his fingers higher under the loose cuff of the robe, stroking her silky skin with his fingers. Her robe had slid open a bit at the throat, but he couldn't see much. Like last night, he had no idea what she wore under the heavy dressing gown.

His shaft stirred. He silently cursed the darkness.

"He was courting her?" she asked.

"No. It's a long story, but he rescued her, and she spent the night in his bachelor lodgings unchaperoned. They married to salvage her reputation."

She clucked her tongue. "How foolish. Forced marriage because of society's judgments—I do not believe in that nonsense."

He could only agree. "Bakeley is the heir. He, more than any of us needed to be sensible. He had to marry sooner or later, and Sirena was an Irish earl's daughter, not good *ton* as they say, but she suited well enough, and he liked her."

"How very practical."

"You do not approve."

The thrumming started up again—his heart, her heart. The very air around them quaked.

Good God, what was wrong with him?

"You require a love match, *Señorita* Kingsley?"

He could almost feel her chest rising and falling as she gulped deep breaths. His thumbs reached the tender creases of her elbows.

She pulled away and stood. "*Señorita*, am I now? Yes, yes, you look at me and say 'Here is a foolish pampered *criolla*, a colonial Spanish girl who is all passion, no intelligence.' You say, 'Let me h-hold her hand. Let me stir her with my tender touches. You think with your pretty hair and big shoulders you are more convincing than all the *caballeros* I've encountered in my life. And you are all seduction because you know I do not care about your society rules, and because you think I'm only a stupid, stupid girl, already, as you say, *ruined*."

Pretty hair and big shoulders—he squelched a laugh. She moved into the light and he rose to follow her. With her eyes flashing, her head tossing, her shoulders squared, she was magnificent. She didn't notice her robe had slipped further, revealing creamy skin and the disappointing lace of a nightrail.

"Love." She sliced a hand through the air. "What does love matter, Charley Everly? Love I feel for...for Reina, for my f-father." She took a breath that sounded like a sob. "It is foolish for a woman to love a man. They are such unfaithful creatures. Between a husband and wife there must be respect and honor. The rest—so common for a man—is merely the physical urge required for mating. A woman who settles for mere love must expect a life of sorrow and regret."

A pain started up in his head. She thought he had no honor.

Or...maybe this wasn't about him. Maybe someone, long before Lord Kingsley and Carvelle, had hurt Graciela.

And indeed, she was trembling again. He reached for her hand, surprised when she allowed him to take it. "You sound like one of the fellows at the club." He made his voice bland and dredged up a smile. It wasn't so difficult since her lower lip protruded like Reina's had earlier. "They decry love until one or the other falls head over ears for some actress or opera dancer and gives her a house and a carriage and carte blanche at the modiste." He'd never speak of such things to an English maiden, but Graciela was no ordinary girl.

Her gaze narrowed. "You have done such?"

"Not I."

"You have not been head over ears then?"

His head swam and the air around them crackled. *Not until I met you.*

He laughed. He was being ridiculous. "No. Nor do I have the funds for such. And as well, I have been on the Continent a good deal of time."

"You are not rich? But I thought your family was wealthy."

"Bakeley is wealthy. Bink has a very comfortable income. Perry and I live on allowances."

"But that doesn't seem fair." She frowned. "So, you both must make your own fortunes, or marry them?"

He suspected that a comfortable income would come when he married, just as Bink's had. Which, in his case, would be never.

"Perry will marry and bring a rich dowry. I plan to make my own fortune."

"How? As a spy? Is spying a profitable trade?"

He laughed. "Not as a spy."

"Were you spying on the Continent?"

She was far too perceptive. She asked far too many questions. He moved closer. "Never did I doubt your intelligence, Graciela." He slid a finger under her chin and tilted her head up. "But from the moment you fainted at your betrothal ball, I knew you were also a woman of great drama and passion."

He pressed his lips to hers, finally. *Finally.* She was soft and warm and smelled like woman.

He kept the kiss tender and brief, and set his forehead against hers. "And when I saw you in Lord Kingsley's kitchen covered in blood, I knew you were resourceful and brave." One hand slid to the back of her head, the other around her waist, and he swept her into a kiss that tasted like sweet mint.

She didn't pull away, wonder of wonders.

He eased closer and deepened the kiss. Her lips opened only a fraction, enough for him to touch his tongue to hers, and he fought the urge to wrap her up and enfold her, to devour her, to force her.

She turned her head and opened her neck to him. His touch there made her shiver and he knew she enjoyed it.

"I should like to hear about your spying, Mr. Everly."

"Call me Charley," he mumbled against her neck.

She huffed out a breath. "Charley."

No fight about that? When he looked, her lips had formed a dreamy half-smile, and he was instantly alert, the brain in his head trying to master the smaller one between his legs.

It was the same expression on a lady he'd met in Vienna, right before she'd stabbed him.

"Will you tell me?" she asked.

A Spanish woman, wealthy and beautiful, the key to a spy.

He hadn't felt any weapons. "I would rather kiss you awhile first."

Her eyes darkened, and her lips opened and closed. The spy, if she was that, would want information, but the woman would rather kiss than talk.

And the woman really did want respect. That pronouncement had been heartfelt. He pressed his forehead to hers again and breathed in her scent.

Egad, but she was lovely.

"I was a mere secretary to an official delegation. Discussing treaties and what not. Of course, I was there on behalf of England, and what I heard in the course of social events, I must pass on."

"Passing on gossip. That is all this spying is?"

The incredulity in her eyes told him she was merely a curious woman, not a spy. He pulled her head onto his shoulder and worked his fingers under the plaited hair, loosening it, massaging her scalp. "It is a boring life."

He became aware of her arms circling his waist, and sliding up his back. With no coats, only the fine linen of his shirt separated his hot skin from her cool touch. The minx. Perhaps she *was* some sort of seductress, but for whom, and after what?

"I don't believe you, Mr. Everly."

He nuzzled her neck and felt a shudder go through her.

"Graciela, it is a matter of honor to keep secrets entrusted to one."

"And you are a man of honor."

"Yes. And I have a great deal of respect for you."

"Especially in this moment." Her voice shook. "You are holding me quite closely and you are...aroused."

Her breathless declaration stirred him anew. Pressed against her like this, the need to rip her clothes off and enter her pounded through him. There was a sofa here. But her poor back—no, he could lift up her skirts, bend her over a desk, part her legs and...

And he would be no better than Carvelle. And she was too young, and no matter the state of her virginity, too inexperienced, too worthy of a kinder introduction. Such ravishment should come later, when she truly knew he respected her. When she trusted him.

He stepped back and took a deep breath. For any of that, he would have to be married to her. And he had no intentions of marrying.

"You are seeing your banker tomorrow. You should get some rest tonight."

Her face fell and she pulled her robe tighter, as though she'd just become aware of the gape in the bodice. "I am well aware of the plans for tomorrow." She knotted her belt, blinking.

He took her elbow. Her body, so pliant before, had resumed its tense state.

"I will escort you up. I promise that, no matter my state of arousal, I will respect and honor you."

"I can find my own way."

"No doubt." He started for the door.

"Wait." She broke free and blew out the candle.

The touch of her hand on his arm stirred him, making his chest swell. He navigated the dark stairs with her in tow, and crossed the landing to go up again.

"My room is on this floor."

"So is mine. We're not going there."

*****

Graciela gripped his arm tighter. Charley Everly rushed up the stairs as if Carvelle himself were pursuing them. These quiet stairs, the twists and turns of corridors and long row of doors. She knew where they were going.

She blinked back tears. That he would understand her needs touched her.

A guard shot to his feet outside the nursery door. He'd not been there when she'd checked earlier.

Was he keeping Carvelle out, or keeping her and her people in?

"This is where I leave, before Juan shoots me with one of his new pistols." Charley lifted her hand and kissed it. "May I have your promise that you will go with me tomorrow?"

"Of course. I am not so foolish as to try to talk to that man alone." Lady Perry had said the banker may not talk, though Mr. Gibson had mysteriously assured them he could persuade the man. She hoped there was no blood to be shed.

"And I will see you at breakfast?" Charley asked.

"I should like to eat here with Reina."

"Of course." He kissed her hand again and disappeared.

Inside, she rested her shoulder against the closed door and allowed her heart to quiet. A lamp had been left burning and a maid dozed in a chair.

His touch had been everywhere upon her, except where he knew it would cause her pain. The kiss had been—lovely. Not forced. Not a plundering of her mouth. Not an act of domination and taking.

Charley's kiss had tasted like brandy and promised pleasure, and had made her want more.

She shook her head. But of course. He had a reputation as a seducer of women, and it was no wonder. He was very good. She had told him what she required—honor, respect—and he had seen fit to pull away and give it to her. He had made her want to reach for him.

She pressed a hand to her heart. And she did. She wanted nothing more than to go back into his arms.

The wonder of that filled her with gratitude and something like hope. Perhaps she wasn't as broken as she'd thought.

CHAPTER TWELVE

"Did I not tell you it was a foolish ploy?" Gregory Carvelle's hooded eyes were those of a lizard. "Bankers do not let go of money so easily."

Kingsley stared down his nose at the man, reminding himself that he was a peer, the latest holder of a very old title. His family had helped rule this island for centuries. And Carvelle was merely the descendant of foreign tradesmen— dishonest ones at that.

In league with a devil, he was. He was being swallowed whole, inch by torturing inch. He rued the day his wife had brought him this plan, and the one that had come before that started the whole damnable mess.

Nay, he rued the day he'd married the woman with her spendthrift ways and her sordid connections. "We shall find her. She could not have gone far."

The beady eyes sparkled. "Perhaps she has run to Shaldon."

"She couldn't possibly know that Farnsworth appointed him guardian in his absence." He had not known himself until this morning.

"The daughter was friendly with her, Blanche said. And I did see Everly out on that balcony where she was found. He might have taken her that night. He is known for seducing women."

"Ridiculous. If the chit could fight you off, Carvelle, she could resist a gentleman."

Carvelle's lips curled. "If she wished to." He rapped the carriage roof and called for the coachman to halt. "I shall wait to hear how your debt will be paid. I shall not wait forever."

"I'll find the girl. The marriage agreements have been signed. Busy yourself with procuring the license."

"Busy myself?" Carvelle raised an eyebrow. "A license? Perhaps a trip to Scotland is in order. Perhaps I'll find her before you." He disappeared into the busy mercantile street, snaking between delivery carts and the storekeepers opening shop.

Kingsley sank back against the velvet squab. The coach was a gem, the newest design, well-appointed and well-sprung, and, like the new draperies and upholstery at Kingsley House, came courtesy of the trust Captain Kingsley had set up for his daughter.

If he controlled the girl, he controlled the funds. The girl was his chip. He needed to find her before Carvelle.

Damn Blanche. She had mishandled her—the girl was as proud as her father. As a boy, every time a fist hit Tristan Kingsley, he'd struggled to his feet to take more. Like her father, the cut of the cane had only made the chit more defiant, more determined.

The coach turned into his square and slowed to a crawl. A plain hackney and two horses blocked the curb in front of his house. Two men in coarse coats and hats stood on the front steps.

The sight sent a chill rattling through him. Tradesmen would not linger on the front steps of a lord's townhouse. This scene wasn't hard to decipher. He'd seen their types enough running about town, poking, probing, and interfering.

They did no more than tip their dusty hats to him as he walked up the steps. Inside, the butler handed him a card.

His blood drained and then surged again pounding in his ears like an incipient apoplexy.

"He is in the front parlor, my lord."

"Lady Kingsley?"

"She has not come down yet."

Thank God. Blanche would only run at the mouth and start quarreling with—he looked at the card again—Sir Henry Laughlin. His mouth firmed. No man tolerated a quarrelsome woman well, but especially not a magistrate.

"Very well." He started for the door but the butler stopped him.

"My lord." He cleared his throat and looked at a spot on the wall. "There are men in the garden, digging."

The garden? Blanche had made plans for the weed-infested space. She'd been studying designs, looking to appoint a new gardener. She'd moved things along much more quickly than expected.

Damn her spendthrift ways. "Very well. Her ladyship will be pleased her gardener has arrived, I'm sure."

More throat-clearing stopped him.

"What the hell else?" he snapped.

"They are not gardeners, my lord." The butler's voice quaked. "They accompanied your visitor. They have unearthed an article of..." The butler paused and looked at his own shaking hands... "bloody clothing. It appears to have been one of Miss Kingsley's dresses."

CHAPTER THIRTEEN

Graciela clutched the firm arm of the large man at her side trying to see through the heavy netting of her veil. All she could discern was that McCollum's Bank was an imposing edifice.

"Mr. Gibson. Mrs. Gibson." The clerk who came to greet them bowed as though she were a duchess or the queen herself.

Or perhaps not the current queen since her husband was famously trying to divorce her, the pig.

A royal duchess then. "Good day," she whispered. Mr. Gibson had recommended she speak very little until they had insured her safety.

"I need a word with Mr. McCollum on a matter of some urgency," Mr. Gibson said.

Through the dark netting, Graciela could only admire Mr. Gibson's command of the bank clerk, who trotted away to find his master. A by-blow Mr. Gibson might be, but he acted just like one of his brothers.

In fact, he acted with more dignity than either of them. Lord Bakeley had arrived in the early morning and she had met him briefly when she'd intruded upon a dispute in the very library where Charley had kissed her a few hours before. Lord Bakely had wanted to come along to the bank, in addition to Mr. Gibson and Charley, or in place of Charley.

Two additional Everly brothers were too many, Mr. Gibson said. Charley insisted that *he* must go, and he would not waver on the point. Lord Bakeley had opened his mouth to protest and then they'd all finally seen her in the doorway. After the introductions, and many sly glances by Lord Bakeley at her and his younger brother, he'd acquiesced to this plan and promised she would meet Lady Sirena who, due to the lateness of their arrival and her delicate condition, was still abed.

The last was shared with great congratulations and brotherly backslapping.

It was all very interesting. She'd been the outsider before on many occasions, Graciela, in the shadows, privy to men's celebrations. Aside from the absence of both alcohol and the most colorful of language, the celebrating had not been so very different among these aristocrats.

And the lord and heir bowing to the wishes of the bastard son—but of course Mr. Gibson was the eldest. She wondered if their father had retained the mother as a mistress after his marriage. It would tell her much about the mysterious Lord Shaldon.

Now, she clung to Mr. Gibson's arm, for in fact, today she was not playing a groom but Paulette Gibson. On her other side, Charley squeezed nearer, close enough that she could smell his soap. The air hummed between them.

Mr. Gibson sighed and muttered, "You are crowding my wife, Charley. Any closer and I shall have to thrash you."

She wondered if there were others within hearing. It was difficult to see through these ridiculous weeds.

Charley laughed and took one step away. "I beg your pardon, Paulette. I am so very grateful to you is all."

It was enough to imply that Paulette was giving him money. There must certainly be others listening.

This money that the Gibsons had at the bank was actually Paulette's. It had been another intriguing bit of information this morning, especially since it was news to Mr. Gibson's brothers also. The Kingsleys had made it clear to her, she needn't concern herself with the money left in trust for her because a wife's money was her husband's. Yet, regardless of legalities, Mr. Gibson talked as if Paulette had money of her own, and he recognized it as such.

The clerk returned, and they followed him into another room. Through the shadows of her veil, she could see that it was an office with a stately carved desk. The man who greeted them stood not much higher than herself.

Mr. Gibson introduced Charley to Mr. McCollum, the proprietor of this bank, who greeted them formally. His English was not like that of the others, and she struggled to understand.

"We are here on some business that involves Charles," Mr. Gibson said. They had agreed to that story for all but the banker himself, which meant that the man's clerk must be lurking. They'd worried that Kingsley or Carvelle might have agents here. They would have no choice but to trust McCollum, once the door to his private office closed.

Mr. Gibson trusted him, as did her papa, who had left his accounts with the man.

"I see," the banker said.

"And how are our funds, McCollum?"

"Well invested, I assure you. Shall I call up the account for your review?"

"Perhaps in a bit. We would like to discuss another matter with you first."

The banker bowed. "I see. Or rather I do not see. Please take a seat. Get us another chair."

The clerk carried over another chair, and she allowed herself to be seated between the two brothers.

"Our discussion must be private," Mr. Gibson said.

The banker made a shooing motion, and she heard the door behind them *click*.

"You may remove your veil, my dear," Mr. Gibson said quietly.

She gripped the lacy edge with shaking hands and tore it back, pulling the attached bonnet askew, trying to right it, and knocking out a hair pin. She took a deep breath. The room was brighter than she'd thought. A lamp stood lit behind the desk, dispelling London gloom and the chilly shadow of money.

And the banker's eyes were a startled shade of blue.

"I apologize for my deception, sir." She swallowed and tried to clear her throat. Her hands moved to the carved wooden chair arms and gripped them as she rushed on. "You see that I am not Mrs. Gibson, but someone else entirely. There have been...attempts. Upon my person.

And I have found sanctuary at Shaldon House and the protection of these good men and their sister, Lady Perpetua. And I have recently learned that you are my banker."

His mouth dropped open.

Mr. Gibson leaned forward in his seat. "This is—"

"Wait. Please, Mr. Gibson," she said. "Mr. McCollum, may I have your assurance to protect my identity and location? It will sound dramatic but it is true that my very life may depend upon it."

"Grace Kingsley." McCollum's throat constricted on her name.

She was that much of a scandal, she supposed. "Yes. It is I." And if she could not trust him, her fate was entirely in Everly hands.

She took a deep breath. No. Her fate would always be in her own hands.

The banker's face grew hard, judgmental, and his eyes began to glitter. It was Kingsley's face before he used the cane. She felt a burning trickle down her back and fought the shiver that wanted to go with it.

She became aware of Charley's large, strong hand upon her own, and breathed again.

"Miss Kingsley would like your agreement of confidentiality and to know the state of her funds," Mr. Gibson said. They had agreed that he would start this negotiation.

The banker blanched. "I assure you, they are in good order."

"She would like to know the details." Charley gave her hand a squeeze and released her to reach into a pocket. "Perhaps you've read this?" He slid a newsprint across the desk. "The description of her plight? Anonymous, but accurate. Our housekeeper has left a sworn testament to the condition of Miss Kingsley's back after her guardian's floggings. It is all ready to be presented to the proper authorities."

The banker's entire face darkened as the blood rose into it, perhaps choking off his ability to speak.

Mr. Gibson leaned forward, like a bear she had seen once in the Alta California hills, ready to attack. The bear had moved more swiftly than his size gave credit for, and this man, big as he was, was all muscle. He could shoot across the desk in moments and fall upon his prey.

"Many a man might think such punishment appropriate for an uncooperative ward," Mr. Gibson said. "If you be such, McCollum, I shall have a note for our funds today."

"Here, now." McCollum sucked in a great breath. "It is...that is...no, I do not countenance floggings, of course not. She should not have to suffer that sort of discipline. You should talk to Watelford, her solicitor."

Her pulse pounded. He spoke as if *she* were not sitting here.

"Do you countenance abductions then?" Charley asked. "We did, in fact, escort Miss Kingsley to Watelford's and found men lying in wait to abduct her."

Taking those men had yielded naught as yet, the man Kincaid had reported. They were hired men from the docks who claimed to know nothing.

Her head was spinning in the currents around them.

The banker's eyes narrowed.

"They did not succeed, of course." Charley squeezed her hand again. "As Miss Kingsley said, she is under the protection of the Earl of Shaldon."

"You knew of the attempt to take her?" Mr. Gibson's voice was a cudgel.

"No." The banker's fingers rattled on the desk. "That is...I was told of it after the fact."

By whom? She wanted to shout the words, but he rushed on in his nearly unfathomable accent.

"There are no men lying in wait at my bank. I would not allow such a thing." He drew himself higher in the chair. "And Miss Kingsley's account is a matter to be discussed with one of her guardians." He drew a file from a stack on his desk and opened it. "Lord Kingsley of course. And Lord Farnsworth...or..." he shifted a paper, "his substitute." He lifted his eyes and glanced at the two men. "The terms of the guardianship allowed for a substitution if one of the guardians was incapacitated or unavailable. Farnsworth has left the country and has duly substituted Lord Shaldon."

Shock slammed her, *whooshing* the air out of her. "Your father?" Farnsworth, who had never bothered to as much as introduce himself or visit her, had put her in the charge of a sick man and had told no one?

She looked from one brother to the other and back to the banker. Or perhaps he *had* shared the news. Perhaps everyone knew except her. "Surely you can discuss the matter of my money with the sons of Lord Shaldon."

The banker glanced at her. "I'm sorry, Mr. Gibson."

He wasn't. She could see that. He was one more man of the Lord Kingsley ilk.

"You mean to say, we must return with Lord Shaldon?" She swallowed hard.

Her voice had risen. She took a breath, trying to regain control.

McCollum closed the file and pushed his chair back.

"Answer the lady, if you please," Charley said coolly.

McCollum's gaze jerked up to him. "Yes, I will speak with Lord Shaldon, or...I was given to understand that the marriage settlements had been signed. I could reasonably discuss this with your fiancé, Mr. Carvelle."

Blood pounded through her. She shot to her feet. "He is *not* my fiancé. *Not*." She pushed at the chair with the back of her legs, needing to walk, trapped by the close-set chairs and the men who'd been in them, who were now standing, and the desk in front of her. Caged.

The banker had stood also, and in his face, she read the conviction that Kingsley had been right to beat her.

The sight of it frightened her back to sanity. She must be shrewd. She must act like she was intelligent. She must exercise some of the coolness these English prized so much.

"Miss Kingsley is correct," Charley was saying. "She will not marry Carvelle."

To the banker, he would appear calm, yet she sensed the tension within him. The honor there.

There was honor in all the sons. It must be in the father, also, her latest guardian, who was on his way from Bath.

She did not have time to wait for his return. McCollum would tell Kingsley where to find her. She must know about her money, now, today, and must take as much of it as possible, as soon as possible.

She looked at Charley, searching his deceptively bland face. His eyes met hers and sent a shiver through her. An idea arose in her. Pleasant, unpleasant. Desirable, undesirable. Possible and yet, not.

She took in a deep breath. What she must do, she could.

CHAPTER FOURTEEN

"You say you will be willing to talk to my fiancé?" Graciela asked the banker.

He tapped the pads of his fingers upon the open file.

Mr. Gibson roused like a sleeping giant. "You've already discussed Miss Kingsley's business with Carvelle." It was a growl, latent with violence. "Really, McCollum?"

"As her fiancé—"

"Wait." She planted her palms and leaned across the desk. "You will discuss my financial affairs with the man I am to marry? Is that correct?"

"In extenuating circumstances—"

"Which these most certainly are." She glanced to Charley and prayed his locked jaw did not bode an unwillingness for more play-acting.

The banker's face was equally grim. He opened his mouth.

"Very well," she said firmly. "It has not been announced." She grasped Charley's hand. "But my guardian, Lord Shaldon, has given his approval. Mr. Charles Everly and I are engaged to be married."

Charley experienced the absence of air that must precede a swoon. The only firm sensation was the grip of Graciela's slim fingers, and the only thing he could see beyond the black dots was the desperate pleading in her eyes. He focused there, willing himself to breathe.

He was a man. Men did not swoon. Not even over an unplanned engagement. He had survived worse moments.

And the warmth in her eyes, the twin pools of emotion there, made him want to cast off his coats and dive in to rescue her.

He laughed at his own ridiculous poetry. "My dear." He clamped his other hand over hers and turned to the stiff banker. "Do you know, McCollum, I cannot even put my arm around my lady for the pain it causes her. I would have called out both Kingsley and Carvelle, if I thought they had any honor to challenge. And if my lady did not object to dueling."

He would, however, make them pay, and enjoy that process.

She was blinking hard, her eyes shining, and it sent a warm buzzing through him. He touched a finger to her smooth cheek.

"Now, McCollum, we will know the condition of my fiancée's finances, or the Earl of Shaldon will hear about your cooperation with the villains who subjected her to *beatings* and an attempted *rape* in order to *embezzle* her funds. Perhaps the next news sheet will even mention her bank. Do you want that?"

All the color drained from the jowly face. Why on earth Bink had picked this bank and this banker, he couldn't imagine.

"McCollum's Bank does not embezzle." He exhaled loudly. "I do truly run an honest business. I have done my best to safeguard the lady's funds and counsel moderation. Please, Miss Kingsley, be seated."

They all sat. McCollum reached for that file again and pulled out an account sheet.

"You have Miss Kingsley's records ready upon your desk." Yet he'd said he would have to call for Bink's.

Under his neckcloth, the banker's throat jumped. "Kingsley and Carvelle called on me early today. Before the bank opened."

Bink caught his eye, looking grim. "To withdraw funds."

"Aye." McCollum rubbed his jaw. "It was three quarters of the balance, they wanted. They brought me that news sheet also, as if I hadn't already seen it and made the connection. They said that Miss Kingsley had been taken and they had received a ransom request. In fact, I saw the ransom note."

"It is a fake." Graciela's voice shook. "Or..." She looked to him. "Who would do this, Charley?" She looked away, and shook her head.

His heart lurched. *Not I.* A ransom note had not been part of their devious plan to undercut Kingsley. "Three quarters of the balance. Why not ask for all?"

"Did you give it to them?" Bink asked.

"No." He slid the paper across the desk. "I told them such an amount would take a few days. Miss Kingsley's trust is quite large, and the money is invested, you see."

Charley took the sheet and scanned it, his head pounding wildly. Graciela's wealth was substantial, even with the series of escalating withdrawals. She was a significant heiress, a prize ship worthy of a pirate king or a smuggling lord. Lord Kingsley might have murdered his wife and married her. A mere quarter of the remaining amount would sustain a lord for years to come or make a man a potentate in some parts of the New World. How the devil had her father amassed that fortune?

He handed her the paper and watched her study it.

McCollum's lips tightened like the line between his bushy brows. "Perhaps it is now time to call in a magistrate, as I suggested to Kingsley earlier."

"No," Charley said, and "No," she said, at the same moment.

He touched her cheek. He could not help himself.

"How quickly do they want the funds?" he asked.

"In two days."

"Or they will ruin your reputation?"

McCollum nodded. "Aye."

"And cause a run upon the bank," Bink said.

"We will not allow that." Graciela scooted to the edge of her seat and waved the sheet of paper. "Mr. McCollum, these recent sizeable withdrawals have bought me gowns, but they have also purchased wardrobes for the Kingsleys and their servants, a new town coach, and furnishings for their house." Her voice shook. "I sailed on some voyages with my father. I know how hard-fought was the earning of this money. And yet, I see, you have waged your own battle against my guardian and his greed. Your investments have been profitable. It is not as bad as I would have expected. It appears you have managed the money to your best, in spite of his mishandling. It is why, I suppose, my father chose you."

McCollum studied her as if he were seeing her for the first time.

Charley's heart swelled. She was a surprise, his Graciela. *His fiancée.*

He found he did not mind the designation.

His eyes strayed to her tight-laced bodice and his mind raced to a wedding night. He could drop her at Shaldon House, head for Doctors' Commons, and marry her tomorrow. He would have to forge her guardian's signature, unless Shaldon had arrived in their absence.

"But what of this solicitor, Mr. Watelford?" Her question brought him back from his ruminations. "He did indeed lay a trap for me."

"He assured me that was not his doing."

"You spoke with him?" Charley asked.

"Yesterday."

Yesterday. And Kingsley and Carvelle had come to the bank today. They would be watching the bank. They would plan a similar trap for Graciela here. He looked at Bink, who nodded.

They had planned for it.

"My staff is trustworthy," McCollum said, "and the bank is well-guarded."

Indeed, it was well-guarded. Most of the bank's customers were their men. Any attempt on Graciela—or Paulette—would be thwarted once again. As to the trustworthiness of the staff, he was not sure. The clerk who'd admitted them had been entirely too curious.

"Go on," Charley said. "What else did Watelford say?"

"He mentioned the terms of the marriage settlement with Mr. Carvelle. Are you aware of them, Miss Kingsley?" He tapped the desk some more, this matter clearly causing him dismay. "Of course not. With Lord Farnsworth gone, and Lord Shaldon away, as someone else concerned with your welfare, Watelford talked to me. Upon your marriage to Carvelle, a portion of your money was to be settled immediately upon Lord Kingsley."

"The same amount as the ransom?" Charley asked.

"No. It would be approximately one-quarter of your remaining funds."

"The rest to Carvelle." Her voice shook.

He nodded. "Once married, your wealth becomes his."

"Unless the trust or the marriage settlement specifies that the wife keep control of her money." Charley took her other hand in his. Her gaze had dropped to the mahogany carving that circled the base of the mammoth desk.

"He s-sold me for a c-commission of twenty-five percent."

He moved a hand to her back, remembered her wounds, and touched her arm. "You will not release that money, McCollum."

"No, I will not."

She pressed a hand to her heart. "When my father returns..." Her head dropped.

"What do you hear about Captain Kingsley?" Bink asked the banker.

Of course—a banker who funded merchants and seamen would have his ear to the ground on such matters.

"Probably no more than what you've discovered. Captain Llewellyn reported him dead in a storm off Tortuga. He's come up to town. I expect a visit in a day or two."

"Captain Llewellyn made the report? He's in London?" Excitement percolated through Graciela, sending an answering rush of emotion in him.

A sea captain who was her father's friend? If she thought to run off and join the man, she would have to knock Charley out of the way first.

"Where is Llewellyn staying?" Charley asked.

"I'll ask my clerk. Excuse me."

He stood. Bink did also, and caught Charley's eye. "I'll go with you and hear what he has to say."

When the door had closed, she stood and tried to pull her hand away.

He held on and snatched up her other hand, rising with her.

Her gaze swept the floor. "I do not wish to marry either," she said. "I'm very sorry but it seemed the best tactic. I could not very well announce my engagement to your brother, Mr. Gibson."

"So, my father has given his permission?"

"Perhaps he will withdraw it." She looked away. "Or you may cast me off."

"My father would not withdraw permission, nor would I cast you off," he said sternly. "How could you presume it? It would be dishonorable of us."

Her head jerked up, concern in her eyes. "You are angry? But you must not be. I will make sail with Captain Llewellyn and you will be free."

"Unless I come along."

Her eyes flashed. "You must not come. Your life is here. Your family—your brothers, and your sister, and your father who is ill."

"And your father will be looking for you here, Graciela." He stepped closer.

"I will release you and go and look for him. This engagement was just a ploy."

His nerves prickled at the challenge. Just a ploy, was it?

He cupped her chin and lifted it. "You are playing with my heart?"

She had begun to tremble and her breathing quickened.

When he claimed her lips and cradled the back of her head, she didn't pull away, didn't resist. She allowed the kiss, allowed him to ravish her with his lips and his tongue, her arms reaching for him, her hands tangling in his hair. He grasped her hips and pulled her closer, trailing kisses.

"You have no heart," she mumbled, her lips vibrating along his jaw.

Stark need erupted in him. *Because you have stolen it.*

He'd never say it—she wouldn't believe him, but he *needed* her. Needed to keep her alive, needed to save her from Carvelle, needed to be inside her. His shaft strained the contours of his trousers, while her touch scorched him, at his neck, along his shoulder, under his coat. She pressed against him, head back, lips open, ready to receive whatever he could give, as if she needed him as well.

The flat surface of the desk, the one file spread over it, caught his eye, and beckoned.

The file. He should peruse the file. His mission...a Spanish woman...it might contain...

Her hand slid down, cupped his arse, and drowned his voice of reason.

"Charley."

His hand had found her breast. He batted back his conscience.

"Charley." Louder now.

Her sweet hands squeezed him and deafened the voice.

"Charley" Two vises gripped him, hauled him up, and landed him across the room into a bookcase. A door slammed. "What the devil," Bink roared. "My wife?" Bink's fist crashed, rattling the desk.

When his vision cleared, Graciela had turned away and was struggling with her veils. And Bink...Bink's eyes glowed with amusement.

"Someone besides McCollum saw us," Charley said. "Oh hell. They'll think Paulette and I...Oh hell. Paulette—"

"Will laugh about it. McCollum is speaking to his clerk right now."

Charley righted himself and smoothed his waistcoat. "I don't trust the man."

"The banker?" Graciela asked in a small voice.

Embarrassed she was, and it was his fault. He straightened her veil.

"Charley means the clerk."

He looked at Bink, who was retrieving a quill that had jumped off the desk when he pounded it.

"I believe we're holding better cards than Kingsley," Bink said. "The stakes are too high for McCollum to side with him and Carvelle. The clerk, however, might be looking to supplement his salary."

"Exactly," Charley said, his head clearing.

McCollum slipped into the room and closed the door. "Your people are in place." He frowned, distressed by all the day's events, no doubt.

"Good." Charley offered Graciela his arm.

"Wait." She gripped her hands at her waist. "Mr. McCollum. I should like to know when I may take my money."

McCollum's eyes widened and quickly narrowed. His lips pursed. "Your guardian—"

"No. I must leave this country. For that I need my money. When may I have it?"

"Until you are of age, your guardian has control of that. Unless you marry sooner, and the decision will be your husband's."

Charley could not see her face under the heavy veil. He could not read her eyes or see the set of her mouth or the twitch of her jaw clenching. He did not need to. Her spine straightened into a stiff line and told him everything he needed to know.

And he decided. They would marry, and he would give her control of every penny and then set her free.

On the way back to Shaldon House, Graciela sat squashed next to Mr. Gibson in this plain carriage, with Charley across from them. Neither man spoke, to her, or to each other. Nor did they look at her. Their attention was divided equally between the windows on each side of the coach.

She longed to rip these veils from her eyes so she could also see properly. All the shadows showed her were the legs of their guards' horses and the men's rugged boots.

The shadows compressed her chest and she fought for a breath.

Charley's hand touched hers briefly, and the edge of the veil lifted an inch. "Deep breaths, Graciela. You must wear this bloody disguise until we are home."

"It is not my home," she spluttered.

"Nor mine," said Mr. Gibson, and she heard in his voice a deep concern that took her out of herself. He had a wife and child he was thinking of.

"Ah, well, until we have reached sanctuary, then," Charley said. The veil stretched at an angle like a jib sail, and she found she could catch some air now. It was, however, intoxicating air, filled with his scent and his attention.

Unless I come along. Warmth expanded her chest and flew up into her cheeks. His presence might be a hindrance, because once she arrived in the new world, she intended to search for her father. Unless he would help her.

But...would he give this up—his brothers, his sister, his father—to come with her and Reina? So tempting it was, to have Reina, and her money, and these deft hands that could manage even this flimsy bit of netting.

She pushed the thought away. He would only interfere and try to direct her.

She must speak with Francisca and Juan, she must prepare them to be ready to depart quickly at a moment's notice, when she somehow had acquired her funds. It would not be difficult. They had nothing left but the clothes on their backs and each other.

The coach jolted, and *crack!* Charley crashed onto her, pushing her into the squab. A horse shrieked and men's curses filled the air.

CHAPTER FIFTEEN

Pain laced her back. She stifled a scream and shoved at the weight crushing her.

More shrieks. More *crack, crack, crack.* Gunpowder filled the air, like it did when Papa tested his cannons.

"Bring her out," a man cried, and they were tugging her. She swung a fist. A strong hand grasped it.

"It's me, Gracie. It's Charley. Hold tight, love. I'll get you out."

Out. Yes. The seat beside her was empty. Mr. Gibson had left.

She reached for Charley and they tumbled out together, and then she was lifted up, up, up, onto a horse.

She felt herself toppling, and then he grabbed her. He'd jumped up behind her.

"Pull up your skirts and straddle."

She did as he said, and he locked an arm around her. Horses swarmed around them, but they were Charley's horses and Charley's men.

Their horse flew like a hellion, down pavements and through the tightest of alleys and byways, splitting crowds, with Charley shouting and cursing like one of Papa's sailors, like a knight with his captured lady.

The thrill pushed out the fear and by the time they arrived in the Shaldon mews, she was shaking with something like mad laughter.

In the stables, two men in plain work clothes backed away, a blonde head peeping between them. Before she could orient herself, Charley sprang down and hauled her with him, losing his balance, crashing them both to the floor.

She landed atop him, her head crooked on his shoulder, and behind her the horse shuffled away. Charley's breath came quick and shallow in her ears and the pounding between them was either his heart or hers, or both. When she tried to move, she was locked against him.

When she tried to speak, she had no breath.

His grip loosened and he shifted, gripping her head, lifting his own to meet her lips, sweetly, softly, soothingly.

Need coursed through her and she fell into the kiss, parting her lips and plundering him. At some point during their ride she'd lost her bonnet with its dreaded veils, and now it was her hair tumbling around her, according them some sense of privacy.

"Charley."

She became aware of footsteps around them and lifted her head. He tugged her back down into another long kiss.

"Charley." The voice was closer, louder.

She pulled away. "It's your brother again."

Charley groaned and released her, helping her to her feet, smoothing her skirts while her cheeks heated.

Twice caught kissing Charley Everly. Even for one such as she, that was scandalous. And the wild ride...she gripped a handful of skirt. "I've given all of London a look at my knees."

"And lovely they are." That voice was feminine.

She pushed back her hair and found a pretty blonde woman next to Mr. Gibson, curling her lips in on a smile. Was this Paulette? But no, Mr. Gibson's wife was in the country somewhere. And this woman's dress was a plain servant's twill.

"Did we catch them?" Charley was arranging his coats.

She heated again and moved in front of him.

"We don't know yet. Let's get you inside, Miss Kingsley."

Mr. Gibson reached for her, but she sank back against Charley and fumbled for his hand.

"Ah, leave her to Charley, Bink." The woman smiled brightly. "But Miss Kingsley, Bink is right. We'll be safer inside while this rumpus dies down, and more comfortable also. Lean then on Charley's arm and we'll move ourselves inside, shall we?"

There was a music to this woman's speech, the accent so familiar.

The lady took Graciela's free arm as they moved down a wide path through the garden. "There now, they haven't bothered with an introduction, but I'm Sirena, James's wife."

"James?"

She waved a hand. "Lord Bakeley. I've already had a tumble with your Reina this morning. Aye, she's charmed all of us, she has, including my James. We've found some old toys for her, and we must buy her more. At the moment, Perry has her in hand so your Francisca and the nursemaids can rest a bit. She'll not nap, though, she won't, that little mite. But I hear Charley has the power to sprinkle the Dustman's powder."

Her head was spinning. "The Dustman?"

Sirena laughed. "It's a fairy character."

"And not an Irish one," Charley said.

"So they say. They say that, like our Charley, the Dustman is not a bit Irish." Another jolly laugh followed. "But I say magic that puts children to sleep and gives them sweet dreams must be Irish." They entered through the servants' door and Sirena leaned closer. "Charley has a reputation as a lady's man, but I don't believe it for a second. He's but sprinkling fairy dust and putting them to dreaming about his great prowess."

"Sirena." Charley turned to face them, aghast. "Don't listen to my bawdy sister, Gracie. She is Irish, you know."

Sirena punched his arm. "So I am, and here's another one."

Mr. Gibson had followed them in.

"My father's surgeon is an Irishman. He does not have your red and golden hair, though." Her heart twisted. O'Malley had always teased her that he was black Irish, descended from the wrecked survivors of the Armada, and they were cousins many times removed. He had sailed with Papa on this voyage. If Papa was lost, so was O'Malley.

Charley lifted her hand. "One skirmish at a time, Gracie. If your father and his Irish surgeon are alive, we'll find them. But we must first deal with Kingsley and Carvelle."

His eyes begged her to trust in him. His gaze, his touch, warmed her.

Mr. Gibson clamped a hand on Charley's shoulder. "Kincaid is here."

He blinked, squeezed her hand, and smiled. "You have straw in your hair," he whispered. "And your gown is ripped. And you've lost that fashionable hat."

"And it is all of your doing," she whispered back.

"Yes." His eyes gleamed wickedly. "A pity we cannot finish it." He lifted her hands and kissed them both. "Will you come with us? Or will you go up with Sirena to change and check on Reina?"

Oh, he was clever—he was offering her a choice. She sensed he did not want her with him when he spoke to Kincaid, yet he would not forbid it. And he knew how strong the pull was to the child.

"Reina must come first, and then I will change and find you, and you will report the news to me."

He grinned and dropped a kiss on her forehead. "At your command, my lady."

And then he was off, knocking elbows with his brother. At the doorway he looked back and smiled.

Her heart lurched.

Qué tonto. What a fool.

She must forget passion. She must reach for intelligence, before she tumbled head over ears into loving this Englishman.

*****

Bakeley and Kincaid sat in the library, heads bent over papers. They both looked up when Charley and Bink entered.

"How did you fare?" Bakeley asked.

Bink cast him a quizzical look and went for the table laid with cold meats. Charley swiped a hand through his brow, went to the sideboard and poured a drink.

"That bad?" Bakeley asked. "Or that good?"

"A bit of both," Bink said. "And a wild ride at the end. The villains ambushed us."

Charley threw back a gulp and let it burn down his throat.

"The lady is safe?" Bakeley's voice held concern.

"Sirena has her in hand," Bink said. "She met us in the stables."

"Any injuries?" Kincaid asked.

"I don't know. Charley and I took horses and left."

"A horse," Charley said. "A horse was injured."

Bakeley stood, eyes narrowed and glinting with murder. Horse breeding was more than one of the family's businesses, it was a shared passion for him and his lady.

"How badly, I don't know, only that I heard the first shot and then the horse's scream."

"I've informed the head groom," Bink said.

Bakeley paced across the room to the window.

"They'll know what to do," Charley said. "By now a crowd has gathered, yet it would not do to draw Shaldon's heir to the scene."

Bakeley's face glowed. "If he's killed an innocent horse—"

"I'll take care of getting you satisfaction." Charley set the glass down. "And not in some twigged-out pistols at dawn. Don't worry, Kincaid, that I don't have the stomach for it."

Kincaid grunted. "Did McCollum betray you?"

"No." Or so his gut told him.

Bink shook his head. "Kingsley and Carvelle had been in to see him that morning. I'm guessing they had people lingering around to see if she would visit."

"We shouldn't have dressed her in black. It was too similar to the disguise at Watelford's."

"No, Charley. The disguise was a good one until..." A smile creased Bink's face and he shook his head again. "McCollum's clerk is in someone's pay, I'll warrant, but whether it's Carvelle, or Kingsley, or both, I don't know. He identified us because Charley here couldn't keep his hands off my wife."

Bakeley's head went up and his eyes narrowed. Kincaid was as usual, inscrutable.

His stomach churned, or maybe that was akin to the fluttering he'd felt after Gracie's announcement. "Yes well, it's a day of good news all around. You're expecting an heir, Bakeley, and I've just become engaged to Miss Kingsley."

Bakeley exchanged looks with Bink. "Have you indeed. And when is the wedding?"

"That's the rub. As soon as I said yes to the lady—"

"*You* said yes?"

"Bink was there. He can attest. Once she learned that Shaldon is her new guardian—"

"Father?"

"Yes. Stop interrupting. Once she learned that Shaldon is her new guardian, she offered for me. I said yes, and then she began plotting how to get out of it. That is what we were discussing when you left us alone for a few minutes."

Bink laughed. "And a very convincing argument you were making."

"Sit," Bakeley commanded, and pulled over a chair. "We have much to talk about but I'll hear this story first."

Upstairs, Graciela shed her torn outer clothing and slipped on a new gown.

A new gown, not a made-over one. Lady Sirena had said so, gabbling non-stop as Francisca did up Graciela's laces and hooks and her ladyship's own little maid fixed her hair. Lady Sirena had stayed with her after her visit to the nursery, following her and Francisca back to her bedchamber.

Now, Francisca's face was a mask of determination, not a bit servile, though out of politeness, the few words she spoke were in her even more indecipherable English. Graciela would have laughed if her head were on right, or even still attached to her neck.

It had been quite the morning.

"Oh, I do like your hair done more loosely," Lady Sirena exclaimed.

The maid had left her curls to their wildness, framing her face, coiling low on her neck, unlike the tight, pomaded style Lady Kingsley had enforced.

"And the dress—'tis a dream. The color makes your skin look like cream. I'm glad, I am, that Madame delivered the start of your wardrobe. She was so disappointed you'd gone out." Perched on the side of the high bed, Lady Sirena swung her feet just as Reina would have done.

With her back to her ladyship, Francisca adjusted a pleat and rolled her eyes.

The modiste she'd visited with Lady Kingsley had been decidedly English, dressing her in whites that made her look swarthy and foreign. Who was this Madame?

She fluffed the skirt of the dress. The blue wafted like soft bay water, the tiny flocked flowers floating upon it. "It is a lovely dress, but let this be the end of them. I fear I cannot pay you right away, and I would not be in your debt."

A rap on the door brought Lady Perry, who clapped her hands together and smiled. "She is sleeping finally, even without Charley's help, and the dress is perfect, as Madame said it would be."

Lady Sirena waved her hand. "She's fretting though, Perry. Miss Kingsley, you're not to worry. 'Tis only one dress, and such a pleasure it is for us to see you in it." She smiled wickedly. "For *all* of us."

Her cheeks warmed. Lady Sirena had caught her sprawled over Charley, and the both of them kissing. And then there was the matter of the engagement, which the ladies could not possibly know about because she barely knew of it herself.

"Madame will be along early tomorrow with another morning dress. She is wishing to measure you in person."

The modiste would come to her in person. Lord Shaldon was indeed powerful.

Lady Sirena laughed. "She's very clever, Madame is, taking a lady's measure from her clothing. But it is better to measure the person, especially when one is addressing needs such as a corset."

"There is no need—"

"I beg you to allow it." Lady Sirena had hopped from the bed and now her small cool hand clasped Graciela's. "It was but a year or so ago that I ran from a monster with naught but the clothes on my back."

"It's true," Lady Perry said. "And a lady must have clothes."

She found it hard to breathe. "I am not a lady." Not here. Not in England.

She had been a lady, or almost so, years before, when she had danced at her older friends' *Quinceañeras* and wondered which of the handsome young men who flocked to the parties would be hers. And then her father had decided they must leave, this time taking them on the long voyage back to the West Indies, dropping them with friends in Tampico and leaving, because what he must do was too dangerous.

And then Mama had decided they must leave there and go to Veracruz. Papa had no notion of that journey, nor the dangers they'd faced. She had never lived so close to the land, so close to the edge of survival. It had cost her all claims to gentility.

Lady Sirena might have fled a monster, but it was to go from one cultured drawing room to another. In this country, Graciela might as well have been an opera dancer, or a flower seller, or one of the Rom threading their wagons down bumpy lanes and sleeping under the stars. She could never meet the standards of these people, especially the ladies.

Well, except for these two, who seemed determined to keep talking. "You're not only a lady, you're a wealthy one, to boot, I hear. Your father had the forethought to put money aside for you and not leave you to running through the woods and knocking on the neighbor's kitchen door to take you in." She patted Graciela's hand.

"There now. If anyone can get you set to rights, 'tis Lord Shaldon and his sons."

Lady Perry eyed her thoughtfully. "Especially his son, Charley."

A bottle crashed on the dressing table, scent filling the air. The little maid rushed to help Francisca mop up spilled liquid.

"It will be all right, Francisca," Lady Perry said in her careful Spanish, and then turned back. "Shall we go below and find out all the news?"

Francisca nodded, her mouth pressed firmly closed.

"Let me join you in just a few moments," Graciela said. "I would have a quiet word with my maid." *In private, so I may stay her hand from throwing more bottles.*

When the door closed on the ladies and the other maid, Francisca turned a shaking finger on her. "That man—"

"Do not worry yourself. I have a plan." *And you are not going to like it.* Graciela swallowed. "And we must prepare ourselves for the opportunity to leave."

Charley paced from one window to the other, another brandy in his hand. Gracie should be down soon, and he was waiting on one more report.

"Carvelle is a cagey one," Kincaid said. "We've knocked on every inn door and brothel and gin mill in a twenty-mile radius. We've traced every place he's known to frequent. Kingsley, however—"

A tap on the library door stopped him. One of Kincaid's men, a brawny dark-haired Scotsman, ushered in Penderbrook and another man.

Charley glanced from Bink, sprawled in an armchair near the cold fireplace, to Bakeley, his elbows resting on the desk. Both men sat up at the intrusion.

He set down his glass and rubbed his hands together. "How did it go, Laughlin?"

A smile crinkled the other man's lips. "It was all I could do to keep from laughing, old man." He brought a package from under his arm and nodded at the glass on the table. "We've earned one of those at least, have we not, Pender?"

Penderbrook smiled. His brothers frowned.

Charley went to the sideboard and poured out two more glasses. "You know Penderbrook. The other fellow is my old chum, Henry Laughlin."

"Sir Henry Laughlin." Bakeley tapped the desk. "Newly appointed magistrate?"

Bakeley *did* have his finger at the pulse of London.

"That is correct, Lord Bakeley." He bowed. "At your service."

"What have you done, Charley?" Bink said. "I thought we weren't going to involve the authorities."

"I'm afraid this was more my doing than Everly's," Laughlin said. "Well, mine and Penderbrook's. That broadsheet and the rumors abounding could not go unremarked." He laughed again. "Great fun to see the look on Kingsley's face. Though I've muddied my new boots, so Kingsley's had his revenge. I've never seen a garden quite like that. It didn't take my men long to find the treasure, though."

Bakeley help up a hand. "Back up."

"Laughlin visited Kingsley's townhouse on a tip," Charley said. "He found a bloody dress belonging to Miss Kingsley buried in the garden."

"Here." Laughlin set the package on the desk. "I thought perhaps her servants could identify it."

Bakeley straightened in his chair. "That's damned devious."

Charley flashed his brother a grin. "Thank you. And now let's hear it. How were you received, Laughlin?"

"Kingsley arrived after the discovery, already in a snit from some bad news or other. His lady had taken to her bed and refused to come down. All but threw me out of the house, the pompous bastard."

First his disappointment at the bank and then the appearance of a magistrate. Kingsley should be good and rattled. He might even lead them to his accomplice. That was the hope anyway.

He saw Kincaid's expression draw in and shutter. "Laughlin can be trusted in this matter," Charley said. This did not involve the safety of the kingdom, only the life of one precious woman. And perhaps a little girl.

"You'll be lucky to have your position by dinner," Bink said. "Kingsley has powerful friends."

Laughlin shrugged. "What a pity. I'd just begun to enjoy it."

"We have a few friends of our own, Bink, do we not?" Charley handed the glasses around.

Voices in the hall silenced the men. The door opened and three ladies entered.

But he only saw Gracie.

Charley experienced that mysterious lack of oxygen again, as if he were struggling up several flights of stairs after a night of drinking. The dots in his vision were there also, outlining her sweet startled face. Even Sirena's voice had stilled.

Bakeley broke the hushed silence with a round of introductions, and when Charley saw Laughlin bend over Gracie's hand and the gleam in his eyes, he roused.

He took her hand away from Laughlin and tucked it into his arm. She'd donned a blue dress, and curls were scattered over her forehead and cheeks. Breathless, it made him. Like a girl. That would not do.

"What is this? The ladies could not find a black gown for you?"

She turned a scowl up to him and grimaced. The faint shadowed bruise still lurked on her cheek, reminding him of the seriousness of the threat posed by her guardian.

"I'm teasing. You're lovely. In all honesty I could not breathe when—"

"Mr. Everly." She slid her gaze toward Laughlin who was studying them unabashedly.

"Miss Kingsley." Bakeley came around the desk and blocked the other men's view. "Charley told me your happy news. You have my sincere welcome and wishes for happiness," he said, too quietly for the other men to hear.

Sirena looked from Charley to Gracie and her face lit. "I knew it," she whispered.

"Sir Henry is a magistrate investigating your, er, disappearance," he said loudly enough for the servant in the hall to hear. "He's brought a piece of evidence. Will you have a look at it?"

"Evidence?" Gracie's voice cracked.

"Perhaps it's moot now," Laughlin said. "Since you are now found, Miss Kingsley."

Her face contorted. "Can you arrest Lord Kingsley, Sir Henry?"

Laughlin's face softened. "Not for murder, it would seem, and thankfully. I am glad to find you alive and looking well."

Gracie pressed a hand to her throat. "I suppose the Kingsleys are untouchable, as great lords are."

"Not untouchable, my dear," Lord Bakeley said. "But sometimes, justice comes outside the law."

CHAPTER SIXTEEN

Outside the law. That concept, she could grasp. Justice had come for her outside the law once before, but that had been in a part of a wild country almost without laws. Perhaps England was not so different from Mexico or the high seas. A man's secret sins could be repaid in secret.

Charley's firm hand on hers transmitted courage. His muscled forearm filled her with strength. She questioned it, doubted it, searched it for falsehood, and could find none. Here was a rock, something certain, some strength that wouldn't waver.

She blinked hard. For her to have found a safe harbor was itself a kind of retribution to the Kingsleys. And if she could take Papa's money from their grasp...

The dress unfurled for her to view, muddied and smeared with another shade of brown. Charley's eyes glittered but his lips did not move into a smile.

"Yes. It is mine." It was the dress Mrs. Windle had removed from her. She had thought they would have burned it. "Where did you find it?"

"It was buried in the Kingsleys' garden." The magistrate's shrewd eyes surveyed her.

"I did not bury it," she said.

"I did not think you did."

He would ask her who did. Or what happened. Or whose blood had soaked the dress. She ran through the possible stories. She would look like a liar, and then she would be unsupported. Perhaps her defense against Carvelle would land her in jail. She was not nobility. She had no protection.

A lie once told must be clung to, no matter the soul-sucking it caused.

Charley shifted her to his other side, his arm draped loosely around her. She found his touch did not sting.

"The blood is Gregory Carvelle's," she said. "Lord Kingsley sent his servants away and allowed him to access my bedchamber. I would not..."

"You defended your person," the magistrate said. "Yes. We questioned all the servants. They had all been from home. His lordship had organized an evening outing for all of the staff."

No. That was not right. "There was at least one maid on duty to lock me into my room."

"I was given to understand by the butler and housekeeper that we spoke to everyone."

"No. The maid is an elderly servant. She and her husband share a room above the stables, I had heard." She'd seen Lady Kingsley abuse the woman quite harshly on several occasions. She supposed the woman had nowhere else to go.

He took down their names in a small notebook and tucked it away. "Forgive me for asking, Miss Kingsley, were you yourself injured in any way. I see a bruise here." He touched his jaw.

"That is from Lord Kingsley before he used the cane on my back. Carvelle bruised me here." She showed him her wrist.

"We have not been able to locate Gregory Carvelle as yet. Were his wounds—"

"Not fatal," Charley said. "He visited McCollum's bank this morning in the company of Lord Kingsley."

"To steal as much of my money as they could get the banker to yield."

Laughlin frowned. "I see."

Charley told him about the attacks at the solicitor's office and on the way back from the bank, but he made no mention of the fake ransom note.

Which pricked her suspicions.

Although, perhaps it was wise not to mention it. They need not complicate an official investigation any more than was needed for her to get her money. These men were Charley's friends, yet she sensed his reluctance to tell them everything.

She understood that. He was a spy—secrets and lies came naturally to such as him.

She searched her heart and found it did not matter. She did not think he would betray the heart of a true allegiance, to, for example, his family, or honor, or someone he loved.

Could he *ever* love her? In spite of her words to him the night before, she did dream of having a love like her parents had.

She shook off the thought. No husband would want her after the wedding night.

The man they called Kincaid, roused himself. "If you'll come with me, Laughlin, I'll fill you in on where we have searched for Carvelle."

Laughlin packaged up the dress and followed him out. Penderbrook went with them.

She opened her mouth to protest that she would like to know also, and said, "Where are they going?"

Charley leaned close. "I'll tell you everything, but all it amounts to is the names of London inns where Carvelle might have been staying and the streets where he allegedly had lodgings. It's basically of no use. His lair now will be one we're unfamiliar with."

"Let us speak of the happy news, then," Lady Sirena said. "Do share the details with Perry and me, James."

Lord Bakeley smiled. "You and Perry and Paulette shall have a new sister. Charley and Miss Kingsley have become engaged."

That brought a round of well-wishing and questioning, and planning on the part of the ladies.

"With a special license you can be married tomorrow, as we were," Lady Sirena said.

She felt herself wobble. Charley's hand slid to her waist and steadied her.

Lady Perry smiled. "And we can host another ball—"

"No balls," Charley said.

His vehemence halted both ladies.

"You don't mean to go to Scotland like Bink and Paulette?" Lady Perry asked.

"No flights to Scotland, either." He squeezed her hip, sending a ripple of sensation through her, and released her. "Gracie is not of age. She'll need her guardian's permission to marry. That means we'll have to wait for Father, and be damned discreet about getting a license if we don't want Kingsley's solicitors taking legal action to challenge us. Which means—"

"No official announcements." Lord Bakeley said. "No articles planted in the scandal sheets. Can you trust the banker?"

A knock at the library door brought a footman and a whispered conversation with Lord Bakeley.

He closed the door and turned to them, eyes gleaming.

"Well?" his lady asked.

"Lord Kingsley is in the drawing room."

CHAPTER SEVENTEEN

Graciela's heart pounded, a great weight like an anchor thrashing inside her head.

"I will see him alone," Lord Bakeley said.

"No," Charley said and "No," she said at the same time.

Charley came and smoothed his hands over her forearms. He opened his mouth, but seemed unable to speak. "You wish to confront him," he said finally.

She nodded, words suddenly failing her also.

"We shall all go," Lady Sirena said. "Miss Kingsley is under our protection. We shall put you between Perry and me and he will see that you have family."

"Paulette will regret missing this." Mr. Gibson had come to stand with them.

Charley chafed her hands. "We won't mention family or marriage plans yet. We'll tell him as little as possible, only that we're keeping you safe, here, under our roof. What say you?"

"Yes." Yes. She would accept their protection, for herself, and her servants and for Reina. For now.

Next to Charley and his brothers, Lord Kingsley did not look so tall, so grand, or so powerful.

She glimpsed him through the door, the side of his face stiffened into the mask that hid angry rage.

In the hallway, Lady Sirena turned her around, taking both of Graciela's hands. "Deep breaths. Head up. Shoulders back. You're a lady among ladies, and no matter the power he thinks he has, you're with us now, and you've nothing to fear."

She shook her head. "I am not afraid. I am angry."

"Anger is good," Lady Perry said. "As long as it sharpens you. We shall outfox this fox."

She wondered how many foxes this lady had dealt with.

When she entered the drawing room between the elegant Lady Sirena and the taller Lady Perry, Kingsley's refined mask slipped revealing the beast within. His eyes bulged and a boiling red seeped from the knot of his neck cloth up to his forehead. His chest puffed under the fashionable waistcoat her father's money had paid for.

A memory flashed—Papa's tense face as they outran a pirate ship. Papa had not worried so much nor fought so hard to buy this fat lord new coats.

He took a step toward her, and was matched by Mr. Gibson and Charley. Lord Bakeley, the lord of this house until his father returned, stepped between Lord Kingsley and her. The threat was not idle, and even Lord Kingsley could see it. Their refined society was not so far advanced. The three Everly men could heft Kingsley's great weight out the front door and onto the cobblestones of the square like her father's men combating a boarding party.

Worse, for Kingsley, they could continue tying him up in scandal sheets and magistrates and gossip, for surely the gossip had started.

How strange these English lords were—aside from Shaldon's sons, words and legal documents meant more to most of them than a fist. Perhaps that was why Papa had left this land.

Kingsley fixed his lips into a tight smile. "You have found her then, Bakeley. I am glad to see she is safe."

Liar.

"She is," Bakeley said.

"Very well, then. If you'll have a servant gather her things, I'll take her off your hands."

Lord Bakeley drew himself even taller. "We've heard some unsettling stories."

Kingsley's eyes flashed again and quickly shuttered. "The scandal sheet, you mean. Lies and nonsense. Probably planted by her." He jerked his head toward Graciela.

"How would I possibly know how to do such a thing?" she said. "I lived like a prisoner in your home."

Kingsley's gaze stayed fixed on Lord Bakeley. She glanced to Charley who gave his head one quick shake and turned away, plucking at some imaginary lint on his coat.

"It was likely a busybody neighbor, or one of their servants." Charley had rocked back on his heels, looking careless, feckless, one would say, almost drunk. "Heard a scream in the night, or some such," he drawled. "Sent a note over to some fellow for an extra quid. It did sell well, I believe. It's all the fellows at White's could blabber about. Had a full page of wagers in the betting book." He laughed, like a fool, like he had nary a care in the world, like her life was not strung in the balance here.

Anger spiked in her until she remembered, he was acting, grandly, consummately, convincingly, and that sent her heart into a flurry. What should she believe of this man?

"You could not imagine," Charley said in that same languorous tone. "Bets on the lady's identity. Bets on the identity of her guardian. Bets on whether she was dead, and if so, where her body would be—"

"Enough, Charley," Lord Bakeley said. "There are ladies present."

Charley straightened, as if snapped back to reality. He bowed toward the ladies. "Oh, I do beg pardon."

"Yes, well, this girl is alive, and I'm taking her home with me, with or without her things."

"Tell us, my lord," Mr. Gibson said, "What happened to the child who traveled with her?"

Kingsley's glare bounced quickly off Mr. Gibson. His face blanched and colored again.

Ah. Here was the next rumor to be planted, that Lord Kingsley had done away with the child under Captain Kingsley's care. "How should I know? Here now, Bakeley, I won't be accused like this. Hand over the chit. She is coming with me."

"I think we must have that answer," Bakeley said.

"I've given it. She was there one moment, and the next, those two black servants had left and taken her with them. I don't know where they went. Back to the West Indies, for all I know. Now, I'll have the girl."

He took a step toward her, and her blood rose, the threat transparent even with Lord Bakeley as an obstacle. Mr. Gibson drew nearer to her guardian, while Charley closed in behind him.

"Oh my," Lady Sirena whispered. "A piece of work, he is that."

The air in the room crackled like the lightning was coming. This would come to a fight, and Papa's knife was upstairs in that pretty blue bedchamber.

But she had these three men as her weapon, and the two ladies as her fellow warriors.

"I think not," Lord Bakeley said. "We are happy to have her as our guest until she wishes to leave."

"Yes, well, I am not happy for her to be your guest, and I am her guardian. She is coming with me."

"Oh, I say," Charley said from behind, startling Kingsley. "Isn't Father her guardian also?"

"He is," Lord Bakeley said.

"He is not. Farnsworth is her guardian, and he is out of the country."

"Well, I distinctly remember Father saying he was stepping up to replace Farnsworth in his absence." Charley had moved to Lord Kingsley's side and managed to make his bored tone sound threatening. "A damned bother, I'd say, all these beautiful young ladies to look after."

Lord Kingsley looked at him then, for the first time, but all he would see was that bored, drunken, careless rogue. Charley's eyes sparkled with an awareness that perhaps only she could see.

"I do wish to stay here with Lord and Lady Bakeley," Graciela said, "and with Lord Shaldon. My father always spoke so highly of him and his accomplishments." She was putting it on thickly, but surely Papa would have spoken thus, if they'd had more time together before he sailed.

"Shaldon is not here. You are coming with me."

"I am not."

"*She is not.*"

The voice boomed from the doorway and she turned to see a tall, elegant man, his hair laced with a few sprinklings of silver at his ears. He was dark like Lord Bakeley, but his strong jaw and straight nose were like those of all three of the Everly sons.

Or rather, theirs were like his.

"Th-thank you." Her tongue stuck in her dry mouth. She swallowed and curtsied.

"Kingsley." The gaze Charley's father turned on Lord Kingsley was as hard and as cruel as the other man's, and the sight of it rattled her.

"Here, now, Shaldon—"

"No." Lord Shaldon shook his head. "Gather all of Miss Kingsley's things and send them here. She is staying with me." He waved a hand. "Hire a flock of solicitors if you wish to challenge me. You may sell your wife's new jewels to pay for them, as you are not going to have a farthing more from Miss Kingsley's account."

A pallor descended upon Lord Kingsley. "I am her guardian."

"As am I."

"Farnsworth—"

"Will return soon. And, as he keeps a bachelor establishment, he will not likely want to take charge of Miss Kingsley's person himself. I've no doubt my daughters will enjoy her company."

"We most certainly do, Father," Lady Sirena said.

From behind Kingsley's shoulder, Charley was smiling. The bored lord had vanished. This was Charley himself, as she knew him. She smiled back, and Lord Kingsley saw it.

"You," he said. "You troublesome chit. You think you have outsmarted..." He took a raspy breath. "We have tried to make you respectable, to introduce you into society as your father wished, to arrange a marriage for you, as your father wished."

"To Gregory Carvelle? My father wished no such thing."

"Did you think we'd get you a duke or an earl or even one of their sons? How hard it was, trying to make you respectable, considering your mother's blood, your foul temperament, and the baggage you brought with you. Where is that child, Graciela? If I find her, you will come back."

Her blood spiked setting her cheeks on fire. "You threaten the child in my care?"

Kingsley's eyes narrowed.

He knew now that Reina was here.

She struggled to breathe. Charley stepped into the breach "I dare say a small child is easier to control than an almost grown woman, eh, Kingsley?"

For that, Charley drew another glare.

"I dare say those beatings were easier to effect on a little one."

Kingsley lunged at Charley. Mr. Gibson grabbed him, locking his arms.

"You whoreson rakehell, don't tell me you've dipped your wick in this—"

"*Enough.*" Charley's fist crashed into Kingsley's jaw.

Hell broke loose. She tried to go to his aid, but a strong hand held her back. "Let the boys handle it," Lord Shaldon said.

The three brothers carried him out of the room with loud clomps, much shouting, and terrible oaths. Soon, a door slammed, and the three returned. Lord Bakeley and Mr. Gibson were unfazed. Charley's neck cloth was askew.

He came directly to her, took her hand from his father's, and pulled her into his arms.

His heart pounded against her ear, and where his hand touched her back, she felt only his strength.

"Are you all right, Gracie?"

When she tried to speak her throat clogged with moisture. She had to break free to nod.

Everyone stood watching them, including Lord Shaldon, whose expression she could not read. It was not the kind greeting gaze, nor the thunderous glare, either. There was a glint of assessment, a hint of pleasure, even humor.

"Father, Miss Kingsley and I have agreed to be married."

Lord Shaldon's shoulders dropped with a grand exhale of breath. And he said nothing, only walked to the window, and turned his back to the room.

Charley felt the quiver that ran through Gracie's body. That look that had crossed his father's face, for but a moment, that turning away, he recognized and his own heart pounded.

Father was pleased beyond punch, and by the habit of years, did not wish to show it. Happiness revealed made a man vulnerable.

What kind of life was that?

Gracie gazed up at him, eyes wide and worried. So unsettled and unsure and unsafe her life had been, and not just these last few months.

What had happened to her? Something very bad indeed, bad enough for Captain Kingsley to yank her out of her safe world and convey her here.

His heart opened at the thought. Nothing in life could be totally settled, yet she could be sure of him. She could. Her heart, if he could win it, would be safe, no matter where they traveled, and as for the rest of her—he would give his life to keep her safe, and the child, no matter where their journeys took them.

Father turned back, his face placid again. "I am gratified to hear it, and gratified that you have informed me before the event."

Unlike his brothers. That part remained unsaid, but he saw the look that Bink, who had eloped to Scotland, and Bakeley, whose nuptials had been equally hurried, exchanged. Though in fairness, Father had pretended to die before Bink's marriage, and had proclaimed Lady Sirena an unsuitable match for his heir.

Charley was finally doing something right. Bakeley had always been the paragon, and Bink was the war hero. He was the feckless younger son.

But Father knew of *his* service, he reminded himself, even if it only involved chasing women, and even if it was Kincaid and Farnsworth who guided him. There wasn't much Father didn't know.

"My dear, I know your father," he said. "He is a brave and stalwart man. What are your marriage plans?"

"We haven't got that far." He studied Gracie's face. The blood had drained leaving her a picture of ivory porcelain, and her lips pressed tightly holding in all her doubt. "What would you prefer, Gracie?"

She cast her gaze down and her grip on his arm tightened.

He leaned close to her ear and breathed, "I beg you, do not break my heart."

A distant shriek pierced the silence. Shaldon sent Bink a pleased glance. Though Father had abandoned them all to dash off in the service of England, he'd embraced his first grandchild with enthusiasm.

"That's not Bink's progeny," Charley said. "That is the tiny despot under Gracie's care, appropriately named Reina."

Gracie struggled out of his embrace. "I should go to her. My lord, will you excuse me?"

And then she was gone. She didn't want to speak of the wedding details. She didn't want to marry at all.

Which meant, he would have to put his mind to the right way to convince her. Sensuality had brought a strong response—good, that. Gracie was no cold, thorny rose. In that regard, there were no thorns at all. It was her heart that he'd have to win.

He knew what to do. He'd done it a few times for Crown and country, bastard that he was. This girl's heart, however was a tight bud with steel petals.

A sensual girl who guarded her heart. That sensuality had led her to be well and truly hurt by some bigger bastard than himself.

And...a sensual girl, who'd been hurt, with a small child of questionable parentage? She had denied Reina, too emphatically perhaps. There was an art to lying that required aplomb. Gracie would never have that.

"I should like a word, Charles," Shaldon said, intruding on his thoughts. Bink and Bakeley ushered the two ladies out.

CHAPTER EIGHTEEN

"Sit." Shaldon pointed at the armchair matching his own.

Charley sat.

"Tell me everything."

He did, starting with Gracie's engagement ball at Kingsley House, omitting only the scandalous interlude in the library, which somehow he thought his father must suspect anyway.

Shaldon listened without interruption, his gaze taking a journey to some place Charley could not follow, and for long moments, there was silence.

"What of the Duquesa?"

"A lovely woman. I have a letter safeguarded for you. Shall I just go and get it?"

Father waved a hand. "He'll be asking for funding or arms. No other intelligence?"

He leaned back in his chair. "There was a tale about Mother's painting."

Father's eye twitched. "You've strayed beyond the scope of your mission."

"The lady offered." *Is it true?* He wanted to shout the question, but one must wait out the spymaster.

"And you trust her?"

Trust a woman willing to let the world see her cheat on her husband in order to spy for her father's faction? "Perhaps if you told me more, I could judge better. But I do not think she is the key to any active plot against the English Crown."

Shaldon grunted. "Yet we may not be finished there, for the letters alone." He turned his full gaze on Charley. "But *you* are finished. The tasks were not too onerous, I hope."

"Was it ever for you?"

"I found your mother's feelings always made it so." That steady gaze pinned him. "It was chivalrous of you to agree to this marriage. You do not have to marry her, you know. It's enough that you're threatening the act. Kingsley will be in a frenzy. He always was that sort."

His heart clacked loudly in his ears. His father's interference had driven his brothers into marriages that had turned out to be quite happy.

If they were present, they would parse Shaldon's words looking for the interfering spymaster's twist.

He should also, but he only detected...love. A father's love.

Love. It was a strange word, and yet so common an emotion now in this household, with Bink and Bakeley so happy in their marriages.

He cared for Gracie. Could she ever love him?

He inhaled deeply. "I'm willing to help her, and not for the money. I don't intend to settle into some grand estate here, and Gracie wishes to go home, back to Mexico. I'm willing to escort her there, and then I'd like to find a posting in the Americas somewhere. Her money will be hers. I can live well and good on my present income."

"I see. And what of her, while you are posted?"

"She may go where she is happiest."

"And what of your children?"

His heart picked up its pace. Blast it, but he wanted her. But there must not be children. He must see to it somehow.

"It's not so easy to be separated from a wife you care for."

His father had spied out his damned *feelings*—well, of course he had.

And wait—he'd *cared* for their mother? Mother hadn't been the sentimental sort, nor was Father by any stretch. In fact, because of Shaldon's long absences, there had been rumors about his own paternity. He could count on the fingers of one hand the times he'd seen his parents together. *Whoreson.* Kingsley's use of the word had touched on old wounds.

He barely breathed, waiting for more.

The silence stretched.

Father tapped the chair arm. "Carvelle's smuggling stretched all the way to the Yorkshire coast and was damned clever. His operation leaned to a bit of piracy, theft of military supplies, and anything else that would bring in a shilling. He knew the state of the coastal patrols and the schedule of shipments. He'd happily steal from one army and sell to the other. He had a contact—perhaps more than one—in the government who we could not uncover, try though we might."

Charley sat up. "Lord Kingsley?"

Shaldon gazed into the empty fireplace. "We don't know. The wars of independence have taken their toll on Spanish shipping. Their ships were always a target, but now...piracy is proving to be very lucrative there. We've had men there reporting." His mouth firmed. "There is something else. One of our men in that part of the world has not made contact in a very long time."

"Was he sailing with Captain Kingsley?"

Father's fingers curled around the chair arms. "Perhaps."

I know your father. He is a brave and stalwart man. Not *knew.* Not *was.*

"Captain Llewellyn reported Captain Kingsley's demise off Tortuga," Charley said.

"Yes."

"Lord Kingsley was pockets to let, and now he's helping himself quite freely to Gracie's money." If Kingsley was engaged with Carvelle's smuggling, he should be just as wealthy. Unless both men had experienced a loss. No reputable insurer would guarantee a smuggling cargo.

And just where did Llewellyn fit in?

"Llewellyn is in town," Charley said.

"At Kirkham's Hotel."

Only a few doors away from Mivart's where the Duquesa was staying. Charley stood. "If you will excuse me, Father."

"Take one of your brothers with you." Shaldon struggled to his feet. "Meanwhile, I shall look in on our nursery guest."

Charley spent wasted moments as the dutiful son looking for Bink and Bakeley. One had gone off for a parliamentary meeting—Bink took his position most seriously. Bakeley had slipped away with his wife.

Charley had been sent to pound on their bedchamber door once. It was not something he would do again.

Consequently, a great deal of time had passed by the time he'd armed himself and reached the stables. Too much time. If Gracie had learned he'd been talking to Father, she'd expect a report on their chat. If she sought him and learned he'd gone out to speak to Llewellyn...

He must hurry. It was no betrayal of her. He would question Llewellyn. He would assess the man and his words and decide how to proceed.

In the stable, a groom went off for his horse, and a figure slipped out of the shadows.

His hand gripped the hilt of his knife and then his breath caught on a groan. "You are not coming with me."

"You are not going without me." Gracie's ungloved hands outlined the small waist under her coats. This set of clothing was cleaner, and newer, and fitted better than Roddy's.

"How did you...Never mind." How she'd found out didn't matter. Neither did the *who* of who told her.

"I like your father."

She moved closer, her chest heaving against the tight coats.

He yanked her cap lower over her ears and hailed the groom. "Change of plans," he said. "I'm taking the carriage."

Charley sat opposite her on the ride to the hotel. In truth, they might have walked the distance there and back in the time it had taken to harness the horses, assemble the guards, and make their way through the late afternoon traffic.

"Do not worry," she said. "I have brought my dagger."

"Have you indeed." He let his gaze trail over her person and watched as a pink blush flowed over her.

She pursed her lips tightly. "Do not forget, it was the veil and the weeds that tempted them to attack. They will not think it is me in this clothing. They did not yesterday when we returned from the solicitor's office."

He turned back to the window. The busy street teemed with carriages and riders, and the pavements were filled with walkers. He comforted himself with the knowledge that the hotel was nearby, and that, if his father knew of Llewellyn's lodgings, he probably had men in place there.

"When we arrive, you must let me do the talking," she said.

"Must I?"

A fellow stood on the street, parting the waves of pedestrians who walked around him, watching their carriage. When a woman and her maid approached the man, he smiled.

Charley's breath eased.

"I know Captain Llewellyn."

Heat colored her words. He'd spiked that Spanish temper. Too bad.

"He is an old friend who dined with us many a time. I've known him all my life." Her breath hitched and her eyes had gone shiny. "He reached us in Veracruz before my father, when I was ill with the fever." She took another ragged breath. "Mama...that is, my mother, and Consuela...Reina's m-mother...when I recovered, they were gone."

Hold her. He battled down his heart—letting her succumb to weepy grief would do them no good. "I see. And I'm sorry, but that means nothing now."

Her head shot up, her eyes burning.

"*I* am not trusting you and Reina to this fellow, if that's what you're planning."

She inhaled sharply. "You are not my master."

"No, but I am your fiancé. Or...are you planning to throw me over for Llewellyn?"

Her face contorted in a way that told him she had no romantic interest in the other man.

You jealous fool. Gracie was certain to run if he tried to hold her too close.

"Of course not. He's as old as my father, and he already has a wife. And *our* engagement was, as you know, a ruse, to get Mr. McCollum to talk."

"So our engagement began. It doesn't have to end that way. I care for you, Gracie."

Deep rose flooded her cheeks and she looked away.

She didn't believe he could care for her, or she wouldn't acknowledge the idea.

His spirits rose. He'd seen this reaction in stubborn women he'd courted for the Crown—too proud to capitulate immediately, too smitten to keep away.

Those women had been unmarriageable—he always made sure of that—and he knew how to make the chase a cat and mouse game, exciting for both parties. Except for the once of course, when the game had turned deadly.

And this time, he reminded himself, was no game. He was not playing with Gracie. She was *his*, she just didn't know it.

"You don't wish to share our good news with Captain Llewellyn?" he asked.

"You are good at pretending, Mr. Everly. You know I do not wish to marry. I know you do not wish to marry." Her gaze skittered to him and moved quickly away.

The girl was a terrible liar. "My kisses didn't convince you?"

Her color darkened to a bright crimson seeping under her neck cloth. How far did the color flow? Over her creamy shoulders? Down to her breasts? Further? He wondered what she would look like naked when they progressed that far. And they would.

"I am sure those kisses have convinced many women and will convince many more. I have no illusions about you."

"You're dodging." They would have to hold the conversation about kissing—and the kissing itself—until later. They'd turned the corner onto Brook Street. "In any event, you wish to get your money. I wish to help you do that. I must either keep you alive until you are of age, or marry you."

"Why? Why would you do that for me?"

He reached across the small space gripping her hands. "Why indeed. You're as hot-tempered as that child in the nursery. You're also as lovely, the loveliest girl I've ever met. Plenty of men would see all of that, but I wouldn't trust a one of them to help you find your way home, to let you have the money that's yours, and to keep your child safe."

And you've stolen my heart. The coach shuddered in tandem with the pounding in his chest.

It was time to put a stop to this melodrama. They had a mission. "Now, Gracie, you're playing a servant, and for the time it takes us to reach a private chamber, I expect you to act your role."

She bit her lip and reached for the brim of her cap.

He clamped a hand over hers. "Except that. You'll spill hair everywhere. The cap stays on."

Graciela stood with Charley in the small, dimly lit antechamber where they waited to hear if Captain Llewellyn would admit them. Two chairs had been arranged on either side of a narrow table in the room's corner, but the rest of the room was empty. It was used for temporary storage of guests' baggage, perhaps. Or for visitors seeking privacy, like them.

The close space smelled of leather and damp. She tugged at her cap. "If you would but send up my name—"

"If *you* would but be silent, like a good servant." He swept out a hand. "It's enough that you've come in coats and trousers that leave nothing to the imagination of anyone who sees you."

She gasped. "I am well-covered. And, of course, I pass for a boy."

"You pass for a beautiful, well-shaped woman dressed as a boy."

Tears burned her eyes. She cast her gaze down. Nothing she did pleased him. He'd been angry from the first moment in the stables. And blast it, she was the one who should be angry. This was her life going up in flames. Papa missing. Papa's money out of her control.

"No tears," he said softly. He picked a spot of lint off his coat and turned away.

She bit her lip to stop it from quivering.

"I spotted no fewer than three of my father's men in the parlor." His voice, suddenly warm, flowed over her. "Have no fear, we shall meet with this paragon of virtue, and I would rather your presence surprise him. His reaction interests me."

"He will be happy to see me."

"Yes, but why? Do you know for a fact he's not acquainted with Lord Kingsley?"

Steps in the hallway rattled her further. She tugged her cap tighter and stood straighter, preparing to traverse the entry again and climb the stairs behind Charley like a docile retainer. Llewellyn had a sitting room where he could receive them privately, the manager had said.

Instead, when the door opened the tall figure that entered was Llewellyn himself.

CHAPTER NINETEEN

Her heart beat crazily against the layers of coats. The sun that had weathered his skin to tanned leather had turned his hair a dark bronze. Had it always been so? She had not seen him in two years, years during which she had grown to a woman. He was old, but not so old she saw now, and the thought made her shiver. He was not as old as some of the men who'd come calling on her and her money.

Older than Charley, older and harder as a sea captain must be. Virile, too, as a man must be when leading a crew of sea dogs.

The skin on her back crawled, as if Lord Kingsley's switch had trailed across it, teasing her, and memories swarmed: looking up from a pallet into Llewellyn's face...Consuela and Mama writhing with fever...Francisca and Juan hurrying a crying Reina away to safety.

She'd heard him talking to someone about taking her aboard his ship but then she'd passed out. And when she woke, Papa was there and Captain Llewellyn was gone.

And Mama and Consuela were gone.

"What is this about?" Captain Llewellyn's voice shook her into the present, his tone as harsh as Lord Kingsley's had been when addressing his troublesome ward.

"I am here on behalf of the Earl of Shaldon," Charley said in his amiable way. "He wishes news of Captain Kingsley and his ship."

"Kingsley? What is there to tell? Captain Kingsley is dead and the ship is lost. The report is in. Tell your master, I have nothing more to add." He turned for the door.

His rude answer crashed on her like a great wave, taking her breath away. This was not the man who'd talked and laughed with her parents at table. Not the man who'd tenderly asked after her welfare.

She moved closer behind Charley and felt the tension rippling off him, stirring the air around her. His arm moved and she heard the whisk of his fingers brushing his coat.

"I say, then, I shall tell my *father*, Lord Shaldon, and his friends at the Foreign Office that you do not wish to add anything to that worthless, sketchy bit of drivel you called a report."

Captain Llewellyn jerked around, eyes glaring.

"Perhaps it will be better to compel your more *thorough* testimony in a more *formal* setting."

The Captain's whole body tensed. If he'd had a cutlass strapped on, it would have been drawn. "*You*. I know of you. You're Shaldon's young pup, the one dashing about with your ramrod in every piece of female—"

"Stop it." Graciela stepped up next to Charley, gripping his arm.

The other man's eyes narrowed on her and then widened.

"*What the devil*." He took a step toward Charley.

She put her hand up as a barrier.

"What has he done to you?"

"So, you recognize me, Captain Llewellyn? You will cease to insult Mr. Everly. He has saved my life, is what he's done. And I want to know what happened to my father."

Captain Llewellyn stepped closer, and she watched his face. The eyes still glowed with a heat that signaled danger, but he pressed his lips and swept his gaze over her clothing. He did not stop at her breasts as Charley had done, but she saw the effort he made to avoid it.

"You should not be dressed like this." He glared at Charley. "Let me get a cloak. I will take you home."

"My disguise was Lord Shaldon's idea. He is my guardian. And I have no home."

"Your home is with us, for as long as you wish," Charley said.

Captain Llewellyn opened his mouth as if to argue and closed it.

"Are you friends with Lord Kingsley, Captain? He tried to *sell* me to a dishonorable man. And when I objected, he tried to flog me into submission, as you would flog one of your seamen." *And if you are on friendly terms with him, you are no friend to me.*

She bit her lip. She must find out first what happened to her father.

"Let me help you, Grace." The Captain made his tone sound tender but she could feel his falseness. "I can arrange rooms for you, a chaperone—"

"Perhaps call in your wife from the country?" Charley interrupted.

Captain Llewellyn heaved a sigh. "Alas. My wife died this past year."

She swallowed hard. So, Charley was right. The Captain might be seeking a wife. "My condolences, sir."

"Thank you. We are both bereaved, you see, Grace."

"Will you tell me what happened to my father?"

He looked around the small, spare chamber. "There truly is not much more to tell than what was in the report."

Which she had not read. Charley apparently had, since he'd mentioned it.

"There was a pirate ship pacing us and heavy seas. A storm came up so viciously we could not maintain our formation. He was boarded and the mast came down, and I saw your father's ship roll."

"You did not fight? You did not take on survivors?"

"Yes, a few. They reported they saw the Captain struck down, fatally, I'm sorry to tell you. We did return to the area and found no one."

"And the pirates?" Charley asked.

"Disappeared also. We'd spotted holes in their keel. That was in my report." He sent Charley a glare and reached for her hand.

His was cold, clammy, the pressure firm. He tugged at her, ever so gently, and panic rose in her. She clutched Charley's arm and pulled her hand free.

"Indeed." Charley's voice was cold. "We should like to know the before and after. In detail. Shall we visit your private parlor?"

The Captain blinked. "No."

"No?"

"No. That is, not at present, Grace. It would not be proper to entertain you in my private chambers, and this man is not a suitable chaperon."

His voice was kind, as it had been when she was ill, but he had fallen back on society's insufferable rules. She didn't want rules—she wanted the truth.

"I have a widowed sister living just outside London. Allow me to arrange rooms for you and send for her. We'll obtain a proper gown for you and have a maid stay with you until she arrives."

"Lord Kingsley—"

"I shall speak with him." His face had become stern again. "I shall smooth over this disagreement you are having with your guardian. You will not have to marry Carvelle."

The air around her crackled and she glanced up at Charley. She could read no emotion there. She prayed he would not announce their own engagement, else the Captain might go retrieve that cutlass from his chamber upstairs.

"Miss Kingsley will not be forced into *any* marriage," Charley said.

"Of course not." Llewellyn took her hand again. "Come along then, Grace."

She tugged her hand, but this time he continued to grip it.

Fear rose in her. Panic. She choked in air and tugged harder.

Charley moved in front of her. "Miss Kingsley, what are your wishes? Will you return with me to Shaldon House, or stay here with the Captain?"

Captain Llewellyn's mouth firmed. She had no doubt he was capable of killing Charley at that very moment. She could not allow that.

The thought calmed her. "My hand, Captain," she said, and tugged it out of his grip.

She took a step back and dragged Charley with her. The two men faced off like bantam cocks each ready to strike. The captain had struck down many a man in his time. In the course of his duties, had Charley killed? It didn't seem likely.

Captain Llewellyn stood blocking the room's only door. Her vision fogged. Whatever she would find with Llewellyn, it would not truly be protection, nor would she be allowed to pursue her own will. She would be returned to Kingsley, or if not, imprisoned in a set of rooms here, without Reina. He had not thought to mention the child.

He would smooth things over with Kingsley and then drag her off to an altar himself.

She put her hand to her chest, teetered against Charley and inhaled sharply. "Please. I must get out of this room. Immediately."

Charley's heart clenched and he wrapped an arm around Gracie. "Move out of the way, Llewellyn." She was about to fake another faint.

"Grace, you cannot think to go with this man. He is a rakehell, a despoiler of young women. Your reputation—what would your father have said?"

She choked for air, her face going pale. Real concern shot through Charley. He slid an arm under her knees and picked her up. "Out of the way. Now."

Llewellyn gave way, glaring. The door opened and Charley marched past two curious gentlemen.

He nodded to them. "My father shall summon you," he said over his shoulder. "And I shall keep the lady safe." He heard Llewellyn behind him, cursing.

At the front door, Gracie wriggled. "Put me down."

"No."

She gripped the door frame. "I'm your male servant. Put me down."

She was right of course. He settled her to her feet and straightened her coats. The lobby clerk was diverted dealing with Llewellyn. Charley's neck rippled with a sense of danger. Llewellyn had not wanted them in his room for a reason. They had interrupted a visitor.

"Hurry, then."

But as they reached the bottom step of the stairs he froze, and Gracie collided into him with an *oof*.

A woman had stopped in front of the carriage, eyes wide. He bowed. She dipped her chin. The dark-clad maid trailing her took a few steps back. Gracie moved up next to him and the lady's eyes narrowed. Her lips trembled, but she quickly firmed them.

"Mr. Everly." Again, the slight dip of the head.

"Duquesa. As lovely as ever." It was true. Her blue gown and the hat that covered her fair hair matched her eyes perfectly. Her gaze traveled to the hotel behind them and returned to the servant next to him. The Duquesa would recognize the woman in a man's coat. A rival—

though theirs had never been that sort of arrangement.

And never mind how hard his heart pounded—he was having none of that nonsense. His pretended interlude with her was over. Father could find someone else to run messages.

"We have not seen you at any of the fêtes, Mr. Everly. Surely you will be at tomorrow night's diplomatic ball. I would be bold and claim a dance with you."

"It would be my great pleasure." He bowed again. He heard voices behind them, and spotted two men approaching. He recognized them as the Duquesa's men, paid to follow discreetly.

It was what lay behind in the hotel that worried him, and they needed to leave. "My father has returned from Bath, and I must hasten to meet with him. If you will excuse me, I shall wish you a good day. It has been a pleasure to see you again."

He skirted around her, climbed into the carriage and yanked Gracie in behind him, settling her onto the seat across from him. "Were you planning another timely swoon?"

She glared back and pleasure sparked through him. She was jealous.

"Not an entirely false one. I cannot abide small spaces."

"How ever did you survive the sea journey?"

"I had Reina to care for. And whenever I could, I went up on deck for the fresh air. So, it is true, Charley."

"What is true?"

"That was one of your women, no less than the famous Duquesa. You *are* a rakehell. A despoiler of women."

"What if it were true, Gracie? Would you throw me over for another man? It appears Captain Llewellyn is eligible now."

She looked out the window, clearly examining the idea.

He steeled himself and went on. "He is handsome, virile, your father's friend. And money is not an issue, since you will bring plenty to any greedy husband's coffers. And I do believe he wants you, as would any man with eyes in his head."

She turned to face him, her eyes shining. "He did not ask about Reina. He had dinner with Papa the night we departed. He knew she was aboard."

Charley eased out a breath. Whoever's child Reina had been, she was Gracie's now. Only a man ignorant of Reina's existence, or a fool, would forget to include her in his wooing. "Perhaps he thought you had delivered her to her grandparents."

"He had to have known we'd had no response to our letters, else we would have diverted to the Peninsula. He had to have known she accompanied us to London. I'm sure Papa would have told him."

"Perhaps he thought you found a place...a home... for her here."

He spoke softly, watching for her reaction.

"I will *never* abandon her, Charley." She clenched her fists. "It is not her fault that she...exists."

He stayed very still. Perhaps now she would tell him the truth of that little girl.

"And you have very nimbly changed the subject. That woman, is she your mistress?"

"I don't have a mistress, Gracie."

"Your occasional lover then? Or something else? Another spy?"

She was hurdling too close to the truth. "You are the only woman in my life now, Gracie."

Her laugh was scoffing. She shook her head. "Why, Charley?"

"Because we are going to be married, and I would never be unfaithful to a wife."

"*Ay, Dios*. She is beautiful, and probably powerful and rich. And likely has state secrets to share. If she snaps her fingers you will not turn away. You are too single minded. About this marriage scheme, about your duty to England, about your family. Single minded here, single minded there. I do not know which Charley you truly are." She sighed. "But I do know the true Charley must feel trapped by my impetuous act this morning. The true Charley does not wish to marry, and if you do, it is not in the nature of any of your selves to be a faithful husband."

A week ago, he would have agreed with her. But now, the sharp words cut.

He opened his mouth and she waved a hand at him. "No. You don't want to marry. You won't like it, not even to please your family. Your father—he was surprised, but pleased, I think. What did he say to you after I left the room?"

"You wound me, Gracie. You are far too cynical."

She colored deeply under her frown. "What did your father say? Tell me."

"Very well. He has sunk his teeth into this marriage scheme, yet he will not force either of us."

He held her gaze until she turned away.

"At least he encouraged me to go out. He did not try to confine me in your elegant prison."

Anger bristled through him. Gracie was no trained operative. "He ought not have. He hasn't seen what that man did to you. He hasn't seen your back."

"Neither have you."

"Mrs. Windle's testimony is enough for me. That bruise on your cheek is enough for me."

She leaned back against the squab. "It is healing well, I think. Still sore, but better. Her ointment is very effective. Were those men at the hotel door yours?"

"Yes."

"What will they do with the Captain?"

Would that they'd keelhaul him into the Thames. "They'll watch him and his visitors."

"Do you suppose he had a visitor above stairs? Do you suppose that's why he would not allow us into his rooms?" She reached for his hand and his heart lurched. "Would Kingsley have been there? Or Carvelle?"

At her mere touch, desire roared through him. "We shall learn very soon." He swept a thumb over her cool, ungloved palm, then stripped off his own glove. "Come here."

She blinked and pursed her mouth, but she did not cross to his seat. He moved his thumb to her lips. Soft, they were, and moist, like she'd just been kissed.

Her breath hitched warming his finger.

"You must know," he said, containing his heart, controlling his voice, speaking matter-of-factly, "These moments of rescue stir my blood. I very much wish to kiss you."

She sent him a stern frown. "You wish to kiss your male servant in a carriage?"

A laugh gurgled up and forced its way out. Of course, she was right. He threw back his head and succumbed to the laughter, and when she smiled and joined in, the urge to pull her onto his lap almost overwhelmed him.

Her smile faded and she gripped his hand. "The Captain must be on close enough terms with Kingsley if he feels confident he can talk him around to his will, and he knew about the engagement to Carvelle. Perhaps you are right about him after all, Charley. How would he know about that horrid betrothal?"

"He could have heard the rumor. Your betrothal ball was the talk of the town."

"True," she said, thoughtfully. "Why did you not share his report about my father's death with me?"

"I haven't seen it."

"You were lying about it?" She grimaced. "Of course you were."

"I didn't much care for his quick dismissal of us. I didn't much care for his story either. Your knowledge of seamanship is surely superior to mine. What did you think of the tale?"

She frowned again. "Papa always said, the pirate captains would calculate their risks. They are facing the forces of nature just like their prey. Papa's preparations for this voyage included extra guns, and many of his men were former marines from the wars. He always tried to pass from afar as a naval ship, and this time especially. I do not believe a pirate would attack them in a storm."

"Not even out of desperation?"

"Perhaps." She shrugged. "And perhaps Captain Llewellyn could have created a better lie." Her gaze turned grim. "You are an expert liar, Charley. What do *you* think of his story?"

He winced at the harsh words, but had to admit they were true. "I think we must get him and the men who claimed to witness your father's death in for a detailed statement, and then pick them apart."

"I should like that. If I found he has lied...I shall be very tempted to make use of my dagger again."

"Leave it to me." He dropped her hands and leaned back. "Let us have our own moment of truth-telling, Miss Kingsley. I am not lying when I say I *do* wish to marry you. I *am* capable of loyalty. I also wish to kiss you, and more. Much more. And I will never force you. Never. We will dispense with fixing a wedding date until you're ready, or until you decide you will throw me over."

The carriage slowed as they approached Shaldon House.

"And until you've decided whatever it is you will decide, there must be no more private meetings for us in the library—my brains were addled last night."

She pulled a face at him and he laughed.

"And you must do me one more favor."

"Cease wearing men's clothing?"

"No."

"Hide in my room or the nursery for all time?"

"No."

"Then what?"

He swallowed a grin. "Allow me to train you in the proper use of that dagger, as well as pistols and other methods. Your next assailant might not conveniently walk into the blade, and if our engagement extends until you reach your majority, I have no doubt you'll have need of those skills, if not for yourself then for Reina's protection."

The light that had sparked in her eyes went out. "Lord Kingsley did threaten her," she said, breathless. Her eyes shone with tears.

It was quite the opposite of the reaction he was trying to engender. Yet...perhaps a good round of tears was needed to clear out the fog. She had been through so much.

But her mouth firmed and small fists clenched, and when she lifted her eyes they were blazing.

How could he be expected to keep his hands off her for another three minutes, much less three years?

"Papa already trained me, but I am willing to learn more. And, Charley, I should like to see the Captain's report as soon as you can arrange it."

He saluted, eliciting a grimace.

"And I should like to be present when he is interviewed."

Upon their return, Lady Sirena swept Graciela away to meet with the modiste who had returned with more gowns, and in the flurry of measuring, and marking, and verdicts about colors, she had trouble keeping to her thoughts and her planning.

The modiste herself was a great distraction. French, and darker than her own half-Spanish self, the beautiful Madame chattered as much as Lady Sirena. Except that where Lady Sirena's chatter filled the atmosphere with comfort, Madame's built great confidence.

"*Eh bien.*" She wrote down a measurement. She had come without an assistant. "*Que linda.* You will shine, Miss Kingsley in the gown I am making you. And here," she smoothed her hands along her side, "shall be a pocket or two. It shall not harm the lines. You will leave it to me."

"A pocket? For what?"

Madame's gaze was intense and intelligent. "Perhaps a small dagger or the tiniest of pistols. It is sometimes prudent."

"Even at a ball, a lady does not always have a gentleman at hand to protect her," Lady Sirena said, nibbling on a meat pie from the tray that had been laid out for the ladies.

It had been only chance that Charley was at hand at her betrothal ball. How lucky she had been to fall into that particular man's arms. She felt her face grow warm. "I see. I thank you, though I do not expect to attend many balls in the future. I am, after all, a scandal."

Lady Sirena exchanged a look with Madame and almost stayed silent. Almost.

"Well, you may change your mind, might you not? Always good to be prepared. And Miss Kingsley's dress will be finished by tomorrow afternoon, Madame?"

"Most certainly, my lady. My girls are already at work on it."

She opened her mouth to say that there was no rush, but Madame vanished as quickly and quietly as she had arrived.

Charley delivered the Duquesa's letter to his father's study, and found him conferring with Kincaid.

Shaldon turned the letter over and handed it to Kincaid. "What did you learn, my son?"

"He's recently widowed. Tried to snatch Gracie right out of the room, and would have done so had she seen him alone. He was as vague as hell about Captain Kingsley's disappearance. Claimed they rescued some crew members who witnessed his death. Have you seen the report?"

"We've sent a man for it," Kincaid said.

"We'll need to bring him in for questioning," Charley said, "along with the rest of the crew. And there's another thing—he kept us waiting in the baggage room."

"He had a woman upstairs," Kincaid said. "Came and went veiled."

"We stumbled across the Duquesa on the street."

"The Duquesa and Captain Llewellyn." Kincaid broke the seal on the letter. "Now there's an intriguing thought."

"He might well have been auditioning a new mistress." Shaldon tapped the desk with his forefinger, staring into the cold fireplace. "Did the Duquesa speak with you?"

"There's a diplomatic ball tomorrow night, which I do not plan to attend. She asked for a dance."

"Perhaps we ought to show up and announce your engagement."

"I'm afraid it might be hard to persuade my future bride. What does the letter say?"

Kincaid skimmed the swirling script. "He asks your father's influence with the new king on behalf of the Spanish people to keep them out of the hands of the French. He fears the influence on your king of the *Afrancesados* attending the coronation, particularly one." He glanced up. "Do you suppose the Duquesa wrote this herself in her father's name? She does hate her husband."

Shaldon grunted. "No request for money or arms?"

"Not yet. I would hate to give up this channel. Might we convince you Charley to—"

"No." He shook his head and stood, pacing the length of the small room. They could put whoever they wanted to it, it would not be him.

The woman in Llewellyn's chamber nagged at him. In all his many meetings with the Duquesa, they'd never frequented a hotel, and for her to meet with an insignificant sea captain didn't seem likely.

If Llewellyn's guest was a lady bird, Charley had contacts on St. James Street who might know, or who might even have arranged the appointment.

And if he and Gracie were to announce their engagement, he must pay a visit to Bond Street.

He excused himself and headed downstairs.

Perry stood in the hall taking a note from the footman's salver. She sent the man off and glanced at the wafer seal, frowning.

"Bad news?" Charley asked.

She handed him the note. "It's for you."

He turned it over, snapped the seal and scanned the writing, and made himself laugh at her glare. "It's the rogue's life, sister. I shall be off."

After the modiste left, Graciela checked on Reina, who was napping, and sought out Charley. Instead, she found Lady Perry and Lady Sirena in the morning room going over household matters.

Charley had gone out, they said, and then both shared a glance.

The hair on her neck rose. "What? You must tell me."

Lady Perry frowned. "Do you truly care for him?"

"I..." *I love him.* She couldn't say that. She couldn't allow herself to feel that. "Our engagement was a ruse, to get the banker to talk."

"Yes, but do you truly care for him?"

"*Ach*, Perry, why are you pressing her? Are you concerned about Charley's heart?"

"I'm concerned about hers, and yes, well, his also. I know my brother, Graciela, and I do think he's smitten, however..." She took a breath. "He received a note a little while ago and went out."

"A note?"

She nodded. "I passed it to him. And I recognized the handwriting and paper. And the perfume. It was from the Duquesa."

CHAPTER TWENTY

Graciela swallowed a watery lump that had sprung all at once into being. "I see. We ran into her on the street. She greeted him most familiarly."

Lady Perry's face darkened. "I shall thrash him myself."

"And I shall help you." Lady Sirena patted a chair. "Come, I'll call for some tea. Or better, some sherry."

"No." She shook her head. Had she not herself stressed to him in the carriage that she had no intentions of marrying him? "It is as it is. And as I said, our engagement is a ruse."

Those kisses, a ruse. His strong hands, available to any willing woman. The passion he stirred, a weapon. Why?

Because he can. Because it was what men like him did.

And perhaps, it was freeing. If she did in fact have to marry him as the only means to collect her inheritance, she could hold him to his promise to let her keep her money and go her own way.

Rigo had wanted to own her. There was nothing of ownership in Charley Everly. He wanted freedom as much as she. And he made her *feel* again, even if there was no heart in it, even if it was just the carnal stirring of a dumb beast.

But if she chose that path, a marriage for money, there would never be a chance at a true marriage, like her parents'. Charley said she was cynical, but she wasn't, not entirely. Love must be possible, perhaps even for someone as damaged as herself. Had not Lady Sirena found it with Lord Bakeley? One could but look at them together and see their happiness.

An arm came around her. "Perhaps you should not have told her, Perry," Lady Sirena said.

Lady Perry's face was grim. "She should know everything."

Here was a true and honest ally.

"And you could have softened the blow a bit. In fact, we do not know he is off bedding her, do we now? Graciela, we do not even know he's gone to see her. He may have gone to the tailor, or off to the jeweler to buy you a bauble, or to the shops for some new toys. Let's not jump into this donnybrook quite yet."

"It is quite all right, as I said. I am aware of his reputation. I have no aspiration to marry him. I merely wish to get control of my funds and go home. He is a means to an end, and we have that understanding between us." She forced a smile. "I shall leave it to some other woman to tame him."

Lady Perry frowned. "You are using him."

"Yes, I am sorry. I was...desperate." Perhaps thoughtless. "I don't wish to hurt anyone. I...I should leave." She must leave, and soon, or this great house would become another cage for her.

The two pairs of eyes watched her, and their feelings had shifted. They were seeing her anew, and not liking what they saw.

"You don't know what it's like to be a woman alone, Perry," Lady Sirena said.

Lady Perry sighed. "We have our squabbles, Charley and I, but he is always kind in his own way. I wish you could care for him, Graciela. And I do think he cares for you."

"Like many men, he cares for many women." It had not been true of her Papa, but there it was. Living amongst men who went to sea, she knew this truth.

Lady Perry shook her head. "I believe the Duquesa was just an assignment."

"An assignment?" More of Charley's gossip gathering? Was that what he had meant?

Yet the woman was so beautiful. No man would resist that golden beauty.

"I shouldn't talk of it. I don't truly know anything, I only suspect. He visited quite often with Farnsworth before he left town."

"Lord Farnsworth? My guardian?"

"Yes. He is Charley's godfather, and Father's great friend. And of course, a spymaster also."

Her head began to ache. "Their war is long over."

"There is always a war somewhere, or a threat of one. And with the coronation next month, well, the powers have gathered. It's a perfect time to collect information. London is swarming with spies." Lady Perry's voice was wistful. "And good heavens, the Spanish colonies have all proclaimed their freedom. Is not your father there helping out with the cause?"

Her father's last instructions had been puzzling. In dire straits, she should go to Lord Shaldon, he trusted the spy lord with her safety. But only if Papa should die, should she hand on the information he'd left with her, and what did that mean? Did he not entirely trust Lord Shaldon?

She wasn't at all convinced of Papa's death. And he had been quite cagey about this voyage. He'd talked only vaguely about his cargo and more certainly about the danger of his daughter and tiny ward sailing with him. With the demise of Spanish power, a pirate war had arisen in the West Indies. He had deposited her and Reina, and the servants at Lord Kingsley's estate, and gone back to London to arrange his business affairs. And she knew he had not shared the details of those with even Lord Kingsley. Had he shared them with Lord Shaldon?

Her nerves prickled. What had Shaldon said earlier? Her father had served England. He *is* a good man.

"I should like to have a word with your father. Is he here?"

"In the study, I think." Lady Sirena said.

"Come along," Lady Perry said, "I'll take you there."

As it turned out, Lord Shaldon had gone out also.

Lady Perry gripped the door handle and rattled it. "I haven't yet been able to pick this lock."

"I haven't mastered that skill, either," Graciela said.

Lady Perry laughed. "Perhaps we'll study it together some day."

With neither father nor son around, Graciela wandered up to the nursery. Francisca was nowhere around, and the nursemaid was happy for the chance to run downstairs for a cup of tea. She spent the rest of the afternoon with Reina, reading to her, cuddling her, playing with her, like they used to do before they'd settled into Lord Kingsley's cold and formal world.

"There you are." Francisca entered the nursery room and settled a dinner tray onto a table. "I must speak with you, Graciela."

Unease threaded through her. "Yes of course." She kissed Reina, turned her over to the nursery maid, and let Francisca pull her into the corridor.

"After the modiste left, no one knew where you were," Francisca said.

"I was with the ladies, and then I was here."

"My heart almost stopped. I asked the housekeeper, and the maids. The footmen, too. This house is so big. You must be careful."

She touched the maid's arm. "What has happened?"

"The footmen were whispering. They thought I didn't understand, but there are strangers lurking around the mews and the square." She took Graciela's hand. "You must be careful. I have spoken to Juan."

She peeked in the door at the child, who was happily gobbling her meal with the cheerful girl's help. Reina was having fewer tantrums and seemed happier here, yet she would have to disrupt her again.

"We must leave here, and soon."

Francisca shook her head. "And go where? I am afraid for you, Graciela. I am afraid for the little one. You must take great care."

The dinner bell gonged. Francisca hugged her. "There will be guests tonight, they said. Go, and I will be along in a moment to help you dress."

A fussy whine came from the nursery.

"No. You stay with Reina. I'll get one of the maids to help me."

When she walked through her bedchamber, door, she found Charley waiting there.

The infernally long wait for Gracie to come dress for dinner had given Charley time to peruse her room. To search it actually.

He loosened his neck cloth against the heat from the coals glowing in the grate, and looked around. Her jewelry was spare, family pieces no doubt, and she had enough money for a few nights on the road, though he doubted she would know that.

The slim volume of Shakespeare's sonnets was interesting. Well-thumbed, it sat beside her bed next to the dagger. The title page of the book made clear it was a gift from Captain Kingsley to his wife. Messages sprinkled the pages, in a lovers' code.

It vaguely depressed him.

Their engagement might be a ruse, but he had found an engagement gift for one lady, and had spied out something else for the smaller one.

It was the only spying that had gone well. If Llewellyn had been entertaining a member of the demimonde in his chambers, no one in that circle was talking about it.

He slipped the dagger from its sheath and examined it. An irregular design had been etched through the hilt and the blade.

He heard a rustle in the hall, and quickly set the blade back.

Graciela spotted him immediately and left the door to the corridor open. He sent the maid who'd followed her away, closed the door, and lounged against it, crossing his arms.

She crossed *her* arms, eyes flashing. "You should not be here."

"Yet here I am. No one will mind."

"I mind."

"Yes, well, Sirena greeted me upon my return home tonight. I did *not* spend the afternoon with the Duquesa."

She turned away. "You do not need a whole afternoon for the things you do with her."

His heart soared. She was jealous. "Except for that brief interlude on the street, I didn't see her today."

"It is not my affair."

"And it is not my affair either. She is not my lover. Will you not believe me, you stubborn woman?"

She turned, her hands on her hips. "Stubborn woman? We are a fraud, Charley. I want to take my child and my servants and leave. I don't have to go with Captain Llewellyn, I can find another ship. I can look for my father. I can go and see what truly happened to him." She clenched her fists and bit her lip. "Your father must get my money for me."

"Gracie—"

"I will not let anyone cage me."

Her chest rose and fell with each choking breath, and he began to sweat under his dinner coats.

A bell sounded below, reverberating through the house.

"I will leave you to dress," he said. "And we will talk more later. I'll send your maid."

"Tell her to go. I don't care to join—"

"I have news about Llewellyn's visitor today." He opened the door and beckoned the maid. "Which I will share—later."

"Tell me now, Charley."

"Later." He bowed. "I shall see you downstairs."

He pulled the door closed and went to find Perry to kill her.

For her first formal dinner at Shaldon House, Graciela found herself seated at Lord Shaldon's right hand and across from Lady Jane Monthorpe, Sirena's kind, older friend who had arrived from Bath while Graciela was busy with Reina. She was also to be a house guest, a permanent one from the way Sirena spoke.

Mrs. Gibson had returned to London also and joined them, along with Thomas, their friend Lord Hackwell's charming young brother, whose presence truly made the evening a family affair.

They'd all greeted her warmly, with many congratulations for her and Charley, sending her head spinning. Charley's smile had been fixed and determined—and false as could be. That she knew. He was angry with her, and she didn't care.

She needed to take charge of her own life.

During such a dinner, even she knew not to question Charley about the Captain's visitor, or push Lord Shaldon for the release of her money. A rude girl she might be, but she knew better than that.

And her intended had arranged to be seated at the far end of the table, so he could not even whisper what he'd discovered that afternoon.

She thrust her fork into a piece of meat, nodded politely at something Lord Shaldon said, and waited for the interminable meal to end.

"What did you learn?"

Charley drew in a long breath of fragrant tobacco and crushed the cigarillo under his heel before turning.

The shivering girl had naught but a thin shawl wrapping her shoulders. He took off his coat as he drew her under a garden lamp.

"There is no need for your coat. We may go back inside."

"And argue in front of family and guests?"

He settled his coat around her, glancing around. The deserted garden was quiet. If there were grooms and footmen out here, they'd all gone to ground.

"All right." He leaned on the stone rail. "Llewellyn's visitor today was a woman, wearing veils."

"Who?"

"We don't know."

"The Duquesa. She was outside when we left."

"That's a possibility. But I don't think so."

Her eyes narrowed. "Because you know her so well."

He paused and studied her. He couldn't yet trust her with the truth. He couldn't trust her not to speak her mind if provoked. "Father has a man on her." Or with her. He suspected one of the

Duquesa's men was also Father's. "Also, I can't see the mutual benefit there. Kincaid thought it might be a...er...mistress."

She huffed. "So quickly? He has only just arrived in town. She was likely a mere prostitute."

He turned away and hid a smile. Gracie had not had a sheltered childhood.

"Yes well, I made inquiries this afternoon and couldn't find anyone who knew something about that."

Her mouth dropped and she huffed again, and then laughed. "Well at least you are honest about visiting brothels."

"I did not visit brothels."

She raised an eyebrow. "No?"

"No. I have sources among...among the people who run that, er, trade."

"I see. And how will we find who this woman was?"

"For now, we are having him followed." As well as the Duquesa, but the less he mentioned her, the better.

"Could it have been a man sent in dressed as a woman, as Roddy was?"

He shook his head. "Anything is possible, but I doubt it. Ours was a ruse to see what kind of trap was laid. In this case, the woman was merely hiding her identity."

"Perhaps." She gripped the coat more tightly around her and sniffed at the lapel absentmindedly.

He bit back a smile. "I did visit a shop today." He rummaged in the pocket near her hip. "Here, my lady."

The lapel flopped back as she took the box and opened it. Her breath caught.

"It is an engagement gift." A damn fine one that he'd spent too much time deciding upon.

She bit her lip and shook her head. "It is a lovely necklace, Charley, but I cannot possibly accept it." The case snapped and she thrust it at him.

Well, and he'd expected this reaction, hadn't he?

Dredging up a dramatic sigh, he took the box. "If this is a ruse, it's one that must be played out. And even if you won't accept that I can love you, desire you, and honor you, you may still show the world that I know enough to buy my fiancée an engagement gift."

She pulled off the jacket. "You are pressuring me."

"I am not." He pocketed the box for a later attempt. "A sensible woman would take a gift of jewelry."

"When I may access my funds, I will buy my own jewelry."

"Of course you may. But your jewels won't come with a promise of love."

"There will be a promise of freedom," she snapped. "And we are finished talking."

In the mews, a horse whinnied, and another answered.

"You are a stubborn, stubborn girl." He shrugged into his jacket. "Inconstant. Fickle."

She stepped back and yanked her shawl tighter, then turned on her heel and marched toward the house.

"And a terrible actress," he called after her.

The door slammed, and he turned back to gaze into the night. A man trundled down the walk with a lantern, and he recognized one of the under butlers.

"Tell Lloyd, best set a good watch tonight," Charley called. With Gracie in a sulk, and Llewellyn aware of her presence here, there might be trouble.

The man saluted and headed for the kitchen entrance.

He pulled his flask from another pocket and tipped it back, the liquor burning a path down his gullet.

Swiving women for the Crown had brought him to this—the one woman he wanted didn't want him. And he was done being used.

But if it was Gracie wanting to use him—well, he'd be atoning for every time he'd led a woman down the garden path. He'd made a promise to her and he damn well would keep it. She was stuck with him, and he would protect her from Kingsley, and Carvelle, and Llewellyn, and—damn it—from herself, no matter the cost.

Tomorrow, he would visit Bond Street and purchase his other gift. Perhaps it would be better received by the queen of the nursery.

In the wee hours of the morning, Graciela heard a child's cry. She rushed from her bed, throwing on slippers and a robe, and ran up the stairs to the nursery. By this time, the crying had stopped.

She found Francisca standing over the small bed, fully dressed. Reina slept, thumb in mouth, curled in upon herself.

Francisca pulled Graciela into the nursery playroom, mouth pressed into a thin line. "She had a bad dream."

A maid hovered in the corner. Juan's pallet was gone.

"Where is Juan?"

"He has gone to the stables to keep watch and to listen."

Her nerves prickled. "Listen for what?"

"I told you. There are strange people snooping about."

An ache started up in her head and she rubbed at it. "We must leave."

"And go where?" Francisca laid a thin hand on her arm. "You have seen Llewellyn?"

They had not had a moment alone to discuss her visit with the Captain. "Yes."

"And?"

She shook her head and sought the right words. She could not lie to Francisca, who knew her so well, but she also did not want her to fear.

"He is in league with Lord Kingsley, then?"

Francisca had always been shrewd.

"Juan said your father always was careful of him," Francisca said.

"He was Papa's friend. Mama's too."

"No. Not a friend. A man he did business with, and a rival also. He had designs on your mother, many years ago, and then when he saw you growing into a beautiful woman..." She shook her head. "You are in grave danger, Graciela. I fear you must marry this lord's son."

"Charley Everly? You hate him."

The maid shrugged. "I do not come to this lightly. I think of the greater good. He and his family are strong. They have treated us well, even down to the servants. The lord himself came up to the nursery and visited with Reina."

"We will be stuck here. You and Juan will never see home again."

"Our home is with you."

Her heart twisted inside her.

"He...he does not love me. And...we have had a great argument."

"Pah." She waved that away. "Even if you did not lie to yourself about this, marriage is not about love. You bring money, and he brings protection. I have looked at it from all angles. No matter that you stabbed that pig with the foul mouth, you cannot stab every man sent by Lord Kingsley. You must remove yourself from his power."

"And put myself in another man's power?"

"Yes. That is the way of the world."

The way of the world was unfair. "I fear he has another woman."

Francisca's face darkened in the lamplight. "It is the way of some men. You must make up your mind to take him to the altar." She huffed out a great sigh. "Do not pretend he does not excite you, Graciela. Go and do what you must. Marry him quickly. Marry him soon, and make him forget his lover."

Francisca nudged her out the door of the nursery suite and closed it behind her. Graciela nodded to the footman guarding the nursery, and found her way to a quiet corridor.

She leaned against the wall trying to breathe. Francisca did not understand. Francisca did not know the truth.

She pressed her fists to her eyes, trying to push down the panic. Charley was wrong about her. She was an excellent actress, shoving the past down so deep, she'd fooled Papa, and Juan, and even Francisca.

She needed to think.

Groping her way down the dimly lit corridor and stairs, she waved away the night porter and carved a wobbly path to the library, to the room where Lady Sirena had been attacked and had jumped out the window, and the room where Charley had kissed her with so much passion, so many nights ago.

So many? It had only been last night. When she pushed open the door, the room was mercifully dark. She felt her way along the shelving, the rich scent of leather and vellum filling her nose and...

Her skin prickled warmly. Another scent. The scent of a man. Not just any man.

He might have just left. Someone had recently snuffed out a candle. The smoke of it still touched the air. She held very still and explored the room with only her consciousness, without seeing, without breathing.

A chair creaked. A large body shifted. A spark struck.

The candle wick came to life and illuminated his face, his beautiful face.

"I thought we were finished talking."

The flat tone of his voice pricked her awareness. He sounded...tired, distant.

Had she, in truth, lost him?

"I-I did not come here to see you. I did not know you would be here. I will leave."

"Don't." He unfolded his long length and came to loom over her. "I shall yield the room."

Do what you must. She reached for his arm. "No. I wish to...."

"What, Miss Kingsley? Will you berate me for faithlessness? Insist you don't want to marry me? Or are you here to tempt me with kisses and then throw me away?"

His hand closed over hers and he drew her closer to the light.

"You are crying."

She squeezed her eyes shut, trying not to tremble, casting about for her reason, her backbone.

"You must know the truth," she said, her voice shaky.

"What truth?"

He was still distant, reserved.

Her heart raced. She struggled to fill her lungs.

No one had known the truth except Mama and Consuela. No one.

Trembling, she shook off his hand and wrapped herself in her own arms.

And Rigo. Rigo, who so many years earlier had been like a big brother. He knew.

"What truth, Miss Kingsley?"

The chill of her English name on his lips brought her out of her weakness. She would share this truth with him. He would reject her, and she would convince his father to get her money for her, and she would go home to look for Papa. If the very worst happened, and she had to stay here, she would find a way to do so until she reached her majority and could go on with her life.

She straightened her back and firmed her shoulders.

"My name is Maria Graciela Kingsley y Romero. That is who I am, even though you English ignore my first name and give no import to my mother's surname." She lifted her chin. "Shortly before we left for England, my mother died of the fever in Veracruz, as did Consuela, who was our friend, and who was known as the mother of Reina."

"The mother of Reina," he said, biting off each word.

She held her breath, watching him. He knew. Charley knew.

Well then. Let him know everything.

She untied her belt and threw off her robe, watching his hard eyes. She untied the string at the neck of her night rail and those eyes narrowed more, focusing doggedly on her face.

"You must know everything." She let the bodice drop to her waist and turned quickly, pulling her plait forward over her shoulder.

His gasp gave her hope. "There will be more scars here on my back, yes? It will never be beautiful."

"As long as I am around, no one will harm you again." He pulled at the nightrail attempting to draw it up, but she slapped his hands away and turned, her breasts bare.

Let him see that her nipples were brown, not pink, like a virgin girl's.

His jaw was an iron clasp holding in what looked like anger. She took a deep breath.

Charley would not hurt *her*.

"You must s-see everything," she said.

After Veracruz, she had never exposed more than her back to anyone, not Francisca, not any other maid sent to help her. With another deep breath, her hands opened and the loose gown dropped to the floor.

Charley's gaze did not fall from her face, nor did he breathe. "I am only human, Miss Kingsley."

"I am not trying to seduce you, Mr. Everly. You must look."

"Stop this—"

"Look. You must."

His gaze dropped. His mouth opened. He fell to his knees and his warm palm covered her there, in that place where her belly swelled, where a hot iron had branded her.

CHAPTER TWENTY-ONE

Dear God. Dear God. Dear God.

The phrase rattled in Charley's brain, and he did not know whether he said it aloud or not. Blood raged through him, and then ran cold, and his rock-hard erection shriveled to nothing. She'd been grievously hurt. She might even now be in pain.

He'd instinctively covered the puckered scar—crossed bars under an oval, much like a Jolly Roger.

"I know. It is very ugly," she said gravely.

He took his hand away and kissed her there, wanting to laugh at her startled gasp, wanting to laugh at himself. He'd kissed his way down many a woman's belly, but never to provide this kind of comfort.

"It is but a scar," he said, drawing on all his very British reserve, keeping his voice calm, making himself study it. The burn had been deep enough that the skin had stretched and buckled around it and across her abdomen, between her navel and her thick thatch of pubic hair.

He was instantly hard again.

"*More* scarring. I see. *That's* what you meant." Hands gripping her hips, he gazed up at her. "Are there more?"

She lifted a shoulder.

He turned her. Her hips, her lush backside had small scars from scratches and cuts, but were otherwise unblemished, as were her shapely legs.

The rest of the scars were not on the outside.

He rose, pulling her gown up with him, helping her arms into the sleeves and tying the ribbon at her neck. His hands trembled in an unmanly way, in anger, and shared sorrow, and lust held at bay. He helped her into her robe and watched her knot the belt with her own shaking hands. He longed to take her, to hold her, to comfort her.

He stepped back and waited.

"Reina has the cleft right here." She pointed to the middle of her own perfectly smooth chin. "Just like Consuela, who was, before her marriage, Consuela Cruz y Ontiveros. Have you noticed it?"

His skin prickled. A truth was coming, but he was not sure what it would be. Reina did have a small fetching cleft in her chin, along with dark auburn tones and eyes more amber than brown when one looked closely. "You have said she is Consuela's child." Consuela Cruz y Ontiveros.

The pounding in his ears started up again. The truth was working its way out like a festering splinter, poking against the back of his eyes. *Cruz*: cross. And *Ontiveros*: O.

"Consuela had a husband...with the same initials," he said.

She shook her head. "Her husband was a fine man who died just before we left Tampico to journey to Veracruz. That was the reason she was able to travel with us." She swallowed hard and fought for a breath. "She and her brother."

He must find a way to bear this story. "Come." He tugged her over to the chair and sat down, helping her onto his lap. "Tell me."

"Rigo. Rigoberto Cruz y Ontiveros. He had come for her husband's funeral and stayed for a while. My mother received some news and decided we must leave for Veracruz and try to meet up with my Papa there. Just before we left, Francisca and Juan were called away to her village to care for her dying sister. And then, Mama couldn't find a ship to take us. Rigo offered to escort us overland, and Consuela came with us."

A long silence ensued before she finally spoke again.

"I had known him as a child, and then he went off to work on a rancho, and when he came back, he acquired a small parcel. He wanted to establish himself, and he wanted a wife."

"You were *still* a child."

"No. I was close to my fifteenth birthday. After that, many girls marry."

Dread stirred in him along with a darker emotion. "Did you want to marry him?"

"To settle forever with a cruel man on a cattle ranch? No. Never. Nor did I even imagine I loved him. And it wouldn't have been what Papa wanted for me had he been there. My mother knew that, but after a very few days, she saw that she must be careful. We were trapped with him on this journey, and she had more caution than I. More experience with rough men, I guess. She told him we must wait to reach Veracruz and speak to my father, and that he must act honorably toward me to have any hope."

"And he didn't."

"My mother was a very beautiful woman. If you say I am pretty, Charley, I am nothing to what she was. The first night he arrived in San Diego on his ship, my father danced one dance with her and went straight to her uncle to ask for her hand."

The beast had attacked her mother also. Somehow, he kept his muscles from jumping from his skin and waited.

"Consuela had not seen him in a few years, and she did not know what he'd become. He had hardened in the company of rougher men. He drank very much, all the time, and one night, he..." She took a deep breath. "She tried to stop him. He beat her very badly."

He forced his eyes to stay open, to see what it cost her to tell him this.

"He beat his sister almost unconscious, and when my mother intervened, he threatened her. I surrendered. I had to make him stop. It was the only power I had."

She spoke matter-of-factly, as if she had rehearsed the words. They were laced with a suppressed emotion he could not identify, but that told him she was telling the truth.

"I was a virgin, but I gave myself so he would not hurt them. I was not strong enough to resist...He was not drunk enough for me to be able to stop him." She shook her head. "I lived on ships. I saw men fight. I'd seen men flogged. I'd never seen such brutality as his. He carried me off, and I was captive for three days. I did try to escape. To fight, I..." She drew in a shallow breath. "He thought I should come to enjoy what he did, and when I didn't, I couldn't, he...he said if I would act like a dumb cow he would mark me like one."

Blood roared in his ears. He would take the next ship and hunt down this beast. He would torture him first, and then kill him. "He is a dead man."

Pain swam in her eyes, rolled down her cheeks. "Yes. He is."

Charley's mouth went dry. "Oh, my love. You killed him?"

"No, not I." She choked. "I was weak. Weak, Charley. I could not..." She inhaled a long breath. "I could barely walk from his attacks. When he showed me the iron, I tried to resist. I threatened him with my father's wrath. I told him my father would kill him, and he said we would be married by then, and he would have my dowry, and my child, and my father would learn to accept it. It was the way things were done when a bride was reluctant. He said Papa would never know the rest, unless I was the one to tell him, and if I did I would not live long past my first-born son. He said he would go back and kill Consuela, and Mama also."

Tears seeped from beneath her lashes. "He said many horrible things. But they tracked us and found us first. The scar is bad, but it could have been so much worse. Mama got to me just as he touched the hot iron to me. She shot him, but he got up. Consuela knocked him down with a shovel, and then she hit him, again and again, until he didn't get up." She gulped in a breath. "Her own brother. Her own brother, Charley. Oh, how her heart hurt. It is all tied together in my memory: my body on fire, the shot, the crack of his skull."

He squeezed his eyes shut, seeing the picture—two women and a sick child fighting a monster.

When he opened his eyes, Gracie was watching him.

"I'm so sorry, my love."

She let out a long breath. "They heaved his body into an *arroyo*. Then they tied me onto a cart and found a village. A padre there helped us. They told everyone I had a fever—which by that time was true—and they must keep away. We stayed there until I was well, and then we stayed longer, and when Reina was born, we said she was Consuela's child."

She braced a hand on the chair arm, preparing to stand.

"Wait," he said. "Wait." He pushed a lock of hair back from her face. "I'm glad that you told me. She's a beautiful child." She would be *his* beautiful child, as soon as they married.

"I do not look at her and see Rigo. I see Consuela. I cannot toss her away. I will never toss her away, not for any husband or any guardian."

"No. She'll be with you always. It is good Consuela's family showed no interest."

"It was Papa's idea to contact them. He...wrote letters."

"Which did not arrive?"

She bit her lip and shook her head. "I made sure they would not."

"So, he doesn't know the truth?"

She went so still, her breath stopping, he wanted to press his mouth to hers and breathe for her. He swept a thumb down her cheek.

"I never told him. And if he truly is dead...there has been enough of lying and enough of secrets. Everyone who knew died. Not even Francisca knows. No one knows but you."

His heart pounded. She had trusted *him* with her darkest—and her brightest—secret. But why, if her plan was to break their engagement and cast him off?

He must cease with this business of feeling and *think*.

She squirmed in his lap. "And so you see, I am what you English call *very* damaged goods. Not a suitable wife for even the younger son of an earl."

Thinking was almost out of the question with her backside twitching against him, making him want to touch her more.

"Please. Sit still a moment."

She jumped off his lap and faced him, wringing her hands at her waist. "There is another reason you will not want to marry me," she said. "I am not a-a good lover. I could not respond. I could not pretend. And I had a thorough education in those three days. I know the English don't expect a wife...well, that is why the husband keeps a mistress, but..." Tears filled her eyes again and her voice trailed off.

He fisted his hand to keep from grabbing hers.

"Gracie." Somehow, he held back the anger that wanted to rage, somehow, he made his voice calm. "You were raped. That was no education. No normal woman responds to brutality with feelings of pleasure." He rested his hands on the chair arms, forcing himself to stay seated. "And you do respond when I kiss you. In fact, every time I touch you, I sense your response. Were you ever kissed before Rigo?"

She nodded.

"Touched?"

She hung her head and still managed a nod.

Someone had shamed her for that also.

"And?" He pushed ahead. "Did you enjoy it?"

She swallowed and slowly nodded.

"There you have it. You're a sensual woman. That doesn't mean you should enjoy being forced. You just didn't have the right man until now."

Trembling shot through her limbs and set her lip quivering and her teeth chattering. "I d-don't know what I am."

"I do." *You are mine.* "And I love you, Gracie, all of you, every part of you, including that little girl in the nursery."

Her head shot up and her mouth dropped open.

He wouldn't claim her though, not until she was ready to claim him. One thing he'd learned swiving women for king and country—a woman's pleasure involved far more than the act. Total surrender was required.

CHAPTER TWENTY-TWO

Gracie closed her mouth and tightened her arms, hugging herself. "I am glad you love me. I have leaned on you very much, Charley." She inhaled deeply. "I was angry today because I was jealous. It is a foolish emotion when so much is at stake. It seems that to be free, I must pledge myself to someone and I wish it to be you. Please m-marry me. I will try not to trouble you about your l-lovers." She chewed on her lip, frowning. "I have shared all my secrets, and I should like you to tell me yes or no, whether you will marry me."

His heart stuttered.

He ought to be happy. But what the hell did she mean about being free? She was fooling herself if she thought marrying him would leave her free to go her own way, have lovers, live apart from him. It wouldn't happen, and he had no need to brand her. She was his. And he was hers. Until she realized that, a marriage like the one she was proposing would be no more than another cage for her.

And—damn it all—it would be a cage for him also. The freedom he wanted was not that sort of arrangement.

He almost laughed at the irony—the freedom he wanted was the trap he'd been dodging. Or...could it be that was the freedom she was talking about?

"Let me be clear on one thing: I will not marry and take lovers on the side."

Her gaze dropped to his feet.

"You say you must pledge yourself to someone, but what of love, Gracie?"

Her head moved from side to side. "To love a husband is dangerous, they say."

"They? Not my brothers' wives. You haven't been talking to them."

"Lady Kingsley—"

"Lady Kingsley beat that convention into you. I don't think you should trust her."

Her eyes sparked, shiny and defiant. "I'm not sure I should trust anyone." She fisted her hands. "Will you marry me, Charley?"

"Without mutual love, Gracie?"

She opened her mouth. Her forehead crumpled. Her lips trembled. No sound escaped.

Oh, this was a stubborn girl, but with good reason. She'd been fighting her way alone through the world for the last three years, carrying a great burdensome lie on her scarred body, all alone.

And he needed to push her just a bit more.

He stepped closer. "Then, no."

"No?" Graciela's heart jumped, her chest constricted and real pain gripped her lungs.

He said he loved her, but he would not marry her. Her shame was too much for him. She must find another way.

By force of will she drew herself taller. "Very well." She turned toward the door.

He reached it before her and blocked the way.

Fear flashed within her, quickly replaced by sense. This was Charley. She did not fear him, and she did not want to leave him. She wanted to be back sitting on his lap, his comforting arm around her.

"That's it?" In the shadows, only his eyes gleamed. "You'd walk away? You won't fight for what you want?"

"I am not a coward. You do not want me."

"Oh, I want you."

A tendril of warmth unfurled in her. Only his scent and his voice and that gleam in his eyes touched her, yet her body had opened as it had before with him.

"I'm not a virgin."

"So what? No man or woman is after the first time."

"I have borne a child."

"A lovely, vibrant, beautiful child."

"I am scarred. I am ugly."

"You are scarred, but you are not ugly, Gracie."

Confusion swirled through her, hope and fear warring.

Fear won. She lifted her chin and steadied her voice. "I will never be used like that again."

"Not by anyone. And definitely not by me."

The steel in his voice cut her and her heart plummeted again, bringing the rest of her with it. Her knees buckled, and he steadied her, his arms like the firm balustrade of the staircase.

Compressed anger had turned him to stone. She had bungled this meeting and insulted him.

He lifted her hand and pressed the fingers between his own.

"You are driving me mad," he said. "No, you are driving us both mad. I won't marry you for your money or merely to protect you. I have enough money for the life I want, and I can and will protect you without marrying you if that's what it comes to."

His hands sent little bursts of lightning through her, addling her brains. Of course, his family was rich. He must have a generous allowance. He was not greedy. He did not need her funds. And his protection would bring them together, and that maddened him because he wanted her and would not be able to take her unless he married her. So why would he not marry her? Why would he protect her until she reached her majority or found another husband?

She caught her breath. Once she turned twenty-one, she could have control of her funds. Marrying anyone but Charley was unimaginable, and she would not need to. If he didn't want her, she'd be free to go her own way.

If he protected her until then...Whatever was to happen between them, she wanted to explore it, in her damaged, fallen, scarred state. She'd never be an English lady. She wanted to be a real woman. To know an honorable man's loving.

He wanted her but he would not use her, so she must persuade him, only she had no skills either in politics or seduction.

"Teach me," she blurted out.

He stilled. She thanked God for the darkness concealing her flaming cheeks.

"You want me, Charley, and I...I want to know, to understand." She huffed out a breath. "Oh, I am saying this badly. You are a man who has had many women—"

"Not so many—"

"And you are right that I do feel...That is, I like when you kiss me. I want to know more."

He moved closer, so close she could feel his breath at her ear, making her shiver. "About?"

"About love. That is, about making love."

He pulled her closer again and she felt his hard phallus against her belly. A frisson of fear went through her, and he stepped back an inch breaking their bond.

She pushed herself close. She must not show fear. Must not. "Help me to not be so afraid."

"And if I got you with child?"

"Oh." Given what happened before, it was a real possibility.

He kissed her forehead. "If I say yes, if that should happen, we shall deal with it."

"How?"

"In the usual way."

Fear raced through her. She had heard whispers of things desperate women did. "I will not get rid of a child. Never."

He walked her into the light and studied her, his eyes very serious. "No. That's not what I meant. I meant, that perhaps, by then, you would love me, and we could marry."

I love you now. She opened her mouth, but the words would not come, and in truth, her own judgment couldn't be trusted. Hadn't she trusted her guardian at first? And Rigo? At first, she had thought her mother's fears excessive.

"So you will teach me?"

"I will."

"After the ball tomorrow night?"

He nuzzled her ear, sending ripples of pleasure through her. "Why no. We'll have our first lesson right now."

CHAPTER TWENTY-THREE

The library candle sputtered and died, leaving them wrapped in a thin stream of smoke and darkness. Charley's hands cradled her shoulders, his lips moved against hers but a moment, and then trailed to her cheek, to her ear, and down to a spot on her neck that sent her wriggling. Pleasure coursed through her, making her heart pound, stealing her breath. She tried to push closer, but he held her away, his touch gentle but strong.

"We'll be more comfortable in a bed," he murmured. "Your bedchamber or mine?"

A servant could enter her chamber any time. Even Lady Perry might come knocking. But that could happen at his bedchamber also.

"Can we not lock the door here? There is the sofa." She squeezed her eyes tightly. Rigo had taken her on the hard ground, many times, many ways, the rocks and pebbles grinding into her back and her breasts.

His lips touched her forehead like butterflies landing, so soft for a man. "I'll lock this door."

Her courage surged. She reached for his arm. "No. We'll go to your bedchamber. Your valet will be discreet?"

"I was only joking in the nursery about my valet being upset. I don't keep one. And I have a sturdy lock on my door."

In mere breathless moments they had reached his chamber.

The heavy curtains were pulled back, the window open to the moonlight and a breeze alive with the city's scents.

He struck a spark, lit a lamp, and then one by one, each taper in a brace of candles on the mantle.

Books and journals were piled atop a carved table near the fireplace. The hangings and upholstery were a dark, manly color; forest green, she would guess. The bed...the bed stood back, tall and not particularly wide. It was a chamber for a single man, and other than the presence of the books, impersonal, as though Charley did not really live here.

He went to another table, poured a glass of amber liquid, and walked it back to her.

"You may turn the key in that lock," he said.

She did.

He extended the tumbler to her. "Brandy. I'm sorry, I have but one glass. I should have thought to bring another from the library."

She shook her head. "I wish to be sober."

He looked at the glass, frowning as if seeing all her secrets in it, again.

Her heart pounded. Charley was not Rigo. He was not. The only time she had seen Charley drunk, at her betrothal ball, he had been but acting.

She snatched the glass from him. "One sip perhaps." The hot liquid burned her lips. She swished it in her mouth, let it coat her throat, and handed it back to him. "Bottoms up."

A small smile curved his lips. He tossed the rest of the drink back, eyes locked on hers, Adam's apple moving in a way that made her shiver.

Everything about him was well made. She shut her eyes tight. Everything about Rigo had been well made also. Everything except the man he was.

Soft lips touched each eyelid. "Don't be afraid. We'll stop whenever you ask."

She opened her eyes and saw that he had moved away, carrying the empty glass back.

She followed him, deciding to be brave. "I am not afraid of you. What comes next?"

He pointed. "The dressing chamber door needs locking."

She crossed the room and did that. "Now what?" she asked.

"I am yours to command."

Her heart pounded, excitement building. His kisses were divine. Perhaps a kiss and then...

He tugged at his neck cloth, unwinding it.

Every nerve in her tingled. Taking off her clothes for him—it had excited him. Underneath her fear, her own desire had answered his.

He had seen her. She had not seen him.

The white linen landed on the back of a stuffed armchair, one he moved to sit in.

"No," she said.

Through it all, his gaze had not left her. It sharpened, like that of a man just challenged.

"Please..." She took a breath. "Please remove your clothes."

Coats flew. His white shirt cleared his head and sailed across the room at her. She caught it and when she looked, he was grinning. She could not help but smile back, lifting the linen to her nose.

Dios. His scent filled her, sent her bones to shaking. He sat and crossed a booted foot across his knee.

"Wait." She tossed the shirt aside and hurried over. He had frozen in the chair, shirtless, his chest as muscled as any well-fed sailor's. A smattering of tawny hair ran to a point below his breeches.

And Charley had scars of his own. The largest one had carved an arc from his center to his flank, puckered from stitching and still in places pink. Older, shallower slices marked a shoulder and his arms. Those were, perhaps, from dueling.

A man with married lovers would have had a duel or two. Because he was experienced, which she was not.

Anxiety crashed through her. Perhaps this was a mistake.

His gaze met hers, sending her a challenge.

For now, she would be brave, and she would ask about his dueling later. "Put out your foot."

Muscles flexing, he complied, clutching the chair arms and extending one long leg. She tugged one boot and then the other, and stepped back, watching him peel off his stockings.

After, he did not move, but sat, richly carved, strong—he was no padded, corseted society dandy.

And he could easily overpower her and force her if he pleased. She could not fight him. Her hands began to shake and she clenched them at her waist.

He would not. He had promised. She did trust him.

"The rest," she said.

"Would you like to help some more?"

The soft words sent a shiver through her. She gripped her hands tighter.

He stood slowly. "Forgive me. I'm teasing you." In seconds he pushed trousers and smalls down about his hips to the floor and stepped out of them.

Graciela pressed her lips together, pressed her hands against her chest to squelch the pounding, to push air into her lungs. In their three days together, Rigo had done no more than open up his fall. She'd seen his cock, but only because he'd made her look.

And everything with Rigo was on a smaller scale. *Dios*. He had torn her apart with that smaller prick, again and again. She could not do this.

Charley snatched his garments and held them in front of him.

"No," she said. "It's...it's all right."

He did not move.

"You said you are mine to command."

"You're frightened, my love. It's too much all at once."

She inhaled and nodded. "Too much, I think. You will hurt me. You cannot help it, but you will."

His grim look eased. "I can help it. And I won't hurt you, if you'll but trust me." He extended a hand.

She shut her eyes again. She had no weapons, had seen none in his chambers, but she could scream. She was not in the wilderness. In a great house, someone would hear. Someone would come to help her.

When she opened her eyes, he had seated himself, hand still reaching for her. "Come. Come sit upon my lap. We won't have that particular lesson tonight. I promise."

His tone was as flat and pompous as any tutor's. She came and took his hand and made as if to sit across his legs.

"No," he said. "That is, if you please, Gracie, you will command me better if you sit..." he pushed her skirts up, lifted her and turned her facing him, straddling his lap, "like this."

His eyes had darkened. His mouth was grim. He seemed to be in pain.

She had heard that men felt pain if they could not relieve themselves. She had heard that lesson: do not excite a man; do not tempt him past a point of justice.

Justice. She'd done nothing to tempt Rigo. She'd done nothing but resist Rigo. She'd all but put a sack over her head to be modest around him. If Rigo had felt pain, it had not been her fault.

Charley's expression shifted again. "It's me, Gracie. It's Charley. I won't hurt you."

She nodded.

"Look at me."

She searched his eyes.

"Now look down." He pushed her skirts higher and left his hands to cup her hips. "You see your power over me?"

"Any woman has this power over you."

"And you have this power over any man."

"Perhaps, but I would not—"

"I know. And I'm not such a tomcat as you might think." His thumbs moved along her hip bones, swirling warmth into her. "Before that monster, you said you'd been kissed."

A shiver went through her, memories rushing in. "There were boys I danced with. There was one who took me outside and kissed me."

"And you liked it?"

Heat rushed her cheeks. What she remembered was her father's anger, and that he'd been right, and later, Rigo's actions had proved what could have happened with that first boy, had proved the rightness of Papa's anger.

But that night, before the shame, she'd felt the pleasure.

She shrugged and he quirked one eyebrow.

"Will you take off your robe?"

She nodded, and he pulled the bow of her belt and pushed the garment off her, letting it fall to the floor.

His gaze burned a path from her eyes to the dark patch of hair between her legs. He had pushed the nightrail high to unveil it.

"Ye gads, you are a dream."

Her heart thudded. She was a dream, until the brand was bared, and then she would be a nightmare.

He leaned in and his soft lips distracted her, pressing, burning, nudging her with his tongue until she'd opened for him. The long, languorous kiss was demanding, convincing. Pleasure sparked through her, melting her tension, and his hands slid higher, circling her breasts. Time stood still and then galloped, mirroring her pulse, her breath. He broke away and kissed a path down her neck, tasting her breasts, taking her nipple, nightrail and all, into his mouth. Pleasure shot through her, a lightning bolt, from her breast to the point between her legs. She bucked against him, and felt his hard rod, and scooted back.

He unlatched from her nipple and touched his forehead to hers. "Did I hurt you?"

"No...I..." She didn't know what to say. "Did I hurt you?"

He chuckled, and drew back to reveal a smile. "I'm feeling no pain. Now, we'll have a lesson."

"That wasn't one?"

"No. That is, we'll do something new, now. May I touch you? Down there?"

Excitement raced through her, curling and unfurling low in her belly.

"I want to see if you are wet."

"Of course I'm not wet. I'm not an infant, or..." Or on her courses. She calculated in her head and looked down again.

"You're a talker." He touched a finger to her and she shot up straight, arching closer. His finger slid down and pleasure arrowed through her from the point where he touched.

Oh. He should not. It was wrong, this sort of pleasure.

She closed her eyes against the pinpoint of sensation. Everything in her squeezed.

His finger inched inward, freezing her breath until she finally gasped.

"Yes." His face was a grimace of concentration as he rubbed her, the touch silky and smooth. "Oh yes. You are just the way you should be. The way God made you to be for the man you love. Give me your finger."

"I won't," she huffed. "It is...shameful."

"Shameful. Did your mother say that?"

"No."

"Francisca?"

"No."

His finger began to move again. "It was someone who didn't know this pleasure and didn't want you to know it. But I tell you, Gracie, between a man and a woman marrying for love there's no shame in pleasure, unless it's forced, unless it causes the other pain. Do you know who taught me that? No of course you don't, but it was *my* mother."

"Your mother talked to you about such things?"

"Yes. Of necessity. Father was gone, and the milkmaid was after me, and Mother very shrewdly saw what was afoot. She told me everything, and let me know she did not countenance liaisons with servants. Did your mother—"

"No. She never got to it before...well, after she said it shouldn't have been like that. *Oh*." He had slid that finger in deeper, making her clench the muscles there.

He drew in a sharp breath and plundered her mouth again, long minutes of passionate kissing while she could do nothing but writhe atop him. New sensations started at her bud—where his thumb swept her gently, steadily, beating a pulse through her. She rose on her knees, bucking against that insidious hand, and the pleasure he stirred.

He dropped from her mouth to her breast, moved a hand to her bottom, under the robe, kneading her, steadying her as she moved and gasped and searched for something, gripping his shoulders, choking for air.

He nipped her neck, swiping the sensitive spot there with his tongue. "Oh, my love," he mumbled. "My love. Yes. Yes." His tongue found her other breast and suckled. "So beautiful." He had pulled her closer, her belly rubbing his hard shaft with each up and down thrust. "That's it. Almost there. Yes. So beautiful."

The murmurs grew faint. The pinpoint of pleasure bloomed in her, growing, all of her fixed on that one place while she struggled, struggled, for something, something, and...

Pleasure burst in her, streaking through all of her nerves, pounding in wave after wave until the crashing subsided, the storm abated, and she found herself sprawled, plastered against him, her head on his shoulder.

She lay there long moments, too stunned to speak, and became conscious that her nightrail was wet.

In front. She sat up and looked down. His erection was gone.

Charley's eyes opened a fraction. "I do apologize. I couldn't help myself." His eyes closed again.

He had...come. That was the word the men used. But not inside her, as Rigo had done. So she would not get with child.

She studied his face. He looked paralyzed. Rigo had paused after each rutting to tie her up and then he had slept. She could leave now. Charley would not detain her.

He had made sure she would not find herself with a baby. Because if there was a baby, they would marry.

If she loved him. He had called her his love.

She shifted on his lap. Her privates touched his leg and she almost jumped from the pleasure. She was still inflamed.

His eyes opened again. "Give me but a few minutes." He reached out to steady her.

She wadded the cloth of her nightrail and wiped them both. Between her legs, there was moisture but no blood. There had been blood every time with Rigo.

She looked into the slits of his eyes.

He smiled. "It can work. You can have pleasure like that every time you are willing. Will you trust me?"

"I am willing to try." She untied the drawstring at her neck then remembered. She would expose the brand.

"Take it off for the next lesson. You're beautiful, all of you, just as you are, my love. My Gracie."

Tears burned her eyes. She cupped his cheek dragging her thumbnail through the stubble there. "My love?" she whispered.

"And I mean it." He pushed at the nightrail. "Take it off."

"Only if you are sure," she said.

"I'm sure."

He buzzed with the tension of holding back, gripped the chair, and gritted his teeth. An honorable man. A man who could exercise self-control. A man who loved her.

She stood and peeled the nightrail over her head.

He was up then, carrying her to the bed, and as he had done before, pressing his lips to the scar on her belly, crawling between her legs to make love to her with his tongue, there, in her scarred, wounded, most private places. Charley kissed and laved and suckled until she was wrenching the counterpane, her moans growing louder, the pleasure building.

Her body itched to take him in.

"Please, Charley,"

He grunted.

"I want you inside me."

He raised his head, his eyes wild. He plunged a finger into her, and then another, making her jump.

"I will go there," he mumbled. "After we're married."

"But...*Oh*."

Pleasure swirled and crested and burst again.

Charley rolled over and grinned at the underside of the bed canopy, tucking her close, the small part of his brain that was still working reminding him why he wouldn't take his own pleasure inside of her.

When he turned his head, she was staring at him, heavy lidded. A small hand touched his erection, sending it bouncing. He clamped his hand over hers.

"This night is for you," he said. "For your pleasure."

"Your pleasure will bring me pleasure."

He groaned and closed his eyes.

His pleasure came seconds later and for long moments, he was lost.

"Thank you." Petal soft lips touched his cheek and she scratched at his beard, reminding him a gentleman should have shaved. He vaguely hoped she was not whisker-burned, but he could barely move much less mumble an apology.

"You are a good teacher," she teased.

He moved a finger along her side and heard her draw in a breath.

"Will you marry me now, Charley?"

He opened one eye.

Her dark eyes burned into him. "For love. Will you marry me for love? I...have grown to trust you. To love you. Not just because of this. But we can do this often, can we not?" She looked away and frowned. "I would not wish to share you though."

He put a finger over her mouth. "Day after tomorrow. No later."

"What?"

"Our nuptials."

She smiled. And laughed. And crawled atop him, kissing him, stirring him anew.

"Shall we skip the diplomatic ball tomorrow night?" she asked.

At dinner, Father had said they would all attend. Her sudden frown and the faraway look told him she was thinking of the Duquesa.

"The Duquesa might be there, but so will her husband. Half the world will be there. We'll go and tell that world our plans." He drew her to him. "Now, before you bring me back to life, I think we should sleep. Our daughter will be up in a few short hours."

"*Our* daughter." A tear plopped onto his chest.

He flipped her over, pulled her bottom close, his chin resting at the point on the back of her head where her plait began.

If he had this every night of this life, he'd have no need of heaven in the next.

He held the hand spread on the sheet in front of her and whispered his plans for their future together until her breaths evened out and he knew she was sleeping. Only then did he let himself drift off.

Gray light was streaming in through the window when he woke.

Gracie was still wedged next to him, her dark hair tickling his chest. He stroked it away and studied her back. The bruises were healing, quickly and well, but the skin might scar where the switch had cut.

Her back dipped gracefully to a slim waist that led to a rounded derriere and hip.

She stirred and lifted sleepy eyes. "Good morning, Charley."

No shock at waking in a man's arms? *Because she's where she belongs.*

He pushed down his desire and said "It's morning. We need to get you back to your chamber."

"Who will care?" She kissed his neck.

Who *would* care? Not his brothers and their wives. Not his sister. Not the men who served his father. Not even his father, likely, if this reached an honorable conclusion. The servants were used to strange goings-on, though perhaps not this sort.

Her servants certainly weren't.

"Francisca will flay me alive, if Juan doesn't shoot me first."

"She wants me to marry you."

"She despises me."

"No. She wants you to keep me safe. She is very pragmatic."

"So you will be safely ensconced as Mrs. Everly, and she will sneak a...a tarantula, or a rattlesnake into my bed one night."

Gracie rolled onto her back and shook with laughter. "Her people *are* fierce."

"She is an Indian?"

"A *mestizo*. Her grandmother was a Yaqui. It is a tribe from Sonora, proud warriors, all."

She talked then about Mexico, the mountains and deserts, the tribes and the missions, and the Pacific, Atlantic, and Caribbean ports she had visited with her parents. She had traveled widely in her world, as had he in his.

"I long to see this new world," he said. "I've been looking for a post in New Spain or whatever it is to be called now."

She raised herself on one elbow and frowned down at him. "You mentioned that before. You would leave England?"

He pushed her hair back where it draped over her face. "Not without you. Not without Reina. Come here."

She ignored him and the frown deepened. "I am not at all sure you should leave England."

His hand froze on her cheek. *You*, she'd said. Not *we*.

Bam, bam, bam. "*Señor Everly.*"

"*Francisca.*" Gracie clamped a hand over her mouth and giggled.

"*Señor Everly, Graciela is missing.*"

"One moment, Francisca," he called. He leaped from the bed, found her nightrail and robe, and while she dressed, tossed on his own banyan and rummaged through his coats.

At the door, he pulled her in for a quick kiss and thrust the jewelry box into her hand.

The pounding started up again, this time more fiercely.

"You will take this," he said.

She nodded.

"You'll wear it for the wedding."

"Yes. Tomorrow."

"*Señor* Everly."

"Will she be armed?"

Gracie laughed.

He kissed her again, turned the key, and pushed her out in front of him, like the coward he was.

Francisca's dark eyes were virtually unreadable, except that he didn't see murder there.

"You are the first to know, Francisca," he said. "The wedding will be today."

Gracie's mouth dropped, a look of panic forming. He kissed her again. "Hurry and get dressed," he said in Spanish for Francisca's benefit. "We must find my father. He must go with me to Doctors' Commons and sign for you, and he'll want to talk to you first before we go for the license."

And then he closed the door on her, leaned against it, and let out a whoop.

CHAPTER TWENTY-FOUR

Charley's strong grip on her hand in this crowded carriage calmed her. The Bakeleys and the Gibsons occupied the plain carriage following theirs, and behind them came a third carriage with Lady Jane Monthorpe and the aristocratic vicar who had joined them in the afternoon, and later for the large family dinner that followed. Penderbrook had even squeezed in next to a teary-eyed Lady Jane. The lady, it seemed, loved weddings.

Graciela had been warmly welcomed into their circle. She'd had a chance to speak more with Bink's wife and felt an instant kinship. Paulette was lowborn, like herself, like her husband, illegitimate. Like Reina. Lord Hackwell's charming young brother, Thomas, also a by-blow, had joined them again at Shaldon House, but was far too young for this night's outing.

That morning, while Charley and his father had gone off for the special license that would allow them to marry privately, and while the modiste had fussed with her extravagant new gown, Paulette and Lady Sirena had shared the hair-raising stories of their marriages with the other two sons of Shaldon. Her situation was quite mild by comparison.

Still, her gown had a secret pocket for Papa's sheathed blade, though to pull such a weapon out at a *ton* ball would be reckless indeed, even for one such as herself.

Seated across from them in the formal town carriage, Lord Shaldon was a silent companion. Lady Perry chattered enough for both of them.

Graciela's stomach danced and fluttered with each start and stop as their carriage crawled with the traffic. The swearing and shouting of grooms and coachmen permeated the thin walls. Beyond their usual guards, she could see throngs of common people crowding to see the great spectacle.

It was exciting and potentially quite dangerous. If Kingsley had learned of Charley's trip to Doctors' Commons, or if it had come to Gregory Carvelle's ears, she could be in very great danger. They were men who did not like to be thwarted.

"It will be worse for the coronation this summer," Lady Perry said. "I shall flee to the country. Will you come with me, Father?"

"Would that I could." A rare smile touched his lips.

"What about you two? Surely you would rather honeymoon elsewhere than stay and be crushed by these crowds. Graciela must see Cransdall. And we can look about the county for an estate for sale. Do you think you will buy a house in the country?"

Graciela looked at Charley. They had not had time to discuss their long term living arrangements.

"Well you could certainly afford it, with Graciela's dowry," Lady Perry said.

Charley's loud sigh reverberated in the carriage. He had explained the hurriedly drafted marriage settlement in precise detail to her before Lord Shaldon had signed it on her behalf. Besides the portions set aside for Reina and their children to come, her dowry would be hers. Whether he himself had enough money to buy a house, she didn't know, but she knew he would not pressure her to use her money.

"Your mother left Charles an estate in the Yorkshire," Lord Shaldon said.

Charley's gaze whipped from the window.

As her only active guardian, Lord Shaldon had unhesitatingly agreed to Charley's marriage terms, so unfavorable to his own son. Now she knew why.

"I had meant to tell you tomorrow, after I retrieved the title from safekeeping, but there you see, your sister is an impatient one."

"An estate." Charley frowned.

Her heart slipped down to jostle about with her stomach. An estate would tie him down, as would having a wife and child.

"Yes. All in good order, as you could expect from your mother and Bakeley. There is a substantial bit of cash also. You should garner four or five thousand a year, if you are wise."

"The same as Bink."

"Yes."

Lady Perry extended her arm and touched Gracie's knee. "Mother was very rich, and a dab hand with investments. What did she arrange for me, Father?"

When he didn't answer she laughed and turned back to Gracie. "He never told Bink or Charley anything until they settled on their wives. Bakeley of course will inherit everything else."

She smiled politely. She had heard the story of Bink's inheritance from Paulette.

"Mother's family was common and grew rich through mining and banking. She saw to Bink's education before he ran off, and she required Charley to live on a small allowance and to be productive. Bink went into the army, and Charley here served in the Foreign Office."

She looked up at Charley and smiled. "You *are* a spy then."

He shrugged. "I told you—I gadded about Europe listening to gossip. Nothing more."

Yes, he had told her that before. And the scars on his body? They had not gone so far as to talk about those yet.

"I can come with you when you visit your property," Lady Perry said. "Shall we go soon? I know it is your honeymoon, but surely you will want to take Reina, and I can happily divert her and play nursemaid. You may put me in another wing of the house entirely."

"Perry." Charley's voice held a warning.

"Or I can sleep in the nursery."

Loud shouting erupted nearby, sending her nerves jumping. "Remind me now why we had to come," she whispered to Charley.

He squeezed her hand, but his other was reaching into his coat, where she knew he had a weapon stored. "Father insisted," he whispered back.

The carriage jerked ahead and the noise subsided. Whatever the trouble, it had been settled.

She clung to his hand, trying to be brave, but the night with so little sleep, the bustle of the morning and onslaught of family and friends, the fitting into this beautiful gown and the afternoon...

She pressed a hand to her throat and felt the jewels resting there. Charley's engagement gift was a necklace of the palest rose quartz beads, polished like pearls and strung between silver spacers. It matched her pale pink gown and its overlay of silver gauze netting. The description of the gown had not sounded beautiful. She had thought to wear it out of obligation.

But then she had seen it, and when Madame slipped it over her head, she became like a princess.

The diamond on her finger dazzled also even in the dim lamp of the coach lights. That had been Charley's mother's. She would treasure it.

"Do not leave my side," she said quietly. "I shall fill up my dance card with your relatives and friends. Your brothers and Penderbrook." She ticked off the names on her fingers. "They can each dance with me twice. Does the Vicar dance, do you think?"

"Perhaps a country dance."

"I will importune him for two. And you, Lord Shaldon—"

"Lame leg, my dear. That will be enough as we are not staying the whole night. Charles must do his duty for the rest of the evening." He nodded at his son and another rare smile bloomed.

Next to her, Charley squirmed. She looked at him quickly and saw his embarrassed nod.

Oh. There had been a second meaning to Lord Shaldon's comment.

It was clear, father and son cared for each other. There was a silent conversation in this moment, an exchange of emotion, a closeness, and no wonder—they were both in the same profession. Neither Lord Bakeley nor Mr. Gibson had followed their father into the spy business. Nor Lady Perry, though if ever a lady was prime for adventure, it was Perry. She was cloaked in a sense of restlessness that her father and brothers did not see.

The lights brightened as they approached the rooms rented for the occasion, and she straightened and closed her eyes for a moment. She must act a lady tonight, for Charley's sake and for Papa's. She must make him proud, even if it turned out that he was truly dead.

Charley exited first, his gaze sweeping the arrival area. Their guards were in place. The footmen hired for the ball were held at a distance. The lights of the assembly rooms beckoned. Now they had only to face the evening and the possibility, the very likely possibility he thought, of a confrontation with Kingsley, or Carvelle, or possibly the Duque himself.

He shook off the sense of impending doom. It wasn't like him to look for the worst. He'd deal with whatever came up, with Father, and Bink, and Bakeley to back him up.

It was Gracie he worried about. Gracie, and the terrible portent that greeted him every time his eyes met his father's.

He knew that look. Father was quite pleased with his choice of a bride, which meant...Gracie was the key to a spy. Perhaps not the spy

Farnsworth had set him upon, the one mixed up in his mother's death, but another one. For Father, the war would never be over. In his devious way, he had used Bink's marriage to Paulette, and Bakeley's marriage to Sirena, to lure old enemies.

Charley assisted both ladies down, and by the time his father was ready to exit, the ladies had moved to stand with the guards, and his brothers had joined him.

Bakeley glanced around. "Bink and I agree. Insisting you go to this ball on your wedding night? Father is up to something."

"Do you know who we're looking for, Charley?" Bink asked. "A bit of intelligence would help."

"Someone related to a Spanish lady," he said.

"The Duque," Bakeley said.

"Or Kingsley." Bink clamped a hand on Charley's shoulder. "Never fear. We'll all help you protect her. Even Kincaid here."

Kincaid had arrived, dressed in Shaldon livery. He would keep track of the guards, the teams, and the coaches. They stepped back to let him assist Shaldon.

"Ten to one, whoever it is, he or she will be here tonight." Bink grinned.

"He," Charley said. "That much I do know."

"As I said, a bit of intelligence might help," Bink muttered.

Charley knew a good deal more than them, some from Farnsworth, some from his father, some from the records he'd dug up on his mother's accident, and those hideous memories, but all he had were pieces of a puzzle. Only his father knew the whole picture being assembled.

"Someone from the old days, so older," Bakeley said. "Right, then. Let's gather these fillies and get off this street."

They entered together, each man tucking a lady's hand into his, except for his vicar cousin. His father, he noticed, had handed Perry over to Penderbrook and was escorting Lady Jane. Perhaps she too had a spy attached somewhere in her past.

He maneuvered them to the back of the group, Gracie offering no resistance, but she was stiff as a royal duchess next to him. "Tonight is our wedding night," he murmured.

She sent him a tremulous smile. "Why *did* your father insist that we come?"

"It is to be our shocking come-out," he said. "I've married an heiress and you've caught yourself a rich earl's son. And he's up to something. I'm not sure what." The last thing he wanted was for her to worry.

She jerked her chin up and gazed at him. "He's after a traitor."

She had spent the morning with his brothers' wives.

"Yes, so I would imagine. And erase that frown, please. This is the happiest day of your life." He let a warm gaze travel over her. "Do it for England."

"Am I English, then? Papa changed sides more than once, and I was not really sure."

"You are now."

She took in a breath that made her fine bosom rise in its silver cage, and he couldn't help smiling. He would ravish her three ways tonight, if he could find the stamina.

"I will do it to honor my father." She waved a gloved hand. "Whatever this is I am supposed to do."

"You are supposed to be just what you are— the most beautiful woman at this ball."

He swept a gaze over the crowd. It was more than the usual assortment of peacocks and peahens, but then, the king peacock of all of Europe was soon to be crowned and no one wanted to miss out on the spectacle.

He recognized many faces from his travels across Europe. The Duquesa was there, glowing and golden. From the tense line of her lovely jaw, he knew she'd spotted him. He easily deciphered the look she directed at a lady wearing a mine-load of diamonds on her neck and a dish filled with feathers atop her head. Her duque had no regard for his marriage vows, was probably right now in a cranny, lifting another woman's skirts. The lady had managed the marriage these many years with the help of her powerful father. And French letters.

She'd asked for a meeting again just that morning. This time, her messenger had waited, and he'd sent his deepest regrets.

But two notes, two days in a row, meant the subject was something important, and with Farnsworth gone, there was no one else to make contact.

He must have that dance with her.

Names of attendees boomed across the room. His father was announced, then the rest one by one. After Bink and Paulette, Charley stepped forward with Gracie and handed over a card.

"Mr. and Mrs. Charles Everly."

There was not much of a ruffle in the room, but looking over his wife's head, he saw one pair of eyes widen. And then two men stepped up with the Duquesa—her husband and Lord Kingsley.

Gracie saw them also. Her breasts rose again. "Bugger the man," she whispered.

"Indeed," he said. If possible, with a very sharp sword.

CHAPTER TWENTY-FIVE

After several sets, Graciela stepped off the dance floor with Mr. Penderbrook and her gaze followed his.

Charley had just released his sister and was leading the Duquesa onto the floor.

Penderbrook moved quickly to block her view. "It's only a dance," he whispered. "Just like ours."

She sighed. "You would say that, Penderbrook. You're a man." Yet, he was right, and she shouldn't be staring like a jealous wife.

She forced herself to turn away. Across the room she spotted another face, and her nerves prickled. Captain Llewellyn had made a late, unannounced appearance. He started their way.

They had reached the side of the room and Penderbrook leaned close to her ear. "I believe he dallied for reasons of national interest. What reasons, do not ask, because I don't know. Who is next for you?"

"Mr. Gibson." Only Mr. Gibson was nowhere in sight, but Captain Llewellyn had almost reached them. "Perhaps I shall beg off."

"No. Go and dance. Give Everly a kick when you pass him."

She sent him a rueful smile and turned to greet the Captain, who bowed and greeted her.

"Are you free for this dance?" he asked.

"It is promised." She spotted Mr. Gibson coming nearer, and the Captain followed her glance.

"Perhaps later." He bowed. "I must apologize for my behavior yesterday, Grace. I'm returning to my ship earlier than expected, but I stand ready to assist you if ever you should need it."

Mr. Gibson joined them, and, hearing the last remark, frowned. "Our dance, Graciela?"

She took Mr. Gibson's arm, made introductions, and said, "Captain, I shall keep that in mind. And you should keep in mind that if you are a friend of my father's cousin, you are no friend to me."

A deep frown furrowed his brow. "I am not in league with him."

She felt the Captain's eyes on her as Mr. Gibson led her onto the floor.

Mr. Gibson looked grim.

"He was a friend of my father and mother," she said.

Across the room, Charley and his partner were bowing and curtseying. She tried not to watch.

"I see. I shall step on her Excellency's toe in passing if you wish," he murmured. "I'm only a great clod anyway."

She smiled and blinked away sudden moisture. He was kind, this brother of Charley's, and anything but a clod.

Several couples away Charley inclined his head to his former lover, listening intently. The Duquesa's eyes glowed, her full lips pursed in a pouty whisper. A large sapphire nestled in her breasts reflecting the astonishing blue of her eyes and the stones of the tiara that rested in her golden hair. The Duquesa was a glittering diamond to Graciela's polished quartz.

Her heart began to race, leaving her breathless. Assignment or not, if Charley thought to keep contact with the lady, Graciela would leave him.

Not with Captain Llewellyn. She need not take ship at all. Now that she was married, she was of no value to Lord Kingsley or Carvelle. They would not come after her. She could find some place in England and wait for Papa to return. And if he didn't come soon, she could hire a ship and go look for him. She had the funds now.

The music started and she tried in vain to turn her attention to the dance. Mr. Gibson blithely rescued her and covered her missteps. As the dancers moved and formed new boxes, she finally met with Charley.

"What did Llewellyn want?" he whispered.

She managed what she hoped was a sweet smile.

"I love you," he said, without lowering his voice, a frown coloring his words.

He was jealous, and when she looked, the Duquesa's eyebrow lifted. And what in the name of God did that mean?

When the interminable dance finally ended, Charley came to join her and Bink, the Duquesa dangling her fingers along his arm.

She pointedly removed them and gave him a little nudge. "There you go, Mrs. Everly. I have returned your new husband to you."

He was never yours to return. Graciela pressed her lips together to hold back the words, her cheeks burning.

"And I wish you every happiness." The woman was still talking. "Such an enchanting gown you are wearing. I do like it much better than your attire the last time we met." That came with a warm smile.

Perhaps she did not need to hate the Duquesa. She eased in a breath. *"Es verdad." It is true.*

Mr. Gibson groaned. "Gowns, Charley. We are to talk of gowns?"

The Duquesa noticed him for the first time, letting her eyes linger on his wide shoulders and broad chest, and Graciela's ire rose again. It was good Paulette was not present.

Charley made introductions.

"I spent a few years in your country, Duquesa," Mr. Gibson said affably. "Ciudad Rodrigu, Badajoz, Vitoria. Madrid was quite interesting."

"You were with your Duke Wellington?"

He smiled. "Yes."

Charley took Graciela's arm. "The quadrille is mine, I believe."

"Wait." The Duquesa looked over her shoulder, and the tiniest of shivers went through her. "Do not forget what I have said."

Graciela followed her line of sight and chilled also. Next to her, Charley tensed. A man approached, parting the huddle of guests, like Francisca's *tlahuelpuchi* searching for a source of blood. All eyes followed, greedy for a spectacle.

Her legs twitched with the need to run.

"Steady." Charley breathed the word into her ear. "Your Excellency." He bowed, as did his brother, and made introductions.

Doubt churned in her. Charley knew the man, and yet had dallied with the wife, or had led everyone to believe so. This was indeed a dangerous game.

Yet one could see why the Duquesa would prefer Charley. Though, he was handsome enough, this Duque, stuffed into his velvet coat and decorated with many ribbons. Gray streaked his temples and deep wrinkles carved the skin around his silver eyes. A paunch marred the line of his coat, but his shoulders were wide, his bearing haughty. His bold gaze sliced her from head to foot.

He was familiar to her, yet she knew she'd never once met him.

"So, you have taken a bride of your own." The Duque's deep voice flowed like honey, but his silvery gaze threatened the sword. "And how lovely she is. Perhaps I should honor you with a dance, my dear."

Those last words had dripped seductively from lips pulled back in a sneer.

Charley held her more firmly. "I'm afraid the next dance is mine."

The first bars of the music were starting, and the Duque was blocking their route to the dance floor.

The man chuckled without smiling. "So, you are the daughter of the infamous Captain Kingsley."

Infamous? Fire ravaged her cheeks and her neck while she sought for a response that would not bring down brimstone.

From the corner of her eye, she spotted Lord Kingsley stepping into this blaze, his wife hovering behind in the crowd.

A trembling started in her chest. All that was needed was for Gregory Carvelle to appear.

She smoothed her free hand along the secret pocket and lifted her chin.

Charley's grip on her hand firmed even more, and she caught his meaning. *Do not speak. I will handle this.*

She squeezed his hand back and defiantly dropped it. "Lord Kingsley," she said.

Her tormenter drew closer. "So, you have married."

"Indeed, we have, today, by special license at Shaldon House." Her traitorous voice shook.

"Or so you think you have married." He ignored her, keeping his gaze on Charley.

"Oh, we're married," Charley said. "With Graciela's guardian's permission."

"I am her guardian, and you did not have my permission," Kingsley growled.

"By the terms of the guardianship, only one signature was required." Shaldon had explained this to her. "Lord Shaldon is one of my guardians."

Kingsley had heard her, no doubt, because his face all but exploded in purple, but his gaze stayed on Charley, as if Charley were the ventriloquist, and she, his doll.

The Duque raised an eyebrow and smirked at both men. "It will make for a pretty English lawsuit, no? The second guardian kidnapping the ward and signing over her fortune to his own son? She is a dainty one, though, Kingsley. Not wild as you described. Perhaps you employed the wrong sort of rod to control her, eh."

Graciela gasped, her temper rising. "You are without shame," she said in Spanish.

"*Si, si.*" Again came that unsmiling chuckle like a groan in his throat. His arrogant face grew hard. "*Cuidado.*"

"It is you who should be careful," Charley said. His eyes had hardened.

Her heart raced. Had she not seen her father stand up to such challenges? Swindling traders, threatening thieves, and rebellious seamen. And a real man must stand up to this devil.

And Charley was a real man.

On her other side, Mr. Gibson moved closer until she was crushed between the brothers. Behind her was the cool wall, in front of her two beasts of the apocalypse, and behind them, the wall of greedy faces.

One of those faces was Captain Llewellyn's. He had offered his help. He was no friend of Kingsley, he'd said. And now he stood and merely watched like the rest.

As the moment dragged on, a heavy fist circled her lungs and began to squeeze. She stood very still and tried to breathe.

"Lord Kingsley. Duque." Lord Shaldon elbowed his way in, pointing his cane at the men. "Come to congratulate my son and my new daughter? How kind, but you are causing a spectacle. Disrupting the dancing."

His words cloaked a pointed message, just as surely as his cane must be sheathing a sword.

"It shall not stand, Shaldon," Kingsley said.

"But it shall. They were married before dinner, before all of the family. It is done."

"It is *not* done. She is *not* of age. I did *not* approve."

"But Kingsley," the Duque said, "let them stay married." He glanced at his wife. "Else the girl will be ruined. No one will want Everly's cast-off."

Nothing changed in the Duquesa's face or demeanor. Her marriage must have dealt her many such dishonorable, undignified insults.

No shame. No dignity. No honor. No wonder the lady had looked for love elsewhere.

"She was brought to me ruined, her and her brat."

"Kingsley." Charley's voice held a warning. He took a step forward.

Graciela grabbed his hand and tugged at him. "No." Let it be said. Let them begin with no lies. "Kingsley is right. The child is mine."

Charley gazed at her a long moment and smiled. "And now she is mine also."

"And a grandchild to me," Lord Shaldon said.

"And a niece to me," Mr. Gibson said. "Like Graciela, she is family now and under our protection."

Kingsley's face purpled.

The Duque's lip curled. "Pah. You see how these colonial women are? Cuckolded already, Everly. How does it feel?"

Charley opened his mouth, but Kingsley spoke first. "How dare your father foist a half-black bastard on me?"

"Easy now." Mr. Gibson said. "There's a fine gentleman. Easy."

The Duque laughed and bared yellow teeth. "Such an interesting night. Yes, Kingsley, unless you are looking for pistols at dawn with the Earl's eldest son, do temper your words. In my time in Veracruz I saw that the lack of civilization drives men to make certain compromises with the natives. In any case to be born on the wrong side of a noble bed is no terrible thing."

His time in Veracruz?

Kingsley huffed. "That was no noble breeding, I'll warrant."

"The Kingsley blood is not noble?" Charley asked.

"Enough." Lord Shaldon's cane lifted again, this time directed at his son.

"Yes, enough," the Duque said. "Well, Shaldon, I take it you and your son have finished with my wife. Have you found the spy you were looking for?"

"London is filled with spies," Shaldon said languidly.

"Yes." He peered down his nose at Charley. "Are you going to send this one again into someone else's bed?"

She gasped, and the silver eyes turned on her. Gunmetal grey, as hard as granite, a Duque. In Tampico, people had whispered of a man with those eyes. A silver-eyed Spaniard known for his cruelty. *El Tlahuelpuchi* some had called him, a monster who had killed even the women and children after he'd let his men rape them.

Dios. If those stories were true, if it was him...he would be a cruel husband. No wonder his wife dallied with others. "Yes, my dear. Your husband searches for information in bedrooms. He has been looking for a spy, who as it turns out, is dead." Those yellow teeth grew larger. "How clever you are to hold onto him after he was done with you."

Her mind was reeling. Charley had pursued her for information? That could not be true.

A cold chill went through her, Papa's last conversation coming back to her. He could not know of that.

Is it true?

Charley turned her to him, and lifted her chin. "No." He shook his head. "We will talk at home." He wrapped an arm about her. "Bink, Father, we are leaving."

"Oh, not yet." The Duque moved closer, pushed by the crowd perhaps. His scent wafted into the air, warring with Charley's. "I am not finished. I have not given my felicitations to your match. So perfect an arrangement—a duplicitous spy, and the daughter of a duplicitous traitor."

The room darkened, her outward vision blurring. Pictures cascaded, her father whispering instructions. The book he had given her to keep safe. The dagger. The instructions to seek out Lord Shaldon in the event of Papa's death or other dire need.

Charley was tugging her away, but she dug in her heels. "I would rather hear out this Spaniard. Say what you wish to say about my father."

"Your father. A traitor to England, and then a traitor to Spain, and who knows who he was betraying when he was killed."

"My father was not a traitor." Her fingers grasped the hilt of her hidden blade. Before she could jerk the blade out of its sheath, another hand touched that arm. Mr. Gibson's hand.

The room swam around her, the lights blurring and hazing. Her father was not a traitor, and why did none of these men who defended her not speak up? Why did they not defend Papa?

He wasn't a traitor. He had taken up Spanish citizenship for love, to marry her mother, and when the Spanish cruelty became too much, he had joined in the cause of independence.

"A traitor. A pirate. A spy. It was he your Mr. Everly was tracking. A pity your quarry, Captain Kingsley, is dead, Everly."

Her stomach roiled. Charley had been after her father? He had used her? A vise gripped her throat and black dots scattered her field of vision.

She drew in a deep breath and choked on the dense air.

"Easy breaths, Gracie." Charley's arms supported her. "Try again."

"Move back." Mr. Gibson's voice created a space around her.

"Deep and easy breaths, my love."

My love. The words were like hartshorn, making her gulp in air, bringing her around until finally her vision cleared.

Charley's gaze burned into her, a mask of concern.

Concern he could easily fake. He was a consummate actor. He had used her to go after her father. He had secured access to her money, permanently.

And yet, and yet...how could she believe this Duque over Charley? Charley had never even hinted an interest in her father's last quiet words.

She didn't believe that anyone knew what Papa had said to her, or that they would understand. She certainly didn't.

But she could bluff. She must learn to be as good an actor as Lord Shaldon and his son.

"You betrayed me," she whispered, and it was not hard to fake heartbreak.

"No. Never." He glanced at the two villains, his eyes blazing as she had never seen them do.

"No," she said, and turned his face toward her. "No duel. I beg you, Charley," she whispered, and then said more loudly, "Everyone can see how little honor is in these men. And," she returned to a shaky whisper, "I shall kill you myself when we are home."

CHAPTER TWENTY-SIX

Charley's heart cheered, and he came close to laughing. She was threatening to kill him, so all was not lost. He held her gaze as long as possible. "I do love you," he said.

Lord Bakeley approached. "The coaches are ready."

She shook her head. "I am not finished." Her voice was far stronger than he would have expected and she drew herself up like a queen in her silver gown. The two villains turned from his father, faces taut, at what Father had been saying.

"Duque. Or shall I call you, *El Tlahuelpuchi*?"

The Duque barely blinked at being called a vampire, but she had struck a nerve.

She nodded to Father. "My lord."

The two villains looked over her head.

Shaldon nodded back, his face an enigma. Their world had just collapsed, and Father looked as serenely satisfied as he had at dinner. The thought angered him.

"Pray, your Excellency, where *is* your dukedom?" she asked.

The Spaniard eyed her, the only sound the shuffle of dresses. The orchestra had even ceased playing.

"San Sebastiano." The Duquesa said.

A liveried footman eased closer, and he recognized one of her guards.

His heart eased. He had used the lady, it was true, as she had used him, an interlude made more exciting for both of them by the danger. And she had risked much to pass notes and whisper secrets, including the one she had shared tonight.

"Yes." Graciela nodded. "You are the one. San Sebastiano. Gray eyes like a frozen river. *Gordo*, your stomach as big as Napoleon's. I have heard the tales." Gracie pulled herself higher on a cord of tension.

He squeezed her hand, transmitting strength, courage, love.

She glanced at him a moment and turned back. "So clever you are, Duque. You are right that my husband is looking for a traitor. And I have the key to one." Her lips stretched in a thin smile directed at Kingsley. "You are not so clever in naming him, however. *He* is *not* my father."

She pulled her hand free and reached for Shaldon's arm. "And *cousin*." She spat the word out like it was poisoned. "After you embezzled my trust, beat me, and tried to force me to marry your wife's pirate cousin, there was no question I would flee, but you might wish to ponder why I sought sanctuary with the lord who set his son to seek out a traitor."

A red glaze was creeping over Kingsley's face. His eyes fixed on her.

She looked up at Father. "May we go now?"

"Yes, my dear. But let Charles take you out."

"See here," Kingsley thundered, and reached for her.

Shaldon stepped between them, Bink backing him up.

Pushed up behind the Duque, Llewellyn looked on, and whispering in his ear was the fellow he'd met at the club: Payne-Elsdon.

Interesting, that.

To their left, the Duquesa was fleeing, flanked by her guards, her survival instincts as excellent as ever.

Charley hooked an arm around Gracie, sweeping her along, through the buzzing crowd, down the stairs, through the ranks of footmen and Shaldon's men to the waiting coach. He spotted Llewellyn in the crowd tracking them, Elsdon following nearby. Were they together?

"Get in, love," he said.

When she balked, he tossed her into the coach and climbed in behind her.

She was shaking, and from the thunderous look on her face, fear was only a part of it. Never mind. They would weather this storm.

"By God, you were magnificent." In fact, she had been quite believable. The reporters would be dashing off their copy as they ran to ink the presses, speculating on the name of the traitor she'd claimed to know. "I am glad you did not pull that dagger on them."

She stiffened.

"Yes, I knew of the dagger. And that was an excellent bluff. Kingsley will be packing his bags and fleeing to his country estate until the smoke clears."

Her stony silence made the air inside the coach hum. Her gaze stayed on the closed window shade, as if she could see through it.

When his father climbed in to join them, surprisingly nimble, and Kincaid followed, both men looked smug and satisfied.

Charley's anger stirred.

"Perpetua will ride with Jane," Shaldon said. "Will you tell us what you know, Graciela?"

He bristled. "Gracie was bluffing, father."

Her gaze dropped to the silver lace reticule she was strangling. And she bit her lip. His heart clenched and froze, and began to heat.

She hadn't been bluffing. She'd known something all along, something she hadn't shared with him.

Farnsworth had set him on this path. Farnsworth had known something. Farnsworth had set him onto the Duquesa and somehow, at the same time, onto Gracie. He was as devious as father.

Charley wanted to laugh. He wanted to punch something—or someone, preferably the missing Farnsworth.

He unwound her fingers from the reticule and gripped them. "By God, Father," he said. "You may not importune her for information. The war is over. It does not matter."

Her chin dropped to her chest, tearing half of his heart with it. They had only just married, and he was losing her, and his father sat calmly looking on.

He forced his hands to relax, to not squeeze hers. None of this was her doing.

He knew now what his brothers had gone through. And what Father must have gone through ten years before.

He squeezed his eyes and tried to blot out his last memory of his mother, broken, bloated, and dead on the Yorkshire cliffs. Gracie was alive, and he must keep her that way.

"Father, it doesn't matter what Gracie knows. Even if we find the man, it will not bring Mother back to life."

Gracie jerked. She gasped, and as if her breath was pumping into his chest he felt her surprise.

"Charley is right," Kincaid said with his usual aplomb. The tension inside the coach hadn't touched him at all. "And we have other fish to snare. Carvelle has resurfaced. Off to Kent he is. There's a boat off the coast we've been watching. We've recalled the revenue officer he had in his pocket. Sent in a new one to give him a little surprise."

Carvelle's absence from London eased his worry.

"So he *is* a smuggler?" Gracie asked.

"Built an empire on it," Kincaid said. "But the war is over, and he's had some losses recently. Calling in debts, he is."

"Debts?" She glanced up at Charley, and then at the other two, and bit her lip. "So, as we thought, my dowry and I were supposed to pay off some debt of Kingsley's."

"Yes."

"Something illegal," she mused. "Something secret."

"Perhaps," Kincaid said, "Or perhaps just a bad investment, a ship taken by pirates or some such."

Or perhaps a ship taken in the West Indies by a privateer?

While she looked away, holding her peace, he pondered the possibilities, and reminded himself, she had more secrets she had not shared, not even with him.

Graciela spotted Lord Shaldon's butler opening the house door before the carriage had even stopped. She had lifted the curtain a fraction while the men talked. Her brain was a terrible blur, her inner vision filled with strong men—dark-haired, red-haired, old and young, and one tawny-haired fellow whose chest bore the scar of a blade, whose hand even now engulfed one of her own and would not let go.

The great bulky carriage stopped with a flurry of action. The man called Kincaid jumped out. Charley cupped some hidden away weapon, still clutching her hand.

"Let me out, Charley." She nudged his unmoving bulk.

Only when Kincaid signaled that all was clear did Charley climb out and pull her into his arms.

"Put me down. I can walk."

Grinning all the way to the entrance hall, he finally set her on her feet. "Lest you've forgotten it's our wedding night."

Memories of the previous night's pleasure flooded her, and she shook them off. She needed some time away from these men. She needed to think about what the Duque had said, about what her Papa had said, and the secrets he'd left in her care.

"I'm going to go see that Reina is alright."

His hands stroked her arms. "You know she's asleep now, else we would hear her."

Lord Shaldon's steps echoed, and he and his men moved down the hall towards the library.

Charley must have seen them with the spy's eyes in the back of his head. "We must go and talk to Father first."

She tried to pull away. "*You* go and talk to your father."

"And what? Manage your life for you? Don't you want to hear it for yourself when Father says the name of the traitor he's after?"

One footman remained in the hall with them, pretending not to listen. She moved closer and whispered, "Who is it?"

"I don't know."

His brown eyes glowed in the light of the entryway lamp, rich, dark, and enticing. Warmth touched her where his hands rested. Only warmth, no pressure.

"The spy is *not* my father."

"I believe you. And I wasn't sent to spy on you." He screwed up his mouth. "As far as I know. But, how *did* I wind up at your betrothal ball? I must ask Perry about that invitation. Very likely, Farnsworth knew that once I laid eyes upon you I'd be interested. That was true, and from the moment you shushed me in Kingsley's garden, I was yours."

Like molten honey, the words trickled in, soothing her.

But—he was a consummate liar. She had to toughen her heart and play at his game. But how?

She could counter that she had become his, but at what moment?

When she'd fainted into his arms? When she'd met him in the Kingsley kitchen the night she'd escaped? Or was it when his eyes had lit up at the sight of her little girl. Or...when he'd kissed Rigo's brand...

She blinked and looked at his neck cloth, still perfectly creased. He had made her forget about the horrible times, had made her feel again. And she still didn't altogether know what he had planned for her. It was too much. It had happened too quickly, and what could she do about it? If she were to escape this, she would have to leave part of her heart behind.

"It seems I am yours also, Charley, at least for this time."

"Let it be for all time." He bent and put his lips to her forehead.

She squeezed her eyes closed. She must not sink into these warm feelings. She must think.

And he was right, she needed to know what Shaldon would say, and then she could decide how to proceed.

"Yes. Of course. As you say. For all time." She shook him off, slipped under his arm and headed down the corridor toward the library.

Charley caught up and she waited for his touch on her arm, her hand, her waist. It did not come. When she glanced at him, he was staring ahead.

A tiny piece of her heart ripped and she straightened her shoulders. Let him be angry. Should the secrets she carried require her to leave, it would be easier if he was setting the first little bit of distance.

Scattered candles brought light to the room. A lamp illuminated Lord Shaldon in an armchair and another man across the library table, his back to the door. Outside the circle of light, Mr. Kincaid stood resting his hands on a chair. Relaxed, but he was the sort of man who could, one second later, pick up that chair and swing it at a threat.

Her skin rippled. He was dangerous, this Kincaid. As was Lord Shaldon. As was Charley. And probably the man in the chair. Not to her, not as long as she stayed in their light. If she stepped out of it...

They heard her approach and rose, tall men all of them. The visitor turned.

Her heart all but stopped—here was another faker. "I know you," she said.

A smile quirked his lips. "And I hope you are enjoying your fine bedchamber, miss." He spoke with an underlay of the east side.

"Mr. Cooper."

He shook his head. "I am sorry for my deception."

Ah now, his speech was all *tonny* Mayfair.

"I am Farnsworth."

Farnsworth? This man had organized workmen in her bedchamber at Kingsley House, hanging paper, varnishing floors, burnishing furniture, fixing windows.

He had sought her out several times, changing the plans to her liking and graciously taking her Ladyship's threats of nonpayment at the results. He had befriended Graciela. He had talked to her.

And just as he was entertaining Lady Kingsley's dreams of a grander redecorating of the rest of the house, he was gone. Shortly after, word came that Papa had died, and a new man had had to be contracted for draperies and paint and wall hangings.

"Farnsworth," she said again, and disliked that her voice shook. He had kept his identity a secret. She was sure the Kingsleys had not known him. But why?

The answer crept over her. He did not trust them. He was spying on them.

Or—on her?

She wobbled and straightened herself. Charley had not stepped up to join her and she must steady her own self. "You left."

The man called Farnsworth took her hand. "Please sit. Charles, pull that chair over." He helped her onto the cushioned seat. "Some sherry, I think, Charles."

Charley's frown buoyed her. He went to do Farnsworth's bidding, as he had done for Mrs. Windle the night Graciela had escaped.

When she looked, Lord Shaldon was back in his chair, his lips turned up ever so slightly.

Dios. She took the proffered glass and only touched it to her lips before setting it away. She would need all her wits about her even among these so-called friends.

"Word came last winter. Napoleon's health was failing. A dreadful voyage, St. Helena is. Have you journeyed that far south, my dear?"

He was making small talk, and being most deceptive. He'd not had time to travel that far and come back. Was this how spies questioned their quarry?

She nodded. "Yes, further, actually. Not on that side of the Atlantic, though. It is a trip of several months." They had traveled around Cape Horn to Valparaiso, and then north, and more than once. She had been but a child the first time, and the storms had been terrifying. "I have never been so cold in my life, that is, until I came here."

"I'm sorry." Farnsworth's eyes were a velvety brown. He was younger than Lord Shaldon, younger even then her father, she would guess. A bit of gray showed above his ears, but the lines on his face hadn't settled. A handsome enough man he was, with the kind of face that would mold into any disguise.

At his age, he might have offered for her himself if he were unmarried. However, Mr. Cooper's interest had never been amorous. Now, as then, he was all kindness.

"Your father counted that family pride and generous access to your trust funds would keep you and the child safe. Nevertheless, he did not entirely trust Lord Kingsley and his lady. Her connections have always been—questionable."

"Gregory Carvelle is her cousin."

"Indeed. When I left, the child seemed well cared for by your servants, and you were outfitted well. I made sure that your rooms were the first stare."

She swallowed a lump. The rooms had been a beautiful refuge, for a while. "Her ladyship never stopped complaining about the changes, but when the news came about my father, she took those rooms."

"Good God," Charley muttered.

Farnsworth's mouth firmed.

She waved a hand in the air. "I am a colonial girl and a sea captain's daughter. I have slept in huts, and windowless cabins, and even out in the open air. The new bedchamber where they put me was better because I was closer to Reina, and I was able to more easily escape. I am not a fairy tale princess."

Charley shifted and her gaze met his. "You are my princess," he mouthed, pointing at himself.

Her cheeks warmed. She bit her lips and rubbed at a spot on the chair arm. She must fight the temptation. Never mind that it was her wedding night. She did not want to be swept away tonight, unless she was swept out the door, with her servants and child—well, and perhaps Charley also—to some anonymous lodging far from this tangle.

None of it had been her doing. She had been good. She had been dutiful. When Papa said he must leave them in Tampico, she'd hugged him goodbye and stayed. When Mama said they must go to Veracruz, she'd gone along on the journey. When Papa said to stay with the Kingsleys until he returned, she'd stayed.

Stay here with my cousin. You will be safe. Should my journey be long or unsuccessful, I've set up a trust for you. I've set up guardians until you come of age. You must be strong, Graciela.

She had tried to be strong. And time had inched on during Papa's absence but it was still almost three years until she reached her majority. And now none of that mattered because she had stepped off the edge of the deck and plunged into marriage.

Lord Shaldon cleared his throat. "I know it has been a very tiring day and night, but will you share with us what you know, my dear?"

More memories crushed her.

Reaching Veracruz had not brought them safety. First there was the fighting between the Spanish and the rebels. Then illness came, weakening them.

And the fever had not killed her mother. Before he left England, Papa had told her the truth, his words turning her grief upside down. While Graciela was sweating and writhing, Mama had recovered and had been murdered, and Consuela with her.

Papa had ordered her to keep the murder secret, but surely Captain Llewellyn had been helping him search for whoever was behind Mama's murder. That was why Papa left England, to sail back and join Captain Llewellyn.

They were all watching her. Only Charley's eyes showed an identifiable emotion, because he hadn't hardened as these men had, because he wasn't really a spy.

Because she knew him and loved him.

She sniffed and twisted her hands. She'd always been able to read Papa, too, until that last day together.

If the worst comes, the book holds all I have found. If you are in danger, go to Lord Shaldon. If I should die—only then—take the book to him, and tell him it is not for the Crown. If the worst comes, Lord Shaldon can be trusted. Until then, you must hold it for me.

Papa was *not* dead. She must not share his words.

"I lied." She eased in a breath.

But who would have killed Mama?

I intend to find out, and there is another matter I must look into. You'll stay with my cousin. You'll be safe there.

She knew Lady Shaldon was dead, but Charley's words implied that she'd been murdered also.

She would share that much. "My father was looking for someone. He was looking for the man who m-murdered my mother."

She looked through her lashes at Charley. His face had set into a tense mask.

"She did not die of the fever as I told you."

Tell no one, Graciela.

The terrible burden of this secret lifted. "I lied then also. Papa told me to keep to that story." *I'm sorry, Papa. I'm just a weak, stupid, stupid girl.*

Her vision clouded and she blinked furiously trying to clear it.

A handkerchief was pressed into her hand, and she lifted it to her eyes, Charley's scent filling her. A great sob rocked through her, and she pressed the cloth to her mouth to hold it back, conscious of the men waiting around her.

The weight of everything—their presence, her father's words, his books, his secrets— pressed down upon her.

An arm came around her, a large hand pulling her head to a broad shoulder, lending her strength while her breathing eased.

She lifted her head and looked into Charley's eyes level with hers as he knelt beside her.

"Would you tell us the rest, please, Graciela?" Shaldon asked. "I promise you, it won't leave this room."

"Father, she's been through enough tonight."

He thought to speak for her? But the tone had been kind. He was not trying to bully her.

She squeezed his hand. "Lord Shaldon, how could whatever I say not leave this room, if it leads you to take some action against..." She shook her head. "Someone. Someone who is a traitor, or someone who killed Charley's mother, or mine?"

Lord Shaldon blinked once, twice. "You will have our promise, daughter," he said. "Mine, Kincaid's, Farnsworth's, and of course, your husband's."

She dabbed her eyes again. "I have promised my father. Unless he is dead...and I will not believe it on the word of those men Captain Llewellyn picked out of the water."

"Llewellyn was there tonight," Charley said, "lurking about."

"We plan to investigate," Shaldon said. "If you have anything that will help us—"

"*It is not for the Crown*," she said.

Charley's hand stilled.

"Papa's words. If he died, go to you and give you..." She swallowed more tears. "And I must tell you 'it is not for the Crown.' But if he is alive, and he comes back, I will have betrayed him."

"We know your father," Farnsworth said. "All of us except Charley. We'll explain to him when he returns. We'll keep his secrets, and if we can, we will use them to help find him, or to find out what happened to him."

She looked at Charley.

"It is a hard choice, Gracie," he said. "But something is very fishy about Kingsley, Llewellyn and Carvelle. Throw in the Duque too, and," his mouth firmed, "another man who I met the other night at the club, a Major Payne-Elsdon, recently in Spain. He was hovering near Llewellyn tonight." He squeezed her hand. "In any case, with or without your secrets, I intend to take action."

"How?" she asked.

"We will all take action," Shaldon said.

"I will know what that is before I speak."

Charley's gaze narrowed on his father. "Does this have to do with Pamplona, Father?"

"What is Pamplona?" she asked.

"Your father had a deep commitment to your mother, my dear," Shaldon said, "and a great loathing for Spain. He has thrown his support to the rebels of New Spain."

They had completely ignored her questions. Very well, she would hold her peace for now and see where this was leading.

"This I already know about my father, my Lord. Do you know who killed my mother?"

"No." Kincaid spoke. "Yet perhaps whatever Captain Kingsley asked you to safeguard might help us discern the truth."

"It is up to you, Gracie," Charley said.

Up to her.

Papa always said, on a ship, the captain decided everything. He was god as far as the gunwale, and then the sea ruled, and one must learn how to roll with old Neptune's changes. Like these men, the sea played its games and hid its secrets. Papa might be alive, or he might be dead, but either way, he'd left this charge to her. And she would have their help.

Forgive me, Papa.

"He told me, he told me, she said, 'the book holds all I have found'. Later, after that, he gave me a prayer book in Spanish with a blade in the spine, but nothing else. I did check the bindings. I read every page." *Dios*, by then she had needed those prayers. "I examined the pages in front of a candle. I washed them in vinegar. I could see nothing."

The men continued their silent study. Charley's arm lent his strength.

"It was big, this book. I could not manage it going out the window. I left it behind."

"Has Kingsley sent over your things?" Shaldon asked.

"Only the gowns I arrived with. Not the new ones, not my brushes and combs, and not the book."

"I'll go tonight for it," Charley said, getting to his feet. "I'll take Juan. He'll know the window to access."

"You mean to break in?" She stood. "Then I will go with you."

"It's too dangerous."

"For you as well. I will not sit here idly while you go climbing the side of a London house."

Charley edged closer, his eyes gleaming. "I have some experience at that. You don't."

"I have climbed ship ladders. I have climbed masts. I have climbed cliffs and I know where we must go."

"No."

"You obstinate man. If you are going, I am going also."

Lord Shaldon cleared his throat. "Graciela, my dear, is that the only book you possessed?"

His lordship almost lolled in his seat, as did Farnsworth.

Charley inhaled sharply and reached for her hand. "*Shall I compare thee to a summer's day?*"

Her heart pounded. The sonnets.

"*But thy eternal summer shall not fade.*"

"The book of sonnets was my mother's. She used it to help her learn English."

He raised her hand to his lips. "*When in eternal lines to time thou growest, so long as men can breathe, or eyes can see, so long lives this, and this gives life to thee.*"

Tears came then, and she could not stop them nor stop from trembling. He pressed her to his chest.

They had been at sea when Papa put the book into her hands. He could only bear to part with it, he said, if she would keep it safe until his return.

Papa's heart had not truly broken. It had hardened with a need for justice.

Forgive me, Papa.

"Might we see this book of sonnets?" his Lordship asked.

"I will get it," Charley said.

"No, I will go." She stepped back and bumped the chair, almost plopping into it. He steadied her.

"We'll be back in a moment, Father."

Charley followed her as she ran up the stairs, her skirts raised high to show her slim ankles. He could see her as a hoyden climbing everywhere, just like Reina, outrunning all the danger around her.

Her mother had been murdered, just like his. He would not let this woman from his sight.

Her bedchamber had been set up for their wedding night, lush bedding turned down, a covered tray upon the table, an open bottle of wine breathing next to it. Francisca pushed through the dressing room door with her customary scowl.

He snagged a biscuit from the tray. "We will not need you, Francisca. You may return to Reina."

Gracie sent him a glare and went to the bedside drawer. "We must return downstairs," she said in Spanish. "Here it is." She quickly hugged the maid. "I shall be all right," she said, and headed for the door.

"She will be." He took two steps and grasped the maid's bony hands. "I will take care of her."

He would. By God, he would. Tonight, he would get her through this next discovery.

CHAPTER TWENTY-SEVEN

A little while later, Charley was seated next to Gracie at the library table, watching as Kincaid took the tiny book apart.

"Never liked a book for messages," Kincaid said. "I much preferred script hidden in a cane or saddle pommel or a boot, or a coded open letter."

She bristled next to him, ever defensive of her father.

"But I do admire resilience and adaptability." Kincaid had noticed her reaction, the wily old trickster. "What do you suppose, miss, he might have written here?"

"I do not know."

She was telling the truth. He glanced at his father and Farnsworth.

A few worn pages held handwritten words, notes by Gracie's mother, words of love in her father's writing. No code in those.

Kincaid's beefy hands were as deft and as delicate as a diamond setter's.

Farnsworth, on her other side, leaned closer. "I should not like to bring up painful memories, but whatever you can remember will help us. Did Captain Kingsley say anything more about your mother's death?"

Charley touched her shoulder, feeling her tense and sent the old spies a warning glare. There was more, he was quite sure, but now that her first secrets were out, she needed time to face this. She needed more time to *trust*.

Lord Shaldon ignored him. "What Lord Farnsworth means, is, it might help to understand the motive, my dear." His voice was gentle. "And that might help us in our search for the killer."

"You do mean to search?" she asked.

"We shall do more than search," Charley said. "We'll find and bring to justice."

She sent him a quick glance, as if realizing he was still there, and blinked, unseeing, frozen to her seat. "Money?" Her gaze went to the window. "Is it not always money that is the cause in these disputes?"

"Sometimes 'tis love," Kincaid said without looking. "Or a need to silence someone who knows the truth." His razor slid through a stitch and he inhaled sharply.

As much emotion as Charley had ever seen in him.

"Clever," Kincaid muttered. With the tiniest of tweezers, he withdrew a folded paper. He slipped on a pair of cotton gloves.

"Let me." Gracie pushed back her chair and stood. "It is mine, after all."

Father nodded, and Kinkaid yielded his seat at the table. Charley went to look over her shoulder.

The filmy paper was so thin, it might have been transparent, but it was new, fresh, and stable. She worked with care, her small hands unfolding the document.

The writing was too tiny to read from here, but he could see handwritten lists marching down the paper in even rows.

She peered closely. "If these are dates, they go back to before I was born."

His father's eyes lit, and Charley's gut clenched. This was a code of some sort.

Codes were not his area of expertise. Codes required analytical precision, and only agreed upon irregularity. "Father, when you have deciphered this, Gracie must know what it is."

She looked up. "You think it is a cipher?"

"Yes." Shaldon pinched his brows together. Charley knew that look. It was the spymaster reflexively holding back from sharing. Father hated revelations, unless they were someone else's. "I met your father years ago. He became a Spanish citizen with his majesty's blessing, though he would have done so anyway to win your mother. He sent reports whenever he could, and we had a code that we worked with. I believe we can work this one out. But Graciela, will you tell us everything he told you about your mother's death? Every piece of information will help."

She dropped her gaze, her long lashes hiding her eyes. "We lodged in a small house in the center of Veracruz and waited for Father's return. And then the fever came and Mother fell sick first. When our friend, Consuela—there were five of us, six with Reina in the small house—when Consuela became ill, we made Francisca and Juan take Reina away, out of the town. My mother, she began to recover. She was so very weak, but the fever broke and she was able to get up and to help with Consuela who by this time was very, very ill. And then the sickness struck me."

Charley crouched by her chair, took her hands, and began chafing them. She had gone cold, trembling as if the fever and chills were still upon her.

"Mama put me into her bed in the tiny bedchamber. Consuela was on a pallet in the parlor and neither of us could move her. How many days passed, I do not know. Mama came in and out, and then Captain Llewellyn was there, and then Papa. He stayed by my bedside and when the fever broke, he told me Mama and Consuela had died. Of the fever, I assumed. He buried them, sent for Reina, Francisca, and Juan, carried me onto his ship, and we left."

The parts she was leaving out, her grief, her father's anguish, were tearing her up inside. Her turmoil churned inside of him.

"Before he left England to return to Mexico, he told me the truth. Captain Llewellyn had arrived in the port hours before Papa and had gone right to Mama's to tell her the ship would follow closely and to check on them. Captain Llewellyn had surprised a man. He found Mama and Consuela dead."

"Who was he?" Father exchanged a look with Kincaid.

"I don't know. Captain Llewellyn killed him. Papa saw that body also. He said he didn't recognize the man. He would say nothing more." She glanced down at Charley. "I wanted to question Captain Llewellyn about this."

"We will do that," Charley said.

"Papa trusted him, Charley, like he trusted your father." Her forehead crinkled. "He is leaving soon. So much happened tonight, I'd almost forgot he said that."

"He won't be leaving until he talks to us." His heart hurt. He wanted to wrap her up and take her to bed and show her that he was her champion now. Whatever was to be uncovered from this code, other men would do it. His job was taking care of her.

The three other men might not have been there, they waited so quietly. Not ones to rush their fences. It had kept them alive for this long.

A distant watchman called the hour.

Father sighed audibly.

"What happened after you left Veracruz?"

Farnsworth's gently prodding question was the third crowing cock.

Gracie's face twisted with anguish. She turned her hands and gripped his. "We left in as great a rush as possible. Papa careened all over the Caribbean, hitting this port and that. He wouldn't say why, and I was too weak to press him, and...shut out. He was grieving and so very angry." She choked in a breath. "He had always been jolly with us. Losing Mama..." She looked up at Father. "Losing his wife, in such a way...We were headed for Spain when we stopped in the Azores. He went off to meet someone, and came back, and we changed course for Portsmouth. Then Papa took us to London, and then to Lord Kingsley's country estate. He went back and forth to London, and one day, he pulled me aside and told me what had really happened to Mama, and that he was l-leaving."

She looked at the men. "Then he gave me the prayer book and showed me the blade hidden inside and reminded me—he had already taught me some things—he reminded me how to use it properly."

"We should get the prayer book back also," Kincaid said, "On the chance the Captain had a backup. Did you leave anything else behind, miss?"

She shook her head. "Only clothing and brushes. I brought my jewelry and the money I'd hidden."

He caught Father's nod.

Charley would go to Kingsley House tomorrow to demand his bride's things. With any luck, the Kingsleys would be out, and he would simply push the servants aside and take them.

"Will you promise to tell me what you uncover?" she asked, "Even if you think the knowledge is not good for me. Will you promise to tell me, on your honor as gentlemen?"

All three agreed, their reluctance palpable.

Charley raised her hand to his lips. "I promise you will know everything I know."

She expelled a long breath, pulled her hand away, and reached for the book.

"We will need that," Kincaid said. "If there's a code, it will likely relate to the pages and writing inside. I shall keep it safe, and repair the loose stitching. I promise that."

Graciela closed her eyes for a moment, fatigue settling over her like another suffocating fever.

"You had better, Kincaid." That was Charley's voice. He had stood. He would want to take her to bed, to consummate their marriage.

She longed for his arms, for his comfort, for the pleasure he stirred in her.

She could not let him think he had won her over. She must see the results of Kincaid's analysis, she must see Llewellyn's report, and speak with Llewellyn.

She must check on Reina. The need to see her little girl gripped her. The whole world knew now that Reina was hers.

"Very well. I will go up."

Charley's hand closed on her elbow. "Good night, Father, gentlemen."

"You may stay, if you wish, Charley," she said.

"It is our wedding night." His whisper warmed her neck.

When they reached her floor, she paused on the landing, planning to send him on to bed.

"I'm going with you to the nursery," he said.

"You may do as you wish."

What he wished was apparently to stay glued to her side. In the nursery's outer chamber, Juan jumped to his feet, saluting them. Francisca, he said, was still waiting in Graciela's chamber. A nursemaid was in with the child.

Her child.

The nursemaid dropped her knitting and rose also. "She's sound asleep this last hour," she whispered, and Graciela heard the implied caution.

She put a finger to her lips and went to the small bed.

Her heart swelled and pushed a smile to her lips. Reina curled around the soft knitted shawl that she'd slept with since she was born, her thumb in her mouth, her thick hair spread over the pillow cover. Tiny puffs of breath spelled out her slumber, and a twist of her lip signaled a dream.

Charley touched the tip of one finger to the round cheek and Reina's grimace relaxed. "She'll have a good life." He whispered the promise, his warm breath stirring her.

Graciela straightened the light counterpane, touched a long curl, and let Charley lead her away.

In the outer room she stopped and spoke briefly to Juan. It was right that he should know the truth about Reina. He listened, his face solemn, and then he lifted her hand and kissed it.

She could not speak then. Charley steered her out into the hall.

"It's good we did not wake her," she said finally. "You would have had to hold her awhile."

"I wouldn't mind, though tonight, I'd rather be holding you."

"Charley, I—"

"Holding you, Gracie. Holding you will suffice for a night such as this." He paused at the landing and cast her a wicked grin. "Unless you want to do more."

She reached for the handrail and started down the stairs.

He quickly caught up. "I shall give her our name, with your permission. Or, if you wish she will be Kingsley-Everly. She will have a good life, with aunts and uncles and cousins, and two grandfathers." He stopped. "Your father probably suspected the truth, do you not think?"

Had he? She shook her head.

"Will he—"

"Accept her? I don't know. I hope so. Even in all of his grief, he treated her fondly."

"She's part of you, so he will love her also. She'll have those connections no matter where we take her. And of course, she'll travel with us. She'll have two parents who love her."

Since the moment she fell into his arms, Charley had chipped away at the wall in her heart, and now it threatened to shatter. She breathed in, beating back tears. He could be such a good liar, her Charley, yet she believed these words. Reina believed in him.

It had been right to acknowledge her daughter, and right to bring her under the Earl of Shaldon's protection.

In the light of a hall lamp, she caught Charley's unguarded look, determined, thoughtful, and fierce.

No, she was right to bring her under Charles Everly's protection.

She reached for him and pulled him into a long kiss before breaking away.

"We did not finish our lessons last night because you were being honorable," she said.

"I was." His hand slid around to her breast and began exploring. "And if you're too tired, I won't ask—"

"I'm asking." She smiled up at him.

She wanted that lesson, and then she had more answers to pry from him.

CHAPTER TWENTY-EIGHT

When they entered the bedchamber, Francisca cast Charley a steely-eyed gaze.

He would lock all the damn doors tonight, he would. They would stay abed until at least noon.

He released his hold on Gracie's arm, went to the table, and poured two glasses of wine.

Gracie went to Francisca and a whispered conversation ensued, Spanish flying between the two women. The older woman's stolid gaze softened, and as her questions were answered went stony again.

The servants had indeed not known about Reina's parentage. How remarkable.

Juan's interest had been heartfelt and circumspect. Francisca wanted answers, so many that Charley was pouring himself a second glass, and both women were crying.

And hugging. Francisca fell into Gracie's arms, and they clutched each other as if both of them had just survived a catastrophe.

It was an entirely un-English maneuver.

Then the wiry maid was gripping his hand, perilously close to hugging him.

He bent over the thin hands and thanked her for her loyalty to Gracie and Reina, and promised to protect all of them, including Francisca and Juan. Francisca whispered back, apologies, best wishes and promises of service, patted his shoulder and disappeared from the room.

He met Gracie's stunned gaze. In the lamplight, her eyes glowed with tears.

"Well," he said. "She took that gracefully."

She inhaled deeply, and let her breath out, her shoulders sagging.

"It's a night for truth-telling," he said.

Gracie straightened and a smile touched her lips. "Yes."

"And, apparently, hugging." Charley opened his arms. She flung herself into them.

The hugging was brief. She pulled his head down, pressed her lips to his, and then her hands went to work, pushing his coats off, untying his neck cloth, unfastening his fall.

Need filled him and drove him, his hands on her clothing clumsy. He heard fabric rip and her dress shimmied to the floor.

She turned in his arms. "Get these stays off me, Charley."

He loosened her lacings, raked his fingers through her hair, letting the pins and combs fly, and turned her around again.

They were down to chemise and shirt and stockings.

She moved close and slid her hand between them, gazing up wickedly. "I shall hold you tonight."

He gasped, and clasped his hand over hers. "Stop." He closed his eyes and took a deep breath, searching for a distraction, something to slow his passion. "Else I will pop like a schoolboy before we've even begun."

"Like you did last night?" she asked, grinning.

Delectable. Beautiful. His.

He pulled her hand away, shed the rest of his clothes, picked her up, and carried her to the bed.

Small hands tugged at his shoulders, surprisingly strong, pulling him in for another kiss. Her hands found his back, caressing him everywhere, teasing him.

He flipped onto his back taking her with him. Her hair veiled them, her breasts plumped on his chest.

"Tonight you must finish the lessons," she said.

"I assure you, the lessons will take more than one night."

He rolled her again and explored her body, finding the spots that brought laughter, those that brought pleasure until she was gasping and he was ready to burst.

"Now, Charley." Her legs came around him like the twin arms of a nutcracker.

Crushing his cock between them. "Wait." He pushed her legs down, positioned himself, and studied her face.

She nodded.

He eased in a bit and watched her.

"It does not hurt." She smiled encouragingly.

He eased in more.

"Still good."

He pulled out and plunged in, halfway. She gasped and said, "Oh," a smile spreading over her face.

With his next thrust she pivoted against him and he filled her. And then he began to move in her, meeting her, matching her, waiting, listening for her until she shattered. Only then did he explode deep inside her.

Graciela stretched on her side and watched a beam of sunlight dance over the carpet. It was surely already late morning.

At the same time fingers tickled her side, trailed a path around to her breast, tapped a message that unfurled warmth from her heart to the overheated spot between her legs. As if having him pressed against her backside was not enough.

Charley had awakened, and it was, by her estimation, based entirely on her woman's intuition, a good time to question him.

She grasped the hand planted on her breast. "Charley?"

"*Mmmm.*"

His fingers drifted over her, and she forced her mind back to her mission.

"Who *is* the traitor? We never truly got to that question tonight."

His hand stilled. His whole body tensed.

A tiny flame of irritation sparked in her. She beat it down. "Are you asleep?" She wiggled onto her back, carefully. The lashings were still a bit sensitive, a good reminder of why she needed answers.

While he gazed at her through slitted eyes, she brushed back a lock of hair from his forehead and trailed a finger over his firm jaw, down to the dusting of chest hair. It was strangely darker than the hair on his head. Not burnished by the sun, she supposed. She tried to move her hand further down.

He gripped her wrist. She smiled.

Once he'd plopped her onto the bed, it had been a true wedding night, one without panic, or pain, or bad memories.

And now they must begin the second day of their marriage with more truth-telling.

"Charley, who do *you* think the traitor is? You must have some idea."

He dropped her hand and touched her breast. "Oh, I have an idea."

"I know you do, but, the traitor—"

"You have worn me out." He rolled to his back.

She curled up next to him and touched him. His shaft sprang to attention. His eyes slammed shut, his lips firmed.

He could not fight this desire, no more than she could, and she rolled atop him.

Mere minutes later, both of them sated, she collapsed onto his broad chest. She found his neck and dropped kisses there, where a scratchy scruff had blossomed, her heart so full she could not contain it. "I do love you, Charley," she whispered.

Fingers laced through her hair, massaging her scalp. "I knew you had fallen for me." He grinned at her, his eyes filled with teasing. "I meant what I promised you yesterday afternoon before God and man."

To have and to hold. Until death did them part.

She'd said the words too, but she'd held a tiny part of herself back. If her father returned...

He pushed a strand of hair away from her face and studied her. "It's all right, Gracie. We'll take this one day at a time."

She was far too transparent.

"Charley, you have distracted me. Who do you think is the traitor?"

He drew in a deep breath and draped an arm over his eyes. "Kingsley."

She sat up and dragged his arm away. "No. It cannot be my father."

"Don't be a nodcock. I'm talking about *Lord* Kingsley."

He gave her the slightest of nods. "You asked my opinion."

"My father would not have left me with him if he was a traitor."

"Your father didn't know."

"But surely—"

"Oh, it's too early for this." He patted her bottom. "Get off me. I'll ring for coffee."

"Not until you tell me."

"My guess is your father was working on something else, something to do with the revolution in Mexico, or maybe the Duque's activities. Something to do with smuggling, or shipping. Spain lost a lot ships and a lot of wealth in that part of the world. Maybe he took a ship full of the Duque's plunder. Maybe he was looking for a treasure, and he didn't want what he found to go to the Crown. He wanted it for Mexico. We shall, I hope, find out everything when Kincaid is done with his deciphering." He nudged her, and she rolled off and stood.

"Stay." She pulled on a dressing gown. What had Father said, exactly? The words were hard to conjure. She'd been so shocked by his report of her mother's death, she'd barely understood what he'd said next. She padded to the bell pull, rang, and went to the table.

Charley was waiting there for her, naked as a pearl diver. He grinned crookedly, sending a ripple through her.

He knew what he did to her, but it was a power to be shared. She let her own robe slide from her shoulders, watched his eyes darken and settle on her breasts.

A knock at the door made her pull up the robe and cinch the belt. "Back into bed," she ordered.

He grinned and plopped into a chair. She shook her head, opened the door a crack and ordered coffee and breakfast, then went back to climb onto his lap.

"We have a few minutes," she said.

"You are blessedly insatiable." He pulled her in for a brief kiss. "But *you've* distracted *me*. I'm anxious to hear Kincaid's report."

"You think he's finished?"

"Perhaps. But we have time to eat." He nuzzled her neck. "And something else before."

A note came with the breakfast, saying that Kincaid had not been able to finish his analysis.

It was a reminder that Charley needed to visit Kingsley House today. The second book might be essential to the decoding.

He'd prefer to stay in bed, but Graciela's protection came first, and finding the truth would be the only way to accomplish that.

"I should leave you to a long bath after breakfast," he said. "We shall have to knock a whole in the wall so I can take the next chamber."

She frowned.

"For my dressing room of course. If you can tolerate my snoring we'll share a bed."

Something had her preoccupied and frowning, and it had nothing to do with the room arrangements.

"Charley," she said, between bites of toast, "there is one more thing I want to know."

His nerves tingled, sounding alarm bells. Her quiet good grace, her delicate tone, her refusal to meet his eyes all signaled something unpleasant. "Only one more?"

"Your mother. What happened?"

An ache started in his head, the familiar sorrow souring his stomach, memories cascading in rapid succession.

Time hadn't healed, nor had time let him forget.

"Mother died in a carriage accident, along with her maid and her coachman."

That was the matter-of-fact explanation.

The reality had been something more stark and awful. Her body had shattered on the rocks below the cliff road. Blood smeared the rocks, blood from the horses, the coachman, the maid. Blood from his mother. So much blood. Even now, he had to catch his breath.

"Father doesn't talk about it."

She looked at him, eyes wide and solemn. "It wasn't really an accident?"

He closed his eyes against the memory of his panic. A rider had come to Cransdall Hall with an urgent message for Lord Bakeley. Only, Bakeley had been away, ferrying some horses he'd just purchased, and Perry was off visiting friends.

Father, of course, was out of the country, exactly where, no one knew.

Charley had tossed the message aside and ridden hell bent for the coast, to a cottage he'd never known existed, arriving first, while the locals were still pondering how to remove the shattered bodies.

He set down his fork carefully. "The axle of the carriage was tampered with. Just enough so that the weight of the cases and people on board, and the roughness of the road would break it in two when she reached the narrowest part of the road on the sea cliff. They plunged to the rocks below."

Or so they had surmised, but it was anyone's guess if that was the truth. The axle might well have broken in two when the carriage toppled down the cliff side.

She rose and came around the table to him, her soft arms circling his shoulders, her breasts pressing against him.

"You are looking for her killer," she said.

He sighed. "Yes."

He'd been looking for years, trying to piece together the truth. Father wouldn't speak of it, Bakeley had shared the little he knew years ago. Only the Duquesa had provided new facts.

She took in a sharp breath. "Your father was the intended victim maybe. Was he supposed to travel with her?"

"We don't know."

"The men after Paulette and Lady Sirena—"

"Were not the right ones. Traitors, they were, though. For every ten soldiers trudging across the Continent and Peninsula, there was one man selling secrets, or shorting supplies, or stealing powder to sell to the enemy."

Fingers slid up and laced through his hair, easing the ache.

"And how does Lord Kingsley fit in?"

He sighed, bringing his thoughts back into order. "In the Lords, he had an interest in the Admiralty. And there's his wife. When you trace down her family, you find a network of smugglers that go back three generations."

Her hand stilled. "Like Gregory Carvelle."

"Yes."

"Your mother was killed on the coast? Is that where your country estate is?"

"No. She had a cottage on the coast where she went to meet with my father, when he could come back. We think she had just left from meeting with him, after..." He looked up at her, his eyes burning.

Graciela watched the tension rise in him again. He'd had as chaotic a childhood as herself, and he'd lost a mother in the same horrific way, the sins of the husband visited upon the wife.

Had the children been threatened also? It would explain the fortress mentality of the household.

The thought of someone going after Charley sent chills through her.

Charley's gaze narrowed. "What I'm about to tell you, the others don't know, well perhaps Bakeley knows, but not Perry. Will you promise me you won't share this with them?"

"Yes, of course."

"Before my parents' last meeting, Father had just escaped from the French. He'd been taken prisoner."

A pain whipped through her. "And tortured?"

"No. At least, not much. He was treated relatively well by his captor. He was in Spain, near the border."

"Pamplona," she said. That's what he had meant.

"Yes. His captor was a nobleman who wanted a painting as ransom."

"A painting?"

"Yes."

"Not money."

"No."

"But that makes no sense. What was this painting? Some valuable masterpiece?"

"I suppose it had value, though I always found it dark and depressing. My father had given it to Mother early in their marriage. Where the devil he got it, I don't know, but I'm making guesses. In any event, his captor had learned the painting was in my mother's sitting room at our country estate, Cransdall."

The private fortress of the Shaldons had been invaded by a spy. "A servant betrayed you."

"No. Or, rather, likely not. An exuberant friend of my mother's got wind, and it was mentioned in a news sheet."

"Who is the nobleman?"

Charley's frown deepened.

"*Dios.* The Duque de San Sebastiano," she whispered. "But no, he was in Mexico terrorizing the people there."

His hand clamped over hers and he turned in his chair. "Was he there ten years ago, Gracie?"

Ten years ago, she'd been but a child. "I don't know. I could believe him capable of holding an English earl for a ransom of pride, but I would expect your father to have killed him by now."

He nodded. "Father plays a long game."

She knelt beside him. "I think my father must do so, also." There was so much left unsaid. And nothing made sense. Who would demand a mere painting for a man's life, in the middle of a war? "What was this painting, Charley?"

He grimaced. "The martyrdom of Saints Perpetua and Felicity."

"*What*?"

"Where do you suppose my sister got her name?"

"Where do any of us get our names? I'd never thought about it."

"Mother's name was Felicity. She was a Papist, like her mother."

"A Catholic?" She'd never thought to ask about their faith, assuming that they were like the Kingsleys, who'd insisted she must leave her Catholic faith behind. "And you, Charley?"

"We are all Anglican. Bakeley must be to take his seat in Lords when he inherits. For the rest of us, she said we must decide for ourselves when we are old enough." He stroked a finger down her cheek. "Should you like to say our vows in front of a priest? I will change my faith for you."

She blinked back sudden tears. "You would do that for me?"

It was what Papa had done out of love for her mother.

The Kingsleys had dragged her off for services at their church, but she had not been to a proper Mass since her mother was alive. But, surely, they had made their vows before the same God.

She did not think her mother would mind.

She shook her head. "Perhaps later."

"And Reina?" he asked.

Reina. The sun was higher now. Her daughter was no doubt awake and having her breakfast. Graciela stood. "The padre in the village baptized her. She is Catholic. We shall decide this later, but for now," she kissed him, "if Kincaid is not done, I shall dress and go and see her. Thank you for telling me what you have told me. It helps me to understand."

His gaze was unreadable, but he rose, gathered his things, and kissed her back. "Later then."

And then he was gone, and she wondered why he had not offered to come to the nursery with her.

CHAPTER TWENTY-NINE

The Kingsley townhouse was located in an area of London rapidly becoming unfashionable, though their street had held up better than others, and Kingsley House, with recent improvements made possible by Graciela's trust, was the handsomest building on the street.

A startled maid opened the door to Charley's knock, and before she could find words, he stepped into the hall.

Trunks were piled in the entry way, with two footmen carrying down more. Lady Kingsley herself was directing the consignments.

Her shocked gaze greeted him, but she drew herself up. "Mr. Everly. We are not receiving visitors, as you see."

"Good day, my lady. Luckily, this is not a social call. I'm here to speak to Lord Kingsley."

"He is not at home."

One footman glanced at the other, and he knew she was lying. "Where may I find him? It is imperative that I speak with him today, and may I add, in his best interests."

"How dare you come calling. He is not—"

"Never mind." The low growl came from the corridor that led to the back of the house. Lord Kingsley stepped out of the shadows, bringing the darkness with him. His complexion had gone a mottled shade of red and his thinning hair drooped. With a terse nod, he directed Charley to an open doorway.

He closed the door on his wife.

The drawing room curtains were shut tight and Holland cloths draped the furniture. Charley went to the window and pulled open the curtains. If Kingsley decided to seek revenge for his violent removal from Shaldon House, he'd best have some light to deal with the man.

"I've come for my wife's things," Charley said.

"Her things?" Kingsley asked.

"When you visited my father, he told you to send her things over."

"I did."

"You sent over the dresses she arrived with. She needs the rest of her wardrobe. The new things she purchased with her money from her trust."

"You've come about her wardrobe? That's imperative?"

"Yes, and whatever other personal items she may have left, brushes and combs, and she also mentioned two books that belonged to her mother."

He waited for Kingsley's reaction.

"Two books?" A shadow crossed Kingsley's eyes and they narrowed. "Two? There was but one, some Spanish Papist twaddle."

"There were two. And you did not find the other one, a book of Shakespeare's sonnets?"

"There was only one."

"Yes, well, I'll have it then, along with her gowns. I'll wait while you have a servant pack them."

"You'll have nothing. The gowns are gone. My lady has taken them—"

"A first season girl's wardrobe?" Charley laughed. "On an elderly matron?"

"That girl was no young innocent, as you discovered." An ugly smile twisted his lips. "My lady can use them for rags or give them to the servants, I care not."

"I see." Wouldn't the scandal sheets like to have that piece of news? "And what of the other personal items?"

"Whatever she had was given to the servants."

"And her jewelry?"

"That went missing with her as you well know. Now leave."

"Not without that book of her mother's, the one with the Spanish twaddle. If you permit me, I'll have a look at her bedchamber. The shabby one you moved her into after your wife took the one Farnsworth remodeled."

"*Farnsworth*?"

"Or should I say, Mr. Cooper. A pity the King needed him elsewhere. It might have spared all of us this trouble. Now, I'll just have a look—"

"You'll do no such thing. Leave. Now."

"Not without the book."

"I burned the bloody book," he shouted.

Accompanied by that much emotion, it was the truth, Charley decided.

"Both of them?" he asked.

Kingsley's gaze narrowed, shifted, and came back to rest on Charley. "Yes. Now, get out."

"Indeed." He laughed. "I'll leave you to manage your retreat from the scandal sheets." At the door, he turned. "And you'd best hope you can run far enough, fast enough, before Captain Kingsley returns to the living."

"He is dead."

"Ah then, until he speaks to you from the dead."

When he opened the door, Lady Kingsley jumped back. He smiled at her. "You'll look lovely in Graciela's white damask and pink ribbons, milady. The matron of the season, a regular diamond of the first water." He dodged around her and out the door.

"Kingsley, what book was he talking—" The door shut on Lady Kingsley's voice.

On the pavement, he signaled his carriage and climbed in.

At the next corner, they stopped and one of Kincaid's men, a tall Scotsman, entered the coach, a package under his arms.

"Well?"

"Stripped bare of clothing and such."

"You had the right room?"

"Aye. As Juan directed. Left a bloody mess— blood staining the floor an' all, I mean. An' I found this in the hearth." He unwrapped the bundle, revealing the charred remains of a large book. Truly, it would have weighed Gracie down had she tried to balance three stories up with it. The leather bindings were singed, as well as some of the pages. The core of the book was intact. Whether it contained secret messages didn't matter. Kingsley would look for it and find it gone.

"Excellent. Wrap it up. Kincaid may have a use for it."

He had one more stop before returning home.

CHAPTER THIRTY

When Graciela arrived in the nursery, Reina's two new aunts were already there.

The little girl flung out her arms and ran to Graciela, making her heart flip, making her laugh.

"Miss Reina, you must say, 'Good morning, Mama'," Lady Sirena chided.

Reina cocked her head and frowned.

Graciela's heart kicked up a fast patter. More truth-telling, and to the most vulnerable person in her life.

She picked the girl up and squeezed her. "You are growing so much. How heavy you are."

Reina squirmed, then leaned back and pressed Graciela's cheeks between both of her chubby hands.

"Ow," she said playfully, invoking a hail of giggles.

Graciela set her down and crouched before her. "Lady Sirena is right. You must call me Mama now." She took a deep breath. Charley had dashed out so quickly and disappeared, she didn't know what to think. Yet she must plunge ahead. "And you must call Charley, Papa."

She pointed a finger at Lady Perry. "*Y ellas*?" And them.

Her little girl must speak English in front of the *inglesas*. Graciela answered in English. "We are going to live with them for a while. And from now on, this is your Aunt Sirena and your Aunt Perry."

A frown twisted the plump lips.

Lady Sirena bent over her. "And you have an Uncle James, an Uncle Bink, an Aunt Paulette, a baby cousin, and two more cousins on the way." Lady Sirena patted the soft mound of her belly. "One of your cousins is growing right now inside my tummy."

Reina touched where Lady Sirena had patted.

"We will all have to wait a few months to see, but, here..." She placed the small hand flat against her. "He is moving."

The brown eyes widened. She groped Lady Sirena with both hands.

"In the stables here, we have a horse with a baby in her tummy."

"Here?" Graciela asked. "In town?"

"Yes, of all things. James purchased her last week. 'Tis not ideal, but I'd rather not move her now." She lifted Reina's chin. "Do you want to see her?"

Reina nodded.

"Do you mind, Mama?" Lady Sirena asked.

"You must be careful, Reina." Graciela said. "You must listen to Aunt Sirena."

"This little mother is gentle, but, yes, you must be careful around horses. They are like people. Some of them are grumpy."

Lady Sirena took her hand and they left.

"Let me take her around the garden after she sees the stables," Lady Perry said. "The day is fine. We can have our tea there and spend the afternoon playing. Will you mind? She needs the fresh air after being cooped up so long, and it will wear her out so she sleeps better. I will bring a guard and the nursemaid."

She felt a weight lift from her heart and she gripped Lady Perry's hand. "Yes. Thank you. I will join you there."

Downstairs, she was headed for the library when a footman stopped her.

"There is a gentleman to see you, Miss—er, Mrs. Everly."

She took the card he handed her. *Captain Llewellyn.*

"Just the one caller?"

"Yes, madam, waiting in the parlor."

"Is my husband in the library?"

"No, madam. He went out."

Tension threaded through her. "Out?" He had not mentioned going out. She eyed the footman. An ex-soldier he was, and shrewd. He might know where Charley went, but she would not stoop to ask.

And, if Charley could go off without her, she could speak to Captain Llewellyn alone.

When she entered the quiet parlor, he turned and smiled.

So, it was the charming Captain visiting today. She curtsied.

"My dear." He took her hands in his clammy ones.

She pulled away. "I am surprised that you would call."

"I hope I am not unwelcome. You look tired, Graciela. Are you well? I was worried after the spectacle you were put through last night."

"You are not unwelcome." In truth she had many questions for him. "And the night was indeed eventful. The Duque's conduct and my cousin's were quite ungentlemanly."

His face colored. "I meant, how could Shaldon and his son expose you so?"

A buzzing started in her ears. "You are referring to my child."

He bit his lips and paced. "It shall not serve. I am leaving sooner than expected, Graciela, returning to the West Indies. You must let me take you away from here. You must let me take you home."

"I am married, Captain. I have a husband now."

He stopped in front of her, unsmiling. "So it is true then?"

"You thought it was not? You thought we would announce it, and it would not be true?"

"How could you let yourself be pressured into marriage to such a rogue?" He swept a hand through his hair. "But it will not matter. I will take you under my protection." He captured her hands again. "I shall arrange a house for us in Veracruz."

Her insides roiled. She looked at his hands, so tightly gripping hers. All pretense of gentility had fallen away. "And what of the money my father set aside for me? Shall I abandon that?"

He frowned. "It's probably lost to Shaldon's swindling son. But no matter. I will set you up and keep you comfortable."

"As what? Your ward?"

His eyes darkened and glittered, the sharpness skittering across her skin.

Bile rose in her. "Your mistress."

"No one need know the truth."

"I would know." She spoke softly. "I would know the truth. And I find that in great matters, the truth matters a great deal to me." She pulled her hands away. "Before he left, my father shared the truth of how my mother died. He was looking for the man behind her murder. I believe Lord Shaldon and my husband can help me finish my father's work."

His mouth contorted in a grimace. "Graciela." He bit his lip, his gaze sliding away before returning. "You don't know? It's one of the reasons I am desperate to take you away from here. The man behind your mother's murder was Lord Shaldon."

She lost her breath and the air around them darkened. "I shall take a chair and listen to this story." His touch on her arm sent shivers through her. He guided her to a sofa.

"No. I said a chair."

"You should lie down."

"No. I will take a chair, and you will take a separate one."

Gripping the chair arms, she asked him to explain.

His jaw firmed. "Your father wouldn't want me to upset you."

"And yet, here we are. You are saying to me that my father and Lord Shaldon were enemies?"

"Let us say, they were at cross-purposes. Your father was spying for a Spanish duke who was under the French thumb."

"The Duque de San Sebastiano?"

"Perhaps. Shaldon, as you probably know, was a leader of the English spies."

"And for this he would send a man from England to kill my mother? You make no sense. The war with Napoleon was over when Mama was killed."

"The war in the Spanish colonies is not over."

"But you believe Lord Shaldon meant to kill my mother."

"I do. His man would have known your father's ship was not yet in the harbor."

"I see. Tell me what happened that day, Captain."

"I don't want to upset you."

Or I don't want to tell you. She watched him, her mind reeling. Lord Shaldon would not send a man to kill another man's wife. She could not believe that about him.

"You have said that already. You have made an allegation that makes no sense. The crime has no motive."

"I know what I know. What do you remember from that day?"

"I was not lucid that day as you know. I remember that you were there, but when I came fully to my senses, my father was with me. Tell me about the killer."

"Your father asked me, if I arrived first, to check on your mother and you. We had heard there was an outbreak of fever. When I arrived at the house, your mother was dead, and the killer was standing over your friend's body, knife in hand. I drew my sword and killed him."

"Who was he?"

He looked away and again bit his lip. "I don't know. The clothing was English. We believe he was also. We traced him to an inn frequented by foreign merchants."

"And the connection to Lord Shaldon?"

Captain Llewellyn shrugged. "Your father's hunch. He was pursuing it."

"He shared those details?"

His sharp gaze turned on her. He had heard the doubt in her voice.

"I mean, please, you must tell me what he shared with you. It would help me to know what to do."

"The only thing for you to do is leave here." He leaned across the space separating the chairs. "I'm staying tonight in Southwark at the Talbot Inn. I've had my ship brought up, and tomorrow I'm returning to it. I'll send a carriage for you."

"That will be too obvious. I can hire my own carriage."

"Do you have access to money?"

"Yes. I have enough, and Juan can find a hackney. My servants—"

"May come also." He pursed his lips. "And the child."

She gripped her hands tightly and held back her words, watching the Captain's lips curl as if he had just sucked a lemon.

"How will you get away?"

Outside, a carriage rattled to a stop in front of the house.

"You must leave it to me, and you must go now. I am not as helpless as you think."

He followed her to the door. She noticed the servant had left it ajar.

He frowned at the open door, but in the hallway, no one lingered. A maid popped out from another room and showed the Captain the way. Graciela watched him go as far as the door.

She all but groped her way to the back of the house and the garden exit, as if swimming through fog. She stopped, took a breath, and looked around her. Rare sunlight splashed into the corridor through the open ballroom door, lighting a few random dust motes. All was in order in this orderly house. The distant sounds of servants at work cleaning were hushed, but it was from contentment, not fear.

Llewellyn wanted her to leave here, to cross the wide ocean on his ship, and set herself up in his bed. When would he want to have her?

Tonight, probably, in his inn room. And once she put herself into his hands, what would become of Reina? Perhaps he would sit a distance off in a squall and watch her baby sink to the bottom of the ocean, just as he'd done with her father.

Graciela hurried along. Her little girl's smile, even her frown, was an anchor, and Reina was waiting for her.

Charley exited his carriage just as a departing visitor reached the bottom steps in front of Shaldon House and turned to walk to a waiting hackney.

He would recognize the hair, the gait, the clothing anywhere.

His heart kicked up. Captain Llewellyn was leaving Shaldon House, alone. That cocky swagger might not signify anything. Gracie might have been ensconced in the nursery. Perry might have entertained the man. Or his father.

The Scotsman watched Llewellyn silently.

"Follow him," Charley said.

He took the bundled book and pulled a long rectangular box from the seat.

Inside, a footman opened the library door for him. Kincaid, Farnsworth, and his father still wore the clothing from last night, neck cloths sharply tied, coats buttoned.

Their work, however was put aside. They sat talking. Plotting.

"Where is Gracie?" he asked.

"We haven't seen her," Farnsworth said.

He dropped his packages upon the table and slid the bundle over to Kincaid. "Your man retrieved this from the fireplace."

Kincaid unwrapped it, his lips curving up.

"Well?" Charley asked. "What did you find?"

"Nothing conclusive," Farnsworth said. "And you?"

"Kingsley claimed he burned both books. He will be tearing the house down to find the book of sonnets."

Shaldon looked toward the window. "He will turn up his own guilt."

"Why was Llewellyn here?" Charley asked.

Three heads came up. They hadn't known about the visitor.

His breakfast curdled in his stomach. "I saw him leaving as I arrived. Where is Gracie?"

Kincaid pushed back his chair, went to the door, and spoke quietly to the footman.

"He'll fetch her," Kincaid said. "She cannot leave without a servant knowing."

"She's not a prisoner." Except, she was, or she might think she was.

"Sit down, my son." Shaldon pointed to an empty chair at the table. "We shall solve this riddle."

He walked to the far window, the one that overlooked the garden. Sirena, Perry, Lady Jane, and a host of servants sat around a woman and child.

The sight of her made his breath return and his heart slow to normal. Gracie was in the garden with Reina, well protected. He watched the footman bow before her and saw her glance up to the window.

Frowning. Charley jerked the window sash up, leaned out, and waved.

Her face settled. She kissed the little girl and followed the servant into the house.

When Charley turned back, all three men were watching him.

"I see I've lost one of my best operatives," Farnsworth said. "Pensioned off to holy wedlock."

"The Duquesa was not a tiresome labor for a single man," Kincaid said. "Was she now, Charley?"

He walked to the table, the comment nudging a memory. "She told me last night, the Duque has ordered his yacht up to London. He has no plans to leave. Rather, he's bringing someone in. Or taking someone out. A debt to pay, she overheard him say."

The door opened and Gracie walked in, striding purposefully toward the table, ignoring him completely. "What did you find?"

Her gaze went to the burned book and she raised her hand up to her throat. She glared at Charley. "You went to Kingsley House without me?"

"You entertained Captain Llewellyn without *me*?"

Her lips pressed into a thin line.

"You were not here. You left and did not tell me where you were going. Not that I expect you to live in my pocket, Charley, but you have no right to chastise me over this, especially not here, not in front of your father."

A laugh bubbled up in him. He'd been expecting a lie, not a tongue-lashing.

He forced his face into a frown but could not speak.

"You did indeed know that I wished to speak to the Captain. I told you that many times."

"And did you?" Charley asked.

"You could have called us, Graciela," his father said. "We would have joined you."

She leveled a gaze on Shaldon, her eyes narrowing, and slowly shook her head.

"Did you get the truth from him?" Charley asked.

Graciela glanced at him. That glint of humor had left his eyes. Having him laugh at her—even if it was inside, in his mind, in his heart, had pinched off her rising anger.

Dios, but she loved him.

Lord Shaldon sat in that strange stiffly erect way of his: unservile, commanding, oh-so-polite. He was cast bronze, from his smoothly cut hair to the long fingers resting on the table.

Yet a pulse jumped in his temple. He was impatient for her to speak. They were all waiting for her, even Charley.

She sat down in the empty chair, and the men seated themselves, all but Charley, who continued to hover.

"Will you tell me the truth, my lord?" she asked Shaldon.

He blinked and finally nodded. "If I am able to."

"Did you send a man to kill my mother?"

CHAPTER THIRTY-ONE

Color rose in her new father-in-law's cheeks, and she noticed how palpably white his complexion had been without it, as if he had long ago opened his own vein to drain off his feelings. The return of blood was upsetting him, she could see that.

His fist hit the table. "Absolutely not. Never. Nor would any of my men."

"Did Llewellyn tell you that?" Charley asked.

Moisture clogged her throat. She nodded.

He flipped a chair around and sat, resting his forearms on the chair back. "That's rather sloppy of him. Quite lacking in subtlety. I'd say the man is desperate, and it's time he came in for that chat. I shall head over to Kirkham's this afternoon."

"He won't be there," she said.

A nerve ticked at the corner of Charley's eye.

"He is moving to an inn called the Talbot in Southwark."

"The Talbot." Lord Farnsworth spit out the word.

"Yes. He is sailing earlier than expected. I told you that."

"*Much* earlier than expected." Farnsworth sat back thoughtfully.

They were on the trail of something.

"What have you discovered in my father's cipher?"

Lord Shaldon nodded at Kincaid. "Tell her."

Kincaid reviewed the system her father had used in the past. The numbers should refer to pages, lines, and words on the page. But that code hadn't worked. They'd learned nothing.

Shaldon nodded again and Kincaid shared that for the last years of the English war, her father had been tracing a ring with branches in Kingston, Cadiz, Calais, and Scarborough. They surmised that the group had access to a highly placed lord who knew the movement of both naval ships and merchant ships.

"Lord Kingsley?" She held her breath at their answer while the question gnawed at her—if her father had suspected his cousin, why had he left her in his care?

"Kingsley was not highly placed in the government," Lord Shaldon said.

"It could have been you then, Lord Shaldon."

"No. I knew the movements of our operatives but not of our ships."

"You could have obtained it."

"Yes, if I needed it. But I am not that source."

"And neither was Kingsley?"

Shaldon rapped his fingertips on the table. "Who was his circle?" He stared off at the fireplace.

"Kingsley had a wide circle," Farnsworth said. "No particular fast friends. He and Lady Kingsley socialized with the usual members of the *ton*."

Charley stood. "Lady Kingsley." He began to pace. "Connected to Carvelle. I wonder, did she have any particular friends among the wives?"

"Would they have known anything? Would they have shared?" Kincaid asked thoughtfully.

"Lady Perry could make inquiries," Graciela said.

Shaldon held her in a steady gaze and shook his head. "She was far too young."

"And she's as subtle as a woodpecker," Charley said.

"Lady Jane," Kincaid said. "She might have been in London with her cousin during some of that time."

A shadow passed over Shaldon, almost imperceptible, and when it lifted left a gleam in his eyes. She shared a glance with Charley. He had seen it also.

"Very well," Charley said. "Gracie, let me return you back to the garden."

Return her. He would leave her with the women and come back to make plans with the men.

She shook her head. "There was more in my conversation with Captain Llewellyn. He...*desires* that I sail with him. He offered to send a carriage to pick me up tonight. I told him that I could arrange my own transportation to the inn."

Charley's face showed no emotion, but his hands had curled into fists.

"Since I cannot legally marry, his plan is to set me up as his mistress. He did agree that my servants and my daughter can come with us."

The room stilled around her. She had shocked them, these hard men, and it left her feeling breathless. She wanted to laugh. Only Charley's face was taking on movement, coming to life.

She pulled a face at him. "Of course, I do not plan to go with him. I would not forfeit all that my father left me. And I find I trust you far more than him." She stood and leaned on the table, looking around at the men. "However, I do wonder what he is up to. Why is he leaving so soon? Why does he want me to come with him—and no, I do not think it's my person he really wants." She sighed. "What is he up to, and what are you gentlemen up to? What are you not telling me?"

Charley brushed up next to her. "What are you not telling *us*?"

Shaldon shook his head. "Children. Farnsworth, Kincaid count your blessings that you have none. There is perpetual distrust."

"And perpetual parental plotting," Charley said.

Like two bulls they were, lowering their chins for a head-butt. They were distracting her from her purpose, which she realized, may have been their intent.

She cleared her throat. "I shall go to him tonight."

"*What?*" Charley shouted.

With what must be the self-control of decades, his father froze, but she saw the same word on the tip of his tongue locked behind closed lips.

"I shall borrow one of your coaches and go to the inn where he is staying. I shall take Juan with me."

Charley's nerves stiffened. "No." It was out of the question. As daft as some of Perry's plots. He couldn't protect her at the Talbot.

She bit her lip. "I shall tell him I could not get all of us out at the same time. I shall tell him I'm sending Juan back to get Reina and Francisca and they will join us posthaste." She clenched her hands together and inhaled, a smile forming. "I shall tell him, we must stay an extra day so I can see my banker and withdraw my funds." She tapped his shoulder and looked at the others. "For that much money, he will stay an extra day, or even longer."

He gritted his teeth. "And what do you suppose will happen in that inn room tonight?"

"Nothing will happen. I shall have my own bedchamber with Juan standing guard."

"No."

Lord Farnsworth cleared his throat. "The Talbot Inn does not have the best reputation, my dear."

"I shall take my dagger."

"I wonder if he knows about the book?" Father mused. "Did your mother or Captain Kingsley talk about it with him?"

"I don't know," Gracie said. "I don't know why they would have."

The hair on his neck rose. "Did the killer search your house in Veracruz?"

She took in a sharp breath. "I don't know. Papa didn't say. But I am determined to do this. I will go with or without your permission."

"I don't like it," Father said.

Neither did he, but she was more likely to listen to his father's reasoning, stubborn woman. "Why not, Father?"

Father's eyes remained open but still managed to shut down. "I like to know what my people are going into. And Graciela is not trained. I would not put her in danger."

His bride's eyes hardened, her color rising, a retort on the tip of her tongue. She was no stranger to danger, but he would not tell his Father that. Those were her secrets to share.

"The Talbot," Kincaid mused. "Right next to Guys Mad House and the George. The White Hart is right there also on Borough High Street, with the stink of the Anchor Brewery drifting over it all." He rubbed his chin. "I do know a man there at the Talbot. We've done some business there."

"Thieves and swindlers," Farnsworth said. "We couldn't be sure they would hold their tongues."

Charley squeezed her hand. "Why not send Roddy in again, dressed as Gracie?"

"No," she said.

He turned her to face him. "I could not bear to see you hurt."

"I don't believe he means to hurt me. I want to know what he is up to."

"Gracie—"

"This isn't a prison. You promised me."

"Gracie—"

"You could help me, Charley. You could pose as the coachman. With you and Juan I will be safe."

"Is he expecting the servants and the child?" Kincaid asked.

"Yes. But we will not bring Reina," she said. "I will not endanger her."

"We'd like him to talk." Farnsworth rubbed his chin. "The child's absence will make him suspicious, and more dangerous. But the maid's presence—there *is* safety in numbers."

Charley's eyes lit on the large box, an idea niggling at him. He reached around her and tugged it closer. "Gracie, look what I have here."

She frowned. "A gift?"

He pulled the string binding it. "It's a gift for Reina, but you must approve it first."

She sighed and lifted the lid.

The doll he'd caught sight of two days before stared up at them, its rich brown hair tightly curled, its lips in a pout. It was too large, too brown-haired, too plainly dressed to fly off the shop's shelf. It had still been there when he'd returned.

"Reina will love it."

"Yes. But I was wondering, when was the last time Captain Llewellyn saw her?"

Her eyes widened. "If he even looked at her, she was not much more than an infant." She smiled. "You will help me then?"

"Help you? We'll do this together."

CHAPTER THIRTY-TWO

Later, Graciela left the library to change to her traveling gown, and ran into Lady Sirena in the corridor.

She rubbed her tummy. "Ah, there you are, Graciela. I'm off for a rest before dinner. Lady Jane has already gone up. She is still tired from the journey and last night's ball. Are you well? You've gone a bit pale."

She took a deep breath to settle herself. They had agreed they wouldn't share the plans with the other ladies, lest they decide they must come along. They'd sent word for Mr. Gibson to stand by. Whether he would tell his wife was anyone's guess. Lord Bakeley was off seeing to some urgent business matter else he would have been involved in the planning, in spite of the fact that he was likely to leak information to his wife.

"Yes, I am fine," Graciela lied. "I'm looking for Francisca. Is she back in the nursery?"

"She went in to order Reina's supper, and Perry promised to bring the wee one up as soon as they're finished picking flowers and making daisy chains." She patted Graciela's hand. "She'll go straight to sleep tonight after all that fresh garden air. Why don't you go up and rest a moment? I'll send a servant to fetch Francisca for you."

In her bedchamber, Graciela ransacked the press until she found the old gown her father had bought her upon arrival in England, the one she'd worn to travel to Kingsley's country estate. She pulled the book of sonnets out of her pocket and set it aside, then contorted herself to unfasten her dress and was down to her stays by the time Francisca arrived.

"Help me," she said, "And then go and get Juan and meet me in the library. We need to talk to the both of you."

Francisca dropped the dress over her head. "What is this about?"

"It's about Captain Llewellyn."

Behind her, Francisca went still. When Graciela looked over her shoulder the woman was frowning.

"Hurry. We are laying a trap for him. I need you and Juan to help me."

"What of the baby?"

"She is staying here with Lady Perry. Go. I'll go down to the garden and check on her."

After she shooed Francisca out the door, she hurriedly packed a small valise, found her shawl and a mantle, and stowed her sheathed dagger in her belt.

The sonnets stared up at her from the bedside table, and she slid them into her pocket. She would meet Charley in the library, but first she needed to see Reina, she needed to make sure her little girl was safe.

Outside, the footman standing guard pointed her toward a side garden. Reina sat on a bench next to Lady Perry, swinging her legs and watching while her new aunt strung blooms together into a crown.

Lady Perry plopped the circlet onto Reina's head and both of them laughed.

"Good evening, my queen," Graciela said.

Lady Perry jumped up, looking relieved. "You are here. We were just about to go in."

"*No*." Reina screwed her mouth up in a pout.

"Sweetling," Lady Perry said. "We've been out here all afternoon, and it will be dark soon. We must go in." She glanced at Graciela. "I must speak with Cook. I promised Sirena and Lady Jane I'd see to the dinner plans. And I sent the nursery maid to check on Francisca. She was supposed to come back."

Poor Perry. A whole afternoon chasing this little one could be exhausting. "I'm sorry. It was my fault Francisca was delayed. Reina, would you like to wear your crown during your dinner? Come along then."

"*No*." The little girl shook her head furiously, the crown flying off. She clambered down from the bench to retrieve it, pushing Lady Perry aside when she tried to rescue it first.

Her little face had fixed in a red scowl. No one at Shaldon House had yet seen one of her tantrums. The least Graciela could do was spare Lady Perry that.

"You go along," Graciela said. "She is overtired from all the excitement and very hungry. I'll sit with her for a few minutes, and by the time we go in, her dinner will be ready."

"If you are sure, Graciela."

The look of relief that crossed Perry's face almost made her laugh. "Yes, I am sure."

Kincaid met up with Charley in the corridor and followed him into the library where Father was waiting. He'd left soon after they'd begun their plotting and now got right to his report.

"We have men in place at the inn, as well as the docks," he said.

"And the Duque's yacht?" Charley asked.

"We have a boat on the river looking for it. Llewellyn's ship is out near the Nore. He has a launch standing by to take him back out."

"Has he arrived at the Talbot?" Father asked.

"Not yet."

Charley walked to the table and picked up the swaddled doll. Graciela was late, and his nerves were prickling.

The door opened and Francisca entered, Juan following her.

Charley's heart raced. "Where is Gracie?"

"We were to meet her here," Juan said.

"She is in the garden with Reina," Francisca said. "I'll just go and get—"

Charley tossed her the doll, pushed past them, and raced down the stairs.

Perry greeted him on the walkway near the kitchens.

"What the devil, Perry?" he said.

"She's not alone. The footman is with her in the side garden."

He hurried past her and heard a child shriek.

Perry snatched at his arm. "Reina was tired. She's having a tantrum."

And then a woman screamed.

*****

The garden bench was still warm from Lady Perry. Graciela watched as Reina plopped down tiredly on the flagstones and began plucking at the petals of scattered flowers. The footman standing guard was beginning to wilt also.

She couldn't remember this placid young man's name. "We shall get you inside for your tea soon," she said. "Have you been out here all afternoon?"

He nodded. "Yes, miss."

Francisca's comments about strangers lurking in the square came back to her with a sense of unease. "*Mija*, Cook told me there might be some chocolate for a girl who eats all of her pudding."

The little head came up, but her eyes looked past Graciela, her mouth dropped in alarm, and the hair on Graciela's neck rose. She flew from the bench, scooped up her child, and the air stirred as the footman rushed past.

"Run," he shouted.

She glanced back. Two men in rough clothing had come over the garden fence and were already attacking their guard.

Reina wailed. Graciela took off toward the house.

A hand grasped her shoulder and spun her around. He was coarse, unshaven, and pockmarked—a man from the docks, she would guess, and that told her all she needed to know about who had hired him.

She clutched Reina tighter. "I suppose the Captain sent you," she said.

He blinked.

Reina whimpered, a choking whine starting deep in her chest. "Let me get the child inside, get my cloak, and I'll come with you."

Pow. Oof, Crash. The footman was down. The other villain brought his boot back to kick him.

"Stop that," Graciela shouted.

He turned his attention on her, and her breath eased, and then hitched up again as he walked her way.

Help would come soon, she prayed. She need only stall.

"'Ere now." Her first captor reached over and grabbed Reina.

Panic roared in her. "No," she shouted. "Stop. What are you...I'll come with you. I'll go to him. Leave her." She held her baby, both of them screaming in this tug-of-war. Hands grasped her from behind, another force too powerful. She couldn't hold on, and Reina was yanked away.

Her baby's look of pure terror sent Graciela flailing.

"I'll go to him."

Charley made out Graciela's words over the screeching child.

A man rushed headlong from the side garden, the wriggling bundle tucked at his side like a barrel of rum.

"Perry," Charley yelled and thrust out his foot sending the man and the child flying.

Charley reached for Reina, but Perry was there, diving to cushion her fall. While she wrestled the man, he grabbed for an urn of potted geraniums and coshed him.

Reina screamed, and kicked, and flailed her little arms. Charley scooped her up and helped Perry to stand.

"He needn't do this." Graciela's voice sounded panicky. "*What—don't touch me,*" she shouted.

He handed the screaming bundle to Perry. "Get her inside."

She hesitated. The man on the ground stirred.

"Go," he said, and she took off.

He picked up the urn and hit the downed man again.

Gracie came around the corner, another man holding her, his hand smashing her breast.

White hot rage roared in him, mirroring the fury twisting her face.

He took in a breath. He was armed with a garden pot. The villain had a knife, not poised at any of her vital spots. Yet blood dripped down the man's knife and his sleeve.

Reina's screams retreated, and other footsteps grew louder. Their men, he hoped.

"Are you hurt, Gracie?" he asked.

She shook her head. "The footman—"

She wheezed as the thug yanked her up tight, that hand taking a firmer grip on her breast.

Blood roared in him. Damn, but he would slice that hand off. "*What the devil are you doing in Lord Shaldon's garden?*" he shouted. "*Let the lady go.*"

"Not 'til I'm out of here. Move out the way and let me pass."

"The footman is—*oof.*" Gracie huffed and gritted her teeth.

Kincaid or one of the men would be going out a window to circle around behind this devil. He just had to keep him talking.

And then he could kill him.

"Shoot him," Gracie said.

"Shut up." The villain gripped her awkwardly, his knife arm trembling. Their footman had sliced him. Some of that blood was his.

"Let the lady go," Charley said. "Whatever the Captain is paying you, we can do better."

The thug's brows lifted, and then drew together. He took a step and Graciela dug in the heels of her sturdy boots.

"*Move*," the man growled.

"More money," Charley said, "for the lady's life."

"An' I should trust a rich swell?"

While he talked, she squirmed, rolling away, her hands moving—

She had her blade.

Charley took a step, raising the urn.

The man yanked on her and stopped, wheezing, eyes popping in astonishment. His grip loosened and he slid to his knees, dropping all the way to the flag-stoned walk.

"Goddamn you." He huffed and wheezed, "Goddamn you, you bitch,"

The urn slid from Charley's fingers, shattering as he reached for her.

"Gracie." He eased the dripping blade from her grip.

"I'll take it." Kincaid had finally appeared.

Charley folded her into his arms and trembled with her.

With her nose buried in Charley's coat, Graciela could begin to breathe again without smelling rot, blood, and death.

Dear God, she'd almost lost her child.

She raised her head. "Reina?"

"Is safe," he said. "Perry has her in hand."

Tears rushed her eyes. "The footman—"

"Shhh. We'll see to him."

Men bustled around them. She could sense them, smell them. They were the Earl of Shaldon's men. Charley's men.

She buried her head again, taking his comfort.

"You did well, love," he murmured, and "Thank God, Gracie," and "I'm so sorry."

"How is she?"

Lord Shaldon had joined them, his voice filled with concern.

She raised her head. "I am fine, sir." But her voice had trembled and more tears came.

She had felt a pop as her blade dove into the villain's back. She had surely killed that man. Her chest constricted, and she gasped, reaching for control, trying to breathe.

Charley held her, stroked her, murmured to her, and she finally managed a full breath.

Lord Shaldon was frowning. "I'm so very sorry, Graciela. This should not have happened. Did you by chance recognize them?"

The arms holding her tensed. He did not want his father questioning her, not yet.

"It's all right, Charley." She shook her head and blinked. "No, but they are sailors or lumpers, someone from the docks, I'd say."

"Yes. This adds a new wrinkle." Charley's father beckoned a man. "We shall see if that one is able to talk. Get a bucket of water."

A child's piercing shriek came from the house. *Dios*, while she sniffled and cried, her baby was terrified.

"Go," Charley released her, eyes burning.

She grabbed his arm. "You come, too. You always calm her."

"It's you she needs now. I'm going to see what this one says."

She glanced at her captor. He didn't move.

The other one, the one who'd taken Reina, was shaking off water and stirring.

Another wail split the twilight and tore into her heart. She dropped a kiss on his cheek and left, vaguely aware of a footman shadowing her. She'd be guarded everywhere she went, and Reina also. She'd have no freedom now at all.

Llewellyn would pay for this.

Inside, Reina sprawled on the kitchen floor kicking, crying, holding her breath, a circle of women around her.

Graciela pushed her way through them and dropped to her knees.

Outside, Charley stood with his father, watching their men help the footman to his feet, as well as the villain he'd coshed. The other...

"Damn it, Father, I don't want her out there tonight."

"I know. Yet she'll *want* revenge."

"Aye," Kincaid said, joining them. "She truly is a colonial girl. That was a poke right to the kidney. Captain Kingsley taught her well." He clapped Charley on the shoulder. "Ye've got yourself a brave lass."

"Braver than either of you could ever imagine," Charley said.

Father cast him a curious look, but held his questions. Not that Charley would share Graciela's secrets.

And...did she have more? *I'll go to him*, she'd said to that bastard.

He shook off his doubts. She'd been bluffing, buying time until help arrived.

Behind them, the man Charley had coshed groaned.

"Ah, very good," Kincaid said. "Let's get this one to spill his guts."

By the time they'd reached the nursery, Reina had slipped into a hiccuping whimper. Settling her into sleep required a hot meal, a posset, and a good deal of rocking, but she finally slipped off.

With Lady Perry and Lady Jane standing watch, a nursery maid on duty, and a footman in the corridor outside, Graciela went to change out of her bloodied gown.

On the walk to her bedchamber, Francisca said nothing. When the door closed on them, she silently pulled Graciela into her arms, pressing her tight to her thin breast.

"Thanks be to God," the maid said.

Her dark eyes shone with tears. Graciela hadn't seen this much emotion since Francisca returned to Veracruz and learned that her mother had died.

She took the maid's hand. "Do not worry, we will get our revenge."

Francisca's mouth firmed and she nodded, and then quickly turned Graciela and began undressing her. She helped her into one of her simple, modest, colonial gowns and was lacing her up when Charley came in.

"How is Reina?" He kissed her.

"Finally sleeping."

Francisca tugged Graciela's skirt into place and turned to leave.

"Wait, Francisca," he said.

"I go back to Reina."

He shook his head. "No. Meet us in the library. Juan is there already."

"But...you do not mean for her to go to him? That man tried to take Graciela. You would let her walk into danger again?"

"I have to go," Gracie said. "Llewellyn must pay for what he did, for what he is planning to do. I am going to go."

Charley's frown told her he agreed with Francisca.

She took his hand. "You know I must do this."

His mouth firmed. "If he's expecting all of you, it would be best if you and Juan went also, Francisca. But if you wish to stay behind—"

"No." Francisca's eyes blazed. "Two times we left you and bad things happened. We will not have a third."

When the door closed on the maid, Charley took her into his arms. "I can't help thinking Francisca is right."

"That man," she said shakily. "Did he...is he...?"

He took in a breath, debating whether to lie. Taking a human life was a burden she shouldn't have to bear.

Yet her mother had borne it to save her daughter, hadn't she?

She leaned back and looked up at him, clear-eyed. "Tell me, Charley."

"Yes."

She bit her lip and nodded.

"You did what you must. You saved Reina's life. Who knows what they had in mind for her."

"For her?"

He took a deep breath. "The man I coshed is talking." He gripped her hands, trying to quell the anger churning inside him. "They weren't there for you. They were there to take Reina."

She stepped away from him and went to her discarded gown, retrieving the small book and stowing it into her pocket. She straightened, then bent over the garment again.

When she turned she held the empty dagger's sheath. "Where is my blade?"

"I handed it to Kincaid. We'll get it back."

"Very well, Charley. Let us go and find Captain Llewellyn."

When she entered the library on Charley's arm, Lord Shaldon came around the table. Lord Bakeley and Mr. Gibson hovered nearby, and Kincaid waited near the window. Juan and Francisca stood by a shelf bursting with books.

It had been a mere few nights ago that she'd stumbled into this room, planning how to run away and find Captain Llewellyn and wondering if they might have a volume of Cervantes to share with Francisca.

What a sea-change fate had wrought—she'd learned the truth of Captain Llewellyn and risked all of Papa's secrets to marry into this spy lord's family. Instead of sharing the plot of a book, she and Francisca were plotting with all of these men.

Or, not all. "Where is Lord Farnsworth?" she asked.

"He's gone ahead to see to things," Lord Shaldon said. "He'll be back shortly."

Charley stepped away, and Lord Shaldon took both her hands in his much larger ones.

"Are you all right then?"

Charley's father, like her own papa, had seen much and had suffered much. Now his kindness almost undid her. She took in a breath. "I am."

"And Reina?"

"She is finally sleeping. Lady Perry and Lady Jane will stay with her. How is the footman? He did try to fight them."

Lord Bakeley stirred. "The surgeon has seen to him and believes he'll survive. And you are right, he didn't betray us."

Us. She was part of them, part of this family, as was Reina. Moisture flooded her eyes.

Lord Shaldon placed the dagger into her hands. It gleamed in the candlelight, the marks etched in the hilt and the blade stark and clearly delineated.

Her gaze dropped. Her hands trembled.

"I cleaned it myself," Lord Shaldon said. "Did your father give you this before he left?"

She nodded, unable to speak.

"The design is quite unique."

She sheathed the dagger and lifted her chin, holding his gaze. "It is an Azteca design, he said."

"Hmm." Lord Shaldon went to the sideboard, poured a sherry, and brought it to her. "Have this."

Out of politeness, she took a sip, praying her heart would slow down before it jumped out of her chest. "What have you found?'

"They staged a distraction," Mr. Gibson said, "An accident the next street over that pulled most of the grooms out to help. Damned clever."

Nodding, she swallowed another few drops.

"Have you eaten?" Lord Bakeley asked. "None of us have. We've sent Sirena off to see about food."

"Truly, I have no appetite. Do we know who those men are?"

"Not yet," Kincaid said. "Most likely they were brought from the docks to do a bit of work."

The door opened with a swishing of skirts and clattering of dishes.

"Come." Charley led her to a chair. "We'll all need some nourishment for the night ahead." He signaled to Juan. "Juan, you and Francisca also."

Shock registered on their faces, and her heart lifted. Living in close quarters during their travels, she'd often shared meals with her servants. If she did not eat, they would not eat.

"Very well," she said. "I'll just have a nibble while we discuss the plans."

CHAPTER THIRTY-THREE

"Cook has gone all out for us." Charley dished up more meat and vegetables for Gracie's plate. She'd push it around a bit before finally eating some of it, staring into space with visions of the nightmare in the garden. Gads, but he wished this night was over.

Kincaid had launched into what was for him a rambling discussion of the pluses and minuses of traveling to Southwark via Westminster Bridge or London Bridge, as though he were drawing this out, killing time.

When Farnsworth burst in, his hair damp, his neck cloth askew, Charley knew why Kincaid had stalled. Bink's temporary ward, Thomas Beauverde, slid in behind him.

They were up to something, these wily old men.

Father saw Thomas also, and glanced at Bink, who looked up from his full plate and sent the boy a glare. Father signaled Thomas to take a seat.

Young Thomas was a cagey one, barely fourteen, and yet Charley would bet his next quarter's allowance, Father had plans to groom the boy for the service.

Bink would not be happy about that.

"I don't like it." Farnsworth took a plate and filled it. "Men milling about in front of every inn on Borough High Street."

Gracie sat up. "They're laying an ambush."

That's my girl. Charley squeezed her shoulder. "Was he there?"

"He checked into the Talbot earlier and went out. No bags. We got a man in to search his room. Not a thing there."

"So where *is* he staying?" Charley asked.

They waited for Farnsworth to swallow.

"My guess? The White Hart." He forked a piece of potato and chewed thoughtfully. "I also saw Payne-Elsdon in the public room there."

"Who?" Gracie asked.

"A fellow club member," Charley said. "An agent. For whom, we don't know."

"We're likely to find out tonight," Kincaid said.

"What do you mean?" Gracie asked.

"If Payne-Elsdon spotted one of our men," Farnsworth said, "whichever villain is missing tonight might be the one he works for."

"But who is there besides Llewellyn, Kingsley, and Carvelle?" she asked. "And you've said Carvelle is in Kent, and Kingsley left for his country estate."

She'd forgotten to mention the Duque.

"Something else," Farnsworth said. "A woman took a suite of rooms at the White Hart this morning. From the description, I'd say it could be Lady Kingsley."

Utensils clattered as Gracie jumped up. "*Lady Kingsley*?"

"Well, well," Kincaid said. "Our man said Kingsley left town today, and she wasn't with him."

"Dear God." Charley pinched the bridge of his nose where a headache was starting. "The woman who visited him that day at his hotel. What the devil could be their connection?"

Gracie stood and began to pace. "And why match me up with Carvelle if she is in league with the Captain. Has Carvelle surfaced anywhere nearby?"

"No," Kincaid said. "Mayhap Kingsley found another way to pay off that debt to Carvelle."

A debt to be paid, the Duquesa had said. But perhaps not the Duque's debt. Perhaps she had found a way to get the Duque to pay Kingsley's debt to Carvelle.

"I don't understand." Graciela turned to him, eyes burning. "It can't be her. Llewellyn is so far beneath her socially, she wouldn't take him as a lover." She fisted her hands. "Let's go. Let's go now."

Lord Shaldon cleared his throat. "There is more, Graciela. The man who talked provided enough details that we were able to send a message in his name. We told Llewellyn they'd got the child safely away, but that she was troublesome and they'd secured her with a woman he knows."

Her eyes searched the room as she took in what Father had said.

"We enclosed a lock of hair," Father said, "contributed by one of the maids."

"And a request for more money?" Lady Sirena asked.

"We hinted at it."

"He'll wonder if she's dead," Gracie said, her voice shaking. "But...it won't matter to him, will it? As long as she's missing, he knows I will come."

"It will matter enough to make him nervous," Charley said. "Perhaps reckless, Father."

"Reckless enough to send a note," Kincaid said matter-of-factly.

Father unfolded a paper. "Yes. This came for you tonight, Gracie. Time being of the essence, we took the liberty of reading it."

Hands shaking, she took the wrinkled paper, and Charley read over her shoulder.

> *My Dear Grace,*
> *Do not be alarmed at your child being taken. I have it on good report that Shaldon has threatened it. I am safeguarding it at the place I told you about on my visit. Bring all of your things, and of course your servants also, and I will get you to safety far from the reach of Shaldon's influence.*
> *L*

"Good God." Charley took the paper and read the note aloud, translating it into Spanish for Juan and Francisca.

Gracie began to pace again. "He wants me to go to the Talbot, but he's not staying there. And there are men at every inn on the street. And he has his woman at the White Hart."

"As you said, my love, they're laying an ambush."

"Do we have more men than he does?" Bakeley asked.

"He will have his ship's crew," Gracie said. "He will need no more than a few men to manage while the ship lies at anchor. The ones with him will not be afraid of a fight."

Lord Bakeley cleared his throat. "May I point out that we have you, Graciela, and your child? We need not send anyone into danger tonight. We simply fail to show up, and send a coastal patrol after Llewellyn when he decides he's waited long enough."

"Bakeley is right," Charley said.

She cast him a look filled with anger. "What is he truly after? Something important enough to try to steal Reina, to force me to appear. If we don't risk an ambush, then what? We do *nothing*?"

His heart twisted. He knew what she wanted— the truth, and revenge. Tonight was her chance to confront Llewellyn in person without the constraints of the British legal system. If they waited, if they sent the authorities, and the Captain was killed on arrest, she would never have that opportunity.

And somehow, he had to give her that.

"There might be a third way," he said.

Father nodded, the crafty old spy, as if he was one step ahead, which he probably was.

"We'll meet with him at a place and time of our choosing."

"And how will we do that, Charley?" she asked. "Send a note and say, 'Here I am, come and get me?'"

"Yes. That's exactly what I had in mind, perhaps worded a bit less directly. We'll need Juan and Francisca to play their parts. And we'll need someone sly to deliver your message to the

Talbot and get away without being snatched up."
He turned his gaze on the boy.

Thomas grinned.

"No," Bink said. "I'll go."

"Llewellyn knows you," Charley said.

"I'm sworn to Hackwell to protect this boy
while he's in my home."

Bakeley laughed. "A risky oath, that."

"Then go along with him, Bink," Charley said,
"but stay in the background and let him make the
delivery."

Father rapped the table. "Before we decide
anything, let's hear the rest of your plan,
Charles."

CHAPTER THIRTY-FOUR

"I do not like this place." Francisca's whisper tickled Graciela's ear.

From his spot near the door, Juan shushed her.

They were in a part of London a far cry from Mayfair, in all ways. The smell of the sea was stronger here, and the bustle of sordid life outside carried in through the window left open in hopes of hearing the Captain's approach. The street had been lined with beggars and drunks who'd spilled out of taverns, some of them Shaldon's men, some of them belonging to the neighborhood crime lord.

In spite of the late hour, the pawn shop below stairs had picked up traffic also, the door slamming and footsteps clomping.

Dios. She didn't like this place either. It was as bad as the worst port she'd ever encountered.

"Don't worry, my love." Charley spoke softly from his position near the window, where he was studying the street below and trying to stay out of view.

"I am not worried," she lied.

To make these arrangements so quickly, Lord Shaldon had strange bedfellows indeed. And yet this set of rooms was likely a brilliant choice—reasonably clean, in a neighborhood likely riddled with pickpockets and thieves, and near the docks. It might be all a desperate woman with very little ready cash could afford.

Charley shifted, and her nerves roused.

Shouting erupted below on the street, a great din of men cursing and squealing.

"Good God," Charley said.

"What?" She started toward him and Francisca pulled her back.

"It's the melee Father promised."

"How many men did the Captain bring?" she asked.

"I can't tell who is who from here."

Lord Shaldon had said they must be prepared for Llewellyn to counter their ruse, either with force or by guile. Apparently, he'd chosen force.

Charley moved from the window, signaled Juan to stay put, and poked his head into the adjoining room. "He's skirting the fight with a couple of men."

"No woman with him?" Farnsworth asked.

"No."

The backstairs creaked as one of Shaldon's men carried the message down to the pawn shop.

Her valise rested on the small table pushed to the side. A narrow tester bed huddled in a shadowed corner, and nearby stood a dressing table. The only privacy the room accorded was a screened alcove for washing and changing.

Charley took his pistols from the washstand and touched his lips to hers.

"Your dagger?"

She pulled it from the sheath and concealed it under her shawl.

He kissed her again and disappeared behind the screen.

Insides quivering, she took a deep breath to calm herself. They had talked about what she would say, how she might draw out Llewellyn's guilt, and how she should use the dagger. She had wanted a pistol, but Charley had said he would carry two and share them if need be, but the room was too small and too crowded for too many firearms.

And perhaps he was right.

Heavy steps sounded on the stairs and someone knocked.

"Who is there?" Juan asked.

"Open the door, Juan."

The voice was Llewellyn's. Lips trembling, Graciela nodded and Juan slid back the bolt, retreating to stand with her and Francisca.

Two other men followed the Captain. She recognized one as his first mate.

She let out a huff that she hoped sounded like relief. "Captain. You came." Her insides were shaking, and the tear she managed was real enough.

Charley was here. Farnsworth and Shaldon were in the next room, and other men, also. She was not all alone with this monster.

But she must play out her part. "I didn't know what to do. When your note came I...I didn't know what to do. We...Where is Reina?" She peered around him. "Did you bring her?"

"She is safe." He glanced at Juan and Francisca, and jabbed his thumb toward the door. "Out," he said.

Tension poured from Juan, and Francisca's skirts rustled against hers.

"*Out.*" It was the voice of command, the one that made stout men of any nationality or language jump.

Juan flinched and still didn't move.

Blood rose in her cheeks, and her lungs tightened. "My servants stay. You did say they could accompany me. And where is my child? Where have you put her? I told you to bring her."

"There now, my dear." Those words flowed like grease off a boiling pig hock. "Do not fret, I'm here now, and your servants must leave. And we'll see to the child later."

She stepped in front of Juan. "You *told* me they could come. Without their help I would not have been able to leave Shaldon House and find these lodgings. They are family to me. I won't leave them here. What would they do? Where would they go?"

"There now. They'll find other work here."

He signaled and his first mate stepped forward. A clattering of boots on the stairs and gruff voices brought the man to a halt.

The door burst open again and a shove sent Thomas flying into the room. The boy's dark frown glittered, and he spat out a string of curses in a cant so thick she could barely understand. One of Llewellyn's men cuffed the boy.

"'Ere now. I'll need more blunt if ah'm to be beat on," Thomas said gamely.

"Shut up boy." A woman had entered, waving a pistol, another man behind her.

"*La bruja,*" Francisca muttered.

The witch. *She was here.* Graciela's heart raced. *Dios.* Llewellyn *had* been setting a trap for her. He *was* a traitor.

"What on..." She took in a breath. She didn't have to pretend this anger. "What on earth is *that cow* doing here, Captain Llewellyn? I agreed to meet *you. Get her out of here.*"

He cast Lady Kingsley a look that said he was as disturbed as Graciela at her appearance, and then he spotted her valise and signaled his man to look through it.

"What...what are you doing? Stop going through my things. Captain, stop your man, and *get that woman out of here.* I will speak with you privately once the witch leaves."

The lady chuckled. "Leave? Why, we are all leaving at the same time, Grace."

"I told you to wait at the inn, Blanche." He turned back to Graciela. "Say your farewells. Your servants are leaving."

"Don't see a book," his henchman said.

"Where is your book?" he asked, all softness gone from his voice.

"What book?"

Lady Kingsley went to the discarded traveling case. "Surely you brought your little book." She set down her pistol and riffled through the contents, pulling out clothing and meager toiletries. "It's not here."

"I left my prayer book at Kingsley House."

"Not the prayer book. Kingsley burned that, the fool. And do not play dumb with me."

"Your mother's little book of sonnets." Llewellyn clipped every quiet word.

A roaring started in her ears, and the crowded room shrank to just her and Llewellyn and the cow. Her hand twitched with the need to drive the dagger through both of them.

She blinked back angry tears, and reminded herself, she was after more than revenge. She wanted a confession first.

"You left it behind at Shaldon House?" he asked.

"What if I did?"

His gaze narrowed on her.

She glared back.

The room went still and a darkness came over him, the look of a captain ready to bring out the whip. No wonder he'd taken up with Lady Kingsley.

And she would die before she let the woman beat her again.

"The book, Grace," he said.

"How do you know about that book, Llewellyn?"

"Your mother told me about it, and I know you took it with you when you left Kingsley House. You treasure it too much to leave it behind when you leave England. I'll keep it safe for you. The time for games is over."

"Indeed. I am also finished with games." She freed a hand, reaching through the slit in her cloak, and slid out a small volume. "Is this what you want?"

Llewellyn's face lit and her jaw ached. She must hold her tongue. She must play this out.

"Give it to me." Lady Kingsley reached out a hand.

"My mother treasured her book. You may get one of these in any book shop."

Llewellyn pried the book from her hand, his face grim. "Ah, but *this* book is the one we want."

She let out a breath and watched him page through it, tracing a fingertip along the bindings.

A weary smile lit his face. "I'm sorry, Grace, but this one we must have. I shall buy you a new one my dear. I shall buy you a whole collection of Shakespeare."

There was kindness in the smile, and something like relief. It almost brought back the man she thought she knew. But the book...Lady Kingsley...Reina...

She must push him to reveal more, to admit his guilt.

Lady Kingsley tried to snatch the small volume from him, but he tucked it into a pocket and said, "Later."

He reached for Graciela's hand. "Come then. I'll take you, and your servants may stay here."

She stepped away. "Where is my daughter?" she asked, in the shakiest voice she could conjure.

"Enough foolishness. I've told you she's safe."

"But she is not here." She gave in to the urge to sob and squeezed out a tear. "I should not have come. This was a terrible mistake."

Lady Kingsley laughed. "Why don't you faint, Grace."

Blood pounded in her ear. She still clutched the dagger under her heavy shawl, but Lady Kingsley had picked up her pistol.

"It's not a mistake," Llewellyn said soothingly. His hand stroked her cheek, smearing her tears, sending a shiver of revulsion through her. "You'll be happy at home. Though we will not go to Veracruz. Perhaps we shall settle in Maracaibo."

"No Spanish hole," Lady Kingsley said. "It must be an English-speaking port."

"English speaking ports will have visits from English warships, Blanche," he said over his shoulder. His eyes bore into her, darkening.

"Graciela shall teach you to get along with the Spanish."

Graciela shall murder Blanche in her bed, and you also if you dare to come near me.

She wiped the back of her hand over her cheeks. "Give me my child, and you may go on your way."

Lady Kingsley moved closer, hemming Francisca in. A low growl escaped the maid's throat.

"Oh, no. *You* must go with us."

"You took her to force me, didn't you, Llewellyn. And why am I so important? Charley Everly has all my money. Do you expect him to pay a ransom for a wife who has left him?"

"A ransom? We're not asking for ransom. You're insurance, Graciela, for when your fa—"

"Quiet," Llewellyn thundered.

Hope lit in her. "Insurance? Because you fear my father. Because he has friends and allies and contacts in every port in the world. Because he'll find you and he'll kill you, both of you."

Llewellyn's gaze flitted over her face, masking whatever emotion he felt.

"Did you lie to the Crown about his death, Llewellyn?"

"Oh, tell her," the witch said. "He may be dead, he may not be dead. We shall need you until he we are sure he is. After that, Grace, well, you are young and pretty and experienced. It is fortunate the Captain likes you because slavery is still legal in some parts of your world. We won't need a ransom from your husband to raise funds."

A shiver went through her. She knew the chilling truth of that. There were men who would buy an unprotected woman, and good luck escaping. "You would *sell* me, Llewellyn? Your friend's daughter?"

His lips rolled into a sneer. "He was no friend to me."

Bile rose in her. Her father had asked Llewellyn to check on her mother and her, Llewellyn claimed. Or had he?

There had been a man, an Englishman, killed by Llewellyn. A man who had supposedly killed her mother.

The truth swept through her with icy certainty. "*You* killed my mother, and our friend, and that man, whoever he was."

Dios. Mama had received news that made her desperate to leave Tampico, to meet up with Papa. The man was probably Shaldon's agent, not sent to kill Mama, but to collect the evidence that drove her to Veracruz.

His eyes slitted, dark and narrow as stilettos.

She put a hand to her breast and sobbed. "Oh, God. You took my daughter and killed her also."

Behind the screen, Charley held his breath. *Spill your guts, Llewellyn.*

He'd cut a hole in the ratty dark velvet big enough for his eyes and the barrel of his pistol, if Llewellyn would cooperate and move closer, and if the *cow* wasn't waving her own pistol about.

Best not to rush his fences. He'd come up with this plan, and he'd promised to let Gracie lead the man into an admission of guilt.

"Stop this, Grace." The bastard reached for her arm, and she stepped away.

"No denial? So you *are* guilty. You murdered my mother because she found out you were a traitor and a thief and she was going to unmask you. You murdered her friend because she was there. And the man there that day? He was not her killer but an agent who you killed. You kept me alive because you thought you would use me as your whore. Admit it."

Sweat trickled down Charley's back. Her voice was strong, but from this angle he could not see her face.

"What if I did," Llewellyn said. "You are coming with us, whether you like it or not."

Not a straight-out admission, but enough for him. He stood and slipped through the shadows past the screen.

"I have something else to show you," Gracie said. "The lamp, Francisca."

All eyes followed the maid who moved a lamp to the dark sleeping corner where a small body lay tightly swaddled.

Llewellyn's back stiffened.

Across the room, Thomas spotted Charlie and looked toward the door. Bink had appeared in the doorway, towering over a better-dressed villain, one of Lady Kingsley's men, probably.

The henchmen were glued to the scene at the bed, the fools.

"With my own hands," Gracie said in a strong voice, "I killed the man you sent to steal my daughter."

"Oh, for heaven's sake, enough of this Spanish drama." Lady Kingsley's pistol still tracked Gracie. "The child will just be trouble." She threw her girth at Francisca, shoving her aside, and grabbed the small bundled body from the bed.

Francisca grasped at the body and a tugging match ensued, Lady Kingsley's pistol waving wildly, Gracie ducking out of the way.

Fighting broke out in the rest of the room, Juan, Thomas and Bink choosing that moment to challenge Llewellyn's and Lady Kingsley's men.

Charley turned on Llewellyn, but spotted Thomas near the window, and one of Llewellyn's sailors raising a knife at the boy. Charley lunged, ripped his hand back, freeing the blade, and kicking it away. The sailor growled and attacked.

Charley brought the butt of the pistol down on his head, but the man got up and charged again.

Thomas swung a chair at him. He parried the blow and turned back on the boy, who retreated to the open window.

"Duck, Thomas," Charley yelled. The boy dove and Charley dropped his pistol, hoisted the villain and tossed him through the window. "Grab it."

He pulled out his other gun and yelled, "Gracie."

"*Right here, Charley.*"

Llewellyn had her by the waist, kicking and fighting, but the two women pulling the baby apart blocked his escape from the room.

Juan had found his way to the far side of the room, and was taking a beating. At the door, Bink parried blows from two men. One landed a solid punch and Thomas raced in, and *pow.* The pistol shot knocked Thomas back, and the man staggered. Bink righted the boy and knocked the wounded man down the stairs.

He turned in time to see Gracie break free and go to Francisca's aid. A sharp crack from Llewellyn sent the maid sailing back into the bedpost where she smacked her head and slid to the floor. Gracie shrieked and dropped with her. Lady Kingsley knocked into Llewellyn, righted herself, and swung the small body against the bedpost.

The head bounced across the floor, the brown eyes wide and staring.

Llewellyn clutched Gracie's hair and pulled her to her feet. "What have you done?"

She twisted and kicked and flailed. "Would I expose a real child to a monster like you?" Her blade flashed down on his arm and he cried out, releasing her.

Charley jerked Llewellyn back and planted the point of his pistol in the man's neck.

"You," Lady Kingsley glared at him.

She tossed the doll's body aside and wove a shaky figure of eight in the air with her gun barrel, stopping at Gracie.

He held his breath. He hoped he didn't have to shoot Llewellyn's head off. It would be an altogether unpleasant experience for Gracie.

He made himself laugh. "You are quite right, Lady Kingsley. The child will certainly be trouble for you. Your other man gave Lord Shaldon quite an earful about the sea captain and the lady who paid him to steal an earl's granddaughter."

Lady Kingsley's gaze narrowed.

"On the other hand, my father is quite a good listener if you have something to share with him. And I imagine you do. Put down your weapon, Lady Kingsley, or your friend here will die."

"My friend?" She laughed.

"Your business partner then. Or is he a lover?"

She laughed softly. "Yes, well, you can reach into my business partner's pocket and retrieve the little book stashed there, and then I will be going. I have a boat to catch."

"You'll not get my crew to take you anywhere," Llewellyn growled.

"Well, not that boat. I will be long gone before you have your turn at the gallows."

"She is going with her cousin, Carvelle," Graciela said. "He was another partner in your crimes, wasn't he, Lady Kingsley. Along with your husband."

"My husband? That fool? All of our hard-won money, invested in a cargo that your father chose to steal."

"Oh dear," Charley said. "A cargo sent under a Spanish flag. Plunder taken from the people of New Spain. Do lower your pistol, my lady."

"Come here, girl." She beckoned Graciela. "You are my safe passage out."

Behind her, Juan and Bink had landed their last punches, and Juan's dagger was drawn.

And Father wanted the woman alive. He shook his head, praying Juan would see him.

"You're a fool, Blanche," Charley said. "So sorry to inform you, that boat you're planning to catch won't be at the dock in Bermondsey."

She glared, and the pistol veered his way.

Fortunately, Llewellyn was in front of him.

"Blanche," Llewellyn said. "Put the gun down."

"Who'll talk first?" Charley asked. "Shaldon won't need both of you."

He heard a rustling and the gun veered back to Gracie.

"The boat's been warned away, Blanche," Charley said. "You really have no choice."

The pistol moved their way again, shaking.

"Now," Charley shouted.

Juan's knife slashed and, *pow*, Llewellyn slammed into Charley, pulling them both to the floor.

He rolled the man off. Llewellyn clutched at his belly.

"Gracie," Charley yelled.

"I'm here." She crawled over to him, dagger drawn and threatening the Captain. "Are you hit?"

"I don't think so." he said.

Llewellyn groaned.

"He's faking." Gracie got to her feet and toed the man's coat open.

Blood stained his waistcoat.

She inhaled sharply. "She shot him."

On the other side of the room, Juan restrained Lady Kingsley, while Farnsworth staunched the wound in her arm.

And Father had made his appearance.

Charley started going through Llewellyn's pockets. "I guess we'll be charging you with attempted murder, Lady Kingsley."

"It'll be murder," Llewellyn said. "I'm gut-shot."

Charley pulled out the book of sonnets and tossed it to Farnsworth. "Here, your ladyship. You may read it in jail while you wait for the hangman. Do not worry, it is naught but a copy from the library at Shaldon House."

She laughed, the witch. "It was accidental. With all of you fighting, the gun went off. I will not be in jail, nor will I hang. I am the wife of a peer. But this man of hers, he may hang for stabbing me."

"I think not, Blanche," Father said. "Since clearly he was defending my son's wife. But if you would like to talk, we will listen."

"Yes, I will talk, Shaldon, and you will not like what I have to share in the scandal sheets about your precious son's wife."

Father sighed. "Ever the bully, Blanche." He nodded to Farnsworth. "See that she's chained. Charge her with treason, attempted child stealing for ransom, and, for now, attempted murder."

"I am no traitor. It was Llewellyn and Kingsley."

"And who else was involved, Blanche? Who were you sailing with tonight?"

"You would like information, and I might have it."

Charley stood and pulled Gracie up with him, making room for the men seeing to Llewellyn. He moved her over to the narrow bed and sat down next to her.

"Is Francisca well?"

She nodded. "She's tending to Juan now."

"Let's clean this blood off." He slipped the dagger from her hand and wiped it on the bedcovers. The blade shimmered in the lamplight. He'd come upon Father examining it earlier, after he'd cleaned it. Her father's gift. "It's done you good service this day."

She nodded and leaned into his shoulder.

She was unable to speak. All of the day's bravery had caught up with her. He pulled her close while he studied the blade. From the hilt to the point was a series of lines and circles, expertly traced, in no particular arrangement that he could make sense of.

His mouth went dry, certainty creeping over him. He'd once studied a code that used these symbols.

Gracie's hand covered his. "I must have that back," she said. "I...I treasure it."

"Of course." He bit back a smile and slipped it into the sheath at her waist.

He'd married a woman who kept her promises.

"Let's go home and check on Reina." He drew her to her feet. "And tomorrow, I'll buy her a roomful of dolls."

They managed a quick change of clothes and a visit to the nursery before being summoned to the library where Bakeley and the ladies waited, demanding a report.

Charley obliged, in great detail, and was all but finished when Lord Shaldon returned with Mr. Gibson and Thomas in tow.

Charley's father excused the ladies so politely, it was a wonder Lady Perry protested before leaving. Graciela got up to leave also, but he bade her stay.

Charley seated himself, his arm finding her, lending her his strength. She'd been very brave, they all said, but inside her heart hurt. She'd ended one man's mortal existence. She'd confirmed another man's grave betrayal. How did men bear this sort of burden?

"Where are Farnsworth and Kincaid?" Charley asked.

"Farnsworth is with Blanche." Lord Shaldon's lip curled and he threw back a whisky.

It was the most emotion she'd seen him display since she'd asked him if he'd killed her mother.

"Kincaid has Llewellyn in hand. He'll last a few days. Bakeley, I would ask you and Bink to get some sleep and then set off after Lord Kingsley. We'll need him back."

Graciela found Charley's hand and clutched it. Her guardian would face consequences, yet this was not over. "What of Carvelle?"

He looked away, frowning. "The coastal patrols are searching. They're bringing in Llewellyn's ship as well. The Duque's yacht is another matter. He'll claim diplomatic privileges, and the King won't want to cause a stir so close to his coronation."

"Did she confirm her plan to escape on that yacht?" Charley asked.

"The Duque's yacht?" Graciela asked. "She was connected to him?" She let out a breath. "They think my father took the Duque's ship, one they'd invested in."

"The night of the ball, the Duquesa told me he was bringing the yacht up to take someone important out," Charley said.

"So that was the whispering in your ear." She looked at their hands locked together.

Charley was wrong. The Duquesa was wrong. The Duque didn't send the boat for someone important—he sent it for some*thing* important. He wanted the book.

He knew what the book contained.

The thought terrified her.

"Lady Kingsley did not mean to leave with Llewellyn," she said.

"No," Lord Shaldon said.

"She meant all along to shoot him."

"That is likely."

"*Dios.*"

Shaldon's faraway gaze had not changed.

Graciela rose, went to him, and touched his shoulder. "Was it she who killed Lady Shaldon?"

The three brothers went still. Lord Shaldon rested a hand atop hers and sighed. "She is ruthless enough. Was she always so? She had relatives in the East Riding. I'd met her at a neighbor's house party when I came back from

Ireland to marry. Felicity loved the seacoast and the wild country." He paused. "Bring over that bottle, Charles, and pour each of us a round."

"Did she pursue you, my lord?" Gracie asked.

Charley's mouth had dropped open. Lord Bakeley's gaze sharpened.

"Blanche wanted a title, and my brother had just died, bequeathing me his. And I wonder if you might call me Father, unless you think Captain Kingsley will mind."

"Oh." She blinked and glanced round the room. Lord Bakeley had covered his mouth, Mr. Gibson was rolling his eyes, and Charley's lips quivered.

The brothers did not mind.

Lord Shaldon's gaze was so much like her Papa's, discerning and wise. He was a man of secrets also, able to keep them, and perhaps able to allow others to keep their own.

She dropped a quick kiss on his cheek. "I call him Papa, so I know he will not mind if I call you Father."

He poured a glass and raised it. "To a successful mission."

She took the glass Charley handed her. "And to Lady Shaldon."

Charley came and touched his glass to hers. "And to Señora Maria Esperanza Romero de Kingsley."

She smiled. "How did you know—oh, from the book of sonnets."

She took a drink and let the liquor burn through her, getting up her nerve.

"My lord...Father. Do not forget to return me the book of sonnets."

"As soon as repairs have been made," he said.

"And the sheet of numbers?" She eased in a breath and held it through his long pause.

"Yes," he said finally, and smiled. "Now let me show you the deed to your property." He stood, all business again. "Come join me in my study."

Later, after a discussion of their new estate in the north, and a long visit by Perry, who claimed insomnia, they were able to get away. Tucked in the high bed with Gracie beside him, Charley drifted into sleep.

"Charley." Gracie's breath tickled his ear.

"Mmm. Best sleep. Reina will be up soon."

"I've been thinking."

He didn't have to fake a groan.

"This is important. I have an idea."

He rolled to face her and flopped his arm over her.

She giggled. "Can you tell me, is your father quite well?"

"When he wants to be. When he needs to be ill, he is."

"He looked very gray tonight." She swept her thumb over his cheek, and he felt it all the way to his loins.

Sighing, she looked away, and he dived in to nip at her neck, just like one of Francisca's *tlahuelpuchis*. She giggled, tasting like good soap and rosewater.

"He was thinking about Mother's death," he murmured into the dip above her collar bone.

She wriggled against him. "Oh. That tickles. Yes, well, I've decided we should not leave yet. You should not leave him. Not yet." She pushed away to look at him. "What years he has left, you must treasure them. And then we shall go later."

"And if later comes a very long time later?"

"That will be a good thing, won't it? He has had a rough patch tracking down spies and killers. Perhaps he will settle quite happily into a retirement. When my father returns, he won't stay long, and perhaps once the Spanish and the pirates are defeated, he can return to a more regular sort of shipping."

"Will that be after you return the book and the dagger to him?"

She blinked and studied him for a long moment.

"Do you have any more secrets you haven't shared with me, my love?"

She looked up at the canopy, blinking furiously.

"I promised Papa." She took a deep breath. "The Duque...he is still very dangerous."

"Look at me, Gracie." He touched her cheek and turned her toward him. "I love you, and I will protect you. Trust me when I say that my father is not done with the Duque." He kissed her nose. "And your secret is safe with me."

"Is it safe with your father?"

He fell back to the pillow laughing. "Yes. Most definitely."

"Well, then, when my Papa returns to his ordinary trade, we can sail with him and I can show you that world. For now, we will stay here and you will spend time with your father. Is that not a good plan? What do you think?"

"I think it is marvelous." He touched his lips to hers. "And I think since you have woken me to share plans," he rolled her onto her back, "I have an excellent idea."

Her eyelids fluttered and a smile touched her lips. "You've had this idea once already tonight."

He covered her with his body and breathed into her ear. "Am I not a genius?"

He stopped her laughter with a kiss.

Two months later, Yorkshire, West Riding

"We're losing our nursemaid, Gracie." Charley looked up from the ball he was lining up. The flat stretch of garden had been perfect for this game of lawn wickets which the Everly family claimed to love.

Perry waved a mallet threateningly. "Don't be ridiculous. I love her prodigiously, but Reina can spare me for a few weeks. Gracie is with her every morning, and Francisca allows me only a little time all alone with my niece. And you have hired a perfectly good staff. And I have not seen my friend Cecilia in an age. Since her father died, she never comes up to London. When will I have this opportunity again?"

Charley eyed the ball and whacked it. He cleared a wicket and bumped Graciela's ball.

"Sorry, my dear." He grinned at her.

A little too brightly, she thought. He was worried about Perry.

"I'm not sure I should allow you to gallivant about the countryside, dear sister."

"You are not my father, dear brother."

"I'm not sure Father or Bakeley would approve."

She harrumphed. "What about Bink? Why not include him?"

Graciela stepped between them. "You must play your ball, Perry. I am getting bored."

While Perry lined up her shot, Charley watched her closely.

Perry had come along with them to their new estate, bringing along the little maid Jenny who had worked for Paulette and then Sirena, to help train the girls they'd hired from the children's home run by Bink's friend, Lady Hackwell. It had been a busy month of settling in, and Perry's help with the staff and the household management had been invaluable.

And now Perry was bored.

Graciela could understand that. Perry had no Charley to go to every night, no Charley to follow every bit of teasing with a kiss. Two nights ago, at dinner, she'd announced her plans. She would travel to East Yorkshire to visit with a friend she'd met her come-out year in London.

Perry's ball cruised through the wickets and struck the post. "There," she whooped. "I have won. I'm returning to the house to direct Jenny's packing. I shall see you at dinner."

Graciela picked up Perry's tossed mallet. "Pack your pistols also," she called.

Perry's hand went up in a wave, but she did not turn or break her stride.

Graciela laughed.

"You shouldn't encourage her." He tapped his ball again.

"It's my turn."

He looked up and frowned. "Come here."

"You are worried. Don't be. You cannot stop her, Charley. She has no husband, she has no home of her own, no child to fret over, she is all at loose ends. She needs an adventure. Perhaps she'll meet a good suitor on this visit. Your father will understand. He will not mind."

"He will mind plenty, as will my brothers. She is up to something. I should accompany her there. I won't stay. I'll return right away."

"You have the workmen coming to install the new stove in the kitchen. You have grooms to hire. You have repairs on the roof to supervise. You have tenants to meet with."

He tossed his mallet, scowling. "Fine. Come here."

She smiled and walked into his arms, looking up into his eyes.

"Drat. I never thought I would be dealing with roofs and tenants and stoves like Bakeley. I always thought, poor sod, I'm glad he was born first. And now I'm a regular sod myself."

"You are. And you have something else in common with your brother."

His brow furrowed and he smiled. "My lack of money worries. In part due to my prodigiously good marriage."

"What else?"

"Some fine horses, though not as many as he has."

"And?"

He truly looked puzzled. She took his hands and placed them on her belly.

"Really?"

"Maybe. I have been sick every morning in the nursery. And there are other signs. I did not wish to tell you until I was absolutely sure, but I couldn't wait. I think it's very possible you have made a baby."

"*We* have made a baby." He pulled her close and kissed her soundly. "Well, then, Lady Perpetua is on her own."

The End

If you enjoyed this story, please consider leaving a review at Amazon or Goodreads

A Note from the Author

In researching some local history of Orange County, California where I live I discovered that one of the early rancho owners, Don Juan Forster, was actually born in Liverpool, England. Then I came across a book, *Testimonios, Early California Through the Eyes of Women, 1815-1848*, fascinating narratives of life in those times.

While history provided inspiration for my heroine's parents' romance, I've taken the liberty of setting their marriage decades earlier. As usual, my characters and story are entirely fictional, and any historical errors are mine alone.

Many thanks go to editor Tessa Shapcott, to cover designer Cami Brite, and to my daughter, Alicia, for helping me brainstorm the title.

As ever, I'm grateful to my husband for his unfailing support and enduring patience. On a recent trip, the dear man ran all over London with me, including a stop at the historical George Inn on Borough High Street where we hoisted a pint to Graciela and Charley.

I love hearing from readers! You can contact and follow me on Facebook, Twitter, Pinterest, and Goodreads, and at my website, AlinaKField.com. For special notices about sales and other news, please consider signing up for my newsletter at my website. I promise I won't spam you or sell your email address!

Best regards and happy reading!

Alina K. Field

Also by Alina K. Field

The Bastard's Iberian Bride
Book One, Sons of the Spy Lord
2017, Havenlock Press

For a chance at true freedom, a spy's daughter dodges an arranged marriage to an earl's illegitimate son and seeks the fortune left by her inscrutable father. When her quest draws a villain's threat, the only person she can trust is the war-weary soldier she doesn't want to marry—but can't seem to resist.

Available in paperbook from Amazon, and as an ebook from Amazon, Kobo, Barnes & Noble, iBooks, and Google

The Viscount's Seduction
Book Two, Sons of the Spy Lord
2017, Havenlock Press

Lady Sirena Hollister has lost everything, even her fey abilities. But when the fairies hand her a chance at a London Season, her schemes for revenge stir up an unknown enemy, and spark danger of a different sort, in the person of a handsome Viscount.

Available in paperbook from Amazon, and as an ebook from Amazon, Kobo, Barnes & Noble, iBooks, and Google

The Marquess and the Midwife
Finalist, 2016 National Reader's Choice Award
2016, Havenlock Press

Uncovering a lie drives a new marquess back from a self-imposed exile at Christmas to find the only woman he's ever loved. Finding her turns out to be easy, uncovering her stunning secrets, a bit harder. But winning her back will be the greatest challenge of all.

Available in paperbook from Amazon, and as an ebook from Amazon, Kobo, Barnes & Noble, iBooks, and Google

Liliana's Letter
Finalist, 2015 National Reader's Choice Award
Havenlock Press

The Matchmaker Meets the Matchbreaker

Liliana Ashford's future as a professional chaperone depends on her wealthy charge's successful marriage, but her own close encounter with a scoundrel years ago makes her determined to save the girl from the same kind of rogue.

Available in paperbook and eBook from Amazon

The Ghost of Depford Hall
A short, sweet Halloween sequel to
Liliana's Letter
Havenlock Press

It's her mother's last All Hallows' Eve.

When family, friends, and tenants gather, goblins, ghouls, and ghosts are banned from this All Hallows' Eve party.

Only, no one told the Ghost of Depford Hall!

Available in eBook from Amazon.

Bella's Band
A 2015 RONE Award Finalist
Soul Mate Publishing

A spinster's secrets tempt a killer—and steal a soldier's heart.

Saddled with his brother's title and debts, nothing about this new life makes the Earl of Hackwell want to stay—until he meets a lady with a secret that can change everything.

Available on Kindle from Amazon

Rosalyn's Ring
2014 Book Buyer's Best Novella Category
Soul Mate Publishing

A Christmas Wish Becomes a Christmas Miracle

When a young woman is put up for auction in a wife sale, Rosalyn Montagu seizes the chance to rescue her—and to recover a treasured family heirloom, her father's signet ring. Her plans are thwarted by the newly anointed Viscount Cathmore who finds her provoking beauty, upper crust manner, and larcenous streak intriguing. Her secrets rouse his jaded heart, including the truth of her identity—she is the woman whose home he has usurped. But more mysteries swirl around Rosalyn's past, and Cathmore is just the man to help her uncover the truth.

Available on Kindle from Amazon

Coming in Spring 2018,
Book Four, Sons of the Spy Lord
wherein Lady Perry proves her mettle.

Find out more at AlinaKField.com